SILENT

FROM THE

SHADOWS

SILENT FROM THE SHADOWS

BY

CRAIG GODFREY

www.penmorepress.com

Silent from the Shadows by Craig Godfrey
Copyright 2021 © Craig Godfrey
Hobart, Tasmania, Australia
Published by Penmore Press LLC

ISBN-13: 978-1-950586-61-5(Paperback)
ISBN:-978-1-950586-60-8 (e-book)

BISAC Subject Headings:
FIC031010 Fiction/ Thrillers / Crime
FIC014000FICTION / Historical
FIC031020FICTION / Thrillers / Historical
The Book Cover Whisperer:
ProfessionalBookCoverDesign.com

Address all correspondence to:

Penmore Press LLC
920 N Javelina Pl
Tucson AZ 85748

DEDICATION

Tasmania's history will never be the same.

Introduction by The Author

In 1804, due to fears of French occupation, Lieutenant David Collins was sent to the fledgling British colony of Van Diemen's Land. In February of that year he set up camp – 'a settlement' – in Sullivans Cove. Sullivans Cove is now bustling with tourists, as is the whole of Hobart's waterfront. His predecessor, Lieutenant John Bowen, had raised the British flag on the opposite side of the river four months earlier, where it quickly became apparent that the site was not suitable for the new colony. From the beginning law and order was an issue. Times were tough in this open-air prison and discipline essential to its success. Criminals in old Hobart Town met with swift 'justice', where short trials often ended with the prisoner at the end of a rope – public hangings were still commonplace.

A decade later free settlers started arriving, attracted by land grants, the government's offer of free convict labour and the chance of a prosperous life. As convicts completed their sentences, more and more destitute souls roamed the streets. Crime was widespread. Summary corporal punishment in the streets was common and even dished out to free settlers who transgressed. With a shortage of volunteers, due to poor pay and conditions, police constables were recruited from ex-convicts. Corruption was rife.

When Lieutenant-Governor George Arthur, of Port Arthur fame, governed Van Diemen's Land from 1824 to 1836, he controlled the colony as an autocrat, creating a powerful police presence. However, this was resented by many citizens, as a number of ex-convict constables abused their authority for personal gain.

By the time Sir John Franklin took the reins in 1837, the British Government refused to fund the police force, ordering Franklin to finance the police force from local taxes and funds. This had a further detrimental effect on law and order.

In 1842 the British Government introduced a probation system. Convicts of good behaviour were offered 'tickets-of-leave' firstly, and eventually, a conditional pardon allowed them into society as free men and women. Some built up businesses and became wealthy citizens.

With this system being moderately successful, the British Government, in its wisdom, sent large numbers of prisoners to the island, including convicts from New South Wales, where transportation from England had ceased after 1840.

But the police force took a downturn in 1843, during an economic depression, under governorship of Sir John Eardley-Wilmot. The pardoned convicts found it difficult to find work, crime rates increased further and bushrangers, who had been suppressed under Arthur, were now roaming free in the countryside.

By 1847, the population of Van Diemen's Land was 70,164, with 517 police constables. The discovery of gold at Ballarat in Victoria in 1851 changed everything. Police constables retired in droves and joined the gold rush.

The life and adventures of Caspian Hunter from Birmingham is fiction. However, it is easy to imagine a small group of men, along with trusty Holly, cooped up in a small dank office, hidden behind barrels of salted meat, at the prisoner barracks storehouse, solving the more serious crimes. There was most certainly a most pressing need for their services.

From the Diaries of Caspian Hunter, Esquire

My name is Caspian Hunter. I am enjoying the third decade of my life, having grown up in Birmingham, where I was educated at Grammar School at the expense of my godfather, Albert Hunter, a reclusive gentleman with no children of his own and a passion for books. He had made wise investments as a merchant. I discovered I had the mind of a sleuth seven years ago, when I solved the mystery of the Birmingham Fair Murders, where four young women in a travelling circus were murdered. Not only did I single-handedly arrest the perpetrator, but I also collated enough evidence to ensure the villain's hanging. With *the world is my oyster enthusiasm* I sailed from my home in Birmingham to Van Diemen's Land, on the other side of the globe, to take up a position as second-in-charge of the newly formed crime detecting agency in the fledgling colony. It was 1855, the twenty-second year of the reign of Her Majesty Queen Victoria. Little could I have suspected how my life would change from the moment I sailed up the mighty River Derwent towards Hobart Town.

An abandoned ship drifting at sea was but the beginning of a mystery that would lead me after villains, the likes of which were rare, even in Old London Town. Within ten days of sailing into Sullivans Cove, I had solved three major crimes and made a name for myself – rather unexpectedly I must confess. Life in Hobart Town for a bachelor lawman was outstanding – the ladies were accommodating, the fare toothsome and the ales made from the fresh mountain water was as good as any I had sampled anywhere.

We made a great team, my colleagues and I. We were enthusiastic; we watched each other's backs. Our commission was dangerous, dare I say adventurous, and my records meticulous...

This is my story.

But first, my 'partners in crime:'

Heading the office is Mr Fabian Winter. What can I say about Fabian? Well, to begin with, he is a rake – a likeable scoundrel, I guess one would say. He will reach his thirty-sixth year this year, god willing. Certainly, he has an ego to match his prowess – after all, who else would name the police sloop *Fabian*, after himself. Fabian enjoys the company of beautiful women, delights in the pleasures of a beverage or two in the inns of Hobart Town, as well as a fine meal. Fabian has a charismatic charm women find irresistible. I imagine 'personable' would be a suitable description. He cuts a stylish figure with his usual smart dress of tartan trousers, waist jacket, frock coat and boater hat. He has the large brown eyes of a Labrador and keeps his hazel hair neat, with a pencil-thin moustache in a straight line across his upper lip. Oh yes, the man *is* a stylish rake.

Under Fabian's and my authority – did I mention I am second in charge? – Fabian and I command four constables. Jasper is the youngest at twenty, an apparently undernourished lad who had been taught the basics in life at Ragged School in Wapping. Yet Jasper is by all means a likeable character with his hooded eyes and slow speech; naïve, yes, but blessed with unquestionable courage, a dedication to the service, and with a hunger to learn. He married young; some say there was no

Billings is of a more sober nature, and dare I say, more dignified. A thirty-year-old gentleman of fine proportions and pleasant appearance. Billings is my age and the only one educated to my standard. He sports thick mutton chops that fail to connect beneath the chin, but he has no moustache; appearing more like a Bow Street Runner in his top hat and wielding his truncheon. Billings has a dry sense of humour, with a neatness of dress about him, becoming of the quintessential lawman.

Holly Villan is no fair maiden. Holly is a sharp-witted, green-eyed, red-haired Irish girl who grew up with six brothers. Six brothers, who treated her... well, like a brother. She is a robust, strapping young lass; the word 'fear', I swear, is not in her vocabulary. Holly is short, four eleven maybe, with the build of a sawyer. She dresses like a farmhand from the country, with a smock coat to protect her undergarments, a simple smock of cotton requiring few seamstress skills. The britches carry on up towards the ribcage to keep her lower back warm; fastened with gaiters wrapped around the lower leg and tied with one piece of string. As I said: fair maiden, Holly is not. Holly prefers to keep her hair short-cropped – *So it is easy for bestin' the villains,* she likes to say. And tackle villains she does. Holly sports a leathered scar across her brow that proves this statement – a blade wound of some sort. But under her no-nonsense façade, Holly conceals a heart of gold.

The latest member to join our ranks is Lantern Jaw Lincoln. No one knows his given name, so we simply call him Lincoln. Six-foot-six Lincoln has, well, a square jaw reminiscent of a lantern. He grew up as a mudlark on the Thames before ending up in the colonies. Lincoln has a lasting, musty smell about him, like the atmosphere of a damp cabin, but there is a comfort in this lingering musty scent. A sense of security accompanies the man, with his towering presence and pugilist's jaw.

Then there is me, Caspian Hunter. Just turned thirty. A little fish in a huge pond; one lawman in a sea of villains. I work hard, and yes, I play hard. The truth is, hunting scoundrels and rogues is a stressful career. I have brushed shoulders with many an innkeeper, fille de joie, felon and malefactor, and have been known to partake of life's many pleasures. But I have also dined with magistrates, taken brandy with the governor and shared company with the gentlemen and fair ladies of the colony.

However, chasing criminals is my priority and I like to think I do not take fools easily. But I will let you, the reader, be the judge of that....

PROLOGUE

I first heard about Zachary Wolf a few months after my arrival in Van Diemen's Land back in in '55. He was a convicted felon serving time at the Saltwater River coal mines on Tasman Peninsula, who had escaped the harsh conditions of his damp, chilling, underground cell in the winter of 1847, the year before the mines were closed and the inmates relocated to Port Arthur. What made Zachary Wolf's escape more interesting was the fact he was accused of cannibalism.

Like Alexander Pearce twenty-five years before him, Zachary escaped with other inmates – Scott White and Ellery Gordon, whom he was suspected of killing and eating, so desperate was he for food. Pearce had been a prisoner at the notorious Sarah Island penal settlement at Macquarie Harbour who had escaped in September 1822 and eaten his companions.

I should explain here that Zachary and his cohorts had spent months saving strips of sheepskin and pigskin from the cookhouse. They gathered wattle branches and finally, in painstaking secrecy, they built a coracle strong enough to get them safely across Eaglehawk Neck, the notorious, heavily-guarded isthmus separating Tasman Peninsula from the mainland of Van Diemen's Land. Unfortunately, the night they made the crossing, on the ocean side of the isthmus, the coracle was swamped by a rogue wave and sank, forcing the men to swim ashore. Wolf always said that a shark had attacked Scott White and that his remains washed up onto the beach. It was then alleged that Wolf further dismembered White's remains and smoked the limbs to preserve for transportation. Ellery Gordon was not around to verify this, as he died of exhaustion ten days later. When caught two months after the escape, Zachary Wolf was found to be in moderate health. And like his counterpart, Alexander Pearce, Wolf was found with smoked human remains in a satchel he carried with him.

So why did Zachary Wolf risk approaching old Ma Bailey's cottage at her vegetable farm outside Sorell on that fateful day when he was recaptured? He certainly was not starving. However, he *was* exhausted and in need of medical attention for festering wounds incurred while trekking through the wilderness of Van Diemen's Land. Ma Bailey tended to his injuries and made him hot tea, after which he collapsed into a heavy exhausted sleep before the kitchen fire. Sometime later, he awoke to the sound of a pealing bell outside the cottage. When questioned, Ma Bailey laughed it off, telling the escapee, Wolf, that she was calling in all the farmhands for their midday meal. Content with the answer, he fell asleep once more, only to be woken later by soldiers and arrested. Ma Bailey was no fool. She knew Wolf to be an absconder and the bell ringing was a local ruse devised to notify soldiers, should escapees be in the district.

'You'll get the five guineas reward for this,' the sergeant-at-arms told the woman.

'Aye, I will, and thart'll buy me a nice new bonnet I'm thinkin'.'

At trial Wolf swore on the Bible that Gordon had been killed by a shark when swimming ashore that night. And indeed, Gordon's ravaged trunk had been found on the beach two months earlier, minus the arms and legs. It was determined that it had been portioned into small pieces with flint tools, similar to tools used by the aborigines. There was no sign of a shark attack. However, foul play could not be proven and Zachary Wolf served his time and another three years for the attempted escape, before receiving his ticket of leave in '53.

Now, in the year of our Queen, Queen Victoria, 1858, Zachary Wolf, forty years old, was a bitter and broken man, eking out an existence around Mountain River, to the southwest of Hobart Town, occasionally finding work cooking for sawyers in the area. The reason I transcribe this man's existence into my journal is that never, in all my years as an investigative policeman, have I had the misfortune to encounter such a man. But allow me to wind the clock back and start at the beginning.

CHAPTER ONE

Mount Wellington's foothills, July, 1858. Early Morning.

Hobart Town had been relatively quiet of late. *The Cessation of Transportation Act,* passed in 1853, meant that no more prison ships sailed for the shores of Van Diemen's Land – now called Tasmania by many, wishing to shake off the shackles of the past. There had been an influx of prisoners in '55 when Norfolk Island Penal Colony was abandoned and the prisoners sent to Hobart Town. But many had been integrated into the community and now, two and a half years later, the guards at the prisoner barracks supervised only a handful of re-offenders. The watch house dealt with three burglaries last week and an assortment of assaults, drunken behaviour, pickpocketing, one case of arson and two arrests for unruly behaviour in bawdy houses. Otherwise, all in all, the township seemed relatively calm.

For this reason, I was unsettled and unprepared for the scene before me. It was July and I stood amongst thick scrubland in the foothills of the sphinx-like Mount Wellington. Although Hobart Town was but five miles distant, I may as well have been in the dense foliage of the Amazon jungle, except that each breath I expelled created a winter's mist before me. I slapped my hands together and rubbed hard, cursing myself for not wearing my gloves.

The body lay half hidden, concealed by a rotted log, where it had been dragged a yard or more across the ground of the remote bushlands. The disturbed leaves of the forest attested to the cadaver's trajectory. I stood in silence, examining the corpse. I could make neither heads nor tails of the senseless killing. From what I could tell, through the veneer of congealed blood, the old trapper had suffered two puncture marks in his neck, above a portion of throat that had been brutally torn away. At first glance I suspected two pistol shot wounds. But the remains of his jugular dangled crudely and the victim's body seemed void of most of his vital fluid – blood.

My colleague Holly stomped into the forest clearing and dry retched. Gore, it seemed from our recent crime scenes, had an adverse effect on the woman. But don't misjudge my courageous colleague. Holly could handle a firearm like the most valiant soldier, or clap a villain in irons before he knew what day it was. Her close friend and another member of my team, Lantern Jaw Lincoln, was immediately at her side. The gentle, six-foot-six giant placed a tender arm on Holly's shoulder. 'You right, Hol?'

'I'll be right in a min...' Holly's words garbled and she gave up her breakfast.

Lincoln gave Holly space and joined me beside the body. He studied the victim a long moment and I allowed the man time to consider, as I was lost for an explanation. Finally, after a long moment, 'I hate to tell yer this, Caspian, sar, but that looks awful like the work of a vampire.'

'A vam— a vampire!' I said, incredulous at the man's suggestion in these modern times of Queen Victoria's reign.

'Aye, sar. A vampire.'

'Tell me something, Lincoln.'

'Sar?'

'You are aware, I presume, that vampires do not exist?'

'No, sar. That's where you are wrong. And yer can see them puncture marks in the neck.'

'You mean bullet holes, small calibre.'

'I beg to differ, Caspian sar. But I lived in Southwark on the Thames for a spell when similar bodies turned up in the river. The dastardly deed of a vampire it were. I seen one, and all.'

'Like this you say?'

'Aye. I was a mudlark, collecting scrap iron along the Thames bank at low tide. One day a body washed up. I seen it before it was carted away.'

'Hmm.' I was unconvinced.

'The stories were printed in the gazette and all.'

'Stories?' I could not help but smirk.

'Aye. Stories o' similar marks on corpses to 'im.' Lincoln pointed to our victim with the toe of his boot. 'With puncture holes in the neck just like this'n. They was washed up by the tide, yer see.'

'I have never heard of this before.'

'Well, with all respect, sar, you're from Birming'am, ain't yer?'

'Yes but...'

'People livin' in the area panicked. 'Vampire' they squealed, and locked themselves in at night.'

'How many bodies are we talking about?'

'Two, Caspian sar.'

I studied the wounds carefully and had to admit they were unusual for bullet entries. They were about three inches apart. The killer would have taken careful aim, if it were not a fluke.

Holly finally joined us. 'Vampire!' she cried out. 'Did you say a vampire done this?'

'N... No Holly,' I said annoyed. 'There is no such thing as a vampire.'

'Well, yes and no, Hol,' Lincoln said matter-of-factly. 'We ain't talkin' fairy tales like in them old books. No sar. This is the work of a real and living person what likes drinkin' human blood.'

'Argh!' Holly retched again.

'I concede I have heard of some people who indulge in this, Lincoln,' I said, 'but it is very rare, rare as hen's teeth, as my mother would say.'

'Rare, aye, sar, but true.'

I rubbed my chin; something didn't sit well with what presented itself before me. I stepped back, better to scour a wider area. 'If this were a murder, what's not right here?'

'Murder?' Lincoln was sold on the vampire theme.

'The man certainly was not killed for his wares,' I alluded to a roll of discarded fresh skins, 'although they have been interfered with.'

'That'd be them wild devil creatures, to be sure.'

'I think you are on the money there, Lincoln.'

I felt the victim's pockets and retrieved his purse, emptying the contents into my hand, counting fifteen shillings and eleven pence in silver and copper. 'His purse is intact. And his double-barrel shotgun, powder and shot pouch are where they were dropped.'

'Vampires 'ave no use for coin or guns, Caspian sar,' Holly offered.

The good Lord save me. 'Not you too, Holly?'

I considered requesting the photographic image-making services of the police photographer Mrs Rowley, but my feet were turning numb from the cold and I was gloveless. The images could quite easily be achieved at the morgue. It was time to return to civilisation and a warm brazier.

CRAIG GODFREY

Hobart Town, Noon.

I knew Hester James, the game-seller, from past meetings. He was an aware and astute man, a loner by all accounts, trapping and hunting game for a living in the foothills around Mount Wellington. A man who drank alone, and in moderation, in the inns, listening to the ramblings of loose mouth drunkards, of whom there were plenty in Hobart Town. Hester still wore his hunting gear; a brown chamois jacket with black neckerchief, moleskin britches beneath thigh-high leather waders and a wide-brim black felt hat to keep the Antipodean sun from his weathered face. Although, this morning his attire was meant to keep the chill at bay. The man was clean-shaven except for a neat beard beneath his chin, with his worldly belongings in a canvas satchel slung over his shoulder and hanging off his hip.

It was Hester who discovered the body in the bushlands.

As I'd guessed, I found Hester James selling his wares on the corner of Murray and Liverpool Streets. When I arrived, he held high a clutch of quail while calling out his wares.

'Brown quail, wild duck, waterfowl, fresh culled ready for the pot.' At his feet on the flagstones his faithful hound, Bullet, curled about – asleep – no doubt exhausted from the day's hunt.

'Hester,' I said in greeting. Bullet opened one eye, saw me as non-threatening and went back to slumber.

'Mr 'unter. Yer found me, then?'

'Well, it is not too difficult is it now? This is Hester James's corner, is it not?'

'I suppose yer right. Truth is I get a good clientele 'ere, what with all the passin' townsfolk.' There followed a silent lull in conversation as he exchanged four quail for a crown. 'I guess you're 'ere to ask me about J. McK?'

'J. McK?'

'Aye. The trapper what got done in the hills? The body I reported to the watch house guard this mornin'.'

'Oh yes.' I was surprised at the name. 'J. McK?'

'Aye. That's McK without the 'ay' as in McKay. No one knows his full name, yer see. He was a bit of a loner.'

'I see. You did not mention you knew the man when you reported this to the guard.'

'No. It's only since I've been standin 'ere thinkin', that I recalled his name, or lack of a name that is.'

'Please tell me how you found him.'

'Dead, sar.'

'Yes, but *how* did you find him?'

'Well, I was on me way back, pretty loaded up with game as yer can see, when I decided to take a shortcut I know through the bush. I know it like the back o' me hand I do.'

'I am sure you do, Hester.'

'Well, I heard them devils fightin' over breakfast...'

'You mean those black devils?' I asked, meaning the angry, furry black cat-like carnivores that eat any carrion left unguarded.

'That's them. Three o' the beggars there were, a mum, a dad and a youngen. They'd just arrived, I figured, and were ripping into his shoulder when I scared 'em off with a single shot.'

The game-seller patted the handle of a two-barrelled pistol snug behind the belt in his britches.

'That would account for the gnaw marks on the man's ankles and arms them,' I said.

The trapper studied me a moment. 'I gotta tell yer, Mr 'unter, I seen them puncture marks in McK's neck and it don't look like no ordinary murder, not to me, like.'

'Oh?' I said, venturing the man's opinion.

'Well, at first I thought they was bullet holes, but when I looked closer I noticed he had bled out and there was no blood on the ground. Well, not much anyhow, so...'

'So what are you trying to say?'

'Devil's blood Mr 'unter. I seen books. I can read, yer know...'

'Excellent, Hester. Say what you mean.'

The game-seller looked about before lowering his voice. 'Dare I say it was the work of a vampire, sar.'

'Now, we both know vampires do not exist, Hester. They are the work of novelists and fairy tales.'

'But that's where yer wrong, Mr 'unter. Make no mistake. I ain't talkin' supernatural. No sar. I come from Baconsthorpe, a village in Norfolk. An' I seen with me very own eyes, a grave what was accidentally found buried in the wall of Baconsthorpe Castle. I was a ten-year-old lad at the time. The wall crumbled yer see, after a storm and heavy rain. Well, some men opened the coffin; it must o' been a couple 'undred years old, they said. An' blow me, the body inside hadn't decomposed.' Hester shuddered at the memory.

'What's that to do with vampires?'

'The body looked fresh as they day it was buried, Caspian sar. But it had an iron rod staked through the heart, the teeth had been removed and several iron bolts hammered into the body to hold it down inside the coffin like. The coffin lid had also been weighted with a pile o' large stones. Yes, sir, that body was secured good and proper. Like they were makin' certain it would not rise from the dead.'

'Poppycock!'

'Sorry?'

'Poppycock, Hester. That's ignorant witchery from people centuries ago, who knew no better.'

I left Hester James with more questions than answers. I had been summoned to the dead trapper's suspected crime scene at the break of day; it was now time to head to the office. And I knew there would be no point visiting the morgue for an autopsy report for a few hours yet, having left Holly and Lincoln to organise the body's removal. As I mentioned, I had also deemed it unnecessary to summon Mrs Royle Rowley to the site this freezing morning, as the bush setting revealed little and she could just as simply make photographic images of the body at the morgue.

Mrs Rowley, you must understand, was the owner of Rowley Photographical Studios in Collins Street. She was a war widow, as her husband, having rendezvoused with a cannon ball in the Crimea, had been reported missing. He would, however, make a disturbing appearance in Hobart Town some time later, and as a mortal, albeit missing one leg. However that saga has been well documented in previous memoirs.

So, thinking herself a widow, Mrs Rowley sailed from England and settled in the colonies, where she purchased the image making equipment from French explorers who were returning to France. For my part, I convinced my superiors that her services would be invaluable, to record crime scenes for the courts. They agreed and Mrs Rowley was now summoned on many occasions to record the crime scenes.

Discreetly though, avid reader – I must look over my shoulder before I write these words – Mrs Rowley and myself found ourselves romantically connected, for use of a better word. The most attractive middle-aged Mrs Rowley, name of Royle, you see, becomes a wild tiger at crime scenes. It is difficult to explain, but the atmosphere, the energy, the turmoil turns the woman into a raging nymphomaniac. And often we are left alone after the initial investigation process, where I assist Royle in her photography, as it is now referred to.

I left Hester James peddling his game on his regular corner and crossed to Collins Street where, trying to be discreet as possible, I ventured into Royle's studio, on the floor above Mrs Adkin's Tea Rooms. There was no escaping Mrs Adkin. The rather jolly woman, who had lost her feminine curves years ago, exchanging them for the spherical shape of a plum pudding, rapped her knuckles on the window in greeting when she saw me approach. She was dressing the shelves with her day's fresh pastries. I waved back and made a mental note to purchase a dozen apple and nutmeg queen cakes on my way to the prisoner barracks office, and took to Royle's studio stairs three at a time. It was still early, and the door was locked. I knocked and heard muffled voices.

Door locked! Voices!

I felt a sudden stab of anxiety. Apprehension. Jealousy even. I thought of retreating back down the stairs when I heard Royle's sweet voice. 'Who is it?'

'Caspian, Royle.' I tried the door once more, rattling the brass knob energetically.

'Wait!' her voice sounded urgent, then more regular. 'Wait a moment Mr Hunter. I'll be there in a jiffy.'

Mr Hunter?

I waited. How long is a jiffy anyway? She must have kept me lingering a whole minute, while I listened to muted voices and the odd soft giggle. Finally the door opened with a theatrical flourish. 'Mr Hunter. What a surprise.'

Mr Hunter!

'What can I do for you?' Mrs Rowley made no sign of familiarity, although she was pleasant and professional.

'May I come in?' She opened the door wider. I entered. 'Royle, I...'

Her expression was one of formality and I was aware that another man was in the next room – in her parlour, no less. I stiffened. 'Mrs Rowley, I am sorry to disturb you at such an early hour.'

'Early hour?' We were both immediately aware of the studio mantle clock chiming half the hour after eight of the morning. 'Well, your door was locked and I thought...'

'Locked! Yes,' she conceded. 'I must have locked it accidentally.'

'Accidentally?'

She made a strange face at me and I think now, in hindsight, she blushed.

'The police department requires your services, madam,' I said in a loud deep voice, unintentionally playing along with her charade.'

'Oh. Very well,' she articulated loud and clear. At that moment a figure appeared from the shadows of the parlour where, I now realised, the curtains had not been opened.

'I'll be leaving now, Mrs Rowley,' the man said, making to push by me for the stairs. 'Oh, Mr Hoffbrand, Cyril. I would like you to meet Mr Hunter from the prisoner barracks.'

Hoffbrand, I noticed, was a bit of a dandy, a gentleman no less, with that prudish air about him customary for those of privileged birth. 'Mr Hunter,' he touched his top hat and ran that privileged eye over my attire with pursed lips. I offered my hand, which was taken with haste in a handshake redolent of a dandy. And he hurried down the stairs, one at a time, in measured steps.

We watched him skip onto the street before I looked Royle in the eye.

'Mr Hunter?' I repeated my name, imitating the dandy and demanding an explanation.

'Oh Caspian, dear boy,' Royle took both my wrists. 'Come in, come in.'

Was Royle inviting me in because she wanted to, or was it because the freezing staircase to the street was drawing the heat from her studio and she was dressed lightly? I entered. Royle closed the door and led me across the studio to the fireplace, where a generous fire had been rekindled from the night before. I always found Royle's studio fascinating; a room full of the props required for her consigned portraitures – like a huge painted canvas trompe l'oeil of English castles, or Roman ruins. There were chests of drawers and a wardrobe full of costumes. Royle and myself often played dress-ups in acts of foreplay before our uninhibited trysts. Lord Nelson and Lady Hamilton were favourites. Now I was confronted by soiled wine glasses and the nibbled remains of sweetmeats on a silver salver on the hearth, where Royle had entertained another.

Royle caught me looking towards the darkened parlour, which led to her darkened bedroom. She crossed the room and closed the parlour door.

'Caspian,' she sighed, taking both my wrists once more. I always assumed there were others, I thought to myself, 'heaven knows, *I* am hardly monogamous.' But when it was so blatantly obvious, it hurt. Was I in love with this beguiling woman nearly twenty years my senior?

'Caspian,' she said more softly, looking me in the eyes, pleading for forgiveness. At least that's what I hoped.

'Royle,' I finally answered sulkily, pulling my arms free and stepping back in a sign of protest. 'I... I apologise for turning up unannounced. But this is police business.'

'Caspian, Cyril... ah, Mr Hoffbrand, was...'

'It is irrelevant Royle. Worry yourself not with such discrepancies. We are not shackled in marriage or... god forbid, we are not betrothed. We were lovers were we not? I have had oth...'

'Were?'

'Sorry?'

'You said were, Caspian. Past tense. Were lovers.'

'Well, I..., you were with what's-his-face... prancing Cyril.'

'Oh Caspian. Forget Cyril. He was just a means to an end.'

'Means to an end!'

'Is that what you think of me? A means to an end?'

'No Caspian. You and I have a special relationship.' Royle took my wrists once more and pulled me close. I felt a stirring in my loins and, god only knows, I was due for some lovin'. Royle placed warm wet lips on mine. Her mouth was open. I stubbornly kept mine closed. I had visions of her with this Cyril, her lips on his. And his lips on her lips also.

'I must get to the barracks,' I said pushing her away, albeit gently.

'Oh Caspian.'

'I need time,' I said lamely, like the jilted young lover, the victim.

'Fine,' Royle regained her dignity. 'Where and when?'

'Where and when?' I looked surprised.

'Police business, Mr Hunter. Where and when?'

'Oh. The morgue. Say... ah... noon?'

I paused outside Mrs Atkins's Tea Rooms a moment. I had not eaten breakfast and I was famished. I purchased a pork pie to eat en route and a dozen apple and nutmeg queen cakes to take to the barracks. Mrs Atkins, who had clearly been aware of Prancing Cyril's attendance, fished for gossip. But I knew the old tyrant to be an addicted peddler of everyone's business except her own and she was not clever enough to crack this sly egg.

Campbell Street Prisoner Barracks

Her Majesty's Gaol, already thirty years old, was a stone fortress style building between Brisbane Street and Bathurst

Street housing, I am assured, one thousand two hundred felons. Five years prior to my arrival in Hobart Town, a chapel and criminal law courts were added at the northern end of the prison, along with the most modern contraption for the resident executioner; the gallows. The resident executioner being the notorious and much hated Solomon Blay. But more about this man later. The fact remains, with public executions now banned, a villain could be imprisoned, tried, executed within the prison walls, given a perfunctory few words from a man of god and then dumped into an unmarked grave on site. How civilised.

There was no arguing the prisoner barracks, where our police investigation office was situated, acted as my second home. Of course, Blue Whale Cottage in Battery Point was my primary residence, but more than fifty hours a week were spent at the prison. And I calculated I spent no more than forty hours a week at my cottage. I was mulling these facts about in my mind as my fly carriage delivered me at a canter to the main entrance.

I stood a moment before the prison gates, better to catch my breath before taking on the challenges of another day. The massive gates of wood and iron were painted a dark green that I found quite pleasing, and were surrounded by fifteen-foot-high brick walls. Square stone pillars either side of the gate supported an ornate cast iron arch that in turn supported a large oil lamp at its centre. An iron door within the gate on the right side boasted a large brass doorknocker, which I recognised from my past studies of ancient Greece, as an image of Dionysus, the god of wine, ritual and madness. I wondered about this choice of entry for a prison full of villains as I put it to service with a thunderous knock.

'Mr 'unter,' my old friend and keeper of the gate, Sergeant Richard Clincher, called out to me in good cheer. Clincher was a wily, ageing soldier with a heart of gold. Always ready with a coffee pot on the potbelly stove or a glass of Weaver's Fluid Magnesia, should one of our team turn up poorly after a night at the inn. He was standing, rather crookedly, in the portal, for the man suffered from gout, arthritis and age.

'Good timing, squire. You've a visitor what's been waitin' the past hour. A visitor what needs your miraculous sleuthing.'

'Oh!' I said, rather irritated. 'Am I the only investigator here?'

'No sar, that you ain't. However, I can't rouse up no one else. Mr Winter's indisposed and Jasper's runnin' errands.'

And I'd left Holly and Lincoln to attend to the dead trapper.

'Where's Billings?' I asked.

'Indisposed.'

'Indisposed?'

'That's wha' I said, sar.'

'Very well. Where is this... visitor?'

Clincher brushed pork pie pastry crumbs from my coat and tipped his head to the interview room within the gatehouse.

'Ah, Mr 'unter sar,' Clincher started again as I made to leave. 'Do yer want me to look after yer parcel?'

'Oh!' The queen cakes were secured in their neat packaging on my arm. 'Yes please. Be a good chap and keep the parcel horizontal.'

'Horizontal, sar?'

'Yes. Queen cakes for the lads. Don't want them spoiled or squashed.'

'Yes, sar. Horizontal it is.' And his nose twitched delightfully as he relieved me of my goods.

First impressions *are* important, so they say. Gideon Hartley was an insipid, timid man; a clerical worker by all appearances. His body was small and stooped, unnecessarily so for a man I imagined no older than fifty. He wore the thick-lensed glasses of a clerk, his eyes poorly from long hours over ledgers in deficient light. His fine grey hair circled his bald pate like that of a monk, reminding me, not unreasonably, of an atoll in a calm sea. His bland coloured swallowtail suit was neatly pressed and his black leather shoes well preserved with a shine of soot black Nugget. As I entered the room he stood politely but had difficulty looking me in the eye.

'Mr Hartley, I do believe.' I offered the man my hand in greeting, which he touched briefly, as if he had come into contact with the famous Portland Vase in the British Museum.

Yes, first impressions are important.

'Hartley, yes, sir,' he answered as his limp limb dropped back by his side. 'Gideon Hartley.'

'Caspian Hunter,' I introduced myself in an accentuated manly tone. 'You asked for me. How can I be of service?'

'It's the wife, sir.'

Ah the wife. Was this the cause of his lack of confidence?

'The wife?'

'Yes, Mr Hunter. Dorothea Hartley, my wife of thirty-five years.'

'Thirty-five years, eh? Well, I must congratulate you, Mr Hartley, Gideon, on maintaining such a long relationship, and I trust in good health.'

'Well, that would be the case, but now my wife is poorly sir.'

Christ, I thought, I'm not a bloody doctor, get on with it.

'Poorly? Is she ill?'

'No, sir. Not exactly. You see, we haven't heard from our son for over fourteen months now and Dorothea is... well she frets something shocking.'

'Sons are like that,' I said sympathetically. 'What I mean to say is, boys will be boys and all that.' I made a mental note to write to my mother back in Birmingham. 'So this son of yours...'

'Albert.'

'Albert. He left home I take it to... go to sea maybe?'

'No. No, nothing like that.'

'Oh?'

'No, sir.' Hartley looked unsteady on his feet, as if he were about to crumble.

'Please sit.' I sat on another chair at his side.

'My son, Albert, loves horses, you must understand, and some time ago he came home excited with the prospect of buying a small horse stud on the Esk River near Launceston.'

'A marketable business, I am sure.'

'Yes, well. Albert is twenty-four, but when he was twenty he inherited eight hundred pounds from his godfather, Dorothea's brother. He's a good lad, sensible. And the idea of a stud farm... well... it seemed perfect.'

'I would imagine so.'

'Albert befriended a man he met while working at Highfield House in Stanley.'

'On the north-west coast?'

'Yes. Albert was an overseer for the sheep stud when he made the acquaintance of a man named Gordon Harper. Ex-army man by all accounts. This Mr Harper knew of Albert's ambitions, and the inheritance no doubt, and told Albert about the horse stud for sale. He asked Albert if he would like to go into a business partnership. Albert was very excited. We encouraged him to think about it, but the impetuous lad went ahead and did not tell us until after he had signed the contract.'

'As in deeds or a lease?'

'Deeds, sir.'

'I see. Please continue.'

'Well, it was then that we discovered Albert put all the money into the property...'

'Eight hundred pounds?'

'Yes, sir. '

'And Mr Harper's contribution?'

'Naught sir.'

'Naught!' I was starting to imagine a picture of gullibility floating before me.

'Gordon Harper you see, was to be the business brains. He had years of experience in business, he said.'

'And Albert was horse savvy.'

'That's correct.

'Hmm,' I did not say so immediately, but the prospect sounded suspicious from the start.

'We also learnt that the day they took over the business, Mr Harper immediately paid the first insurance premium, valuing the business at two thousand six hundred pounds.'

'Would that be with The Van Diemen's Land Insurance Company?'

'Yes, Mr Hunter.'

'Then how can I help you, Mr Hartley?'

'Well, if I may just explain, sir.'

'Yes.'

'Everything operated smoothly for the first two months, as they settled in, like, and what moderate income there was, was re-invested back into building up the stud – investing in breeding stock and the like. And initially Albert was happy with the arrangement. He wrote home frequently. His letters spoke highly of his partner's business skills. But after a while, Gordon Harper took to journeying.'

'Journeying? Journeying where?'

'Melbourne, mostly. Well, so he told Albert. He told Albert he had other investments in a brewery in Ballarat and a hotel in Bendigo, but whenever my son queried him about them he was evasive. After six months Mr Harper journeyed more and more often and for several months at a time. This caused aggravation between the two partners.'

'I am certain it would.'

'In their second year, they started to lose money, which they argued over constantly. They decided to put the stud farm on the market and Albert took the opportunity to take a month's furlough.'

'I am certain that he needed it,' I stifled a yawn and thought *I will need furlough should this story continue much longer.*

'He sailed to North Adelaide in South Australia, where he has a cousin.'

'I see.' *Yawn.*

'But while he is away, the stud farm suffered a serious fire.'

I sat erect. 'A fire!'

'Yes, Mr Hunter. Quite damaging, as it turned out. And this Gordon fellow wasted no time demanding the insurance money. The insurance company sent in the investigators to review the damage and could you hazard a guess of that outcome, Mr Hunter?'

I looked pensive. 'They refused outright to pay the claim.'

'That is correct.'

'Suspicious circumstances afoot, I must say.'

'Yes, sir.'

'So how does this affect my office Mr Hartley?'

'Well, my son returned to hear the bad news, and what really surprised Albert was the fact that Gordon Harper refused to sue the insurance company.'

'Sounds like he knew he would lose in court. Maybe even face charges.'

'Exactly.'

'Albert and Harper fought. They had terrible arguments. Albert wrote us everything. Dorothea and I felt terrible; there was naught we could do and our son had lost his investment.

The last letter we were sent spoke of the partnership souring, but ...' Gideon Hartley's eyes welled and a lone tear rolled down his cheek. He took out his handkerchief and cleared his nose. 'I'm sorry sir, Mr Hunter.'

'Your son, where is he now?'

'Missing, Mr Hunter.'

So that's why you have come to see me.

'We have had no contact with Albert for fourteen months now.'

'Oh.'

'He sent us a letter over a year ago. It read, *I will be coming to see you Saturday one week.* He never arrived.'

'Do you think him ashamed to face you? Embarrassed? Angry with his own foolishness?'

'My wife thinks he is dead.'

I was silent a moment while the sorrowful father wiped his nose and eyes.

'Why would your wife think that?' I asked, surprised at such negativity.

Gideon Hartley looked me in the eye for the first time. He thought long and hard and cleared his throat to speak. 'She's had dreams, sir.'

'Dreams!' I wanted to laugh out loud.

'I know you'll think this daft, Mr Hunter. But my Dorothea, well she's a little spiritual like. Psychic, I think the word is. And she has seen Albert in her dreams. The dreams have been repetitive, sir; at least once a week. Then last night she saw him, clear as you like, lying at the bottom of a well. She was certain he was dead. Dorothea was most insistent I come to see you.'

Jesus Christ, I thought. *First vampires, now telepathic, clairvoyant, psychic lunatics.*

'You don't believe me, Mr Hunter.'

'Oh I believe your wife Dorothea has had dreams, yes, sir. But you cannot tell me you think your son dead because of a vision.'

Hartley expelled a loud sigh. 'I told Dorothea it would be useless coming to the police. I said they would never understand.'

I stood. 'Sir, Mr Hartley, have you not taken the coach to Launceston and inspected the property yourself? Asked questions? Your son is probably taking time to get over the embarrassment. He is probably working with his precious horses in Melbourne or Sydney.' I had a thought. 'Or what about in Adelaide, with his cousin?'

'Dorothea is an invalid, Mr Hunter. She has difficulty getting about; bedridden most of the time, and the only outings she manages are when I can borrow a cane wheel chair from the invalid hospital at New Town and push her to the docks. We are but poor folk, sir.'

'Oh. My apologies.' I resumed my seat, fielding ideas of how to rid myself of this problem. At least with a murder scene I had a dead body to contend with – something I could sink my teeth into; which reminded me, I had an appointment at the morgue, hopefully with a full report on our *vampire* victim.

'Mr Hartley,' I started, 'I have an appointment and I am late, sir.'

Hartley grew irritated. 'You don't believe me, do you?'

'I did not say that. I am a police investigator. It is my duty to serve you. But I do have prior arrangements of the utmost importance. I am going to leave you with my colleague, Jasper, and I want you to tell him everything. He will make notes. Where do you live, sir?'

'Warwick Street, West Hobart.'

'Then leave your details with Jasper and I promise I will be in touch. Now wait here please.'

I had spent more time with Mr Hartley than I intended and noted that it was nearly ten in the morning already. I had an appointment with Royle at noon and I wanted to talk to the coroner-come-mortician before she arrived.

Sergeant Clincher assured me Jasper had returned, so I sent a guard to fetch him. The lad had had few duties the past three days and I was keen to see what he could make of Gideon Hartley's dilemma. Clincher lingered on duty, back at the main entrance. He watched me approach, his back aching and his gouty foot giving him grief. He straightened his black leather shako and dusted his red coat as if on parade.

"Mr 'unter,' he said, pulling his Brown Bess musket parallel to his side in an act of duty. Or was it for support? 'Off again so soon?' he noted.

'Yes, Richard. I have business at the morgue.'

'The morgue eh!'

Already I had said too much. 'May I ask, sar, what draws your busy person to the morgue?'

'Later, Richard. Now, if you don't mind...' I alluded to the exit.

'Of course, Mr 'unter.' He lifted the heavy iron latch. 'How did yer go with Mr 'artley then, sar?' he said in a throwaway manner.

Not that it was any of the guard's business, however he was a harmless and helpful man who showed a healthy interest in his surroundings of twenty years.

'Fair, Richard,' I said. 'Fair.'

'Fair, huh? His wife sounds a bit o' a dreamer, if'n yer don't mind me sayin' like.'

'Dreamer?' Had Gideon Hartley been talking to the guard before my arrival?

'Aye. Them dreams about 'er dead boy, sar.'

I nodded to the prison's main entrance and the old soldier wheezed and groaned and tugged at the door within the iron studded main gate. It squealed on rusty hinges and the sergeant made the usual comment about Hobart Town being a whaling port, yet there was no oil for his damned gate. 'Thank you, Richard.'

'A penny for yer thoughts, Mr 'unter.'

'Pardon?'

'A penny for yer thoughts, your thoughts on Mrs Hartley's dreams?'

Christ, I thought. *The man knows everything.* 'I should have appointed you to solve the case, Richard,' I answered, stepping back out into that southerly gust blowing up Campbell Street from off the harbour.

'Me solve the case, sar. Golly gosh. Do you really think so, really?'

'Yes.' I pulled my coat lapel up about my ears to tackle the chill, thinking I should add gullible to the sergeant's repertoire, and strolled vaguely in the direction of the morgue.

'Mr 'unter.' My name was screeched against the incoming wind. I turned back to face Clincher, who by all appearances, had urgent business.

'The queen cakes, sar?' he shouted.

Oh, I had forgotten. 'Take them to the office, if you would be so kind.'

Clincher saluted and slammed the gate shut.

CHAPTER TWO

Of course, I was too early for the coroner-mortician. As I passed St Mary's on my way to the docks, I saw two hired help carrying the dead trapper from a cart on the street and up the front steps of the hospital. Arms and legs hung loosely on each side of the stretcher, but at least his mauled torso was hidden beneath a shroud. All the same I could not help it smile to myself, imagining the head matron catching them using the front entrance instead of the rear stairs. Dullards.

This suited me fine. I needed time to think, I needed space. I walked directly to the docks, making my way through the ever-increasing industry of whaling ships, which had replaced the convict transports, ever since *The Cessation of Transportation Act* was passed. I never tired of the sounds and sights of maritime commerce about the waterfront: coopers, blacksmiths and carpenters forever hammering, the cursing, timbers creaking, gulls fighting, clinking of chains, snapping of sail, the bosun's whistle and the singing crew hauling ropes as a ship sets sail. Then there are the smells, from Stockholm tar to week-old fish. I passed timber yards and shipyards where vessels small and large rise from timber piles. These shipwrights swear Tasmanian timber is superior to Australian mainland timbers of the same species. The blue gum for shipbuilding, peppermint and stringybark for general construction, Blackwood, Huon and King William pine for the cabinetmakers and fine furniture carpenters. All shipbuilders agreed the Leatherwood, Tea Tree and the Native Ironwood were noted for toughness, especially the Ironwood that they compared with lignum vitae, used for sheaves in ship's blocks. I personally favour the pungent smell of fresh wood shavings from the Huon pine tree – sometimes referred to as the Macquarie pine; Huon pine is a conifer native to the wetlands of south-western Tasmania. I should note again here, for the discerning reader, that Van Diemen's Land is increasingly becoming known as Tasmania; since the *Cessation of Transportation Act,* as I mentioned earlier, the good folk of the island are keen to rid reminders of the colony's dark past. As I mentioned, even public hangings have been prohibited and such executions are now conducted behind prison walls. Far more civilised.

The docks were crowded. Sullivan's Cove was peppered with craft from the Royal Navy to merchantmen, to whalers and passenger ships. Tenders, wherries and ferries weaved amongst them, taking passengers and luggage back and forth. You see, the goldfields of Victoria, or 'The Rush' as it was called, was settling somewhat. Unsuccessful miners were returning to Hobart Town.

I headed straight for the Sailor's Rest on New Wharf, passing sailors conversing and arguing in a foreign language. How cosmopolitan Hobart Town seemed. And the future looked bright from where I stood, now at the taproom bar of the Sailor's Rest.

'Bit early for a tipple ain't yer, Caspian?'

My good friend and innkeeper, Bonnie Nettle, always watched my back. We became close friends when I arrived in Hobart Town in '55, when I lodged at the inn for several months. I should mention here that the Sailor's Rest was a bordello, a whorehouse, but a clean and well-run enterprise. Bonnie was now innkeeper and madam, having retired from the profession of her youth, years earlier. And before you ask, keen reader, our friendship was platonic.

'Early?' says I. 'Not today Bonnie. It is brass monkeys outside.'

Bonnie poured me a brandy. 'Then this'll warm yer cockles.'

'Thank you.' I drank the measure in one draft.

'My word,' Bonnie smiled pouring another. 'And this one'll clear the head.' I drank half and returned Bonnie's warm smile, as the French brandy fired my belly. Bonnie was not her usual jovial self, and I noticed the thick ledger on the bar where she had been inspecting the inn's figures of late.

'Everything shipshape?' I alluded to the tome.

'I guess so, Caspian. I can't complain. But with the Hobart Gasworks now in full production, I fear for the whaling industry.'

I knew Bonnie spoke of the use of gas in street lighting and the increasing use of spirit oils for fuel, both of which were having a detrimental effect on the whale fishery. My guess was, though, that the whales would not complain.

'But there will always be industry around Sullivan's Cove, Bonnie. You worry needlessly.'

'I suppose. It's just that I have commitments; many girls rely on old Bonnie.'

'Enough talk of being *old* now, Bon.'

I must have looked preoccupied myself, for Bonnie asked me, 'Well, are you goin' to tell Bonnie *your* woes?' as she slammed the ledger closed. The woman could read me like the *Hobart Town Gazette*.

'I just have this feeling, Bonnie, that today is going to be fraught with complications.'

'Oh?'

I told Bonnie about my brush with vampires and mystic dreamers.

'There are people out there, Caspian, who drink human blood. I've heard about it before. And, like it or not, they are called vampires.'

'Jesus, Bonnie. Not you, too.' I swallowed the rest of my brandy and shuddered, sliding a silver crown onto the bar and bidding her farewell. Bonnie pushed the coin back at me with long black-glazed fingernails. 'You hang onto that crown and come spend it with me on yer way back to yer cottage tonight. All right? Take care.'

I was about to leave when Holly came through the parlour door, barking like the town crier. 'Sar, sar, Caspian sar,' she gasped for air.

'Holly!'

'Bonnie,' Holly panted, touching her cap to the innkeeper in greeting. 'Excuse the interruption.' Holly swung about to face me. "They said I'd find yer here.'

'Who?'

'Sergeant Clincher.'

'How on earth... never mind. What is it Holly?'

'You better come quick, sar,' Holly gulped a lungful of air. 'We got another deaden.'

'Oh? Really?'

'A body, sar... on the wastelands.' Holly snatched another breath.

'Wastelands?'

'Aye... behind the slaughter yard near... Queen's Domain.' Holly doubled over with her hands on her knees gulping mouthfuls of air. 'Jaysuz, an' I thought I was in fine fettle,' she bemoaned her health. 'It's a woman, sar...'orrible sight an' all. Attacked... her womanhood assaulted, I'm thinkin'.'

'Lead the way, Hol'.'

11 AM

We passed the slaughter yard and tanneries, deserting the stink of the morgue for the reek of the Hobart Town rivulet. Unfortunately, the pure springs of sweet drinking water, originating at the top of the mountain, filtered through the township where it spilled into Sullivan's Cove, curdled into a soup of daily life and all its waste. I hurried after Holly, across a narrow footbridge and climbed a shallow hill with a clear view down the estuary and all its environs. Apart from the macabre scene waiting, the view was imposing. Tall ships anchored with furled sails, others about to embark into the blue yonder on their next adventure and lighters and wherries weaving amongst the anchored craft, going about the daily business of a busy port.

Two constables were having difficulty keeping the ghouls at bay. A dozen or so morbid onlookers gathered about, each voicing their own conclusions.

'Back off!' Holly yelled. 'Move it. The lot o' yer.' Holly ploughed into the circle, shoving bodies this way and that whilst flashing her brass badge to assert her authority. The two constables, javelin-men who were once guests of Queen Victoria at Port Arthur and now had their 'tickets', took a leaf from Holly's book, poking and prodding disgruntled sightseers with their lead weighted coshes.

'Garn,' Holly shouted. 'Bugger orf, all o' yer.'

The ghouls moved away only to gather together on a grassy knoll ten yards away. I looked at the victim where she lay dead on her back; eyes open, staring blindly towards the heavens. Her skirts were saturated with blood. I dropped to my knees and felt for a pulse but she was clearly deceased.

'She hasn't been there long, eh?' Holly asked.

'No Holly. Not long at all. A few hours maybe, before dawn.' I stood and looked about to take in the scene. Familiar as I was with the area, it seemed to me someone would have seen something. It was broad daylight. At that moment I saw Lincoln appear from over a rise in the hill, pulling behind him a handcart.

'How did you know she was here?' I asked Holly.

Holly turned to scowl at the ghouls. 'One o' that mob came to the barracks... after the watchmen 'ere arrived.' Holly tipped her head to the constables standing by dutifully. 'She's been... you know...' Holly lowered her voice. 'Defiled... assaulted, ain't she?'

'It looks that way, Holly.' I walked over to the gathering. 'Did anyone see anything?'

'It be thart damned vampire!' some ignoramus cried out.

'Aye!' another uneducated sod concurred.

'How on earth did they hear about it?' I snapped.

'Small world, Caspian sar.'

'Small all right.'

Holly looked at me with that questioning face of hers. A face I had witnessed before. 'Do yer think that...?'

'Holly! There are no such things as vampires!'

'Yeh but...'

But the locals did not agree. 'Margery Waters's cat jumped over the body of 'er dead father two day ago,' one shuddered.

'Aye,' another agreed. 'Thart be the makings of a vampire. Everyone knows thart.'

'An Betty Norris's little bastard bairn were born with teeth.' An old hag stirred the pot. 'Born wiv teeth I say!' Her eyes were wide with gullible fear. 'We all know what thart means.'

'I said, 'Did anyone see anything at all worth reporting, besides the undead sneaking about before sunup?' I added with a measure of sarcasm.

Low murmurings, incoherent mumbles. 'Come now,' I said. 'Someone must have seen something.'

'Edgar 'ere found 'er,' one woman offered, stepping away from Edgar as if he would launch an attack on her for pointing the finger.

'Edgar?'

'Aye.' The man looked sheepish. 'I was headin' down to the water to do some fishin' when I seen 'er lyin' there. Thart's all, sar, honest.'

'It's alright Edgar, I'm not accusing you of such a dastardly crime.' Edgar shot the woman a filthy look. 'Does anyone know her name?' I asked.

'Aye. Thart be Lizzie Burke. She be a scullery maid. She used to live at Wappin' with the rest o' us.'

'Aye. But she moved out some time ago.'

'Is she married?' I asked, and was answered with a dozen sniggers. 'Well, what does that mean?' I scowled.

'She were single, sar, but thart don't mean she didn't enjoy the company o' men.'

'Are you implying the woman was a... a streetwalker?'

'Nay, sar, she weren't no whore. She just liked men, thart's all.'

'Not against the law is it, likin' men, thart is?'

'No. Of course not. Does she have children?'

'No sar.'

'Does anyone know where she lives... she lived?'

There followed much foot shuffling and down-turned heads, before one woman huffed at her neighbours and offered, 'Aye. Last I heard, Lizzie be scullery maid at the Nightingale.'

'You speak of Florence Nightingale Inn I take it?'

'Aye, sar.'

'Innkeeper Cecil Condon give 'er lodgin's there too, sar.'

'Cecil Condon, you say?'

'Aye.'

I knew the grossly overweight Cecil Condon, the innkeeper, to be a difficult man, a tyrant, too, by all records. So I insisted Holly accompany me to the inn facing Morrison Street on Hobart Town's waterfront, while Lincoln transferred little Lizzie to the morgue. I was also aware that Condon shared his bed with a like-minded, corpulent gold digger named Elvina Hedwig. Hedwig was an opportunist, an ex-prisoner from the women's factory at the Cascades who was transported for larceny and had been in and out of trouble ever since she was released, eleven years passed.

Holly and I walked the docks briskly, more to warm ourselves with a fast pace, rather than in haste, this freezing July morning. We hurried across the narrow footbridge of Victoria Dock towards the Mariner's Church, a delightful sandstone chapel for seafarers, where the Florence Nightingale Inn fitted snugly between chandlers and providores behind the church. Here, we turned the corner in time to witness a most unusual scene.

'Oh dear,' I said to Holly. 'It appears we are too late.'

Holly and I stood before the inn as the colossal body of Cecil Condon was being winched from an attic window.

The undertaker's horse and cart waited below, while Colbert Lemmings, the undertaker, directed the procedure. His assistant, a little old man I knew was named Charge, whom it was said was a powder monkey on Nelson's *Victory* at Trafalgar, smiled away, showing off his lack of teeth. He pulled hard on a block and tackle; double tackled to take the weight, hopefully. And he looked the grizzled old sailor of some vintage and experience. Lemmings recognised me immediately. 'A good mornin' to yer Mr 'unter,' he said, tipping his pipe stack topper.

'And a good morning to you, Lemmings.'

'Old Cecil 'ere wouldn't fit down the stairs,' the undertaker said of the innkeeper. ''e's too heavy a gentleman to carry. So I come up with this 'ere mastery of engineering.' As he spoke the rope slipped through his assistant's fingers and the door being used as a stretcher, on which the body was fastened, tipped dramatically.

'I can't watch, Caspian sar,' Holly said quietly in my ear.

'How did he die, Mr Lemmings?'

'Coronary thrombosis; the doctors are touting it these days, Mr 'unter.'

'You mean a heart seizure?'

'That's the one, sar. Seizure o' the ol' ticker.'

'Well, 'e *were* a big bastard,' Holly offered.

I shot Holly a look... *little more respect, please.* But somehow it was lost on a *fat old bastard* I knew to be a tyrant.

We left Lemmings and his aged and grizzled number two to lower the behemoth onto the cart, and let ourselves in a side door to the inn. Cecil Condon's partner in licentiousness and portly lover, Elvina Hedwig, was sitting at a table by the fire grate counting the takings from the day before. I had been warned she was a strong old bird who could fight like a man, and she looked far from the grieving widow. 'We ain't open,' she scowled as we entered.

'Elvina Hedwig?' Holly asked.

'Who wants ter know?'

Holly planted her feet apart, hands on hips, exposing her Tower pistol wedged behind her britches' belt. 'Obart Town police department,' she said.

Elvina slammed the cash tin closed, twisting the key in its lock. 'What d'ya want?'

The sound of pouring liquid drew my attention to the bar, where a timid young girl funnelling slops from last night's tankards into a stoneware crock reminded me why I did not partake of the inn's surprisingly cheap drink called 'sailors' trousers'.

'We came to talk to Mr Condon,' I told Hedwig. 'But he is kind of indisposed, isn't he?'

'Indisposed!' Hedwig coughed a laugh. 'Yer mean dead!'

'I was not going to be quite so blunt, Miss Hedwig.'

'Lizzie Burke,' Holly started. 'She lived here, eh?'

'Lived,' Elvina answered. 'You tellin' me she's indisposed also?'

'Sadly,' I said. 'Yes.'

Suddenly she looked grave. 'Yer serious, ain't yer?'

'Yes madam.'

'How?'

'We think she was brutally raped and plundered...' Holly divulged, without choosing her words carefully.

'Thart'd be 'er lover Samuel Groundwater,' Elvina spat the name with vitriolic hatred. ''e be no good. Jaysuz Christ, I told thart girl; Lizzie I says, stay away from the cunny mongrel.'

'Strong words, Mrs Hedwig,' I was shocked. 'Strong words indeed.'

''e be trouble from the start that one. Oh, 'e tell little Lizzie 'e love her an' all thart shite, but 'e were only after one thing. And then she went an' got herself with child, didn't she?'

'With child?'

'Aye. She were havin' the bastard's baby. I was real mad when she told me.'

'So where can we find this 'ere cunny?' Holly asked.

'Holly!'

'Sorry Caspian, sar, I'll rephrase thart. So where can we find this bastard, Samuel Groundwater?'

''e works the slaughter yard yonder.' Hedwig waved a hand in the direction from whence we just came, near the domain.

Oh. He's a slaughterman, is he?'

'Aye, he boasted 'e could draw and quarter a bull in ten minutes.'

Back on Morrison Street I blew warm breath into cupped hands and lifted my collar high, watching Lemmings's toothless offsider rope old Cecil Condon onto his cart for transportation to the undertakers. The gnome-like assistant, agile for his age, hopped onto the back of the cart, dangling his legs over the back for the ride, like a playful tyke. Coronary thrombosis victim Cecil Condon was barely hidden beneath a canvas shroud. Lemmings tipped his topper to me for a final salute and tapped Ned the draught horse on the rear, and Holly and I watched in silence a moment, as the macabre scene played out to the first corner.

'Slaughter yard, sar?' Holly words drifted before my reverie in a condensed mist.

'What was that?'

'Slaughter yard, Caspian sar? Will we go talk to this 'ere Samuel Groundwater? Little Lizzie's lover?'

'Oh... ah... I need to pay a visit to Doctor Crawley at the morgue first,' I told Holly.

'Rightio, then.' Holly made to head for St Mary's Hospital, only a brisk walk away.

'Ah no, Holly. You go to the barracks.'

I spoke of our office, knowing Royle Rowley had been summoned to the morgue to make photographic images of the *vampire victim* for the courts and police record. And I certainly did not want Holly there as an unwelcome chaperone, should the occasion arise for Royle and myself to indulge in a little hanky-panky, as they say.

Just the very thought warmed my cockles.

Holly studied me a moment. She knew what I was up to, I know she did. There had been rumours of late. And where there's smoke there's fire.

'I'll see yer back there then, Caspian sar,' Holly said obediently, hooked her fingers together, cracked her knuckles and marched away, whistling the tune to a whorehouse ditty.

St Mary's Hospital morgue, corner of Davey Street and Salamanca, 11.45 AM

One never becomes accustomed to the morgue. Especially this poorly vented underground dungeon entered by a spiral stone stair, with only two lanterns pinioned within wall sconces to usher the unwary into the pit of death.

I always said that any man whose prime interest in life is death has to be a little peculiar. Dr Ernest Crawley was no exception. He was tall and slim, slovenly in his dress although clean in hygiene, with mutton chop side burns joined by a moustache, but no beard. Long silky strands of snow-white hair were combed clumsily over his baldpate in an attempt to deduct a few years from his appearance. Nevertheless, he was seventy-one and looked even older.

The trapper's cadaver lay on the mortician's stone slab, a large sandstone worktable carved in one piece with a convenient gutter surrounding its perimeter and angled to allow blood to drain into a well-positioned bucket.

Doctor Crawley worked alone and appeared inundated with death of late. The dead trapper was not his only body this day. Already, I noted two other bodies in shrouds on the floor awaiting his expertise. I was aware Crawley had acute hearing and made my steps purposeful, wishing to warn the man of my approach. However, my shadow, in the ill-lit morgue, passed over the naked cadaver before I had a chance to announce my arrival.

'Jesus Christ,' he shouted, rounding on me with a scalpel in his hand. 'Must you always creep up on me like that?'

'I... I did not mean to alarm you Doct...'

'What? Alarm me? Yes you did.'

His hearing was definitely deteriorating. It was easier to simply apologise. 'I have a name, Doctor Crawley.'

'Yes, I know. Caspian Hunter.'

'Not me, doctor. The victim,' I nodded to the body.

He peered over his pince-nez. 'What?'

'The victim, sir, I know his name.'

'Oh. What is it then?'

'McK.'

'McKay.'

'Yes but it is spelt 'Mc 'with a capital 'K', not McK-a-y.'

'And I'm supposed to write that on the death certificate am I? Ridiculous.'

'It is all I have, sir. So, tell me Doctor Crawley. What are your observations?'

'Heart failure!'

'You mean coronary thrombosis?' I said, feeling pleased with myself for knowing the most modern terminology.

'What?'

'Coronary thrombosis.'

He looked at me as if I had used vulgar language in church.

'I was just recently talking to the undertaker, Colbert Lemmings,' I quickly added. 'And he explained the new terminology.'

'Coronary thrombosis? Never heard of it, Mr Hunter. And I'm telling you now, this man died of heart failure.'

'Yes of course.'

'Now pay attention Mr Hunter. He has dropped dead and been mauled by those abominable devil creatures.'

'Oh.' I moved closer and shifted the lantern to light the wounds in the cadaver's neck. 'Those holes, at first I thought they may be small calibre bullet entries.'

'Bah!' Crawley made a half laugh. 'Well, in all fairness I can understand you thinking that. They do look a little like bullet holes, but they are the canine teeth of those furry scavengers.'

'Are you certain?'

'I'll pretend I didn't hear that, young man.'

'Sorry. It is just that... well...' I was lost for words.

'Well what, Mr Hunter? Spit it out.'

'I know this sounds ridiculous, but someone suggested it was the work of a vampire.'

'Huh! Vampire, eh. You better go back to the inn and have another brandy.'

Was my breath that obvious?

I felt myself blush. 'It was but a theory, Doctor. Ah, I have been told there are those, a rare few thankfully, who enjoy drinking human blood.'

Crawley's mockery returned to a face of academia.

'If you refer to the lack of blood at the crime scene – for the use of a better word, as I am signing this off as natural causes – and the loss of blood in the body, it is due to the devils drinking it.' I must have looked a little vague. 'Vampires are just fodder for horror stories, Mr Hunter. Warded off with garlic. Live in castles. And all that. It's simply a fear of the dead, once buried, coming back to harm the living.'

'I agree, Doctor.'

'Ignorance spurns the myth,' he went on. 'As a corpse decomposes the skin shrinks, making the teeth and fingernails appear to grow longer in death. As the innards, the organs that is, break down, they purge a dark fluid from the mouth and nose and in all appearances, to the ignorant, it appears they have been drinking blood from the living. In medieval times, vampires were also accused of spreading disease amongst communities.'

'I am glad we are on the same page, sir.'

'Good. Give your friend the recipe for an anti-vampire cure,' Crawley offered with a cheeky grin, referring to Lincoln, who had started this vampire caper.

'Recipe, sir? And what may that be?'

'Burn the vampire's heart and mix the ashes with a portion of grog, to be drunk by the victim. That is, the fool that believes such poppycock.'

'Did you make that up, Doctor?'

'No. I read a lot. You will find that written in *The Vampyre*, printed back in 1819.'

'Aha. I see.'

'Now if you will excuse me, I have a meeting with the hospital board at noon.' He gathered his coat and made for the stairs.

'I meant to tell you, doctor. There will be another body delivered here shortly.'

'Good god man. What now?'

I explained the discovery of Lizzie Burke.

'I've no room here, as you can well see. See she is taken to the Electric Telegraph Hotel. I'll have to send my assistant, Doctor Kingsley, to do the autopsy. Now, are you coming, Caspian?'

'No, sir. I have an appointment with Mrs Rowley.'

'Oh the photographic images. Jolly good. I'll leave you to it.' Crawley was on his third step when he called back, 'Watch that fellow will you.' He pointed to the cadaver.

'Sir?'

'Yes. Watch he doesn't sit up and go for your throat!' Echoing laughter faded up the spiral stairs.

I waited in silence. My mind wandered. My imagination worked overtime. It would be easy to imagine ghosts and ghouls lurking in the shadows here, and I was considering waiting up top for Royle when I heard the struggles and clatter as hospital orderlies dragged Royle's equipment down the stone steps.

'Caspian, you are here, thank goodness.' She was in high spirits.

'Of course. We had an appointment, remember,' I answered, trying not to sound curt.

The workers dumped the crates and left us to work alone. I helped Royle set up the camera, the tripod and prepared the flash pan. We said little. Finally Royle peeled back the sheet covering the trapper's body.

'Dear me,' Royle let out an inappropriate snigger. 'What got to him?

To be honest, I think Royle makes light of these events to disguise the horror of it all.

'Not you, too.'

'What's that?' Royle asked, her focus locked on the trapper's upper body.

'Vampires. Everyone thinks the man was killed by a vampire and had his blood drained.'

'Well, he does look rather pale.'

'He *is* dead.'

'Yes, but paler than most I have seen. And I've seen a few.'

'I bet you have.'

'What was that? Caspian, are you still angry with me?'

'Royle, can we please just make the images and vacate this awful place?'

'Argh,' Royle saw my weakness and pounced. 'My little soldier isn't scared of the dark, is he now?' She pushed herself against me.

'Royle. Not now.'

'Oh Caspian,' she purred, and nibbled my ear whilst exploring my inner lobe with her warm tongue.

I was butter in her hands. Blood rushed to my loins. I felt my britches stretch... so did Royle, and she thrust her body hard against mine. 'Caspy, Caspy, I've missed you so.'

'Oh Jesus, Royle. It is impossible to stay vexed with you, you little minx.'

'Guess what?' she said suddenly.

'What?'

'I seem to have forgotten my knickerbockers.'

'Oh behave... you wicked little girl.'

I lifted her skirts and groped her perfect round tight white buttocks. Royle fumbled for my naughty soldier who was standing at attention waiting to be punished.

'Mr Hunter!' My name echoed about the walls from the top of the stair. It was the duty matron, Eudora Cabarge. 'Mr Hunter, are you still down there?'

'Y-yes,' I answered weakly, cleared my throat and repeated in a deeper baritone. 'Yes. Mrs Cabbage, is it not?'

'Cabarge, Mr Hunter. Cabarge.' We heard her heavy steps clip and clop as she descended. 'You are with Mrs Rowley, I take it.'

'Yes,' I replied as we frantically straightened our clothing. 'We are about to commence, madam.'

The matron's generously rounded head appeared about the stone stairwell. 'Very good. I am just in time then. I have always wanted to watch this image making process as it happens, so to speak.'

Well, that was the end of that, then. The naughty soldier went AWOL while Royle's round, tight, white buttocks disappeared back under her skirts.

Bugger!

With any thoughts of a tryst with Royle thwarted, I came to the conclusion that, to take my mind off such forbidden fruits, I should make an appearance at the Electric Telegraph Hotel.

'Caspian, sar.' I twisted about to see Jasper already here.

'Jasper. What a surprise.'

'Yes, sar. Fabian sent me down here to make notes,' and he held up his leather-covered pad and lead pencil.

'Very well. It appears I am just in time.'

With the morgue fully occupied with cadavers, Doctor Ernest Crawley had ordered the body of Lizzie Burke, the young woman whose body was found in a ditch on the domain, to be taken to the parlour of the Electric Telegraph Hotel, on the corner of Morrison and Brooke Street, a stone's throw from Waterman's Dock. This newly opened hotel had taken its name from the Hobart telegraph office directly opposite on Franklin Wharf.

There were witnesses aplenty, filling the parlour with their persons and pints and all offering their two bobs worth of what happened to the young lass stretched out on the dining table. As promised, the indisposed Doctor Crawley had sent a colleague from the hospital in his place.

Doctor Edward Kingsbury was in his mid-fifties and an excitable man with a tremulous disposition. He was five-foot-two short with a thick neck and blotchy red complexion. I got the impression that the man was fond of alcoholic libations, for I smelt gin on his breath, although the ever-present formaldehyde permeated his clothing.

Following a preliminary inspection, and after hearing some of the more reliable witness reports of Lizzie, seen staggering across the wastelands clutching her belly, Dr Kingsbury cleared the parlour to afford the victim some modesty before hitching her skirts high to inspect her private parts. For this was from where most of the blood had seeped. He inspected her internally, turned to me and said, 'You can write on her death certificate, death by misadventure whilst inducing a miscarriage, possibly self-inflicted,' he told me matter-of-factly.

'An abortion.'

'Yes, Mr Hunter. The foetus has been removed and she has died an agonising death of acute peritonitis, consequences of her punctured uterus. She has bled out.'

'How sad.'

My mind went to charlatan abortionists who should be held to account.

'Sad, yes, but unfortunately, not uncommon. Women use sharp instruments such as knitting needles, boot hooks or heaven forbid, I have even known hat pins to be used.'

'God no.'

'Others use abortifacients like juniper oil and herbs like pennyroyal, tansy and ergot of rye, or womb cleansers like lead pills or savin.'

'Savin,' Jasper said. 'Known as bastard killer.'

'That's correct.' Doctor Kingsbury washed his hands in soapy water brought to the parlour for his benefit. He dried his hands on a drying cloth and scrawled his signature across the bottom of Lizzie Burke's death certificate.

'Now I suggest you send out men to trap that vampire of yours.'

'Not you, too,' I said curtly.

'Vampire!' Jasper was suddenly alert. 'I told yer.'

'I hate to ruin the moment, Jasper,' I said, 'but the doctor is talking figuratively.'

'Figuratively?'

'Yes.'

Doctor Kingsbury slipped a pewter spirit flask from his back pocket and took a long draught. 'The dead house is full,' he said nonchalantly.

'Well, the body can't stay here,' I said.

'No, but I spoke to the innkeeper earlier, and he said she can spend the night in the scullery.' This was not exactly an unusual state of affairs when the morgue was full.

'She'll be fine in this weather,' he added, buttoning up his coat.

'Aye,' Jasper agreed.

That she will, I thought to myself, 'but the scullery?'

'The inn is not serving food this day.'

'Oh. That's fine then.'

12.25p.m

I looked at the hotel clock in the parlour. 12.25. *My, the day's getting away with me and I haven't even been to the office as yet.*

'You coming back to the barracks, Caspian sar? Cos I'll walk with yer.'

'Shortly. I should pay a visit, sooner than later, to Samuel Groundwater, dead Lizzie's lover, at the slaughter yard.'

'Then I'll see you back there. Fabian told me to come back directly.'

Slaughter Yards

Hobart Town's slaughter yards cover six acres I am told, running along the rivulet where all the unusable material is discarded. For this reason it is said the area where the rivulet meets the River Derwent is prolific with the bull sharks that breed further up river in front of government house. There are fifteen private slaughtering pens within the yard, each capable of holding fifteen head of beef or one hundred sheep or a large number of pigs. Butchers who pay slaughtering dues in advance hire these. As the area is washed regularly with lime wash, the smell was not overly malodorous, yet the odour of blood and guts does dominate. And the racket! The mooing, bleating and squealing tugs at one's conscience. Unfortunately though, for the beasts, they just taste so good dressed, cooked and served on a plate.

I passed half a dozen aborigines at the entrance; here, they assembled waiting for refuse. Sadly, it was them or the sharks, I thought. Although I wore the day-attire of a middle-class gentleman, my position as policeman was immediately noted. Hobart Town is not an overly populated town by any means, not like some similar towns in England, so my presence as a lawman was made aware. By the time I sought out Samuel Groundwater, the man had time to prepare himself.

'Aye, I'm Samuel Groundwater.' He was a pint-sized man with a furrowed brow, a receding chin, a brush moustache and oiled hair parted in the centre. For some reason, I thought him well suited to Lizzie, sadly deceased.

'What's this all about then?'

My, he was defensive.

Immediately I was aware of an older figure working alongside Samuel, who by all appearances, was teaching Samuel a cut or two. They stood together alongside a rather large pig, also recently deceased, hanging by its back trotters, where its blood poured into a leather bucket, ready to make blood pudding. The other man had unwashed shoulder length hair and sunken narrow, dark eyes and I could not help to notice his left ear was missing. Probably lost it through a fight, I fancied. He was also a large, well-built man whom I would not like to meet on Kelly's Steps on a dark night. *Built like a brick shithouse,* as Fabian was fond of saying. He avoided eye contact and made himself scarce.

'I've not done nuthin' wrong,' Samuel said defensively. 'You're with the constabulary ain't yer?'

'Yes, I am. Look Samuel, I'm here about Lizzie Burke.'

'Wha' about 'er?' he said far too readily.

'Well, when did you see her last?'

'Yesterdee.'

'What time yesterday?'

'Bit before noon, 'cos I 'ad to be 'ere at twelve o'clock.'

'And you did not see Miss Burke last evening?'

'You deaf? I said I last seen 'er jus' before noon.'

'You saw her most nights, I've been told. Why did you not see her last night?'

Samuel thought a little more carefully this time before answering. 'Cos we 'ad a row, didn't we?'

'About what?'

'Does it matter?'

'Answer the question if you please.'

'If'n yer must know, we found out she were with bairn.'

'She was having your baby?'

'That's what *she* said.'

'What does that mean?'

'Well, Lizzie weren't exactly keen on bein' with the one fella, was she?'

'Oh. So you thought the baby could possibly be someone else's?'

Samuel Groundwater looked out towards the river. His face reddened. 'I told 'er to get an abortion. I told 'er I knew a woman in Wappin' what does 'em for five bob.'

These charlatans were not exactly strangers to me either.

'Do you know her name, this woman?'

'No.'

I had deliberately held back on telling Samuel Lizzie was dead, and now felt a little awkward having left the sledgehammer moment this late in the conversation. All the same I looked him in the eye.

'Samuel.' Nothing. 'Samuel!'

He reluctantly turned to face me.

'I am sorry to have to inform you, but Lizzie's body was found this morning.'

He did not flinch. No eye twitch or look of surprise, before he burst into what I could only describe as bad acting.

'No!' he cried out. 'No. Not my Lizzie. How? What happened?'

'She was found on the Queen's Domain early this morning. She had died due to the loss of blood, from a less than satisfactory feticide.'

I looked at Samuel long and hard. He covered his face with his hands and lowered his head, better not to be scrutinised by the law, and I had a nagging feeling that he knew more than he let on.

Surely it was not he who had attempted the termination, I thought.

'I loved her,' he sobbed, his words muffled through his fingers. 'I was truly in love with Lizzie. Oh, I know she saw others, but none were like me.'

This was in contrast to his insisting she had an abortion.

'Some say you merely used Lizzie.'

'What! Who?'

'I... I'm... I am not at liberty to say.'

'Did you talk to that fat bitch Hedwig at the Nightingale, where Lizzie lived?'

Now it was my turn for bad acting. I must have blushed.

'Yer, did didn't yer? She tried to bed me once and I turned 'er down. I was drunk an' all, told 'er she were too fat an' I would 'ave to roll 'er in flour to look for the wet bits.' Samuel laughed nervously at the memory.

I wanted to laugh myself, but this was serious business.

'She's had it in fer me ever since, fat cow.'

With doubts about Samuel Groundwater's integrity, yet uncertain if it was he who had accidentally killed Lizzie, I threatened him with arrest, should he try and leave the island.

And finally walked to the barracks.

Campbell Street Prisoner Barracks. Two'ish in the afternoon

It was early afternoon by the time I finally presented myself in our office, a first-floor room above the prison stores, where we were afforded the tight space for our investigative travails. We enjoyed a desk and chair each, albeit small, a large painted blackboard on the south wall for recording clues, a chest of drawers for stationery that doubled as a bookshelf and a potbelly stove to heat the room and stew our coffee. This however was more a hindrance in the warm summer months. However, one small window opened onto the prison courtyard, offering a clear view of the gallows.

Famished, I fetched some cold cuts of meat and fresh baked damper from the officers' mess before returning to an office where the full team were present.

Fabian balanced on his chair's back legs, boots on his desk, stared at the blackboard where Billings had been making notes. Jasper was showing Lantern Jaw Lincoln how to disassemble his Tower pistol, clean and re-assemble it, while Holly sat by the potbelly stove cutting and pasting articles of interest, pertaining to her achievements at the barracks, from the *Hobart Town Gazette*. There was also a soft side to Holly I did not know existed. For Holly was pasting a Christmas card and a gilt-edged Valentine into her scrap-book, as well. The Christmas card, dog-eared and well loved, I recognised immediately. It was made up of three panels, the outer two showing people caring for the poor and the centre panel showing a large family enjoying a sumptuous Christmas dinner.

I knew the illustration well for I remember my mother in Birmingham railing at the image of a wee child being fed a glass of wine. But it was the Valentine that caught my attention. Was this from Lincoln? I was sorely tempted to take a peek when Holly's eyes warned me otherwise. And I noted that her trusty Tower was within easy reach.

Outside Hobart Town had turned bleak. Winter, it seemed, had arrived with a vengeance. Although in all fairness, I must say winter in Van Diemen's Land rarely is as bleak and miserable as England. I had walked into the office amidst a spirited debate. Holly was animated. ''tis the truth I say.'

Fabian, Lincoln and Jasper stood by as Billings weighed in. 'Truth? I doubt it Holly,' Fabian argued. 'You jest, surely.'

'On god's honour, it's the truth.'

'What is?' I asked.

'Ah,' Fabian released his feet from his desk and swung forward on his chair. 'Welcome stranger.'

I nodded acknowledgement to all, and noted the parcel of queen cakes untouched on my desk.

'You've been unfortunate enough to have survived a shipwreck, Caspian sar,' Holly said.

And yes, I had survived a shipwreck, but that story is in another memoir. 'How do you mean Holly?' I asked. 'I was *unfortunate* enough to survive a shipwreck?'

'Oh Jaysuz sar, you know wha' I mean.'

'If you meant I was *fortunate* enough to survive a shipwreck, then the answer's yes.'

'Well, I was jus' tellin' the lads 'ere about a shipwreck victim what was washed up on the beach down Dover way and a local cove what found his body tried to claim the man's knee high boots...'

'Was 'e dead?' Jasper asked.

''course 'e were bloody dead. But 'e couldn't get the boots off 'cos the cove's legs were swollen up like.'

'Then what?'

'Well, 'e chopped 'is legs off at the knee...'

Billings face screwed like a ball of paper. 'Chopped them off!'

'Sawed 'em, chopped 'em, hacked 'em. What's the bloody difference?'

'I hate to tell yer this, but he's dead, eh Hol?' Lincoln smiled at Holly in admiration.

'Why try to remove them if they was stuck?' Fabian asked. 'If they was stuck, they was stuck.'

'He took 'em home and ...'

'What, the legs an' all?'

'Aye. He took 'em home and tied them boots upside down, up the chimney and left 'em there until the meat shrank and fell out.'

'Lovely,' I said. 'Anyone for a queen cake?'

With little to occupy our sleuthing requirements, other than a trapper dropping dead from heart failure, the dreams of an invalid woman who agonised over the whereabouts of her foolish adult son, the death of poor Lizzie Burke, we took the advantage of an early afternoon and moved camp to the Sailor's Rest. This was after all, a rare occurrence. Bonnie was most excited. It was scarce that she had us all under her roof at the same time.

'So, you've come back to spend that crown huh?' Bonnie singled me out as we filed through the taproom door.

'Yes, my dearest Bonnie,' I answered, 'and we're all thirsty.'

'Good. Mr Wallis's latest brew o' porter is ready to be tapped.' Bonnie cleared a table for us by herding drunkards to other tables. 'And it's Friday.'

'Every day's Friday here, Bonnie,' I said.

And there was no arguing that. Bonnie Nettle ran the finest inn on the waterfront. But Friday was entertainment night, when one end of the taproom was furnished with a raised floor for a stage, with thick velvet curtains falling from the ceiling either side. A trompe l'oeil of a London street scene painted on canvas hung at the back of the stage. Bonnie even supplied limelight on the stage floor to light her merry troupe. Bonnie styled her taproom on music halls in Covent Garden, where she had trod the boards before being arrested for prostitution and transported to Van Diemen's Land for seven years. That was back in 1839, when she was just thirty years old. Bonnie served four years at the Bothwell women's prison in Van Diemen's Land's central highlands. Here she met Captain Rogers of the 40th Foot Regiment. They fell in love and married. And should have lived happily ever after, however the good captain was killed in a coaching accident in '46. Bonnie inherited a small amount of money and a cottage on fifty acres, which she sold and moved to Hobart Town. Now in possession of a full pardon, Bonnie leased the Sailor's Rest in '47 and was in a position to purchase the building in '49, all the while operating a fine establishment with good entertainment, toothsome food, good ales, unadulterated spirits and above all clean girls.

'I have four new ladies on the menu tonight,' Bonnie said with a wink, as she shuffled a tray amongst us with ewers of porter and clean tankards.

'Any men on the menu?' Holly yelled over the banter.

'Jamaica Black will be here later,' Bonnie teased.

Holly whooped, only to earn a downcast look from Lantern Jaw Lincoln.

'I only jest,' Holly said, elbowing her friend in the ribs.

By six o'clock we had not a care in the world. The fiddler entertained with ditties as the docks were draped in winter's darkness, and seafarers and Hobartians stepped out of the mist to fill every available space in the taproom.

By seven, scantily dressed dancing girls kicked up their heels on stage in the latest dance moves from Paris. The low-beamed room filled with the aromas of cook's rabbit and carrots at one shilling and sixpence, a plate mingled with the bouquet of hoppy porter; while the vapours from Old Tom gin and navy rum tackled smoking pipe tobacco. The mood was merry. By eight o'clock, Lantern Jaw Lincoln propped up an inebriated Holly, stumbling out onto the waterfront, while Bonnie's latest assemblage of filles de joie made themselves comfortable at our table.

'Lulu Darling,' I heard Fabian say. 'What a delightful name.'

'I like yours, too,' she replied.

'What, Bunty?' Fabian feigned surprise.

'Bunty? I fort yer name was Fabian.'

'Oh yes. You're right, love.'

Bewitching Sugar Bare helped herself to my knee. She sat. I certainly did not argue. She had long hair; so long she sat on it. The twenty-one-year-old brunette was a slight, attractive girl who was slender but full bosomed. We were instantly attracted to each other, me through my rum spectacles and Sugar, in hindsight, was attracted to me through my purse strings. What the hell. We had fun.

I have a vague recollection of Jasper leaving mid-evening; he is, after all, a married man with a young wife and bairn, but a rare night of frivolity should not cause too much unease in the family home. Fabian finally disappeared into the fug of smoke and vapours, sweat and odours. I seem to recall him, arm in arm, unsteadily negotiating the treads to the upper floors of the inn, Lulu Darling a lather of giggles.

CHAPTER THREE

Saturday

I woke having my face licked. It was a wet and viscous lick from a generously large tongue. Then I smelt the bitch's breath before I opened my eyes. 'Vicky!' a voice barked. I opened my eyes as Vicky, the Irish setter, backed away from the bed within which I lay spreadeagled, my head pounding and my throat parched with a taste not dissimilar to soiled carpet.

'Vicky, get 'ere.' The huge canine chased a roast bone from Bonnie's cook's kitchen to a corner of this modest cabin in which I had awakened. Sugar Bare sat at a pine table in the middle of the one room dwelling, where she shared the table with a teapot, chipped mugs and what looked like, from where I lay, a large damper. 'Yer awake then.'

'Jesus,' I groaned. 'My head.'

'Up yer get, then. Take some tea. That'll bring yer right squire. Tea an' damper.'

'Where are we?'

'Christ! Don't yer know?' I shook my head gently. 'This's me home sweet home, Caspian Hunter.'

She knows my name.

'Vicky?' I asked, staring at her from where I now propped on one elbow.

'No, you silly sod. Vicky's me dog. Named 'er after Queen Victoria, she's a bitch an' all.'

Harsh words, and words that could see her back in prison for a spell. However, I could understand her resentment; after all, it was Queen Victoria who had sent her here in irons in the first place.

'Yer don't remember me name, do yer?'

My look of helpless guilt said it all.

'Sugar. Sugar Bare. That's the name Bonnie give me any'ow. Me real name's Rose McGuire. Come on, up yer get. You gotta be at work don't yer, it's eight already.'

'Oh, Sweet Jesus. Eight, Really?'

'Aye.'

I emptied my bladder in her garderobe, a small jetty-like structure with a seat and a hole directly into the Hobart Town Rivulet, which ran briskly below as snow melted up on the mountain top. Now I knew – I was in Wapping, a Hobart Town's shanty town for the poorest of the poor.

I joined Rose at the table on the only spare chair. She poured tea. 'Tea?' I spoke without thinking. Tea was a rich man's beverage and not for consumption in hovels like this.

'Yes tea. I pinch some when I get the chance.'

'From Bonnie?'

'No. I do domestic work at the barracks.'

'Barracks?'

'Anglesea. I clean the officers' mess. Some o' me... ah... clientele, officers like, help me out time to time.'

'And you pinch their tea?'

'Jesus! Always the policeman, huh.'

'Sorry Sugar... ah Rose. Force of habit. I did not mean to judge you.' I drank the now tepid tea and Rose poured another while I picked at the damper and some hard cheddar. 'How long have you lived at Wapping?'

'Too long.' She lifted a pottery dish of hot water onto the table, drawn from an iron and brass water fountain hooked over the open fire. 'Here. You can wash, tidy yerself up before yer go to the barracks.'

'How kind.'

Rose passed me soap and a clean drying cloth and I stripped naked and washed freely, uninhibited, as we had been intimate. At least, I assumed we had. Rose and Vicky watched me with interest. 'You got a lady friend?'

'Um... no. No, I have not.'

'Why? A nice handsome cove like you should 'ave a woman in his life. 'ow old are yer anyways? Twenty-eight, nine?'

'I've recently turned thirty.'

'Well there you go, Caspian. Time ter get hitched, I reckon.'

I was about to answer I was a free spirit and not ready to *get hitched*, also assuring her that I was not cheating on another this day, when a knock came at the door. Vicky the Irish setter near bowled me over, barking at the door loud enough to wake the dead. I covered my ears.

'Mr 'unter, Caspian sar. You in there?' Jasper's words were articulated between barks. Rose restrained the animal.

'Jasper!'

'Aye, sar.'

'One moment, if you please.' I dressed hastily.

Rose opened the door. 'Miss Bare,' Jasper touched his cap in greeting as his eyes danced about the shanty taking in as much detail as possible. Oh well, I did train him so. *Take in the surroundings, lad. Look and note.*

Jasper stood grinning. This wasn't the first time he had disturbed me first thing in the morning with a scarlet woman. 'Have a good night, sar?'

Cheeky sod. 'What brings you here?'

'We have a deaden' sar.'

'Oh. Not another vampire attack, I hope?'

'Vampire?' Rose's eyes widened.

I looked back over my shoulder to my host. 'I jest, Rose.' Back to Jasper. 'A killing you say?'

'Aye, sar. A murder.' I heard Rose suck in a breath. 'Give me a moment, Jasper and I will join you in one minute.' I closed the door and turned to Rose. 'Thank you Rose for a lovely evening... ah night. I must leave, duty calls. Thank you for the breakfast and wash.'

'Here,' Rose handed me a half sovereign.'

'What's this?'

'Your money, sar.'

I vaguely remembered having a gold half sovereign amongst the silver and copper in my purse last evening.

'But that is now yours, Rose. You earned it.'

'No, sar. We got back here and you was so pickled yer fell asleep.'

'Oh! Really?'

'Really.'

I pushed her hand away still holding the coin. 'No Rose, it would be remiss of me to accept it. Keep it. You have a good soul.'

She looked coy and suddenly I felt like throwing her back on the bed and taking ten bob's worth. 'Well, thank you, Caspian,' she smiled. 'I really can use the money.'

'Buy something nice to remind you of me.'

'Caspian, sar,' Jasper called out through the closed door. 'Fabian's waitin', sar.'

'How did you find me Jasper?' I asked as we weaved through the maze of alleyways and shanties of Wapping Town.

'Bonnie, sar; she told me.'

Makes sense, I thought.

'An' how did you find Sugar Bare, Caspian sar?' Jasper asked as he scurried ahead towards Campbell Street. 'A little sweetie I should imagine?'

'None of your business, Jasper. We enjoyed each other's company; that is all.'

'Yer... right.'

There was no denying this was a murder. And it had happened only two hundred yards from where I lay *pickled*, as Rose put it. The victim was a woman, found by the night soil man who almost rode over the body lying in a narrow alley off Sackville Street, a part of Wapping Town. Now in the light of day, soldiers had placed a barricade around the scene to keep prying eyes at bay.

I stood over the body; she was lying on her back, her arms stretched either side, with her head twisted and her left cheek resting on the cobbles. Her skirts had been folded neatly to expose her private parts and there was no sign of undergarments, but neither were there any outward signs that the woman had been sexually assaulted. Her bruised neck pointed towards strangulation as the cause of death. There were no signs of violence on the body, except for scratch marks amongst the bruises on the neck. At a glance, she looked about thirty years old.

Fabian joined me from a nearby vendor, where he had purchased a stone bottle of William Champion's ginger beer. He looked as exhausted as I, making my situation more bearable.

'Good morning to you, Caspian,' he croaked, struggling to untwist the wire holding the cork in place.

'Do we have a name?' I asked.

'Molly O'Neil.' Fabian looked back to a group of onlookers peering from behind the backs of soldiers keeping order. 'They all knew her.'

'Lives nearby, huh?'

'Aye.'

Rigor mortis, a stiffening of the limbs caused by chemical changes in the muscles after death, had well and truly set in, suggesting death occurred in the early hours of the morning, 2a.m. maybe.

Jasper stepped forward, knelt next to the corpse and lifted one arm.

'What are you doing Jasper?' Fabian asked.

'One moment, Mr Winter.' Jasper rolled the victim gently onto her side, touched the cobbles beneath her and let her roll back into position. 'I'd say you are spot on, Caspian sar.'

'What, 2a.m.?'

'Aye. Yer see it rained early this morning, a real downpour about 2a.m.. The cobblestones under this body are dry, so she has lain here before the rain.'

Fabian and I were impressed.

'Downpour?' Fabian asked. '2a.m.?'

I personally do not recall rain. Apparently, I was sound asleep.

'About 2a.m., aye, sar. The wife left washing on the line yer see, she forgot like, and made me bring it in when she heard the rain.'

'Oh.'

The sound of a horse and cart drew our attention to Holly and Lantern Jaw Lincoln, who had fetched the transport from the prisoner barracks to remove the body to the morgue.

'We need photographic images before we disturb the scene,' I said. 'Jasper, fetch Mrs Rowley and her equipment, smartly now.'

'Aye, sar.'

Billings appeared from Sackville Street. 'I've been to the deceased's address and by all signs, her husband appears to be home.'

Fabian could see I was confused. 'The husband, Caspian; he's our main suspect and lives just two hundred yards from here.'

'Right.' I was a little behind this day.

'Also, Caspian,' Billings said, 'you may like to read this'. He handed me a copy of *The Courier*. 'Front page news, sir.'

'Oh Jesus! Who wrote this poppycock?' I read aloud for the others, 'Vampire stalks Hobart Town.'

'Aye,' Fabian nodded. 'I was goin' to talk to you about that. Everyone I passed this mornin' has been agitated. News travels fast in a small town.'

'It is so… so ridiculous,' I spat. 'Vampires. The town will be fighting off werewolves next.'

'Werewolves!' Holly near shouted.

'I jest, Holly. Christ! Townsfolk will be hiding old shoes in the walls of their homes next, to ward off evil spirits.'

Holly's jaw dropped wide open. 'But Caspian sar, it is a custom, to keep the devil away.'

'Do not tell me you have old shoes in the walls of your cottage Holly. Please.'

'I… ah… well yessar.'

'I hate to tell yer this, Caspian sar,' Lincoln said, 'but I think it works.'

'Oh please. Not you, too, Lincoln.'

Fabian simply stared at me, rubbing his chin. 'Best we go talk to the husband, huh?'

Number 47 was a tenement residence where four families rented bedsits above the owner's four-bedroom residence on the ground floor. The landlord allowed us to enter and gave us direction. We climbed the stairs to a landing where a passage, four foot ten inches wide, ran the length of the building, with the bedsits running off either side of the passage. I noted back stairs led down to an unloved garden and a shed above a cesspit. This convenience was shared by all residents.

Fifty-year-old Mr Hilbert O'Neil did not answer his door, but called out that it was unlocked. We entered. It seemed clear to me that he was expecting us. The slightly built man lay on one side of his bed with the blanket pulled up to his chin and I suspected he was fully dressed. He also had had a big night by the looks of him, with at least one empty gin bottle by the bedside. He was bedraggled and unkempt; he looked quite ill with fever; his eyes sunken, his skin jaundiced and his eyes red and teary. The atmosphere was redolent of illness. I observed him closely, and although he was fully clothed under the blanket, he was shaking from the chills. Was this illness or signs of guilt? It was difficult to tell. Most of all, he seemed blasé about his wife's death, and I thought first impressions were not aiding his protestations of innocence.

O'Neil, or Lloyd to those few that knew him well, had been a labourer at the various whaling stations along the River Derwent estuary. But with whales becoming scarce in the area, he was made redundant. Now he lived in poverty in this bedsit with his wife, the diseased Molly O'Neil.

'Mr O'Neil,' I started, 'your wife, sir, she is...'

'She's dead.'

'You heard them?'

'Aye. Mrs Pratt down the 'all, she come to me earlier.'

'I see.'

O'Neil coughed and his chest rattled.

'We need yer to come and identify her, official like, Mr O'Neil,' Fabian ordered. 'So if'n yer please... I can see yer already dressed.'

O'Neil smiled slightly at our observation and it was then I noticed that he missed two teeth on the side of his upper jaw. O'Neil came without question. Out in the laneway, Billings, who had managed to find a sheet to cover the body, lifted the corner covering her face. 'Aye. Thart's 'er.'

I alluded to the fact she was not wearing underclothes and there was no sign of them at the crime scene. I added that we were of the opinion she had not been sexually interfered with.

'She were in the 'abit o' not wearing pantaloons, especially if she didn't have a clean pair, and as far as I know she 'adn't worn any for months.'

Much of the rainwater remaining in shallow pools amongst the shadows of the lane had iced over. We were all cold and miserable and my body craved hot coffee.

'I suggest we continue this investigation at the barracks,' I suggested.

'The barracks, sar?' O'Neil grew animated. 'You aren't suggestin' I done this 'ere mischief.'

'At this very moment sir, you are helping us with our enquiries only.'

Once back on the street I excused myself briefly, leaving Fabian with O'Neil, as I made a cursory examination of the backyard at number 47, which was overgrown with grass and weeds and sprinkled with rubbish. Something had bothered me when I had taken a brief look out the rear window on the first floor. The weeds looked trampled in a straight line from the back door to the gate at the rear of the property and fresh cobwebs over the door had been disturbed recently.

Silent From The Shadows

By the time we arrived at the barracks, Jasper had run his errand to Mrs Rowley and gone on ahead to our office, where he stoked a glowing fire in the potbelly stove. Our large coffee pot bubbled and percolated as we entered. The day was looking up. On the premise that we were preparing our questioning, we left O'Neil in the hands of the guard downstairs at the gatekeeper's watch house. This was not a lockup per se, the man was free to move about... have time to think, while we lawmen drank hot, steaming coffee.

Fabian was first to speak. 'What do you think, Caspy?'

'Caspy, Caspy?' I pondered. Fabian knew I hated being called Caspy. 'What do I think? Well for starters I do not know a Caspy.'

Billings and Jasper choked a laugh.

Alright. Jaysuz. What do you think, Caspian?'

'I think he is guilty.'

'Aye, I tend to agree.'

Jasper and Billings nodded emphatically.

Fifteen minutes later, sated on dark black coffee with four sugar lumps apiece, Fabian and I sat opposite our 'guest'. I took notes. 'Your full name, please.'

'Lloyd Edgar O'Neil.'

'Lloyd,' I started. 'You do not mind if I call you Lloyd do you? I mean, we are all friends here.'

'Fine.' This relaxed O'Neil and he began offering information immediately. 'She's been highly strung o' late, sars.'

'Oh? Please continue.'

'Aye. She's been a bit cranky.'

'How do you mean?'

'I cannot sate the woman in bed. She wants it every night an' I just can't do it. And when I do, she likes me to lie on top o' her when I finished like, and bite and suck her nipples, for half hour after. The woman is insatiable.'

Fabian and I looked at each other stunned. We weren't expecting that.

'You are twenty years her senior, thereabouts, are you not?'

'Aye, but every night, and for hours at a time.' He went silent a moment and wiped his brow. He most definitely had a fever. 'Only last week, she told me I was no good for her... she wanted a man every night. Can you imagine your wife telling you that?'

'I am not married.'

'Well, you are better off, in my opinion.'

'Where were you last night, Lloyd?'

'Home all night.'

'And your wife?'

'She went out about eight o'clock and never came home.'

'Oh.'

'Aye. She done it often o' late, never come home till the mornin', eight, nine o'clock sometimes.' The chills set in and the man started shivering, although a fire burnt in the watch house grate.

'Did she say where she had been?'

'I didn't ask, but I knew she been with other men.'

I conferred with Fabian briefly in the next room.

Finally, on our return: 'Lloyd O'Neil, we are detaining you here for a short period while we make further investigations at your lodgings.'

'Am I under arrest?'

'No, Lloyd. You are free to bide your time here. The guard will give you refreshment; we will be two hours, thereabouts. But for your own safety and peace of mind, we request you remain here in this room.'

'Do you understand?' Fabian added. Lloyd nodded sheepishly.

On our way out I ordered the guard to fetch the prison doctor and evaluate O'Neil. He clearly was not well, but this could possibly be brought on by guilt.

'It don't look too good for 'im, eh?' Fabian told me as we strolled briskly back down Campbell Street to Lloyd's bedsitter.

'I tend to agree,' I said. 'Poor beggar. Miserable life with an ungrateful doxy.'

We were within a stone's throw of the Theatre Royal when a fly carriage galloped alongside.

'Caspian,' a familiar voice yelled out through a lungful of chilly morning mist. 'Caspian, a word if you please.'

'Mr Boyles, sir, Warren,' I was surprised. This was the editor of the *Hobart Town Gazette*, a man I knew well, a friend even, with whom I liaised regularly on police business to be published in his paper. Upper-middle-aged, Mr Warren Boyles had been a handsome man in his youth, but now he enjoyed the dignity and personable appearance of maturity; by all means, an intelligent man full of wit and wisdom with whom it was a pleasure to share company. What he lacked in stature he made up in strength of character. A respectably aged Stilton came to mind; subtle, hard crusted yet soft in the middle, an intellectual, sharp and deliciously satirical accompaniment at any dinner table.

'What do you know of this, young man?' the editor was less than pleased. Greeting formalities were abandoned and Fabian ignored. He shook a paper vigorously before my face.

'What is it?' I asked.

'*The Courier!*'

Oh, Christ. He had read the vampire story. 'What is all this humbug about vampires... this deceitful claptrap?' Warren's pince-nez balancing on his nose had fogged up. 'It's horse shit... yes, that's what it is, horseshit.'

'I agree, Mr Boyles... Warren. I had no clue they were printing that story. And I certainly do not know who leaked the information to them.'

'Well, it's irresponsible. Damned irresponsible.'

'I can only agree with you.'

Warren took a deep breath, rearranging his tartan scarf and buttoning his open collar against the cold. 'Maybe you will come to see me when you have time.'

'Certainly.

'They told me at the barracks you were on an investigation. Another killing?'

'I'm afraid so.'

'Not another vampire victim, I hope!'

'Ah... no.'

'Another time, then.' Warren had rolled *The Courier* into a cylinder, which he now used as a prop to poke the driver in the back. 'Back to my office, if you please.'

We watched in silence a moment, as the fly broke from a trot into a canter. 'He does not condone fake news,' I told Fabian.

'Clearly.'

The fire in the grate had burnt out and the O'Neil's bedsitter had an unpleasant smell of urine, something I had noticed but not identified on the first visit. It was then we noticed the two bed sheets thrown over a chair in front of the fireplace. They were both clearly stained with urine and left to dry.

'He must o' pissed the bed,' Fabian muttered.

We searched the room carefully, but found nothing untoward. Their possessions were few and the lodger's frugal lives of poverty were evident.

'Not a lot to go on,' I said.

'So let's see what old Crawley's got to say about the body.'

The morgue. St Mary's Hospital. Twenty minutes later.

Doctor Ernest Crawley was in fine spirits, mainly due to his successful analysis of Mrs Molly O'Neil. The cadaver lay on the slab before him, naked, and the doctor had already made an incision in the abdomen where the skin was folded back neatly, exposing her intestines and other vital organs. I felt the need to purge my stomach but fought it, my attention drawn to her breasts. The nipples were red raw, and teeth marks were clear. 'Yes, Caspian,' Crawley followed my line of vision. 'She has bite marks on both nipples.'

'The husband told us she liked to have her nibbles bitten after copulation,' I told the doctor.

'Really. There's no limit to the bizarre that I see down here in my little dungeon. Does her husband miss any teeth? Premolars per chance.'

'Yes. Upper jaw.'

'Well that explains that then. However, gentlemen, this woman was not murdered where you found her.'

'Oh?'

'No. She has been murdered elsewhere and carried to the laneway and set up to appear like she was strangled in the open.'

'How's that?" Fabian asked.

'Both forearms have been tied with cord.' Crawley pointed to the marks on her wrists, something we had not seen before, as they were covered by her sleeves.

'And we saw no sign of this when we inspected her in the alley.'

'No. The cords must have been removed.'

'They are quarter inch cord marks,' Crawley said. 'Both the bite marks and the rope marks were inflicted before death. The pattern of bruising also indicates to me that the assault most likely took place on a soft surface, and not on the cobblestones. There is no evidence that the body was dragged either.'

'The cause of death?' Fabian asked.

'Asphyxiation.'

'The throat marks, eh. She was strangled then.'

'Yes. As you can see, I have examined the contents of her bladder, or lack of contents I should say.'

'Empty?'

'Yes Caspian. But I suspected this; the emptying of the bladder is a common occurrence during strangulation.'

'Yer learn somethin' new every day eh?' Fabian said dryly.

'Doctor Crawley,' I asked. 'There were no signs of a struggle at the crime scene, and there were certainly no pools of urine. And the weather is too cold to evaporate such evidence.'

'Then that confirms my observation that the woman was killed elsewhere.'

'The sheets,' Fabian spun to face me. 'The sheets with urine stains, drying by the fire.'

I nodded. This fact had already occurred to me. 'We need to inspect that bed once more before we return to the barracks,' I said. It was only ten minutes out of our way, after all.

Back at number 47, in the O'Neil bedsit, Fabian ran his hand under the bedclothes. 'Dry.'

'Try under the mattress. He may have turned it over,' I suggested.

'Ah!' Fabian pulled a face and withdrew a dampened hand. 'You were right.' He hurried to a washbasin and jug on the sideboard and washed his hand. 'The side closest is wet,' he said. 'But only one side. It's been turned over, which means she would have slept on the right side of the bed. When we first saw O'Neil he was lying on the left side.'

'Yes. Fully clothed.'

While Fabian washed, I inspected the fireplace, often a convenient place to dispose of evidence. 'Hello,' I sighed. 'What is this?'

I pulled the remains of cord from the ashes. 'She had her wrists tied, did she not?'

I carefully folded the evidence in a paper envelope I carried, especially for such occasions.

'It's a foregone conclusion. The man's guilty.'

'I'm inclined to agree.'

Campbell Street Prisoner Barracks.

Fabian and I returned to the barracks and walked into a fray. A rabble of three dozen or so were pushing and pulling each other vying for a position to look at something on the back of a bushman's cart outside the prison gates. The bushman, a stooped old man struggling with lumbago by all account, stood on the tray, desperately trying to calm his spooked horse. Sergeant Richard Clincher had started duty for the day and was not happy with the state of affairs outside his prison.

'Stop it!' he shouted. 'Stop it immediately or by Christ, I'll shoot some bastard.'

At that moment, as we hurriedly approached, we watched Holly rise from the rabble, given a leg up onto the cart by Lincoln.

'Quiet yer mongrels,' she screamed out.

But the crowd were having none of it. Billings saw us and rushed to meet us.

'It's anarchy I tell you. The crowd's lost all sense of propriety.'

'What's the problem?' I asked him.

'There's a body on the cart,' Billings had to shout. 'Brought here by that fool trapper.'

'And...'

'Quiet yer firkers! Holly screeched, freeing her Tower pistol from her britches belt and firing into the air. The explosion brought extra soldiers from the barracks. But it had the right effect. The crowd hushed. Holly blew smoke from the muzzle of her gun. 'That's more like it.'

'What in the name of hell is goin' on?' Fabian rammed into the crowd dispersing Hobartians in every direction. The crowd backed away as Holly reloaded and Clincher threatened those standing too close to the cart with a fixed bayonet on the end of his loaded Brown Bess.

'It's 'im, sar,' a toothless old woman screamed. Gaping with eyes the size of goose eggs, she clamped onto Fabian's arm,

Fabian tore his arm free. 'Him who?'

'The vampire!' the woman shouted the word.

'The vampire!' the crowd squealed in unison. 'It's the work of the vampire!' The medley of the ignorant threw themselves into a terrified lather once more.

'Shit!' I heard Fabian growl over the increasing rabble. 'Holly!'

Holly didn't hesitate. She pulled back the hammer and another ounce of lead punched a hole in the clouds. The crowd fell silent once more. 'Now, get back,' Holly snarled, aiming the smoking barrel at those nearest. 'Get back, the lot o' yer.'

Then soldiers marched through the gate and onto Campbell Street and I had to laugh. From where I was standing, the scene was most comical, as superstitious fools, dullards and the totally ignorant scattered, only to reform across the street like a gaggle of tormented geese.

'You there,' Fabian spoke to the bushman who had managed to settle his mount.

'Sar.'

'This your cart?'

'Aye.'

'Name?'

'Tom, sar.'

'And what is this... this body doin' here?'

'I found 'im in the foot'ills o' the mountain, squire, an' thought to bring 'im here for you lot to investigate, like. It's the devil's work, sar!'

'Poppycock!' I stepped up to inspect the body, twisting the head to one side.

'Yer can see the teeth marks, sar, in 'is neck, jus' like McK got taken, recent.'

Indeed there were two puncture marks, three inches apart and a large portion of the man's shoulder had been torn away.

'You knew McK?' I asked calmly, as if all was right with the world.

'Aye, 'e be a trapper like me and Frank 'ere,' he nodded to the body.

'You knew this man too, eh?' Fabian studied Tom like he suspected him of skulduggery.

'Aye. Frank an' me often work together. We mostly trap up north around the Western Tiers, but the brush and ringtails 'ave been plentiful in the foot'ills this winter.'

I knew he spoke of possums, for which the brush tail skins fetched the best prices, at fifty shillings per dozen.

'Then what happened to Frank?' I asked, as Lincoln joined me.

'Well as I said, me an' Frank usually trap together but this trip we split up, two weeks ago. Frank 'ad more skins than 'e could carry an' made camp in the 'ills. I went after platypus up behind the Dromedaries. Any'ow I had some luck, caught me quota and returned to the camp.' I knew older Hobartians still referred to Hobart Town as the camp. 'That's when I 'eard about the vampire from *The Courier*. Anyways, I went lookin' for Frank; 'e were camped near the Ferns and that's when I found 'im, all messed up as yer can see.'

'I hate ter tell yer this, Caspian sar,' Lincoln whispered in my ear. 'But' e's drained o' blood.'

There was no blood spilt on the cart either.

'And your point is?' I whispered back.

'Well, vampires do like drinkin' the stuff, that's all I'm sayin sar.'

'Lincoln,' I said curtly. 'Go and see the coffee is brewing,' and I tipped my head towards the prison.

'Now, Mr...'

'Jacks, sar, Tom Jacks.'

'Mr Jacks, do you realise you have possibly disturbed a crime scene?'

'Aye, but I couldn't leave Frank lying there, sar. The devils'd eat 'im.'

'I hate to say this, Caspian sar, but he's got a point there.'

'Lincoln!'

'Sar?'

'The coffee!'

'Yes, sar.'

'What of this man's possessions at the camp site?' I asked Jacks.

''e has a small trapper's 'ut there, sar. I buried his guns and valuable chattels – not like there were much – in a hole beneath 'is bed and secured the 'ut best I could.'

'Then, give directions to Miss Villan,' I ordered, pointing to Holly.

After the kerfuffle, Fabian and I retired to our office to write up our report on the O'Neil case before arresting the man, and to warm ourselves, with the help of the coffee pot. Meanwhile Holly and Lincoln took charge of the bushman's cart and supervised the removal of trapper Frank's body to the morgue.

On our return to the watch house, at the gatekeepers, we discovered O'Neil's health had taken a downward spiral. The prison Doctor had sent him to the Hobart Town infirmary.

''e's been sedated, sar,' Clincher told us, removing his coat and shako. He lifted his coat tails and parked his backside in front of the potbelly stove, warming himself by the fire. 'In the tender lovin' arms o' Madame Laudanum, 'e is.'

'He must have been more ill than we figured,' I said.

'Well, we can't arrest 'im while 'e sleeps, Caspy... ah, Caspian. Let's go to the mess and avail ourselves o' some vittles.'

Good idea; I was starving. But it was never to happen. Our presence was requested at St Mary's Hospital, immediately.

St Mary's Hospital.

Doctor Jacobs met us in the corridor, where we could talk privately.

'He sleeps still,' the doctor said. 'The man is quite ill. He has consumption, I am afraid, or tuberculosis as it is called these days. TB for short.'

'Hence the chills, the fever,' I said.

'Yes. He has been coughing blood also, and purulent expectorations.'

Fabian screwed up his face. 'Pure what?'

'Purulent expectorations,' I answered for the doctor. I had read of this before. 'Mucus from the lung.'

Fabian groaned. Too much information on an empty stomach.

'And,' Jacobs continued, 'I do not know whether you noticed, but he has trouble breathing.'

'Aye,' Fabian agreed. 'And we thought it was the guilts.'

'He has all the signs, I am afraid. Gastro-intestinal infection, aching bones and joints, caseation, abscesses, fibrosis formation of tubercles. He suffers terrible pain when I touch on these areas.'

"When will he be well enough to arrest?' Fabian asked in his usual sledgehammer style.

'He needs rest, guilty or not, Mr Winter, if he's to stand trial at all. Frankly, I feel he is not long of this world.'

'That bad, huh?'

'Yes.' Doctor Jacobs stroked his coiffured beard, pinching it into its tapered point. 'Ah... Mr Winter..., Caspian, may I speak freely?'

'Certainly.'

'I believe Doctor Crawley told you the victim was murdered and her body moved to the laneway, where she was found in the early hours.'

Fabian and I looked startled.

'Oh,' Jacobs explained. 'I read a copy of your report before you arrived.'

'Oh,' I said. I was thinking, *news travels fast around here.*

'And there are no drag marks, I read also,' Jacobs noted.

'Correct.'

'Which would seem to imply the body was carried?'

'Aye.'

'Well here's my point, gentlemen. This is why I wanted to see you urgently. You've seen how frail Mr O'Neil is. He couldn't lift a pet cat, let alone a solid built woman.'

'He's got a point there,' Fabian said.

'So,' the doctor continued, 'there is a chance the killer is still out there.'

I had to concede, it seemed nigh on impossible for O'Neil to have moved the body. Did he have an accomplice or was it someone else entirely? But all the evidence we had, incriminated the man.

Hours later. Prisoner Barracks. Campbell Street.

Keeper of the gate, Sergeant Richard Clincher, entered our office without knocking. 'A messenger delivered this 'ere letter, sealed an' all, fer your privacy like.'

He passed me the envelope and stood casually looking about, finally slipping a gnarly finger under his shako to scratch at a troublesome nit. Clearly, this action irritated Fabian. 'You waitin' for a reply or a gratuity, Richard?'

'Oh Lordy no, sar... I jus'... jus... I'll be off then.'

'It is from Doctor Crawley,' I told Fabian, and the others soon filled the office after Clincher told them I had news. 'He writes that the second trapper's body has pieces missing from the shoulder and neck...'

'Which we knew.'

'Yes, but also the buttocks and lower calves. He says the puncture marks are similar to the other trapper's, which he is certain belong to scavengers who have ravished the body after death and drained the body of blood.'

'The black devils,' Holly shuddered. 'Savage bastards.'

I read on, aloud. 'In my opinion, this man has died of heart failure brought on by severe shock, but at his age, he would most likely have had a weak heart.'

'Heart. Teeth marks, drained blood. It's the work of some deranged villain,' Fabian said.

'It's almost cannibalistic,' I suggested.

Billings stepped to the filing cabinet. 'Do you remember that felon who escaped Saltwater River some years back, and he was accused of eating the prisoners he escaped with?'

'Alexander Pearce,' Jasper looked pleased with himself.

'Not him; he was incarcerated at Macquarie Harbour.'

'And that closed years ago, decades even.'

'Aye, an' he was executed decades ago, also,' Fabian said.

'Yeh, I read about him,' Holly followed Billings to the cabinet.

Billings opened the bottom drawer and started searching the files. 'Wolf, his name was. I remember because, well, I thought at the time, a cannibal called wolf.'

'Aye,' Fabian sat up. 'I remember. He got his ticket only a few years back.'

'There! Wolf,' Billings busied himself at the filing cabinet, finally pulling the file free. 'Zachary Wolf. Got his ticket in '53 and a full pardon in '55.'

'What?' Holly looked incredulous. 'He got a full pardon after eating a fellow escapee. How's that work?'

'The man had already died, it was seen as an act of self-survival and as abhorrent as it sounds, it was not deemed a criminal offence. He did, however, do extra time for escaping.'

'Then what are you suggesting, Billings?' I asked.

'He might just as well enough be our vampire,' Billings scanned a keen eye over Wolf's file. 'He may have lost a few marbles late in life and had a relapse, a taste for human blood.'

'Possible,' Lincoln said. 'I've heard of worse.'

'Like what?'

Lincoln thought hard. 'Can't answer thart, I'm afraid.'

'Hmm, it is a long shot,' I said. 'Where is he now?'

'Doesn't say. But Hobart Town is a small community. It cannot be too difficult to find out.'

'Then you 'ave your day's work laid out for you, Billings,' Fabian said. 'As I am certain your search will take you to many inns of this colony, take Jasper with you. I know he won't lead you astray.'

And Fabian looked at Holly, displaying her disappointment with a downturned lip.

With the stairs to our humble office being unwelcoming to arthritic Sergeant Clincher, the old guard sent a younger colleague to fetch us this time; that is, Fabian and myself. Constable Ned Tinley was an unkempt lad, a few months shy of twenty. His blue-grey winter issue trousers were already filthy and the front of his red coat showed signs of clumsy eating. His large and solid figure filled the doorway as he touched his shako in a lazy salute.

'Now what?' Fabian asked, his pounding head having returned, requiring rest. My head fared no better.

'It's a coach outside, sars, from Government House.'

'Government House?'

'Aye. Thart's wha' I said.'

'What... a coach? Outside? Now?'

'Aye, sar. Gov'nor wants a chat wiv yers, the coach driver said. Said 'e ain't to return empty 'anded.'

Chapter Four

Government House. Queen's Domain.

Governor Henry Fox Young had moved into his new residence in January, I can confirm, a seriously happy man. The old Government House, built near on fifty years ago, was literally falling apart and the governor ordered it demolished. He even hinted at a social gathering to celebrate the occasion, such was his lack of regard for its continued existence.

Designed by architect William Porden Kay in the neo-Gothic style, the new residence, overlooking the wide expanse of the River Derwent was immediately regarded as the most fashionable vice-regal address in all the colonies. And at a cost of 120,000 pounds so it should, I say.

The governor's coachman dropped us at the eastern entry where we were ushered into a sunlit visitor's drawing room, away from the main and formal entrance. Although Sir Henry and Lady Augusta had moved into the residence, there were still carpenters busy finishing interiors, their banging and brushing echoing through the lightly furnished mansion.

'How thoughtful.' Fabian gazed upon a table of silver salvers of sandwiches neatly quartered and filled with bloater paste and preserved potted meats brought from England. These silver salvers were accompanied by blue and white Spode platters of fruit jam pastries with jugs of whipped cream.

'I'm starved.' Fabian launched into the spread with the finesse of a famished glutton.

'I am not too certain you should be doing that Fabian,' I said, looking about as if awaiting the school headmistress to enter the room with a cane.

'Nonsense. Who else would this lot be for?'

'The women's Christian Temperance Union,' a voice behind us said sternly. 'That is who.'

Fabian mouth dropped open, which was not a good look, being that it was full of macerated fish paste sandwiches with another wedge poised at chin level. He allowed the cream cake in the other hand to fall back onto the platter, where it missed its destination, landing on the Persian rug.

'Lady Young,' I smiled with a half bow. 'Sir Henry summoned us.'

Over the past two years we had grown to know the governor's wife, Lady Augusta Sophia Young, a handsome woman only two years my junior, and had enjoyed a cordial relationship, but this afternoon Lady Young looked less than impressed. She was immediately joined by a woman ten years her senior, who by all appearances had just bitten into a grapefruit.

'This is Mrs Fairfax-Hatton, president of the Christian Women's Temperance Union, Mr Winter,' Lady Young said sternly, 'and you, sir, are helping yourself to the afternoon tea set out for our meeting.'

Immediately a gaggle of voices followed as a dozen other society women filed into the room. The room silenced noticeably. I was about to apologise on Fabian's behalf when Sir Henry himself appeared behind the women, like a farmhand herding the honking geese forward. On seeing us, he rolled his eyes, motioning for us to follow him back outside. We bade our farewells to the Temperance Union and joined him.

'Terribly sorry, sir,' I started, as the drawing room door closed haughtily behind the female gathering.

'Do not apologise, Caspian. It's Charles's failing,' he said of the footman. 'He was supposed to show you to my study. But come, it's noisy in here with all the workmen so busy, let us talk outside.'

We strolled lazily a short distance from the house to where a large stone quarry gouged into the embankment and dropped away sharply.

'This is where much of the sandstone came from to build the new government house,' Young said. We stood at its edge. 'I must have a fence built here before someone does themselves a mischief,' he said. I had to agree. 'Now, where were we? Oh yes.' The governor turned to face us. 'Dorothea Hartley, do you recall that name?'

'Yes. Gideon Hartley's wife,' I said. 'The woman who grieves for her missing son.'

'Ah, the horse stud,' Fabian remembered.

'Yes. We have not met, however.'

'No, neither have I,' Young said. 'But my wife has, gentlemen. And Dorothea Hartley is a member of my wife's beloved Christian Women's Temperance Union.'

'Oh!'

'Yes, oh! Mrs Hartley has been hounding my wife to hound me to hound you, Fabian and Caspian, to search for her missing son.'

'Well, he's at the bottom of a well somewhere, isn't he?' Fabian said heartlessly, picking at his teeth with his little finger. 'According to her dreams that is.'

Governor Young kicked a few pebbles over the edge into the quarry where they splashed into a pool of water at its base.

'I'm hoping this will eventually fill with water and we can start breeding ducks,' he said. 'I am quite fond of duck. The French roast them with cherries, I have been told. Sometimes oranges, also.'

We all stared into the shallow pond a moment. The governor stroked his full-length beard and finally spoke. 'Mrs Hartley has had visions or dreams yes, and she believes her son has been the victim of skulduggery and is, indeed, lost at the bottom of a well.'

'There is no evidence of foul play,' I started.

'He *is* missing however, a year or more now, I do believe.'

'Yes but...'

'I would request that you at least interview the woman. At the least, it appears this Albert Hartley was swindled out of his inheritance. It may be that he simply has gone AWOL, too embarrassed to contact his parents. Who would know? See if you can't track down this partner, Mr Harper, I think his name was.'

Fabian and I exchanged discreet frowns.

Sir Henry hooked his thumbs into his waistcoat pockets and went on, 'There is something else that bothers me.'

'Sir?'

'What is all this nonsense about vampires stalking Hobart Town?'

'Huh! Vampires!' I feigned a mocking laugh. 'You read *The Courier* then, sir?'

'Yes. And I am not amused. Such nonsense has no place putting the fear of the devil into simple townsfolk.'

'We agree, Sir Young,' Fabian said. 'But rest assured, we have leads already.'

'Leads?'

'Aye, sir.'

Now I knew Fabian had hit a brick wall. We were no better informed than we were two days ago. Fabian pinched a stubble of hair he had started to grow on his chin, in an attempt to appear contemplative. 'We fear we have a cannibal loose in the colony.'

'Cannibal!'

'Aye.'

Personally, I would have kept the cannibal theory to myself, right now, at this moment. The governor looked to me for a more rational explanation, but I was suddenly overcome with the spectacular view. Fabian floundered for my support. I ignored *him,* also. *You climbed into the privy matey – you can climb back out.*

Fabian explained our suspicions of Port Arthur escapee Zachary Wolf. The governor sighed and pinched his lips. Clearly, the jury was out on this one.

'I dare say, Ophelia will forgive you, Fabian,' Sir Henry said, heading back to the warmth of his new abode.

'Ophelia, sir?'

'Ophelia Fairfax-Hatton.'

'Oh.... The sandwiches.'

'Yes, the woman is tiresome, a temperance crusader. She will have forgotten you by now and be preaching her beliefs to the white-gloved, bonneted flock, boring my poor Augusta to tears. The Temperance Union,' the governor tut-tutted, but left his thoughts there, refusing to be drawn into the argument. 'By the way Fabian...'

'Sir?'

'How *were* the sandwiches?'

Silent From The Shadows

Warwick Street. Hobart Town.

We found the Hartley's modest red brick cottage in Warwick Street, a mile and a half west over the hill behind the prisoner barracks. It was just after five o'clock in the evening but the township was already dark and Mount Wellington hidden under heavy cloud. Although it rarely snowed in the streets of Hobart Town, I was certain it had snowed, up on the mountain. Gideon Hartley opened the front door, but was hesitant, at first, to invite us in.

'We are here to talk about your son, Albert,' I said, to break the ice.

Immediately a voice shouted down the hall. 'Who is it, Gideon?'

'It's the police investigators,' he called back, standing with the door half open, as if waiting instruction.

'Well, let them in. You're letting all the heat out.'

The wife had spoken. We entered, and the cottage felt just as cold inside as it was out. Gideon Hartley led us down the dark passage to the kitchen where the older and solidly built woman sat in a wicker chair built to include armrests and wheels. She was parked before the kitchen fire; a sad affair of one smouldering log. An iron pot sat on the coals, heating what appeared to be a left-over stew, and I now caught the aroma of stewing mutton and potatoes. Against the tiny kitchen wall a small table was set for two, with breadboard and a half-eaten loaf. Hanging over the table a lone lantern struggled against the darkness. A book of scriptures sat bookmarked on the table, no doubt in preparation for Grace.

'At last!' the woman said briskly. 'It's been several days since Mr Hartley came to see you at the barracks.'

'Yes,' I started. 'Please accept our apologies, Mrs Hartley but...'

'But you're being harassed by vampires,' she coughed a laugh. 'Vampires from the pages of a silly novel. You should know vampires don't exist. Try reading the Bible instead.'

Mrs Hartley was understandably upset. We chose to ignore the vampire comments. 'Which of you is Caspian Hunter?' she grumbled.

'Me, Madame.'

'Hmm.' The woman ran a dark eye the length of my body. She looked to Fabian and harrumphed.

'Your son Albert, Madame,' I said.

'Yes?'

'We would like to ask you some questions, like when did you last see him?'

'It's been over a year now.'

'There was a letter... you mentioned a letter Mr Hartley... informing you your son would be home, Saturday week, I believe it said.'

'Yes.'

'Do you still have that letter?'

'It's right here Mr Hunter.' Gideon Hartley fetched a stoneware salt crock from the mantle with several letters scrolled neatly inside. 'Here.'

I ran an eye over the note. 'Do you mind if I borrow this?'

'Certainly. I will want it back as soon as you have finished with it,' Mrs Hartley said bluntly.

'Of course... Now this business partner, Mr Harper,' I asked. 'Did you ever meet the man?'

'Gordon Harper!' Mrs Hartley answered. 'No. A vile creature, I am certain.'

There followed an awkward silence and I distinctly heard Fabian's stomach rumble as he weighed in to the questioning, trying to ignore his hunger. 'So yer don't have a description, then?'

'How could I? I told you I have never met him.'

'He was older,' Gideon Hartley said meekly. 'In his late thirties, by all accounts.'

'Where exactly is this stud farm?'

'On the Esk, about a mile south of Evandale. You'd have to ask in the township.'

Gideon Hartley looked at his wife as if waiting permission to speak. 'The previous owner lives in the town, doesn't he Dorothea?'

'Smith, his name is.'

'Was it not Jones, dear?'

'Smith!' the woman spat, although I could see her thinking hard. 'Smith, Jones, some common name like that.'

I looked at Gideon, who mouthed *Jones* silently out of his wife's eye line.

'These dreams, Mrs Hartley?' I asked.

'What of them?'

'Well, could you explain what you see in these dreams?'

For the first time, the woman lost her hard edge. Her eyes welled slightly. 'The dreams started about six months ago,' she said. 'He came into my mind as I slept; it was as if he was trying to warn me of something. But then, only last week, I had a most vivid dream. My son was lying at the bottom of a well and....' A lone tear rolled off the woman's cheek. 'And he was lying very still. I had the distinct feeling he was... he had passed.'

'I shall require your son's bank details and the names and addresses of any acquaintances. Can you help me?'

'The bank was the Van Diemen's Land Bank, but as for acquaintances, I'm afraid he never confided in us.'

'What about Henrietta, Gideon?' Dorothea said.

'Oh yes, Henrietta Myles.'

I looked on expectantly.

'We never met the lass, but she was a farmhand whom Albert often spoke highly of.'

'Do you have an address?'

'No. I do know however that she lives in Evandale.'

'I shall journey north myself,' I said, 'and make enquiries. But at this stage, it is a missing person's investigation, you must understand.'

Gideon Hartley showed us to the front door with the light of a half candle. I'll swear the night had become darker in the short time we had been at the cottage.

'Albert's cousin in Adelaide...,' I said, 'is it possible he resides there? I mean, have you had correspondence from him?'

'We have had correspondence from Eddy – that's his cousin. He has seen neither hide nor hair of our Albert.' Mr Hartley stepped onto the front cottage steps with the door ajar. 'I fear there is some truth in what my wife says, gentlemen. Dorothea is very religious and righteous and the Good Lord has visited her before in her hours of rest.'

'Oh?'

'Yes, like the time her cousin was drowned at sea some years back, Dorothea was even able to name the ship she saw in her dream, the *Kenley*, a merchant ship. She could not have possibly known beforehand.'

'Yes, well,' I said. 'I must admit some people do have that gift. I will keep you informed.'

'I'll send Holly and Lincoln,' Fabian said lifting his collar high, slapping his hands together and blowing warm breath into them.

'If you have no objection, I will go.'

'Why?'

'I said I would see to it personally. Besides you sent Holly and Lincoln to search for Zachary Wolf, the cannibal.'

We walked to the Elizabeth Street corner where two noisy patrons spilled cheerfully from the Lord Raglan Inn and onto the street yonder. Here the window into the taproom told of a busy inn, a log fire, hearty food and porter. We crossed the street with haste and pressed into a bar room of warmth and joviality... and the hair of the dog.

Chapter Five

Heading North on the highway through the central highlands.

With less than a clear head, I was on Samuel Page's 6am coach to Launceston. I do not recommend this journey; and how I let Fabian talk me into the extra Genevas after rabbit stew, potatoes and carrots washed down with several pints of porter at the Lord Raglan Inn, I will never know.

The journey north was as comfortable as one could expect for a common bush roadway cleared of tree stumps and smoothed with flattened soil. However the gullies and river crossings and broad stony fords where bridges had not yet been built could be most uncomfortable.

Since the *Cessation of Transportation Act* became law near on five years past, Van Diemen's Land had been renamed Tasmania and had shaken off its shackles, literally. The last convict transport had delivered its human cargo the same year. Now Tasmania, governed by my mentor, Sir Henry, was self-governing. This came with its own public debt and Tasmania had to impose its own tax system, as the colony had forfeited its 350,000-pound a year handout from England. I only mention this, as labour for road works and public buildings now had to be purchased at the market price, and unfortunately this was evident, beneath the coach's less than efficient suspension.

We arrived at Launceston after dark, a community of near on ten thousand people and soon to be incorporated as a township, I was told. It had been a most tiring journey and my priority was to find a bed for the night.

I was directed to Bentham House in Bathurst Street, short-term lodgings for refined gentlemen. With that said, the name *Bedlam* House would have been more suitable. Refined gentlemen may have resided here once upon a time, but this winter's day in 1858, it was less than salubrious. I threw my carpetbag on the bed, locked my door and left for the nearest inn, where I could cure my sore head with a hearty meal and a porter or two.

The Three Jolly Settlers Inn was near the esplanade. So, like a moth to a lantern, I followed the sounds of the inn's rampant fiddler and the aromas of a spit roasting sheep, being turned by a young lad of nine or ten in the alleyway next to the inn.

On the marshy riverbank I passed a group of Chinamen. Two of the men loaded possessions and supplies into a sloop, while the other four men sat about a campfire eating. The aromas sharpened my appetite. While large bamboo steamers cooked their rice, the men helped themselves to some kind of wildlife, fried with Oriental spices in a dish-like pan. I slowed to watch this unusual sight of men eating ravenously with their Chinese eating sticks. How they managed without forks was beyond me. A local cove caught me staring.

'They're off up the river to a place called Beaconsfield.'

'After gold, eh?'

'You've heard of it then?'

'Certainly.'

'Well, they found gold there back in '47 and now it's rumoured that more has been found.'

Launceston

I found the Three Jolly Settlers like I found the spit-roasted sheep, a challenge. But after a porter and a plate, I retired to Bentham House and slept like a wee babe.

The next morning, feeling brighter than the day before, I strolled the short distance to Charles Street to visit bank manager Toby Tombe at the Bank of Van Diemen's Land. I arrived right on 9am as the huge iron-studded double doors were pinned open for business. Disturbing, however, was the sight directly across the street from the bank of a young man looking bedraggled and thoroughly distressed, on his knees with his arms and head locked in stocks. He had been secured there since dawn; removed from the watch house especially for the occasion. Some rotten fruit, vegetable projectiles and dung lay on the dirt beneath him. He looked at me with pleading eyes.

Too bad, I thought, *the law's the law.*

Toby Tombe was indisposed, so I was told. The man kept me waiting for twenty minutes and by the sound of strange noises emanating from his office, I thought he might have an ailment. Finally, I was summoned by a junior clerk who, after knocking, threw the door wide open, presenting me with a most unusual sight. Toby Tombe sat on a kitchen chair balanced on top of his desk, swinging a long handled wooden mallet; the ageing bank manager was practising his polo swing.

'More wrist, Toby,' the assistant manager applauded. 'More wrist.'

I can truly say the two were having a gay old time.

'Come in, come in,' the manager cried out with cheer. 'Caspian, is it?'

'Yes, sir.'

'Well, do come in. Don't mind Mr Beasley and me. I've a polo match with Sir John Reynolds and Captain Little on Saturday and Mr Beasley was just giving me some guidance. Mr Beasley offered the manager his hand and Tombe dismounted his hobbyhorse with care. Toby Tombe was taller than me, six three at least. His face was full and mapped with laugh lines. Although a man of sixty, he had a complete head of unruly hair. Curls formed thick mutton chop sideburns meeting at his various chins. His eyes were hooded and weary, his nose large, with ears to match and the shoulders of his black frock coat were well salted with dandruff. I wanted to tell the man not to use soap to wash his hair and do what my mother did to prevent the flaky pest – smear the hair with whipped eggs.

'Well, Caspian, how can I be of service?'

'I'm from the prisoner barracks in Hobarton,' I answered, referring to Hobart Town's new title.

'Hobarton eh?'

'Yes, sir.'

'Tell me,' Tombe said, 'what's the best part of Hobarton?'

I was perplexed at his enquiry until he answered his own question.

'The best part of Hobarton is the road to Launceston.'

Toby Tombe snorted a laugh and whacked Beasley on the backside as he left the office, carrying the kitchen chair.

'Sorry, old chap. I merely jest. Now let's start again, shall we?' He kicked the door shut. 'What can I do for you?'

I was about to launch into my investigation when a loud scream came from across the street. Tombe moved to the window and together we could see the prisoner in the stocks had just collected a bullseye in the face from a rotten mushy cabbage. There was a moment of silence in the office.

'What has the man done to deserve such barbaric treatment?' I asked. I had not seen the stocks used in Hobarton for some time.

A thin smile crossed Tombe's lips. 'What did he do?'

'Yes, sir?'

'Last Saturday we had the Newcomers' Ball at the Town Hall, for newcomers to Launceston, you understand.'

'Yes.'

'Well, he released a bag of rats onto the dance floor.' Tombe's generous paunch wobbled as his mirth rose towards his multiple chins. I stood open-mouthed. That was hardly the answer I'd expected.

'He was only caught last night and the watch house wanted to make an example of him.' Tombe noted my expression and he repeated the charge, before exploding with laughter. I joined him, and for a brief moment, I forgot myself.

Tombe sat behind his desk, teary eyed from merriment. 'Sit, Caspian, sit.'

'Thank you, Mr Tombe.'

'Call me Toby. Now, where were we?'

I explained why I was in Launceston, listing my concerns, and Tombe called for the relevant files.

'I only ever met Gordon Harper once,' Tombe spoke of the missing man, Albert Hartley's business partner. 'Came into this very office to sign some documents. If I am to be honest with you, I didn't like the man. Wouldn't look you in the eye, you know the type.'

'Indeed. How would you describe him?'

'Sneaky.'

'I mean in appearance.'

'Tall, handsome features, tanned skin of the outdoors type. Oh, and he had a gold tooth, upper left.' I made notes. 'He was a confident beggar, too. Ran rings around Mr Hartley, as far as worldly goes.'

'Oh? In what way?'

'He seemed to wear the britches, if you know what I mean. It was, after all, an equal partnership, although Mr Hartley financed the entire business while Harper had the business savvy. Being the major financial shareholder, one would think Hartley would have the upper hand. But as I said there was something... sly, yes sly about Gordon Harper. Now, Hartley's missing you say?'

'Yes. His parents have put pressure on my department to investigate.'

'Then I fear there is good cause, Caspian.' Tombe looked serious once more.

'Oh?'

Tombe signalled to a bank clerk. Moments later, a knock at the office door heralded the clerk with Hartley's records.

The manager placed the relative documents flat onto his desk. 'You are not going to like this Mr Hunter, Caspian.' He explained that a year ago, Albert Hartley's bank account held a healthy balance of 826 pounds. However, three months later, the bank received a letter from Hartley to transfer 400 pounds to the bank's branch in Sydney, with the request that arrangements be made for Gordon Harper to draw on it with no limit.

'There is Hartley's specimen signature, Caspian.' And Tombe showed me the neat and readable signature of Albert Hartley. 'Here is the bank's copy of Mr Hartley's signature.'

They looked exactly the same.

'Do you think it is forged?' I asked.

'Well, it's a damned good one if it is.'

Hartley's signature was never questioned and the instructions were accepted.

'Over the next few months the account was drawn upon, and here,' Tombe pointed to the relative figures, 'here you can see the final balance was drawn from this bank after we received additional instructions, from Mr Hartley, to allow Harper draw on them.'

Once again the signature matched.

'What is the balance, or would I be correct in saying it is depleted?'

'Exactly. And something else set off alarm bells also,' the manager informed me.

'Yes?'

'We know Gordon Harper journeyed to Adelaide in South Australia, as cheques there were overdrawn on the Hartley account.'

'Adelaide?'

'Yes, it is my guess that he has travelled there, attracted by the copper boom, and has used his charm and confidence to defraud the good honest citizens of South Australia.'

My heart sank. I really did not feel like another sea journey, especially after travelling to the goldfields of Victoria so recently.

By noon my coach, full of locals, trundled noisily into Evandale. I sat alongside our driver in his vivid red livery, taking all caution not to be plastered with mud as the four-horse carriage, with damaged mudguards, ploughed through puddles. Passing the watchtower, which I was told was built twenty-five years earlier, to warn of aboriginal or bushranger attacks, the coach left me at the corner of High and Russell Street, where I made enquiries at the corner inn, the Clarendon Arms.

I was soon to learn that Evandale was a small community.

'Henrietta Myles.' The jolly innkeeper, Edgar Lewis, welcomed my inquiry with red cheeks and an ale-induced smile. 'I'll fetch 'er for yer.'

'Fetch… fetch her?' I gasped not expecting such ease and generosity. 'What of your taproom, sir? You cannot vacate your business now, surely?'

I looked across at the only three patrons standing about the fire and watching on, tankards near empty.

'Nay, sar, Henrietta be me scullery maid. She's out in the yard; I'll be back in a jiffy, squire.'

Henrietta was a comely wench, and she was not too shy, either. She stood before me, her long blonde curls pinned beneath a maid's bonnet. Her deep blue eyes were bright and watchful and I estimated her age at eighteen or thereabouts, a woman in full bloom, and not that much shorter than me. Although she wore long skirts covering her ankles, my discreet eye imagined long slim legs beneath the tight-fitting garment. She smiled in greeting, displaying teeth intact and white as chalk. With the innkeeper as chaperone, we exchanged introductions. Immediately, I had the impression that visitors were scarce in these parts, and especially visitors who asked for you in person. Henrietta joined me at the bar. I stated my profession and feeling obliged, I purchased her refreshment, a pint of small beer, and a quart of the Clarendon's own porter for myself. With inquisitive eyes at the fireplace also within earshot, we adjourned to the only high-backed booth for privacy.

'So Henrietta,' I asked, 'you worked at the Hartley stud?'

'Aye, I mucked out the stables. Bloody awful work, sar, if'n you'll forgive me French.' Henrietta slurped her beer and wiped her mouth on her grubby sleeve.

'And what of Mr Harper?'

'Gordon? Couldn't keep 'is 'ands to 'imself. No, sar. Regular octopus, that one.'

'When did you last see Albert Hartley?'

'Over a year ago. I was supposed to see him a month before the stud closed. After the fire, like. Gordon, that is Mr Harper, said 'e and Albert was off overseas to Melbourne on business – said somethin' about insurance business – and that they was to leave soon. But when the time came, he arrived alone...'

'Harper? Here at the inn?'

'Aye.'

'Then he proceeded to show me a letter from Albert, excusing himself...'

'Excusing Albert?'

'Aye. Sayin' that he couldn't make it. It seemed weird to do that like...'

'Showing you the letter?'

'Aye. Well, I no longer worked for 'em for one thing, and it were like he wanted to prove somethin'. But what I thought strange was when 'e said *overseas*, normally he would just say I've gotta sail to Melbourne.'

I swallowed the rest of my porter. 'Henrietta, can you take me to the stud? I believe it's not far.'

'There be naught much there, sar.'

'So I believe, however I would like to see it.'

She looked towards the innkeeper, content with a tankard in his hand, surreptitiously sampling his latest brew of porter. 'It ain't busy, I'll let Edgar know.'

Edgar was in better spirits than I had imagined and lent us his trap and pony. Actually, the scullery maid's familiarity with the old innkeeper led me to suspect she had the man wrapped around her little finger.

Hartley's Stud was less than two miles from the township and, as Henrietta had warned me, there was not a great deal surviving. The property was fenced at the approaching roadside with a chained and locked gate, and I could see from where I was perched upon the trap that much of the remaining twenty-acre property was protected with split-rail fencing the height of a man. I imagine this was to keep the horses secure. The stables were completely destroyed. Only burnt oak framing remained and just one of two cottages stood to tell the tale. How the fire spread, if not deliberately induced, was beyond me. No wonder the insurance company refused to pay out. Henrietta waited on the trap while I inspected the gate.

'Are there any wells on this property?' I asked.

'Yes, sar. One next to the stables and one behind the second cottage. But Mr Hartley never used that one 'cos a privy was dug too close to it and 'e always said 'e could smell shite in the water.'

'Oh, how unpleasant.'

'Aye. 'e preferred to fetch water for drinkin' from the river.' And Henrietta jerked her head towards the Esk half a mile away.

I ignored the *Caution to Trespassers* sign and climbed over the gate. The well behind the cottage, although overgrown with foliage, looked as though it had been filled in. The safety wall was missing. The other well, closer to the stables was also overgrown with weeds, otherwise intact. Boards had been nailed across its opening, for safety reasons, I dare say.

Any signs of a pleasant morning soon evaporated as dark clouds turned the sky a dull pewter grey. I remembered the magnificent pink sky out my window as I awoke at my lodgings this morning and remembered a saying my dear mother would recite, *Red sky at night shepherd's delight, red sky in the morning, shepherd's warning.*

'Are yer through 'ere, sar?' Henrietta's voice reached me on the chill of a sudden gust. She wrapped her shawl tighter about her shoulders. 'Rain's comin'.'

I joined her back on the trap and we picked up pace back towards Evandale.

'Thank you Henrietta, most generous of you to give me your time,' I said, pulling my own collar high against my neck.

'Oh think nuthin' of it, squire.' I sensed Henrietta studying me as we journeyed at a fast trot along the dirt road. 'Say,' she finally said. 'Yer coach back to Launceston ain't for two hours yet, do yer fancy warmin' yerself by the fire and enjoyin' a bowl of Scotch broth?'

'At the inn?'

'Not the inn. Me cottage. Edgar won't be wantin' me back until the farm 'ands finish for the day, and come in fer a drink late afternoon.'

'Oh,' I thought. *What is this little minx suggesting?*

'Don't feel obliged, sar, 'twas just a friendly suggestion like. Me pa and bairn will be there to chaperone us if'n yer worried.'

'Me. Worried?' I blushed. 'Sorry Henrietta, I did not mean to... I... that is most kind of you.' *Why is your mind always in the gutter Caspian Hunter,* I admonished myself. 'Most kind indeed.'

The scullery maid's cottage was only two hundred yards from the inn. We arrived just in time. The heavens opened up and the rains came. We stabled the innkeeper's pony and ran back to her cottage, bursting through the door at a giggle.

'My my,' Henrietta laughed. 'We barely made it, sar.'

'Barely!' I laughed, drenched.

Standing near the fire was an older woman, a red-haired lady in her mid-thirties, I guessed. She was by the fire, folding clothes. 'You just made it, by the looks o' yer.'

'Yes,' Henrietta caught her breath, as did I. 'Has Master Jack awakened?'

'Not yet.' The redhead ran an inquisitive eye over me and, by all impressions, I was not exactly a surprise. 'This is Mr 'unter, Felicity,' Henrietta introduced us. We exchanged friendly nods – well Felicity's was more of a curt gesture.

'Well, I'll be off then.' Felicity made no effort to linger, threw an oilskin over her head and shoulders and hurried away. Henrietta watched her a moment before closing the door. 'Felicity minds Jack when I work. She's me cousin and lives just across the road.'

'Jack's the baby?' I asked.

'Aye, me wee bairn. Eight months 'e be.'

'Oh.'

'Here. Give me yer coat and I'll hang it near the fire.' She looked to our muddy boots. 'Better we get them off too, can't be dragging sludge through the place. I only cleaned this mornin'.'

And I had to agree, the cottage was clean and tidy, with three rooms; two being bedrooms leading off the main kitchen living area. A steady fire burned in the kitchen grate and overall the home was cosy, warm and inviting. Henrietta removed her shawl and jacket and, along with mine, she hung them over a clotheshorse before the fire.

'You live here with your father you said.'

'Papa Will, aye.' She nodded to a closed door off the kitchen. 'But me pa is an invalid. He's old and deaf and bedridden, I'm afraid. He stays in bed most o' the time. Unless I aid him to the fireplace.'

Invalid, eh! Suddenly I felt more than warmth in the cosy confines of this young wench's kitchen.

'Please call me Caspian,' I said. 'And your husband?' I fished.

'Oh, I ain't got one... Caspian. Me bairn was born outa wedlock, I'm sorry to say.'

'Oh,' I answered, strangling a smile. 'You need not apologise.'

'Gets pretty lonely in these parts, especially for a scullery maid with a bairn.'

'I... I am certain you are right.'

There was a brief moment of awkward silence when Henrietta suddenly flustered.

'Golly,' she said. 'Where's me manners? That blouse o' yours is awful wet too, sar... ah... Caspian. Take it off and I'll give you a drying cloth to cover yourself.'

Now, I am not one to be backwards, going forward, but if I did not know better, this wench was up for more than company. I feigned a reserved, almost bashful manner and unbuttoned my blouse exposing my – even if I do say so myself – my masculine chest. Henrietta watched on, letting out an involuntary gasp, and I could not help notice her bosom rise and fall. She noticed. Our eyes met briefly but Henrietta broke off and snatched my wet blouse, passing me a drying cloth whilst fumbling to make room on the clotheshorse. I stepped closer to the fire and Henrietta noticed me staring at the rug on the floor. By all appearances, it was the skins of four Tasmanian striped hyenas, or Tasmanian tigers as the pesky sheep killers were becoming better known.

'Papa shot them back in the days when he was a strapping young man. Good 'unter was me Pa Will.'

I had seen the skins for sale in Hobart Town when I first arrived. The wild animals were a menace to settlers and grazers, killing livestock, and now the government had a bounty on them.

'They make a cosy rug,' I said, suddenly hoping I did not sound too transparent. Another brief silence was broken by baby Jack, crying.

'I'll have to feed him,' Henrietta said. 'There's a bottle of ale on the bench there.'

'What! For the baby?'

'*No*, for you. Open it and make yerself comfy.'

Don't mind if I do.

I eased the cork from a black glass bottle and poured the dark ale into a stoneware mug from the dresser. Taking a long draught, I sat on one of two chairs at a small pinewood table. Immediately I was aware of soft whimpering. I turned and was pleasantly surprised as mother joined me at the table, one plump, firm breast exposed, feeding little Jack. I tried not to stare.

'He is adorable,' I felt compelled to say. Truth is, I have not much time for infants, but my guess is that that instinct will possess me with the passage of time.

Meal completed to the sound of smacking lips and a loud burp, little Jack was placed between cushions near the fire. Useless creatures at that age, I thought, as I gazed at the tiny, animated arms and legs kicking about like a turtle stuck on its back.

But something else caught my attention. Henrietta made no effort to cover her exposed breast. In fact the blouse dropped, exposing them both. I sipped at the ale and stared at the fire when Henrietta could wait no longer. She stood next to me collapsing her skirts to her ankles.

Yes, sir, those legs were long and slim.

The pantaloons, it appeared, had been abandoned while she fetched little Jack. Now it was my turn to suck in a quick breath. Standing before me where I sat, the tight blonde curls of her womanhood were in my face. I was speechless. Excited as a rampant whaler after two years at sea. I was putty in her hands. Lost for words. Henrietta ran her long, thin fingers through my hair and pulled me to her. I could hardly breath. Instinctively I locked my arms about her derriere, pulled her tighter still, before launching her off the floor and onto the rug. Words were not necessary. Henrietta let out a squeal of delight. I expelled a groan and with my britches unfurled to my ankles we went at it like long-lost lovers.

My God, that was unexpected.

We lay before the fire uninhibited, entangled flesh to flesh in each other's arms. The rain was now heavy on the shingled roof. Extra logs crackled and spat sparks and cinders up the chimney like celebratory fireworks. I had not been so relaxed in weeks. Sated, our breaths restored to normal, conversation returned to business.

'Did you know Gordon Harper well?' I asked.

'Well enough.'

'What does that mean?' *Well enough.* I had a brief twinge of jealousy. Was this woman intimate with him also? Did he lie before the fire on this same rug? Henrietta leant up on one elbow, elevating her head above mine. Her bewitching blue eyes were glossy with emotion. Baby Jack stirred, gooing and giggling, blowing bubbles and kicking his little limbs in complete contentment.

'I don't know if'n I should be tellin' yer this,' Henrietta started.

'Then if you are about to tell me what I'm thinking, you may wish to remain silent.'

'Oh! And what am I thinkin', Caspian 'unter?'

'Jack is Gordon's child?'

Her eyes answered. Words were not necessary. And making love with me was an attempt at finding a husband. Damn! And I thought it was my charm alone.

'Does he know?' I asked.

'Aye. 'e knows, all right. Bastard up an' left.'

Yes. And he up and left with Hartley's inheritance, as well.

'I am sorry Henrietta, you deserve better.'

She took advantage of those words instantly, 'Do you think so?' She rolled her naked body on top of mine. Her womanhood pressed against me and I felt a stirring once more. I pushed her back to the rug. I had questions that needed answering... *first.*

'Can you describe him?'

'Are you goin' after 'im? Cos if'n you are you can tell' im from me, I think 'e's a low-down bastard.'

'I will. But I need a description of the man if I am to arrest him.'

'He were handsome, tall, dark skinned with a gold tooth...'

'Upper jaw?'

'Aye. An' 'e had a thin moustache. Pencil thin, I think they call 'em.'

'Did he ever mention Adelaide?'

'Aye. 'e did an' all. Why do you ask?'

'Oh, it was just something the bank manager told me. Albert has a cousin in Adelaide, also, does he not?'

'Aye. But 'e told me they ain't close.'

'Oh?'

'No. Albert never spoke high of Eddy, that's his cousin. Apparently, Eddy was real jealous of 'im.'

'Jealous. Why?'

'Well, it were Eddy's father what was Albert's godfather an' 'e left the inheritance to Albert, and Eddy got naught. Bit of a swindler was our Eddy, I 'eard.'

'From whom?'

'Albert told me. An' his father disinherited his own son.'

Aha, I thought. The dots on the blackguard's map of deceit started to join up. I rolled over, leaning across to slip my turnip from my waistcoat pocket, when I felt teeth bite gently into my buttock. You saucy minx. I flipped the lid of my watch. The coach would be thirty-five minutes. *In for a penny in for a pound.* I grinned to myself and mounted my pony once again. Tally-ho!

The coach left me in the main street of Launceston, where I made my way immediately to the esplanade to enquire about a passage to Adelaide. I was in luck; the *Adelaide Packet* was leaving first thing in the morning. I was about to return on foot for the Van Diemen's Land Bank to draw funds for the trip when a kerfuffle on the riverbank caught my attention. A crowd had gathered around the deserted campfire left by the Chinese miners I had seen the night before. Local constables already had the scene secured. I made myself known and was shown to the crime scene.

An older man, a coolie, lay sprawled dead amongst the reeds of the marshy waterfront, where he had remained well hidden until now. He was naked from the waist up and his long-plaited queue was wrapped around his neck, almost like a noose. But what caught my attention were puncture marks over his heart – neat and clear puncture marks surrounded by purple, congealed blood. They reminded me of the so-called *vampire bites* in Hobart Town of recent. However here, there was no suspicion of a vampire. Here were three wounds, all made with the same weapon – a Chinese eating stick, which still protruded from the last stab wound.

One of the constables noted my interest. 'Chopsticks, they call 'em.'

'Pardon?'

'That stick in his chest sir, it's called a chopstick, named after the pidgin English, chop-chop. Eat fast, you see.'

'Pidgin, eh?'

'Yes, sir.'

I left the local authorities to conduct their investigation and walked back into town wondering at the possibility of a mad Chinaman in the foothills of Mount Wellington racing about stabbing people in the neck with chopsticks.

Absurd.

At the Launceston Post Office I sent a telegram via the new telegraph wire service to Hobart Town, notifying the barracks of my decision to sail to Adelaide, and to request funds to be released to me at the Bank of Van Diemen's Land. I could only guess at the angst my being away some weeks would cause, but this was at the request of the governor, and I now had reason to believe skulduggery was afoot involving Albert Hartley.

Is not modern technology a wonderful thing? My reply came within the hour, along with a second telegram to the bank, affording me fifty pounds advance for expenses. It read:

Permission granted STOP Make haste STOP Cannibal Zachary Wolf not found STOP Gods speed STOP Signed Fabian.

Chapter Six

At sea

God's speed!

God's speed maybe, but the journey across Bass Strait and west over the gulf and onto Adelaide was not all beer and skittles, and it would be remiss of me not to digress briefly to explain.

The *Adelaide Packet* was a three-masted clipper of around six hundred tons. It had seen better days. I stepped aboard with trepidation, my recent shipwreck experience off Tasman Island clouding my thoughts. And to reinforce my fears, we sailed from Port Dalrymple into a squall, albeit briefly, but enough to loosen my foundations. The squall dissipated, followed by a robust southerly. It was whispered on deck that we might arrive in Port Pirie, South Australia, sooner than later. Excellent.

We were barely out of sight of land when one passenger, Anthony Brighton from Liverpool, decided, against all wisdom and in a moment of exhibitionism before the young belles of the voyage, to climb the ratlines. Now, unbeknown to me, and I'm a reasonably seasoned traveller, sailors do not, under any circumstances, allow passengers to climb the ropes. Never. Full stop. Well, maybe under very special circumstances, like if the ship was foundering. So it was, with the approval of Captain

George Alberton, that nineteen-year-old Brighton was secured to the ratlines, legs and arms spread-eagled like a convict about to be whipped, and left to hang for a good hour, long enough for him to lose face amongst the other passengers; including the young ladies, of whom there were several. *One less competitor,* I chuckled to myself, especially since he wet his britches in the process. It finally cost him a bottle of rum to be set free, purchased from the passengers' saloon bar at the inflated price of one sovereign.

One less competitor, did I hear you say?

I forgot to mention there were forty-six single women on board. All Irish. These female emigrants had been temporarily residing in Sydney. They had been destined for Adelaide aboard *The Goodwin. The Goodwin* had lost a mast passing through Bass Strait and they were forced to change ships at Port Dalrymple. They all travelled in steerage, below the main deck, and were segregated from the families, and certainly from the single men. The berths for steerage passengers were fastened along the walls of the hold with one long mess table running down the centre.

I had, however, treated myself to a second-class cabin – albeit a compact one – and with several days at sea to endure, I was glad that I did.

On the first night, the head flooded and the contents washed everywhere. As if this was not enough discomfort, many passengers suffered seasickness, and I could not help but feel the angst of the *slop boy*, fifteen-year-old Nelson Sawyer, whose duty it was to clean up all such mess; including the head!

Still at Sea

I was woken by a pitiful scream. I rushed on deck and wished I hadn't. One of the young ladies had had her fingers crushed in a winch. It was a dreadful sight and I learnt later that the ship surgeon had to amputate the hand at the wrist. Awful business. It was also at this moment that I learnt the ship surgeon was addicted to opiates and that he was an alcoholic, frequently seen imbibing on the brandy and other spirits locked away for his patients. Fortunately this day, the man was sober enough to amputate the hand and cauterise the horrific wound.

At breakfast, which I chose to eat in the steerage mess in the hope of making the acquaintance of some of the Irish lasses, I heard a child had been injured the night before. Falling down a companionway, he had broken his thigh. And when the family sitting next to me started complaining of large boils that were appearing on the body of the father and his son, I decided to have my breakfast in the saloon in future.

For the moment, I ate alone. Soon, I discovered how overcrowded the steerage was and how the passengers were allowed to store their luggage wherever. This meant that several sleeping berths were blocked up with chests, ventilation hatches were obstructed and few if any of these hatches could be opened for fresh air and light. In fact, most hatches had been sealed with white lead to keep the seawater out. Other ventilation was so obstructed that it was necessary to keep lanterns burning for light. Hygiene aboard ship was the surgeon's responsibility and clearly, on the *Adelaide Packet,* it was being shirked.

Another day at sea

First Mate Christian Calvert's morals were far removed from the morals of a good Christian and his namesake. The man, somewhere in the middle of his fourth decade, had taken a particularly obsessive fancy to a not so unattractive emigrant lass – seventeen-year-old Bronagh O'Farrell, a nursery maid from Cork. Whether it was seasickness related I do not know, but Bronagh fainted on deck and Christian Calvert came to her rescue. She was pale and sickly, and *good-hearted* Christian suggested she lie down in his cabin so as to enjoy a better rest in the quieter environment, rather than the steerage bunks. Innocent or naïve, Bronagh accepted the offer and was duly escorted to the first mate's cabin. Meanwhile Christian continued his duties. Later in the day Bronagh was well rested. Christian was most helpful and kind. So kind, in fact, that he suggested Bronagh stay the night in his cabin. It was, after all, far more comfortable than down in steerage. Bronagh accepted, on the condition she had her good friend, Anne Byrne stay as well. Christian agreed and now, two seventeen-year-old Irish lasses shared his cabin; Anne asleep in the bottom berth, and Bronagh in the upper berth.

What happened during the night is conjecture, to say the least. But someone, anonymously, tipped off the captain, who held an immediate inquiry.

'When I awoke early this morning,' Anne told the captain, 'to my absolute surprise, I found Mr Calvert in bed with Bronagh.'

This state of affairs precipitated the first mate being dismissed for the remainder of the voyage, confined to his cabin.

And how tongues wagged. *I* would have to be discreet.

It soon became apparent that the captain was not a threat, in the sense of liaisons on board. Yes, he had made an example of his first mate, but it appeared to be a vendetta rather than shipboard law. For the captain, no stranger to maturity in his mid-sixties, had taken a lover of his own. Mary Wetherford – Mrs Mary Wetherford – was forty-nine, a somewhat cuddly matron, employed to look after the young ladies on the lower deck. However, once persuaded by the captain to share a more enjoyable voyage in his stern cabin, the matron rarely ventured down yonder to check on the moral wellbeing of her charges.

This could hardly go unnoticed on board a ship, and one evening at dinner in the saloon, the captain went to great lengths to tell myself and a dozen other second-class passengers that he had the right to invite whoever he wished into his cuddy. And he rightly did so, including the matron, who happened to have a husband awaiting her in Adelaide. However, he insisted, he enjoyed their company only, and never took liberties with these women.

Yes, right!

By day three of the voyage, most passengers had acquired sea legs; that is, they were no longer suffering seasickness, all very well, if the pickled pork and pickled beef on board did not cause stomach ills. On investigation, it appeared the company purser had purchased several hogsheads of aged, barrelled meat at a bargain price. It was later learnt that these barrels had already made the journey from Melbourne to London and back again, and god only knows how much further, festering in brine in a dank warehouse. With stomach woes, it seemed passengers had much more on their minds – like inadequate heads – than socialising or, god forbid, romance.

To try and placate the complaining passengers, Captain Alberton authorised the sale of wine and spirits to the steerage, but this turned out to be a mistake also, as passengers became the worse for drink and starting quarrelling. Fighting followed. Then one male passenger was hit in the eye with a swinging hook and badly injured. While the surgeon was too drunk to administer medical aid to the unfortunate, the responsibility came down to one of the older female passengers to do so. Another messy state of affairs.

Being a cabin class passenger, my cabin was below the poop deck, where I had access to the deck above, should I wish to lounge about, play cards with other passengers, read or write or, god forbid, participate in social activities. I preferred to keep to myself. For this reason, the pretentious first-class passengers soon branded me a cad for my choice of entertainment. Shipboard life is rarely private.

Nessa Byrne was an eighteen-year-old feisty redhead from County Donegal – an experienced farmhand by all accounts and a seductress to boot, especially when it meant being upgraded from steerage to the cabin of yours truly. Here, in cabin number 14, we played cards, mostly euchre and cribbage, and for an extra two guineas I was able to have dinner brought to the cabin – better cuts of meat, of course – with wine. After dinner we enjoyed additional cabin entertainment; the nature of which I will leave to the reader's imagination.

Last day at sea

One of the single women, nineteen-year-old Sorcha McCarthy, died during the day, giving birth to a baby girl, who, sadly, died four days later. It was a melancholy moment as her body was cast into the sea. The body was sewn into canvas with a cannon ball placed at her feet. This *sack* was placed upon a wide plank, feet foremost, where she was rested on the bulwarks, while prayers were read, before tipping her over the side, committing her body to the deep.

We hit bad weather half a day out from Port Pirie, when a rogue wave washed over the ship, swamping the steerage berths down below. *Poor devils,* I bemoaned their discomfort, as Nessa burrowed even deeper beneath the bedclothes.

Finally, land appeared on the horizon and I heard one sailor tell a passenger we were about fifty miles away. We were at our destination, at last.

Chapter Seven

Adelaide

We disembarked mid-morning at Port Pirie, a seaport on the east coast of the Spencer Gulf, where there was little else but wool stores and a landing jetty. A regular coach service transported us to the township of Adelaide.

Adelaide is a neatly planned town, laid out with purpose and precision, and not yet twenty years old. But in those twenty years much has happened. The discovery of gold in Victoria slowed development in South Australia somewhat in the early '50s, but successful miners are now returning with their wealth. Copper was discovered here in the '40s and there is speculation that much more is to be found, adding to the state's prosperity. Many farmers have also found a prosperous market for their wheat in Victoria and New South Wales, creating wealth for the South Australian settlement, which is growing rapidly on the income from this staple.

Like Tasmania, South Australia is self-governing – two years now, since '56, – and with the Murray River joining the Darling River, steamboat transport has aided trade immensely.

This was my first visit to Adelaide and I found the settlement thriving. The buildings, a mix of stone, brick and timber with shingle or slated roofs, were handsome and neat. The main streets were the standard width for the period, wide enough to fully turn around an oxen team with their drays. I noted a presence of red-coated soldiers to help keep the peace and, all in all, the citizens went about their business in a respectable and sober manner. Noticeable were the ever-present gatherings of aborigines with their many dogs.

I was directed to the police headquarters near the corner of Franklin Street and King William Street, where I was informed that two hundred and fifty policemen were registered to cover South Australia.

Tall slim Constable Denis Sullivan; with his tanned skin, thin face made thinner with a moustache to his chin line, and receding hair, was an amicable young man and particularly helpful. We met at the front desk, exchanging a firm handshake in greeting.

'Twenty-seven of those two hundred and fifty are local natives Mr Hunter,' he informed me of the police numbers. 'They are mounted police from the Moorundee tribe. Mostly trackers. They get one shilling a day plus rations.'

'Fascinating.' I dared not mention how shamefully the Tasmanian aborigines were treated, but my guess was, he already knew.

'The native police are stationed at Port Lincoln.' Denis was clearly having a quiet day with ample time for idle chitchat. 'I'll tell you something else,' he said. 'Most of the police here were once soldiers and...' He looked over his shoulder. 'Most are illiterate.' Clearly he was not.

'Really?'

'Aye. Really. Many can't even read the time on the clock.' I must have looked suitably shocked. 'What's it like down in Diemen's Land,' he asked. 'Same?'

'Pretty much, I should imagine. But I have little to do with the general police force per se, being in the crime investigation office.'

'I wouldn't mind detective work. What's it like?'

'Sorry, Denis. I do not wish to appear rude, but I am pressed for time.'

'Oh. Right then. How can I help you, sir?'

As smartly as possible I explained the situation. 'Mr Gordon Harper you say?' Constable Sullivan now looked serious, his brow furrowed. Something clearly triggered his memory.

'Yes. He is in his thirties, tall, good looking, dark skin and a gold tooth top left jaw.'

'That doesn't ring any bells, Mr Hunter. But we did have an incident here two days ago.'

'Oh?'

'One of our investigators was shot.'

'God, no. Was he killed?'

'No. But he is in a stupor. He was shot in the neck you see, and is comatose at the barracks infirmary; he cannot be woken.'

'I am sorry to hear that. But what has that to do with my case?'

'Well Sergeant Carlin, that be the man's name, was investigating a number of worthless cheques being passed about town, and the word is that there was a man frequenting the inns and taprooms as far as Port Lincoln, a free spending loud mouth, throwing his money about. And he was not a gold miner.'

Now I was interested. 'And?'

'Well from what we can ascertain, Carlin found his man and was shot for his efforts. But our leads have come to a dead end.'

'Did Sergeant Carlin have a file on the case?'

'Certainly. I'll fetch it.' Minutes later I was shown into a small room and left with the file. There were nine cheques, all signed A. Fitzpatrick and filled out for various amounts, along with the investigator's black leather covered notebook and newspapers; all *Adelaide Observers*. I studied the cheques; each signature was neat and precise. I opened the first newspaper. Why would a police investigator file these? There were three in all. Then I realised. Circled in lead pencil amongst the classified advertisements I read:

Men of the highest integrity should apply to me, Albert Fitzpatrick, for details of employment with very bright prospects.

This was suspicious, very suspicious indeed, and it occurred to me that for a man passing false cheques and whose deception had come to an end, this advertisement smelt of corruption. The advertisement called for persons of interest to make an appointment at the Criterion Hotel for an interview. Even more suspicious was the request that applicants should only arrange for the interview if they had twenty pounds on their person to invest. Why this had not been investigated already was beyond me. In fact, Constable Sullivan was most red-faced for his own colleagues neglect when I pointed this out.

'Where is the Criterion Hotel?' I asked.

'Rundle Street. It's only a brief walk Mr Hunter.'

The Criterion Hotel was indeed a five-minute walk from the police headquarters, where I found the two-storey stone building facing north. It was bathed in South Australian sunlight. The sign read Wine and Spirit Vault and a smaller sign advertised clean accommodations for the discerning gentleman. The bar was grand, with generous dark wood all pleasantly carved, some framed huge mirrors in the style so popular in London these days. The bar-room was busy and the barman clean and friendly, with greased-down hair over a round, clean-shaven happy face, however, he wore a noticeably bristling moustache. He finished serving two prosperous looking gentlemen and turned to me.

'What will it be, sir? Today we are offering a fine cognac from France at the exceptional price of two shillings. Care to partake?'

Resisting the beverage, I slid the *Adelaide Observer* across the highly-polished counter and opened my lapel to expose my identification. The man took one look at the advertisement, lost his smile and nodded to a man in a clean-cut suit sitting at a table under a window reading *The London Times*. So engrossed was he in his newspaper, he did not see me approach.

'Gordon Harper,' I said loud and clear. Startled, he dropped the paper and looked me in the eye. He did not flinch.

'You have the wrong man my friend. My name is Albert Fitzpatrick.'

I saw the gold tooth immediately.

'Maybe today it is. But you are known as Gordon Harper in Launceston.'

'You have the wrong man, sir.'

His brows joined in annoyance. Heads were turning. Harper looked to the barman for support but he was wisely pre-occupied.

'My name is Caspian Hunter. I am from Hobart Town police barracks. I am a criminal investigator, and I am here to ask you about the whereabouts of your business partner, Albert Hartley.'

'Hartley? What about him?'

'So you are Gordon Harper?'

'Evidently.'

'Hartley is missing. His parents have heard nothing of him for over a year. You are the last person to see him. I also have irrefutable evidence that you have misappropriated funds from Mr Hartley's account and what's more, I have His Excellency,

Sir Henry Fox Young, the governor of Tasmania, breathing down my neck. I am not in the mood for shenanigans.'

'Sir. Mr Hunter,' he interrupted, his face the colour of Madeira wine. 'Must you humiliate me in public? Can we continue this discussion in my room?'

'Room?'

'He jerked his head towards the ceiling. 'I have lodgings upstairs.'

I looked about the room and acknowledged that we had an audience. 'Fine.'

And I must admit, the man was calm and collected, showing no sign of guilt. However, we never reached his lodgings. On the landing at the top of the stairs, I observed my suspect reach discreetly into his pocket.

Evidence, I surmised. Was he about to try to destroy incriminating evidence? 'Harper!' I yelled, leaping forward. Harper turned to meet me and it was then I saw the barrel of a small pocket pistol.

'Jesus Christ!' I shouted. 'You scoundrel.'

I snatched at the gun arm and threw my full weight at him. We crashed into the wall. Harper yelled some obscenities at me and struggled violently. The pistol twisted within his grip. Harper bent double, trying to free himself, but I had a firm hold, when... the pistol discharged.

Harper let out a groan and went limp in my arms. God no! He fell to the floor clutching at his chest. The man had shot himself in the heart.

Management was not happy. A death in the hotel – in a respectable establishment. And with the Adelaide police headquarters so close, I was soon in the company of half a dozen policemen. I was angry. I was shaken and angry. The situation would never have come to this if Sergeant Carlin's case had been pursued. But my guess was that, with a largely illiterate police force, how could they have? I turned the tables, laying responsibility on the useless law enforcers surrounding me. Although I had not the jurisdiction in South Australia, I gave the men a piece of my mind and ordered them to see to the body.

'And for god's sake, someone bring a bucket of water and towels.' I alluded to the considerable amount of blood pooling on the landing and threatening to cascade down the carpeted stair.

'You, Madam,' I spoke to a sad-faced woman in her fifties, whom I had discovered was the manager's wife.

'Yes, sir?' she answered rather sheepishly, her eyes fixed on the dead man, while a bunch of keys on an iron ring jangled at her side.

'The deceased. What room did he occupy?'

'Seven, sir.'

'Seven. Very good. Open the door for me if you please.'

I was relieved to find more evidence, a gambler's eyeshade and a mask, a gold pocket watch and chain with the monogrammed initials A. H. on the lid. In a chest of drawers I found a bank chequebook from the Bank of Van Diemen's Land with thirty blank cheques remaining. Many had the name Albert Hartley pencilled on the signature line. To me the signature looked traced in preparation to be inked when required. I found other personal items also, like a gold miner's pin, with the initials A.H. and the date 1852 engraved on the shovel. It appeared my suspect was guilty as hell of fraud. He had run out of money and the people he had swindled were closing in. His ruse to find gullible investors in *a very bright prospect* was a drowning man grabbing at straws. He had already shot one police investigator and I was to be the next. I could only think myself lucky I pounced when I did. But the question remained, where was Albert Hartley?

And my thoughts returned to the two wells at the stud farm in Evandale, back in Tasmania.

Note to self: do not travel over the high seas in winter. The sail back to Launceston on the *Adelaide Packet's* return trip was horrendous, terrifying and treacherous. The mountainous waves rolled relentlessly beneath the keel of the hundred and eighty foot steam and sail ship. There was no respite. No hot meals could be prepared, as the galley shuddered and rattled, accompanying the sounds of the ill and the stomach churning stench of the retching wretches. The only positive was the wind in the sails. *God speed!*

I remained confined to my small cabin, alone with stale bread, cold corned beef and cheese. Never again, I thought. I had survived one fatal shipwreck by the skin of my teeth. I would rather crawl across the Sahara Desert than repeat the experience.

Late afternoon. The day of arrival back in Launceston

Corporal Hulbert Shaffer stood in the doorway of his cottage, a sturdy sandstone block residence with a slate roof, which belonged to the police department. The lawman frowned, looking me up and down while scratching at his private parts, oblivious to the comedy of his ways.

'Dig a wha'?' he asked me.

'A well,' I answered rubbing my hands together to warm them. 'Two of them. in fact.' He looked at me as if I had asked him to build a replica of the Taj Mahal in the middle of Evandale, when I realised the error of my demands.

'Oh, I do not mean for you to dig them from scratch. I mean you to empty two existing wells. I have reason to believe a missing person will be found, at the bottom of one of them.'

Corporal Shaffer was one of three policemen stationed at the small village of Evandale, a village usually at peace with the world now in the 1850s, since the decline of bushrangers – which were prevalent in the past.

'A body down a well, huh? Jesus,' he finished scratching and began picking at his teeth with a long splinter of wood. 'Can't yer jus' toss a grapple hook down yer well and hook the beggar out?'

'No.'

'Why?'

'As I said, we must dig. The wells have been filled back in. Look,' I grew annoyed. 'Can I come in, it's freezing out here?'

A woman's voice yelled from within. 'Let the man in, Hulbert, Jaysuz, he'll catch a death standin' out there.'

'Oh yeh, sorry.'

Inside, the small cottage was much larger than Henrietta's abode across the street and down the road. With a low beamed ceiling, the room was pleasantly warm, with several logs burning fiercely. No wonder the man was barefoot and dressed only in a sleeveless undergarment, with britches held up with braces.

'Hello, I'm Alva,' the woman said, smiling contentedly while bouncing a baby on her hip. 'Hulbert's wife.'

'Caspian Hunter.' I forced a smile.

'Caspian huh? I have a friend called Caspian.'

'He wants me an' the lads to dig wells,' the husband interrupted.

I explained the situation and my suspicions.

'Can't it wait 'till mornin'?' Hulbert asked, stabbing an iron poker at the fire, creating a galaxy of sparks.

'No, it cannot. So, if you please, fetch your constables, and we'll need two extra labourers, lanterns, rope, grapples and any other equipment you think we might require for the job.'

The rain had stopped for the moment, but the winter's day was drawing to an end. With the overcast sky crowding over, it would be dark in an hour. We unchained the gate, removing the lock, and I entered with a cartload of equipment, two paid labourers from the village and three disgruntled policemen. We had also commandeered the town fire engine: a four-wheeled cart with a pump handle and canvas hose for drawing water, should we encounter any water that might hamper proceedings. A dozen leather buckets were fixed along the sides of this engine.

First, I led my team to the well near the stables, where the skeletal remains of the building, reduced to blackened ribs, looked more unwelcoming as darkness approached.

'We'll start with this one,' I ordered. Planks had been placed across the opening and large rocks placed on top, which I thought most suspicious. However, the labourers, promised a guinea each, were keen to start work. But when the planks were removed, they realised the well was filled with rubble. It would be a long night. With the darkness came a bitter chill, and a haunting mist crept up from the river. The fog circled our lanterns, in turn casting eerie shadows across the overgrown terrain, shifting shapes as the men went about their macabre business.

Soon, we had a human chain in process: two down the well, feeding rubble into a cradle on the end of a roped hoist we had rigged. Hulbert and his constables, aloft, lifted the rocks free, tossing them aside.

At eight o'clock, I called a break. Rum for warmth and small beer for our thirsts. I leaned over the edge, holding a lantern to ascertain the drop. We had cleared fifteen foot, by my reckoning.

'How deep do you think the wells are around here?' I asked. 'Anyone have any idea?'

'Twenty-five, thirty feet, sar.'

Three hours later.

'Water, sar!' one of the labourers called up. 'We've hit the water table.'

This is where they earn their gold guinea, I thought to myself, as I knew the water would be six foot deep, at least.

'Hulbert.'

'Sar?'

'Bring the fire engine cart close. Stand by to pump.'

The pony harnessed to the engine needed prodding, but once it started, pumping began immediately. Although the well continued to flood, the rate of extraction was faster. Another two hours passed. Finally, the labourers hit the bottom.

Nothing.

It was a huge disappointment. Eight hours toil and for what? Naught. But there was still the other well.

By now the constables had lit a bonfire, using old timbers from the stables. The men stood about thawing. It was half the hour after midnight and I sensed a mutiny. But I felt so positive.

More rum and beer.

Hulbert hastened to his cottage to raise his wife, but she had anticipated his calling. The two returned with hot damper, jam and a large kettle of coffee. I was as tired and exasperated as the rest, but sure as hell I was not giving up. The food filled our bellies and a second crock of rum was poured into the hot coffee. But five pairs of tired red eyes stared at me in the firelight and I still smelt mutiny.

'Another guinea each,' I finally said. God only knows the difficulties I would have securing these funds, but I bit the bullet.

'That's one each for us too, sar, I take it?' Hulbert spoke for his constables. I nodded and stood briskly.

'All right, men. Let us move camp to the other well.'

Then the heavens opened up and down came the rain. As if we weren't miserable enough. Fortunately, we had brought canvas and sailcloth and a tent of sorts was soon rigged over the site.

The second well, fifty yards from the stables and next to one of the cottages, was as laborious as the first. But the promise of a month's remuneration for one night's toil, accompanied with rum, produced results. It had taken half an hour to clear the site of overgrown vegetation and debris, much of which I knew had been deliberately thrown there.

The hours passed. Dawn approached and with it more mist. Lanterns cast elongated shadows over the cottage, where the reflected figures of the workers reminded me of dancing marionettes. Yet the only sounds were of shovels against stone and the heavy breathing of the exhausted workers. At the halfway point, maybe fifteen feet, compact earth replaced the rocks. This fact alone gave me confidence. At thirty feet the earth became mud and with the mud came an offensive odour. If I had been at the goldfields, this would be a Eureka moment. But in reality, it was something sinister, something almost supernatural.

'Jaysuz!' the worker's voice called up through the miasma below. 'It stinks, sar.'

'Quick, get buckets on ropes down to those men.' I stood at the edge with a lantern and strained to look down into the well. The water was becoming viscous and slimy. Suddenly a human foot appeared above the slime.

'Mother Mary!' the first workman, up to his knees in this vile muck, jumped backwards and crossed himself. I leaned over the edge, lowering my lantern beneath the mouth of the well, twisting it until my light reached the crime scene. A heavy fetid and putrid stink rose to greet me.

'It's 'im, sar!' the man called up.

'Excellent,' I said in a soft, reverent voice. It was barely a whisper. As Dorothea Hartley had dreamt, her only child and son *was* at the bottom of a well. I had succeeded where weeks earlier, I'd thought the notion ridiculous. Unfortunately, the thrill of success was tempered by the next step: to extract the decomposed remains and identify them as those of Albert Hartley.

Chapter Eight

Ship Hotel, Collins Street, Hobart Town

Mack Ryan, the coachman, was not happy. He spurred on his mounts from his livery perch atop the coach, sharing the luggage rack with a leather-bound chest containing the dismembered, putrefying remains of Albert Hartley. As tightly as the lid fitted, the malodorous airs still escaped, often encircling the coachman as the winds took their fancy.

I had sent a message to Hobart Town via the telegraph wire, and on arrival I was more than pleased to be met by Jasper, Holly and Lantern Jaw Lincoln. It was great to be home.

The trunk was hefted onto the roadside outside the Ship Hotel where I watched my colleagues' noses twitch. Being accustomed to the unpleasant odour, I smiled at their reaction, Jasper and Lincoln taking a handle each as they slid the chest onto a handcart borrowed from the morgue.

'I hate ter tell yer this, Caspian sar,' Lincoln said. 'But that there trunk don't half stink.'

'Tell me something I do not know Lincoln,' I grinned.

'That vampire's struck again,' Lincoln said.

I was not expecting that. 'What?'

'I said that vampire...'

'Yes, yes. I heard you the first time. What do you mean? Where?'

'Up near Collin's Cap, sar,' Holly said.

'Mrs Mary Kelly. A trapper's wife,' Jasper continued. 'She were found dead outside their cabin. Found by her old man, Horace Kelly.'

'Another trapper eh?'

'Aye. Well, the trapper's wife, any'ow.'

'What happened?'

'It were like the others,' Holly said. 'Vampire bites in 'er neck, half 'er face torn off, half 'er upper body missin', torn away by the look of it...'

'And all her blood sucked dry.' Lincoln shuddered.

'Her body's at the morgue,' Jasper said. 'We've gotta deliver this 'un,' Jasper spoke of Hartley in the trunk, 'So you can come with us if'n yer see fit, Caspian sar.'

I thought a moment 'Where's Fabian?' I asked.

'At the barracks.'

'Right.' I looked to Holly and Lincoln. They had become quite the couple; Holly short and stocky and Lincoln the tall rake, looking ten foot tall in his weathered top hat. 'Then you two return to the barracks, and Jasper, you help me with this cart to the hospital.'

The Morgue, St Mary's Hospital, 8a.m.

The suffocating odour of formaldehyde crept up the spiral staircase to meet us like some spectre from the dark side. It was as if the spirit in the bottle felt a responsibility to the remains of our deteriorating cadaver in the trunk.

'Doctor Crawley,' I called down the stairs. No response. I knew the man was down there, alone in the company of the dead. But like the dead, the doctor was hard at hearing. Jasper and I had negotiated the handcart to the top of the stairs. All we had to do now was manhandle the trunk down into the morgue.

'Careful,' I commanded as Jasper jostled the trunk with impatience. Leading the struggle, I held my end of the chest as high off the steps as possible, whilst Jasper groaned and gasped, his end thumping heavily on the treads.

'Go easy Jasper. Careful...'

Whether Jasper's leather handle snapped while he was carrying the trunk or whether it happened after, I do not know. What I do know is, suddenly Jasper sat heavily on the step. The trunk launched itself towards me. Instantly, I bore the full weight. To avoid crushing my foot, I dived aside, cracking my head on an overhead lantern. The light swung wildly. The trunk crashed, end first, at the bottom of the stairs. The straps parted and the lid flew open.

Our violent entrance was mimicked by our shadows on the wall, the flames of the lanterns flaring from the unexpected boost of methane. Doctor Ernest Crawley turned from the cadaver on the slab before him, the moment Albert Hartley spilled onto the flagstones in a gelatinous state of decomposition.

Jasper vomited.

Seventy-one-year-old Crawley glared at me over his pince-nez through watery formaldehyde eyes. 'Christ man!' he covered his nose with a handkerchief. 'What's the meaning of this?'

I was not amused either. Jasper deserted me for the crisp fresh winter's air of Davey Street. Meanwhile, I was forced to shovel the hapless victim unceremoniously back into the trunk with the use of a hearth shovel, but I was pleased to see the lid fit back into place and at least a portion of the stench with it. All the while, I explained the history of the dismembered body to the incredulous coroner, who watched my every move with interest. Apparently, by all appearances, Doctor Crawley's nostrils were as useless as his hearing, as the stench did not overly disturb him. Not more than my intrusion, anyhow.

'Gideon?' Crawley harrumphed. 'Did you say the father's name was Gideon?'

'Yes Doctor Crawley. Gideon Hartley.'

He tilted his head to look over his glasses at the trunk. 'Who calls their son Gideon anyway?'

'Gideon's parents I guess.'

'Who?'

'His parents, doctor.'

'And this *Gideon* lives at Warwick Street you say?'

'Yes.'

'Very well. I will have Mr *Gideon* Hartley identify the...' Crawley poked the trunk with the toe of his shoe, 'that... that mess, later,' Crawley muttered absent-mindedly.

'Really?' I was shocked that an already traumatised father would have to see his son in such a horrendous condition.

'Oh fear not, Caspian. I'll doctor him up somewhat. Maybe just have the head showing.'

You're the mortician.

'I heard you were in Adelaide,' Crawley spoke as if all was well. 'Shot the villain dead, eh what? '

'Not really. I...'

'Good sport I say. It'd save the government funds if all the beggars took a bullet instead of elongated costly trials and the such.'

'Some are innocent,' I argued.

Crawley didn't appear to agree.

'Well, get over here then,' he said offhandedly. 'I haven't got all day.'

The doctor lifted a lantern off its wall sconce, shifting shadows and darkness from one side of the morgue to the other. He cast light over one whom I guessed to be Mrs Heather Kelly, the trapper's wife and latest *vampire* victim. She lay on the stone mortician's slab. I stepped closer into the light when...

'Careful!'

Too late. I tripped. 'Jesus Christ!'

I looked down where another body lay on the floor in the shadows, awaiting room on the mortuary slab for the coroner's pleasure. It was not so much the shock of a body on the floor; this was a common practice when the slab was occupied. But I had had enough contact with the dead of late, and tripping over another body unnerved me.

'Who's that, then?' I asked.

'No name. A sailor by all accounts. Drowned.' The semi-naked cadaver was a Jack Tar, wearing purplish grey three-quarter britches but little else; exposing his generous belly, a flaccid and loose overhang, like a giant blancmange.

'DAFI.' the coroner spelt out aloud.

'What's that?'

'DAFI, Mr Hunter. *Drunk and fell in*. There's been so many of late I've abbreviated it.'

'Oh.'

'Yes. He was found face down in Waterman's Dock this morning.'

This was not a suspicious death, just another drunken seafarer who did not make it back to his ship.

'Oh,' I muttered. 'There's more.'

Another pair of feet protruded from the darkness, also lying on the floor, awaiting the doctor. Crawley, a little absent minded of late, looked nonchalantly at the rather fat shape in the darkness.

'That's... ah...' he leant down and read the card tied to one toe. 'That's Lizzie Burke, cook from the Morrison's in Macquarie Street. Suspected heart failure.'

'Oh... so,' I said, stepping over no name to finally reach the slab. 'And this is Mrs Kelly, huh?'

'What?'

'I said, this is the body of Mary Kelly, the trapper's wife from Collin's Cap?'

'Yes.' Crawley lifted the lantern high onto a hook overhead and it was then I saw the side of her face that had been mutilated. I pulled a suitable face. The cadaver was waxy white, depleted of blood. One side of her chest had been mauled also, torn away violently. Crawley followed my eye.

'And right there Caspian,' he paused for effect. 'You can see puncture marks in her neck where the vampire sucked her dry.'

'You jest sir, surely?'

'What?'

'You jest sir.'

'Good god, man. Of course I jest. And what's more, I know who your murderer is.'

'Oh?'

'Yes. It's... goodness me, is that what I think it is?' Crawley lifted some black and red anomaly from a stone dish sitting on the mortuary slab.

'It's who, Doctor Crawley?'

'Black sausage, my breakfast, I was wondering where it got to. Fancy some?'

'Ah... no thank you. Doctor Crawley,' I repeated. 'It's?'

'It's with tomato relish; my wife made that last summer also.'

'No doctor. The murderer?'

'What? You'll have to speak up, lad.'

'You said you knew who the murderer was.'

'Did I?'

'Yes, you did.'

Doctor Crawley used his mortuary scalpel to slice a portion of blood pudding, sniffing at it.

'Well at least I think it's my wife's black pudding,' he said before popping it into his mouth. 'You sure you don't want to sample a piece,' he said, savouring the morsel of cold blood sausage as if it was his last meal. And by the look of him it possibly could be.

'Look Doctor, I'm indisposed this morning. Do you have any clues as to the murderer?'

Crawley looked at me long and hard, his brow furrowed and he frowned as if something untimely worried him. 'No,' he finally answered.

'No?'

'That's what I said, Caspian. No.'

Prisoner Barracks, Campbell Street 1p.m

'Seven guineas and five shillings!' Fabian stared at the promissory note owing to our northern brethren for labour, and gulped. He jammed tobacco into his pipe with his thumb. 'Seven guineas and five shillings, Jaysuz Christ, Caspy.'

'It is Caspian, remember? Just sign it please. You can take my word for it – the men digging the wells earned every penny. And Governor Young would agree it was money well spent.'

'Aye, but seven guineas. What was the five bob for?'

'That's to reimburse me. I gave the corporal's wife a crown for preparing supper.'

'Well I don't care what the others say about yer, me and the lads think yer done good, Caspian sar,' Holly grinned, defying Fabian's complaint and defying gravity by swinging back on her office chair and hooking her hobnail boots on her desk.

I heard an ominous creaking as the chair adjusted to her weight.

'That Gordon Harper must have had help, to fill them wells in, that is.'

'He did.'

'Oh. Do I detect more arrests?'

'No. They were innocent fools. I spoke to two young brothers, fourteen and sixteen, who were given a sovereign each to fill the wells in one night. Harper told them the wells were polluted and all water in future would have to be carted from the river. But there is possibly another party to be investigated.'

'Who's that?'

'Albert's cousin Eddy, who lives in Adelaide. I suspect he was in cahoots with Harper. He certainly had a grudge against Albert Hartley, Eddy's father having short changed his inheritance to favour Albert, who was his godson.'

I looked to Fabian, who knew exactly what I was talking about.

'Aye. And it ain't our problem,' Fabian said. 'I have filed a report to Adelaide. It's their problem now.'

Billings walked into the office, beaming with success. '

I have managed to track down the cannibal Zachary Wolf, gentlemen.'

Holly shot Billings a scowl. *Gentlemen!*

'Ah,' Billings apologised. 'And you too, Holly.'

'And?' I asked.

'He's residing at the Sea o' Graves.'

Of course, Billings spoke of the Sea o' Graves Inn at Browns River, a four-hour sail down the Derwent Estuary.

'And what, pray tell, is the limb muncher doing at the *Graves?*' Fabian lit his pipe grinning at his acquired brand of humour.

'You'll never guess,' Billings grinned back.

'Try me?' I said.

Billings paused. 'Well,' Holly shook her head impatiently. 'Tell us then.'

'Wait for it,' Billings thought it a great joke and kept us all waiting. 'He is the inn's butcher.'

'The cannibal's a butcher,' Jasper started to laugh. 'Well my guess is 'e has had enough practice.'

'He has been working in the galley with Lynch Savage's cook, Jean Pardon, three months past.'

'So he has an alibi,' I said. 'He could not be our *vampire*.'

'Ah, but that is where you are wrong,' Billings said. 'He has a close friend, another lag from Port Arthur who got his ticket about the same time as Wolf, and guess what?'

'You and yer firkin' *guess whats,* Billings. Spill, fer Christ sake.' This outburst from Holly.

'Well, the friend lives behind the mountain. He is a fur trapper. And Zachary visits him often, usually once a week on his day of rest.'

'Then we need to talk to this Zachary Wolf immediately,' I said slipping my turnip free to read the time. 'It is one o'clock. Billings.'

'Yes, sir.'

'Since you were the man to locate our suspect maybe you will accompany me down river.'

Fabian bounced to his feet. 'There's naught much else afoot this moment, I'll be joining yer,' he said.

And I knew why. The colony's best filles de joie, the colony's best porter and the colony's most amicable and generous innkeeper all reside at Browns River, at the Sea o' Graves Inn.

Chapter Nine

The Sea o' Graves Inn, Browns River

Police skipper Swain met us at Waterman's Dock where the police sloop, *Fabian*, named *Fabian* after Fabian by Fabian, was permanently docked. With a good wind in the sail, the inn was usually a three to four-hour journey down the Derwent Estuary. This day, dusk was already upon us as we sailed around Browns River headland into a scene of industry, where retired and scuttled craft were stripped of anything of value. The beach here was usually busy with vendors or those procuring; all haggling for a bargain or to make a large profit. But with winter upon us most merchants had retired from their tent village to the inn taproom. Swain sailed up onto the beach where the waves were slight and it was possible for me to leap over the bow and secure the anchor into the sand.

The Sea o' Graves Inn was well appointed, and well named, being the heart of this ship graveyard. Sloops, cutters, tenders and every smaller craft imaginable lay moored or beached in various states of repair or desertion.

Innkeeper Lynch Savage operated a successful chandlery here on the beach as well, a chandlery of pre-owned maritime goods – a cover up, so the word goes, for many other nefarious activities. Small craft from Hobart Town plied back and forth, looking for a bargain. Usually, all along the beach, steam hissed, tar smoked, smithies pounded anvils and the ever-present gulls circled overhead, singing their song of the sea.

The Inn itself, the remains of a whaling barque wrecked by a rogue whale in the Derwent Estuary several years earlier, was built into a steep embankment alongside Browns River. To a naïve traveller it looked like the abandoned wreckage of a tidal wave. The stern cabin had been rebuilt 'arse about', as Fabian described it, so that the stern windows faced over the bow beneath it, looking back along the beach; one atop the other. The bow jutted over the river, its bowsprit snapped above the figurehead – the figurehead of a rampant wolf. The stern nameplate was nailed over the doorway, a low hatch in the port bow facing the River Derwent; it read *Sea Wolf*. But painted along her hull were the words, 'Sea o' Graves.'

The Sea o' Graves was a gathering place for lawless rogues and villains, sealers, absconders, whalers, lost sailors and a trickle of law-abiding citizens like myself. There was naught a vice a man could not find to pleasure him here, as long as he had coin in his pocket.

Lynch Savage himself was an obese man; so fat in fact, that he hired four bearers to carry him in a sedan chair from one location to the next. The man was a legend. Born in England in 1795 he was now in his sixty-third year, as generous as he was enormous. But he was a man of many talents, all of which made him a rich and envied man. Flamboyant in appearance and hopelessly theatrical, drugged by the fancy of the stage, Savage insisted on attiring like Captain Morgan, the 17th century pirate, complete with a tricorn hat resplendent with ostrich feathers.

Lynch liked nothing more than to entertain visitors at his table – a *hair-loom* as he called his ancestor's oak banquet table shipped all the way from Cornwall, and over two hundred years old. These feasts were always a sumptuous affair; served in the stern cabin, they included shameless amounts of near extinct local game, prepared by his *stolen* French cook, Jean Parton. Fine wines and obliging women were also necessary accouterments. Secretly, I envied the man.

And *my* relationship with Lynch Savage, I hear you ask? We had become friends over the three years I had known him. The man took a shine to me as an intelligent ally, albeit a naïve one, within the police force, although I refused frequent offers of remuneration, usually in the form of employment within his situation. I imagine he respects me for this. However, I had been known in the past to reveal snippets of exclusive information in return for assistance in catching a villain or two.

And on this chilly overcast day, I hoped to solve another mystery. We negotiated the gangplank from the embankment to the inn door; a precarious bridge to the main entrance cut into the port hull. I say precarious, as to miss a step here one would end up in Browns River amongst the sludge and swill seeping from the bilge into the waterway. Not to mention the waste from the inn's garderobes.

Once inside the taproom, it was how I will always remember it: tobacco smoke yellowed walls, permeating vapors of Old Tom, Navy rum and tuppenny gins, a soupy fug of warmth with fire grates burning generously, the comely welcome of loose women, along with enough unwashed bodies and unsavory language to make any seafarer feel at home.

Old hand at the game, Fanny Peach, greeted us in the taproom. Fanny was one of the inn's resident doxies who had taken to Fabian and his rakish charm in the past. She led us up a wide stair companionway to Lynch Savage's stern cabin.

'Caspian, my boy,' Lynch was his usual jovial self. My guess was the roasted leg of some animal and the near empty jug of French Bordeaux he had consumed as an aperitif to his evening meal had something to do with it. 'What a pleasant surprise. It's so nice to see you.' He caught sight of Fabian on my heels and muttered flatly, 'Mr Winter.'

The innkeeper had never taken a shine to Fabian and I was yet to figure out why. Fabian nodded politely and eyed the wine jug.

'And you have company also,' Lynch alluded to Billings who removed his topper and nodded respectfully. As Billings had not met the great man before, I remembered my manners.

'This is Billings, Lynch, one of my hard-working colleagues.'

'Aye. Good day to you, sir.'

Billings made to cross the cabin floor to take the great man's hand in greeting, but was abruptly stopped, by one of Lynch's men placing a firm hand on his chest. Protection for Lynch Savage was always a priority.

'Please excuse Jack, Billings. He can be overprotective sometimes.' Lynch waved his men away with the back of his great paw.

'So,' Lynch ran a keen eye along the remains of his roasted leg bone, harumphed, and threw it back onto its pewter charger. His guard dogs, chained to barrel kennels along the riverbank, would enjoy that. 'You are here on business, eh?' he said, using the long nail on his little pinkie to prise stubborn meat from between his teeth. 'When will you come for a social visit?'

'Sorry Lynch, but we have urgent business in...'

'Sit.' As I expected, Lynch cut me short. 'I'll not listen to your business until you join me in some refreshment.'

He tugged on a velvet servant's cord within reach at his table and platters of food appeared. Clearly he was having one of his late lunches this day and the galley was awaiting his demand. We three sat whilst Fannie charged our tumblers with wine and delegated the distribution of the food being delivered by two most attractive and toothsome wenches.

And what a fine feast it was. Kangaroo tail stew and kidney pudding was followed by a fish dish called kedgeree, jellied calves feet and lashings of souse – better known as headcheese or brawn. Claret jelly and lemon dumplings followed this delicious repast.

Absolutely sumptuous.

After some time, I managed to wrestle Savage's attention away from the banquet before him. 'Zachary Wolf,' I said aloud.

'Aye,' Fabian joined in nodding his head profusely. Apparently, he had just remembered the reason for our visit.

Savage leant back in his carver and wiped the grease from his hands with a cloth. 'What of 'im?'

'He is engaged in your service here at the Graves, is he not?'

''e were me butcher, aye. Jean trained 'im in me galley. 'e be a real natural at it an' all.'

'Oh?'

'Aye. Hacking' away, butcherin' meat. A real natural 'e were. But 'e ain't no more, lad.'

'Pray tell,' Fabian was determined to restore some respect. 'Do you know his whereabouts?'

Lynch Savage bided his time before giving Fabian one of his chary looks. 'Why do yer want to know?'

'I'll be up front with yer Lynch,' Fabian answered. 'We need to ask 'im a few questions.'

'Questions about what?'

'There've been three deaths of late, around the Mount Wellington environs...'

'What sort o' deaths?'

'Nasty. Quite savage, in fact,' I said, immediately realising I could have chosen a better word.

'Savage!' Savage leant back in his carver slapping the chair arms and roared a laugh.

'Ferocious,' I corrected. 'Almost predatory.'

Savage wiped a tear from the corner of his eye. 'Oh. Do go on.'

I explained the vicious attacks, the mauling, the puncture marks and the draining of blood without trace, finally mentioning the words vampire and cannibal.

'And you suspect Zachy boy's been up to 'is old tricks. Killin' and eatin' 'is victims.'

'This did cross our mind Lynch,' I said seriously.

'Well, it's impossible,' Lynch's bottom lip folded in serious contemplation.

Fabian answered. 'How's that?'

'Well I feed 'im well here, lads. As yer can see no one goes hungry 'round the Graves. Why would Zachy want to eat humans?'

'That is a point, but we would still like to have dialogue with the man, if you please.'

'Well I would love to help. But I can't.'

'Can't or won't?'

Fabian's comment was answered with a raised eyebrow.

'Can't. The fact is, 'e is in the ground.'

'In the ground... you mean...'

'Dead Caspian. Dead an' buried. He fell off the perch a month ago.'

'Oh!'

''e were no spring chicken, yer know. The girls went to wake 'im one morning and 'e'd slipped off in the night.'

'And you buried him?'

'Aye.'

'Did you give him a funeral?'

'O' course, lad. We give him a grand ol' send off.'

'Did you register his death with the coroner?'

'I do know the law, Caspian,' Savage said, his expression indignant. 'I got papers an' all, just 'aven't had time to register 'em in Hobart Town as yet.'

'It was your responsibility to have registered his death with the coroner within thirty days.'

'I am aware, but have been otherwise occupied. Maybe you could deliver them on your return.'

I looked at Savage and nodded in agreement. Heaven forbid, I owed the man one or two favours. 'Who signed these papers anyway ... his death certificate?'

'We had a sawbones off HMS *Friendly*, down 'ere at the time. Making use of the Grave's facilities like. A jolly officer, Douglas Cromwell was 'is name.'

'I do not mean to be rude, Lynch,' I said tactfully. 'But we will need to see the certificate.'

The papers were in a chest in the cabin and were all in order. Lynch had, indeed, done the lawful thing.

'Well that excludes him from any mischief then,' I said. 'We are back to where we started.

'Aye.'

'Where is he buried?' Fabian asked.

'Along the riverbank,' Lynch said. 'There be half a dozen coves what have a peaceful resting place there.' Lynch studied us carefully. 'You'll not be diggin' 'im up I hope?'

We stood on a steep incline with a lantern in hand. Along the bank, six graves denoted the whereabouts of six lost souls, no doubt strangers to each other, yet now united in death on the picturesque riverside. And yes, one grave was freshly dug. The air was full of chill and a mist lingered. I read aloud the inscription painted onto a modest wooden grave marker. 'Here lies Zachary Wolf, Butcher. Who died peacefully. Second day of June in the year of our Queen Victoria, 1858.'

'Butcher!' Fabian smiled. 'I reckon he would 'ave appreciated that.'

Behind us the tall gums of Browns River groaned. A southerly was picking up. 'We've got the wind in our favour.' I said, not in the mood to impose on local hospitality further. 'We best find our skipper.'

Prisoner Barracks. 8a.m.

8a.m. sharp, Fabian and I were summoned to witness a hanging in the new gallows within the prison system, public hangings having being abolished as a medieval practise. I say new gallows, although the scaffold and the trapdoor are from the old gaol in Murray Street. Now, in these modern times, hangings are conducted in the presence of the sheriff, the under-sheriff, the gaoler, gaol officials, any officials deemed necessary by the sheriff: men reporting for the newspapers, Fabian and myself, clergy and of course the hangman, Solomon Blay.

But what was particularly macabre about this execution was the fact that the prisoner was eighty-four years old. Ned Baxter was born in Scotland in 1774, left home when he was nine, travelled to England and spent the next twenty-five years working as a thatcher. He was a frugal man who saved a moderate fortune before sailing to Sydney Cove where he opened a brewery. Five years later, now married to a Janet Fletcher, he sold the brewery and became a grain-trader. By 1830, at the age of sixty-four, he was a wealthy man. He then sailed for Hobart Town where he speculated – one might say gambled – with his wealth. Unfortunately, he lost more than half his fortune. However, he still had enough money to maintain a decent standard of living and run a large house with four servants in Davey Street, overlooking the River Derwent.

Then, one month ago, a neighbour heard Janet screaming as Ned, now eighty-four, beat his wife. The next morning, the wife was found crouched on her bedroom floor, covered in blood and bruises. She was taken to hospital but died the same day. No one will ever know what happened to make old Ned behave the way he did. Found guilty, he was to hang.

The warder told us that throughout his trial Ned seemed cheerfully indifferent to the case. Even when the judge donned his black cap and sentenced Ned to death, he smiled peacefully. But as the day of execution arrived, it appeared that Ned realised his life was about to end and began weeping hysterically. The warder said that the night before, he was heard weeping in his cell. He refused a last meal and then, by the time the guards came to fetch him, together with Solomon Blay the hangman wearing his black hood, Ned collapsed and had to be carried to the gallows.

As he stood, hands tied behind his back, on the gallows trap door, he started ranting and raving that he was innocent and condemned those who spoke against him at his trial. Ignored, he finally harangued those witnesses before him, including Fabian and myself. The moment he paused to draw breath, Solomon Blay stepped forward and drew the bolt. The trapdoor dropped open noisily. But as his body disappeared through the trapdoor, I saw a hand, apparently not pinioned securely, seize the rope at the back of his neck. It was a futile attempt to save himself. His body jerked violently and he started to choke to death until the hangman managed to lower himself into the drop and kick the Scotsman's hand free. He died soon after.

It had not been a pleasant sight – not that any execution is.

Billings caught us crossing the courtyard back towards our office, within the prison storeroom. 'I just got the verdict back from the priority court hearing conducted for Mr Hilbert O'Neil.'

'Oh.' We were aware of the priority court hearing, on account the man was on death's door, dying of tuberculosis. 'And?'

'Not guilty.'

'Not guilty?'

'That's right. He couldn't lift a pumpkin, let alone drag his wife's body all that distance and dump her in the alleyway.'

Fabian was philosophical about the outcome. 'Well, it was a forgone conclusion, was it not?'

'I agree. So now what? We still have her killer on the loose'

We climbed the rickety wooden steps to our humble office above the prison stores only to walk into an argument on capital punishment.

'Hang the bastards,' Holly voiced her opinion in no manner of restraint. 'An eye for an eye eh, doesn't it say that in the Bible?'

'Wouldn't know Hol',' Jasper said. 'Never read the Bible.'

'Neither 'ave I, but that's wha' I 'eard, anyways.'

'I think you will find the Bible also says we should forgive,' I suggested. But I, too, had not read much of the *good* book.

'I'm not so certain anymore,' Fabian said, stepping back from the window, from where he watched Solomon Blay, the hangman, take a pipe of tobacco in the sun. Without his hood, he was a hard and bitter man with a cadaverous face. The hangman seemed to be muttering to himself, also. As it was protocol to leave the body swinging for one hour after the drop – to be certain the prisoner was dead – the hangman had all the time in the world.

'All the time in the world and no one to share it with,' Fabian made his observations public.

'What was that?' I asked.

'Solomon Blay down there, all alone,' Fabian nodded out the window. 'It's a lonely business being a hangman. Look at him, will yer, he chatters more and more to himself these days.'

With a father transported to the colonies for fourteen years for stealing two coats, Solomon Blay had not long been in the free world himself, Fabian informed me.

''e were caught stealing three bushels of potatoes from a field near Oxford in '33 an' given twelve months' gaol with hard labour, includin' time in a solitary cell.'

Fabian went on to explain that eking out a life in poverty led Blay to team up with two other desperate men he had befriended in prison, and together they had forged the King's coin. But they were caught and sentenced to fourteen years' transportation, arriving on the ship *Sarah* in Hobart Town on the 29th of March, 1837.

On arrival, Blay had been described as prisoner 2598, height five-feet-eight-and-three-quarter inches, sallow complexion, head large and long, hair dark brown, visage long, eyes blue, and with a deeply pock-pitted, small lump under the right eye.

Three years after arriving in Van Diemen's Land Solomon Blay, by all reports a loner, was desperate to keep out of chain gangs, lashings and solitary confinement. 'So 'e took it upon himself to volunteer as the colony hangman, a position the government had trouble filling.'

'I wonder why?'

'With 'is only skill being a boatman in little demand, and 'is other option to abscond and become a bushranger, and end up on the end of a rope himself, Blay applied for the position. He was accepted at a monthly salary of seven pounds one shilling and seven pence. That was back in August, 1840.'

'And he's been hangman ever since.'

'Aye. An' a good one, most o' the time.'

Of course, capital punishment had been debated in the newspapers in all the colonies for some time. Many religious minded folk felt it barbaric, a throwback to a darker age. Maybe they were right. A good public hanging, if I can use the word *good*, had not been proven a deterrent to crime. 'Many suggest,' I continued, 'that what is needed to deter violent criminals is the prospect of a lifetime in prison with hard labour and the promise of a regular flogging.'

Only recently, Joseph Connors, who had turned Queen's evidence by admitting his own guilt in a rape charge whilst implicating three others, had his death sentence commuted to a life sentence of hard labour. The first three years are to be spent in chains and he is to receive three floggings of twenty-five lashes each, at stated periods. In his case, maybe hanging would have been kinder.

Chapter Ten

Blue Whale Cottage, Cromwell Street, Battery Hill

It was such a pleasure to finally make it home this day, back to my abode in Battery Point. Blue Whale Cottage being a leased dwelling, once belonging to a sea captain whose murder I solved over two years earlier. His distraught wife was only too happy to let me have the property at a modest rent, as she could no longer bear to live there.

The bluestone cottage has three rooms downstairs with two attic bedrooms with large dormer windows and wooden shutters. It sits on a long narrow grant of land, with its own well at the rear and a moderate stable; not that I could afford the luxury of a horse. The neighbourhood was pleasantly quiet except for the constant clack clack of the sail cogs operating Cowgill's flourmill opposite. But in all fairness, that is during daylight hours.

Mrs Rumball – Emma, my housekeeper – had prepared me a roasted pigeon, leaving it in the meat safe hanging outside, under the back porch, where the winter's chill kept it in good order. I would like to note here that I can only afford Mrs Rumball four hours a day, three days a week. Emma is a big-boned lady, strong willed, not afraid to speak her mind, yet her big-bosomed chest harbours a kind heart. She was to be married late in life to a Captain Seabrick Philbrick, an army captain posted to Port Dalrymple, but sadly, the army captain was drowned off the coast before they had a chance to wed. I took Emma Rumball back into my employ without hesitation, and now my waistline was evidence of our happy relationship.

With extra logs thrown onto the fire grate, I ate the pigeon with pickles, cheddar cheese and Emma's freshly baked bread, and thought of my mother and how she would have connected with my housekeeper. Outside Jack Frost stalked. But I sensed another presence. Call it policeman's intuition, I had a feeling I was being watched, and decided that I must have curtains fitted.

I was lost in my thoughts, nibbling the thigh meat from a reasonably fat pigeon, when there came a thumping on my door. I looked to my pocket watch sitting on the table. It was only seven in the evening, but in the middle of a Van Diemen's Land winter, it was dark by half the hour after five.

'Fabian!'

'Caspy.'

I hate being called Caspy. Fabian knows this, yet he persists. I have given up, mostly.

'What brings you to Blue Whale Cottage this freezing night?' I asked. A chill off the River Derwent swirled at my feet and I motioned Fabian to step inside, the better to keep my cottage moderately warm.

'O'Neil's about to fall off the perch,' Fabian panted. He must have walked here in haste. O'Neil being the husband of the dead woman in Wapping.

Fabian stood before the fire, rubbed his hands vigorously before turning about and hiking his coat tails high to warm his backside. 'The hospital sent a message to say he is gravely ill, he will not make it through the night, and he wants to talk to us.'

Now this was good news, yet awkwardly timed. 'I will avail myself of the privy, then fetch my coat.'

'Hurry Caspy, the clock's tickin' as they say.'

In the backyard, my lavatory looked as inviting as the scaffold. The dark shape stood sentinel in the back yard in the moonless night. I had no lantern. Over the fence I could just make out my neighbour, Mrs Rust, in her kitchen. But our properties were in blackness, so I relieved myself on the lemon tree. *Should help the fruit,* I quietly chuckle to myself when I heard movement in the shadows. I *was* not alone. 'Who's there?' I called out.

Nothing.

Silence.

Whatever it was, it remained still. And it was not a dog or cat or possum even, for I knew it sounded large. Much larger. I buttoned my britches and ventured forward into the darkness. I must confess, my courage was boosted with the knowledge that Fabian was inside.

'Who's there?' I said, in my most authoritative lawman's baritone. 'Come out immediately.'

I remembered a rake, left leaning against the back fence, and armed myself before venturing, rather bravely I thought, into the darkness of the fruit trees at the bottom of my garden. 'Show yourself...'

Instantly a dark shape lunged towards me. I was struck in the chest and thrown aside by burly arms. I swung about with the rake, slapping the prongs into the escaping figure. 'Stand to!' I yelled.

But he was powerfully built and tall. He ran for the fence and seemed to fly over it, a long cape chasing after him. An incognito covert shape in the pitch black of night.

'What took yer so long?' Fabian said through a mouthful of pigeon. 'Actually, I don't want to know.' He stuffed a large piece of bread and cheese into his mouth.

'I was just attacked!' I said, my heart pounding.

'What? In the shithouse?'

'No, in the backyard.'

Fabian saw I was distressed. 'Yer serious, ain't yer.'

'Damned right I'm serious.'

'By whom was yer attacked?'

'A man, a figure dressed all in black, by all appearances.'

'Well? Well what happened?'

I explained. Fabian went out into the yard. Nothing. 'Christ Caspy, yer better lock yer doors proper like.'

St Mary's Hospital

Disturbed by the intruder, I could only hope it was a random attack and not someone targeting me for a past arrest. Moments later, Fabian and I took the brisk walk through the village of Battery Point, where we hurried down Kelly's Steps leading us onto New Wharf. Here we headed north – bypassing the Sailor's Rest that, as usual, was doing a roaring trade – and passed the cemetery opposite St Mary's Hospital. This never failed to amuse me, a cemetery opposite a hospital.

Matron Hope Benedict was expecting us. Well into her forties, Matron was an attractive older woman whose beauty had followed her into middle age.

'I've been expecting you,' Matron said in an official and professional tone. 'Give me a moment would you please?'

We watched as the woman removed leeches from a rather waxy-white patient, wearing only a napkin. Leeches, I knew, were used to relieve pressure and release toxins in order to achieve the body's natural balance. Supposedly. I had often wondered at the practice. Since 1838 a fully qualified medical practitioner had to have one or more of the following: a university medical degree, a license from the College of Physicians in Great Britain, a membership with the Company of Apothecaries of London, or be an experienced military medical officer. But leeches?

'Mr O'Neil is not long of this world, I fear,' the matron warned us of her patient. 'He was asked if he would like a priest, but he asked for you gentlemen instead.' This fact alone had the woman roll her eyes. My opinion was that she would rather see the man in the company of god's followers.

We followed the lady with the lantern to a men's ward at the rear of the building on the first floor. Passing the spiral stair leading down to the morgue, I could not help but notice the lantern flame brighten as we passed, feeding off the gasses rising from below, I imagined.

Matron Benedict used a taper to light a candle next to O'Neil and the crackling and spitting as the wick took hold woke our patient.

'Sorry to startle you Mr O'Neil,' matron said. 'But Mr Winter and Mr Hunter are here to see you, as you requested.'

It took a moment for O'Neil to focus, or maybe return from whatever darkness surrounded him. Finally he nodded silently in recognition.

'I'll leave you be then,' the matron said, and left.

'The court hearing found you not guilty Mr O'Neil,' I said when I was certain I recognised life in the man's eyes. 'Mr O'Neil... Hilbert, is it not?'

'Aye. How could I kill me own Molly?'

'Quite.'

'You wanted to see us Hilbert,' Fabian said, subtle as a ship of the line rolling out its cannons.

'Aye.' Hilbert O'Neil tried to sit up. I helped, sitting him semi-upright with the aid of a folded blanket. 'Water,' he barely whispered, his voice weak and croaky.

I fetched a pannikin of water while Fabian thumbed tobacco into his clay pipe and sparked it alight with a wax-headed match.

O'Neil sipped, coughed and sipped again. 'Samuel Groundwater done it,' he finally said.

'Samuel Groundwater, the slaughterman?'

'Aye. I'm certain of it.'

'What makes you say that?' I asked.

'Cos 'e threatened my Molly, earlier in the week.'

'Now why would 'e do thart, Hilbert?' Fabian demanded, his face temporarily cloaked in smoke.

'My Molly...' Hilbert O'Neil looked about weakly, better his words be for our ears only. 'My Molly... well she were a... ah...'

Fabian hooked his pipe into the corner of his mouth. 'Spit it out Hilbert.'

'She were an abortionist, squire.'

'An abortionist!'

Hilbert's face winced at the word repeated aloud.

'Are you saying your wife conducted abortions, Hilbert?'

'Aye. She were a good woman, honest she were. Then this 'ere Lizzie Burke, a youngen who works as a scullery maid at the Nightingale, by all accounts. Well she come visit my Molly. Desperate she were. But soon after, this 'ere Samuel Groundwater, the bairn's father, well 'e come an' threaten Molly, tells 'er if'n she even touched Lizzie, well 'e'd kill 'er 'e said. Nasty bastard, if'n I ever seen one.'

'I spoke to Samuel Groundwater, Hilbert. And he told me he wanted Lizzie to terminate the child.'

'Thart's a lie, sar. I were there, sick as a dog I were, lyin' in me bed. But I heard Samuel clear as day, sar, threaten' my Molly if she went ahead.'

'So what happened to Lizzie Burke?'

'It were a botched job. Molly cut into the womb. There were blood everywhere, she told me. Molly was real upset.'

'Where did she conduct these operations?'

'In an outhouse, down back o' number 47. The landlord, 'e closes a blind eye long as Molly give him some coin.'

'Jesus.'

'And Lizzie?'

'She ran away. She must 'ave walked across to the Domain, where she died. Thart's the honest truth, sar.'

Matron Benedict showed Fabian and me onto Davey Street, bolting the huge oak door behind us.

'I suspected Groundwater all along,' I said, blowing warm breath into cupped hands and wondering why I didn't wear my gloves. Fabian tapped spent tobacco on the iron fence and rubbed his chin.

'It ain't even eight yet, Caspy.' He tipped his head to the Waterloo directly across the street. 'Fancy somethin' ter warm yer cockles?'

The Waterloo Tavern was a soldiers' inn. And with the army barracks less than a mile away on the hill, it did a brisk trade. Fabian bought two quart tankards of porter and a generous Irish whisky each. We quaffed the whisky and took a decent draught of the porter before I went over my interview at the slaughterhouse with Samuel Groundwater.

'Groundwater told you he wanted Lizzie to have an abortion?' Fabian said. 'Not the other way around. Why?'

'I think he was trying to point the finger at Molly O'Neil by saying the opposite.'

'Jaysuz!' Fabian drank, smacked his lips and discreetly pulled back the flap on his jacket. 'You armed, lad?'

'No!' I looked about me anxiously. I did not consider it wise to show off a firearm in a taproom full of soldiers 'You're not thinking what I think you are thinking, are you?'

'Aye. Finish yer drink and we'll go ask about the inns; someone 'll know where the bastard is.'

'Do you really think that's a good idea?'

'Yes I do. Now drink up.' Fabian drained his own glass and turned for the door. 'Besides,' he cast a disapproving eye over the regimental clientele. 'There's too many firkin' officers in 'ere,' he said, and it was then I remembered how he disliked army officers.

The Sailor's Rest Inn was our most obvious choice, back down to New Wharf, where the docks were deserted this cold night, but the inns and taverns were booming. Bonnie Nettle was enjoying a rare night away from the bar, but Sally Twinkle her manager for the night, assured us she had never heard of a Samuel Groundwater. The Lord Rodney next to the *Rest* was more a hotel for gentry, so we spent no more time than it took to drink another whisky in there. As Fabian suggested, we should be enquiring at the more shady establishments.

'Maybe over on Old Wharf on Hunter Island and around Wapping,' he said, his eyes alight with expectations.

A whisky here, a whisky there. I was soon warming up. In fact I was on fire. We stopped in at the Electric Telegraph Hotel, bypassed the Florence Nightingale, as we knew he would not be there, and paid our respects to the Howard, the Commercial, and the Steam Packet Tavern. So, by the time we arrived at the Shades Tavern under the Theatre Royal, a dark, cramped taproom patronised by the steerage ticket holders in the theatre above, I found myself joining in on the sing-along to the fiddler's tune.

It was after ten, but any regard for tomorrow's pain had flown the coop.

'Samuel Groundwater,' the cove repeated the name when Fabian asked. 'Who wants ter know?'

'Coupla mates,' Fabian lied, his brow rising high as his eyes widened, enjoying the fabrication.

'Mates, huh?'

'Aye... mates.'

'Well, little Sammy usually tipples at the Cutlass an' Keg.'

I had heard of the Cutlass and Keg up Elizabeth Lane on the Hobart Town Rivulet, and it *enjoyed* an unwholesome reputation for rowdy drunkenness and fights.

'Perfect!' Fabian slurred in my ear in a mist of whisky. 'Just the sort o' nest to catch our rat.'

With the frost settling on the waterfront, we made our journey as briskly as possible; only having to pass the Derwent Hotel, All Nations, The Rock, The Albion and The White Horse. Each innkeeper welcomed our increasingly unruly presence when silver crossed their palm. From The White Horse we crossed Elizabeth Street to Elizabeth Lane when we were both caught short.

'Will you look at that?' I said aloud to Fabian as we *crossed swords* relieving ourselves on the butcher's window. 'Pork four pence per pound.'

'Aye, lad, it be more expensive than mutton.'

Now, with the streets empty and a numbing breeze inhabiting the town in off the Tasman Sea, we were only too pleased to patronise the Cutlass and Keg.

The Cutlass and Keg was a tiny inn down a narrow lane running parallel to the rivulet, a muddy lane rutted from the hand-hauled carts laden with ale barrels, and all but forgotten by the progressive sandstone and red brick erections on the opposite side of the alleyway. It was a shanty inn, wedged in amongst the decrepit abodes of the poor living along the rivulet, with the mountain's water rushing by behind the flimsy dwellings.

The innkeeper, forty-five-year-old Henry Staghorn, was a retired sergeant major from the 101st Regiment of Foot, also known as the Royal Bengal Fusiliers. He was wounded during the first Anglo-Afghan War in July '39, when one of his own men accidentally shot him in the face. The musket ball took out most of his right cheek. It had healed, but at what price. The man now looked like a demon, like a gargoyle clinging to a church spire. The cheek was a leathery saddle of cured, but grotesquely distorted, skin, welded to his skull. He was in constant discomfort, surviving on slop food, as he had lost most of his teeth at the time of the dreadful accident. Henry Staghorn was not to be underestimated. One does not stare at his injuries, for he takes offence easily, and rightly so.

'It's been said 'e's killed more men than the plague,' Fabian giggled as we threw open the door to a welcoming fiddler's tune and that fug peculiar to inn taprooms. The small room was packed but, forgetting our mission for the moment, we pushed our way to the bar where the innkeeper watched our approach with a flinty eye.

'Gentlemen,' he said with an element of suspicion. *Gentlemen?* Was this a title reserved for the likes of Fabian and myself only? I looked up into the face of a man who had been through the wars, literally. I had seen etchings of gargoyles hanging from the Notre Dame that were more attractive. 'Jesus!' I said involuntarily. Fabian elbowed me hard in the kidney, knocking the wind from my sails.

'And a good evenin' to you, innkeeper,' Fabian said.

'I 'ope you haven't come to the *Keg* ter cause no trouble?'

'Goodness gracious me no,' I said, all serious like.

'What'll it be then?' Staghorn drawled.

I was about to say whiskey until I saw a fancy clear bottle with an appealing lime green liquid within. 'What's that then?' I said.

It seemed he had sold a few this night, for he did not even look to where I was pointing. 'Green fairy,' he answered, and his mouth turned up at the corners into a huge, albeit ugly, smile. 'A crown for two. Does sir wish to partake?'

'Green fairy, huh.'

'Also known as absinthe. It's a frog grog made from anise and sweet fennel.' What he did not inform us was absinthe was the stuff of ruination. A potent spirit derived from botanicals, including flowers and leaves of *Artemisia absinthium* or ground wormwood to the less informed. Ideally, it is diluted with water. Henry Staghorn failed to advise that little titbit as well.

I tossed a silver crown on the counter.

Fabian sniffed his proffered glass and made a suitable face. 'Up yours,' he said and drank the liquid in one mouthful, smacked his lips and exhaled with satisfaction. I did likewise. Gasped. Snatched a breath. Whistled. Before I could manage a word or two Fabian's crown spun before the innkeeper.

'Up yours?' I questioned Fabian. 'What vulgarity is this?'

'Caspy, Caspy, where yer been, lad? Yer soundin' terribly, terribly English tonight. Up yours is what all the lags 'ere say. It means cheers, or here's mud in yer eye.'

'Oh, like a salute?'

'Aye.' Fabian passed me my glass, and lifted his to his mouth. 'Now it's your turn.'

I pirouetted on the spot, lifted my chin high, clicked my heels and raised my glass to the room. 'Up yours,' I shouted to all the inebriates and reprobates within earshot. And I drank the lot. 'Whooh!' I gasped, pumping the air. And earned a cheer for my adventure. 'Up yours,' a handful yelled back.' And the fiddler leapt onto a stool launching into a tune.

What do we do with a drunken sailor?
What do we do with a drunken sailor?
What do we do with a drunken sailor
Early in the morning?

'Oh – my – god!' I gasped.
 'What?'
'The fiddler!'

I could not take my eyes off her beguiling smile, her doll-like face, her pixy legs, and her long ponytail of amber hair; shifting shades in the smoke-filled inn. Her eyes were a mystifying green I fancied, and she was the most beautiful woman I had ever seen. Or was that the most beautiful fiddler I had ever seen? Or was it the green fairy talking?

'The fiddler, Fabian. Look at her.'

He turned to face the lone musician. 'Aye, lad, she sure is pretty.'

'Pretty? Pretty?' I was like a schoolboy in the confectioners with a whole florin to spend. 'Pretty? She is... gorgeous... bewitching... captivating. All of them together. A delight to behold...'

Hey ho and up she rises,
Hey ho and up she rises,
Hey ho and up she rises early in the morning.

I was mesmerised, smitten. The young Irish lass worked that fiddle like a master, dancing on the stool and drawing that bow across the strings with the agility of a humming bird. The crowd jigged. And as everyone was familiar with the words, they sang along. I stood enthralled, my green fairy slopping to the tune as I too was compelled to do a little dance...

What will we do with the drunken sailor?
What will we do with the drunken sailor?
What will we do with the drunken sailor
Early in the morning?

As I bounced and bobbed, drank and sang, I became aware she was turning in my direction, playing the room like the professional she was. With the fiddle firm between chin and shoulder she too bobbed to the lively ditty.

The chorus ended...
The verse continued...

Throw him in the hull with the captain's daughter,
Throw him in the hull with the captain's daughter,
Throw him in the hull with the captain's daughter,
Early in the morning.

And then she looked directly at me. Our eyes locked and she smiled. But it did not end there. She launched into the chorus once more, her eyes still focussed on mine. My heart skipped a beat. I was in love. I raised my glass to her and she raised her chin, mid fiddle, to acknowledge me.

She acknowledged me!

'I think she likes yer, Caspy,' Fabian called out over the music and drunken banter. I simply nodded, not wishing to take my eyes off this most alluring seductress.

As sudden as it started, it ended. The crowd cheered and clapped and cried out...

More... more... more...

And the little darling broke into another ditty, an Irish ballad I had not heard before. Instantly an upturned boater was thrust before me, distracting my reverie. I looked into the dark recesses of the hat, where its owner rattled several pennies and threepences. The hat belonged to a male figure, about the same age as me. Amongst the hustle and bustle I was poked impatiently with the hat.

'Some coins, sar, for the fiddler's melodies.' The man's accent was Irish. *Oh, I hope this is not the husband,* I thought, dropping a silver shilling in amongst the copper coins.

The taproom seemed even busier since we arrived. Maybe it was the music. Awkwardly, I faced Fabian, who stood grinning at me, holding two fresh glasses of green fairy.

'You all right, lad?' Fabian yelled in my ear. *I think he slurred.*

'I could not be better. My, that fiddler is the most beautiful woman I have ever seen.'

'Aye, I'm with yer all the way there, lad. Go an' introduce yer self.' And Fabian undertook a rendition of how such an introduction should proceed. *'Hullo beautiful, my name's Caspian 'unter Esquire, I'm from Birming'am, don't yer know.'*

I was sorely tempted, but we were here on business were we not.

Maybe I will introduce myself when she stops fiddling.

And there lies my problem.

The evil drink.

By now Fabian and I were propped up at the bar by a dozen other drunkard anchors. With everyone propping each other up, we continued drinking, waxing lyrical about nothing of importance. *Dribbling shite,* someone said. The music stopped and my heart-throb left with her male companion. I was so under the influence that I did not notice the transition from noisy taproom with entertainer, to just noisy taproom.

The time passed.

There was no sign of our mark, Samuel Groundwater the slaughterman. Henry Staghorn the innkeeper opened another bottle of Green Fairy. I felt a stirring in my stomach. I had only eaten half a pigeon and some bread. Now it was after midnight, and the remnants of a pork pie caught my eye, deserted on the bar amongst puddles of spilt ale. It looked back at me expectantly. I think it may have even winked at me. I reached out...

'Nay lad.' Fabian's hand enclosed about mine, crushing my fingers together in defiance. 'Avoid eatin' anything offered 'round 'ere, as yer likely to suffer a pain in the guts for your indiscretion.'

I felt my stomach rumble in protest. 'Oh!'

'Aye, Caspy.' Fabian eyed the innkeeper to be certain he was out of earshot. 'This 'ere publican, Stag'orn, he be a frugal bastard. I hear stories. He scrapes patron's plates of leftovers back into the cook's pot. He will waste nuthin', purchasing tainted produce unwanted by other victuallers and orders the inn cook to spice up rotten meat with curry spices he learnt about in India.'

It looked inviting, all the same. Damn. I swallowed hard. The green fairy had befuddled me. I nursed a small porter – a cleansing porter I hoped would undo my befuddlement. Now the inn was in full swing. A new busker had arrived, playing the accordion, and he too played a lively tune. I watched Fabian jigging with a grotesque woman whom, I assume, he thought looked like the crown princess, when I finally remembered Samuel Groundwater. We were supposedly here to arrest the man. Now I was drunk and the taproom was spinning. The inn's beams seemed to lower upon me, the walls appeared to compress. The music, the dancing, the drinking, the inn fug; they all took their toll, when suddenly I saw Samuel

Groundwater. He walked through the inn door, a late arrival, attracted by the drunken joviality.

'F... Fab... Fab... bian,' I slapped about, trying to reach Fabian, who was now cuddling the grotesque woman and leaning in for a lascivious kiss, his lips puckered and eyes closed. I was pressed amongst Hobart Town's most depraved. Jostling to reach Fabian, I was doused in ale, slopped with porter and sprayed with drunken laughter. 'F... Fabian!'

But Fabian, high on absinthe, was an octopus, a lecher, a carnal fiend whose attention was fixated elsewhere.

'It's him!' I screeched at Fabian, finally reaching him halfway through a slow jig.

'What?' he shouted over the racket.

'It's him. Groundwater!'

They say if one's name is spoken in a busy room, even a noisy gathering, one recognises it over the rabble. Samuel Groundwater turned from where he had pushed to the bar. He saw me and read my lips as I was shoved and shouldered:

You are under arrest!

Underestimating my drunken state, Samuel heaved into the tightening crowd, making a beeline for the door.

'He's getting away!' I screamed at Fabian who was now embraced by this particularly ugly woman. 'Fabian!'

No response. He was away with the green fairy.

'Jesus Christ!' I lurched forward, hoisting Fabian's pistol from his britches' belt and roared at our escapee. 'Stop in the name of the Queen.'

Samuel made it to the threshold.

I cocked the pistol, stabbing it towards the ceiling... and pulled the trigger.

It was as if a cannon had fired. The ball shredded the ceiling and the floorboards of the upstairs room. I heard a squeal, then screaming. And the taproom fell silent. Samuel Groundwater did not wait for a re-load. He bolted.

The activity sobered me, a little.

'Stand back!' I yelled. 'I'm law here. Stand aside. Let me through.'

I instantly had the strength of ten men, or so I thought.

'Shite! Caspy!' The altercation had sobered Fabian as well, and together we shoved our pathway to the front door.

'Firk!' Fabian laughed as we stumbled out into the fresh air. 'Firk! Caspy, that was amazing.'

I twisted about in circles, Fabian's smoking pistol at my side. 'Where is he? Where the hell did he go?'

Instantly, the inn door opened and Henry Staghorn stormed towards us, wielding a huge Maori club. He roared some gibberish, his distorted face in the lamp light looking like that of a demon raised from Hades. He took a swing. I ducked and heard the whoosh of the knotted wood close overhead. The club was so heavy, it continued a full arc, slammed into the architrave and wedged there. It was then I saw the nails protruding from the end. I raised the pistol and stabbed it towards the innkeeper. 'Back!' I yelled. 'Step back, sir, or I'll put another hole in that ugly head of yours.'

Staghorn wrenched the club free and stood erect. He was the height, and sight, of a rearing Grizzly bear.

'Back!' I shouted.

He leapt forward and I decided a warning shot might halt his behaviour.

Click! Damn! I'd spent my shot. 'Jesus!'

'Jesus ain't goin' to help, Caspy,' Fabian charged at me, tackling me aside, as once more the behemoth barkeep swung his log of death in my direction. This time the club ploughed into the quagmire at my feet, the very spot where I had stood one second earlier.

We took flight, rushing away in the direction we hoped to pursue our prisoner. One thing was certain, we would not want to wander back into the Cutlass an' Keg any time soon.

'Did yer hear thart?' Fabian held a finger up for silence.

'What?'

Fabian leant forward, hands on knees, gulping air. 'Listen.' Immediately we heard the sound of someone floundering in the dark. A dog's bark seemed to increase in fury. We stood at the entrance to a narrow lane between shanties and leading towards the rivulet. Then there was a shouted warning...

'Oi! Who goes there?' The sound of metal cans rattling. 'Bugger off or I'll fetch the watch.'

Fabian snatched my shoulder and together we slipped into the blackness of the alleyway. A dozen steps led us to a dilapidated fence. On the other side we could hear the rivulet.

'There yer are yer bastards!' A little old man with a toothless snarl appeared in the light of his own lantern. He was armed with a broom. 'Garn... git,' he threatened.

'Stand down, sir,' I said. 'We are lawmen.'

'Law!' he held the lantern high, which was my chest height. 'Lawmen, huh? Well some bastard just crashed through me yard 'ere.'

Immediately we heard a splash.

'Christ!' the old man said. "e's in the shitter!'

It was then we realised we were standing next to a communal garderobe. I turned to the now ajar lavatory door. I rushed inside.

'Bugger!' Fabian was at my side, and in the light of the old man's lantern, we could see our man had slipped through the seat of ease, dropped into the water and escaped down the fast-flowing rivulet.

'Christ, he's a nimble bastard to slip through there,' Fabian said.

'Well he is rather skinny and short,' I added. 'Now what?'

I had sobered somewhat, but could feel the little green fairy lingering. Fatigue threatened.

'One fer the road?' Fabian said.

I was not convinced I could drink another thing and said, 'Where to, then?'

'Thart's the spirit, Caspy. White Horse. It's right there across the road.'

I stepped into the White Horse and experienced a déjà vu moment. Surely, Fabian did not wish to do the inn crawl all over again, backwards?

The barkeep took our money, pulled two porters and yelled to the dozen imbibers remaining. 'Last drinks.'

Thank god.

I took one sip of the heavy black beer with its creamy head, told Fabian I was going to the privy, walked out the back door and kept walking. Or I should say, kept staggering. For now, the sobering rush after chasing our villain had worn off and fatigue and the green fairy threatened to leave me in the gutter. I vaguely recall seeing a clock somewhere, noting it was 2a.m..

New Wharf was eerily quiet. The whalers all moored to the dock were riding on a tide-changing swell, in off the estuary. I did not even see a night watchman, although I imagined one would be there somewhere, cosy inside his sentry box on a night as cold as this. I passed the warehouses, negotiating the neat hogsheads full of whale oil stacked in orderly piles and turned into the lane leading up Kelly's Steps that would take me onto Battery Hill and home. Instantly, I sensed I was being followed. I twisted about in time to see a shadow dissolve into the stonewall. Sobriety challenged me.

If that was possible.

'Who's there?' I called out, but my tone sounded feeble. I cleared my throat. 'Who's there?' I repeated in a deep baritone.

Somewhere a cat answered with a miaow. Immediately I had a vision of Staghorn with his Maori club charging towards me. *Damned hallucinations.*

I made a dash for the steps. Tripped and fell. Instantly, I was aware of a figure rushing towards me. A dark, caped figure silhouetted against the lamp light from the docks. He was tall and lean and fast. I leapt to my feet unsteadily. Unarmed, I took up a pugilistic stance. One foot in front of the other, balled fists high.

'Come on you bugger,' I managed a little pugilist's dance. 'Give it your best shot.'

He charged me. I saw the glint of steel. He thrust the knife forward. I ducked aside, throwing a punch but missing. The blade sparked against the stone wall. I rushed at my assailant, throwing my arms about him in a wrestling tactic. With his arms pinned, he could not wield the dagger. I shoved him hard against the wall, surprised at my own strength. He fought hard, and for a brief moment I had him secure, when he kneed me in the groin.

Argh!

That old chestnut.

I doubled over in pain. I caught his shadow, the knife lifted high. He was one move away from bringing the stiletto blade down into my back when an almighty explosion disturbed us. A musket ball slammed the stones behind us. In a shower of shattered sandstone, the attacker twisted about to catch the night watchman running towards us, screaming something like 'Halt!'

I grabbed at his cape trying to restrain my attacker, when I saw it. The oddity – one ear missing...

'Zachary Wolf!' I cried out.

For the briefest of dark moments, I saw recognition. I saw cold, black eyes. I saw hatred. I saw the devil.

'Halt in the name of the Queen,' the watchman shouted, coming at us at the run. Wolf spun to face him, his black cape swirling about, enshrouding him. Two against one. The odds were in our favour and so, with the agility of a wild cat, he fled up Kelly's Steps and was immediately lost into the night.

'By golly, I near shot the mongrel, sar,' the nightwatchman was on high alert. 'If'n I had me bayonet fixed, I would 'ave skewered the bastard.'

I was exhausted. I had thought it was lights out for Caspian Hunter.

'Is that you, Mr 'unter? From the barracks?'

I nodded, still short of breath. Short of breath from the altercation, along with my inebriation, it had taken its toll.

'Did you see him?' I gasped. 'There's your vampire.'

'Vampire!'

'Yes. All this fuss about vampires and there he was. Right before us.'

Of course I *was* speaking figuratively. And he was supposed to be dead and buried.

'Vampire? My God.' The guard crossed himself. 'I've heard stories, aye, but... vampire!' He stared off into the blackness after the escaping assailant. 'Here, let me help you. It's Aldrich Kent, sar,' the guard stood to attention. 'From the watch 'ouse.'

'Thank you, Aldrich. I fear if you hadn't come along I would be a dead man.'

'Nonsense, sar, you were givin' him a right what for.' And the man mimicked a right hook. 'I can't believe yer tackled a vampire.' I was about to correct this assumption when he reeled back, 'Cor, yer don't 'alf stink o' grog, sar, if'n yer don't mind me sayin'?'

'It's been a long night.'

'Yer well. You headin' home, was yer? Battery Point?'

I nodded once more, emitting a long sigh followed by a wide yawn.

'Come then, I'll see yer 'ome safe 'n sound, sar.'

I looked the kindly old soldier in the eye. He was most likely only ten years my senior, but looked older with his St Nicholas beard, and I drew encouragement from his courage and company.

'You know what, Aldrich?'

'What's thart, sar?'

'I'll take you up on that offer. I fear the green fairy sneaking up on me.'

'Green fairy eh?' He must have thought me crazy. 'I'll just reload and fix me bayonet, sar, jus' in case we come across that there vampire again; then I can skewer the bastard through the heart.

There we go again. The vampire story perpetuated. But I was too exhausted to explain.

Chapter Eleven

Blue Whale Cottage. Battery Point

I awoke to the sound of Cowgill's Windmill across the street. They had unleashed the sails of the mill, regular as clockwork... Clacketty clack... clacketty clack. It must be 6am.

Argh! I tried burying my head under my pillow, but to no avail. Immediately, I heard pots and pans down stairs and smelt frying bacon. Mrs Rumball, my housekeeper.

But only three hours a day, four days a week mind. The woman was as reliable as the windmill. I sat, swinging my legs over the side of the bed and waited a moment for the blood to drain from my aching head, and wondered how I managed to make my way home. Suddenly, my near-death experience filled my mind, as did a thumping ache in my head. Groaning, I slipped off the mattress into my piss pot, brimming with last night's overflow.

Damn!

I always kept the receptacle in the same spot, in a corner next to the wall so I can religiously climb from my bed in the dark of night and piss in the same spot. I wanted to reprimand Mrs Rumball, but then realised it was most likely me who moved the darn thing.

I washed – especially my feet – and dressed and freshened my breath with Maw's Cherry Tooth Powder, took in a deep breath, and descended into a warm kitchen of motherly delights.

'Good morning, Caspian.' Emma Rumball was always a figure of sobriety and good cheer.

'Good morning, Emma.' I sat at the kitchen table before I fell.

'My my, will you never learn?' Emma tutted.

'Pardon?'

'The demon drink will be your ruination.'

'Oh. How so?'

'How so? I was talking to Aldrich Kent, the night watchman. I met him in passing this morning at the end of his watch, and he told me you were merry weather and talking about a green fairy and vampires. And at two in the morning, no less. Dear me, what would your mother think?'

'I was on duty, Emma.'

'On duty. Well then, I must commend you on taking your profession so seriously.'

I made to protest further, but my head was pounding.

'Drink that mint tea,' she said pointing to a pottery tea pot. Now I realised what that pleasant smell was before me. Emma's failsafe remedy for headaches: fresh mint tea.

The Prisoner Barracks, Campbell Street, 8a.m.

The morning was chilly but the sun shone brightly, as is common in Van Diemen's Land in winter. By the time I had walked to the barracks in Campbell Street I was reasonably clearheaded and had managed to piece together most of the events of last night. In particular the altercation with Zachary Wolf ,who was supposedly dead.

Richard Clincher, at the front gate, was particularly concerned.

'Mr 'unter sar,' he greeted, saluting me, his shako standing to attention, which was most unusual. 'Well ain't you just a sight for sore eyes?'

'Good morning, Richard.' I could not help but smirk.

'I'm so proud o' yer, sar. Tackling that firkin' monster single 'anded. Goodness me, sar. That were a brave man yer be.'

I stood, incredulous. 'Are we speaking of my altercation on Kelly's Steps last night?'

'Aye. Last night?' He looked through the gatekeeper window to a clock in the watch house. 'I should say this mornin', for it were only six hours ago, sar, an' look at you. All armed and ready to go,' he said proudly.

It was then I remembered that I armed myself before leaving the cottage, rapier at the side and my trusty double barrel Yale pistol in my britches' belt.

'Yes, well,' I answered in all modesty. 'Must always be at the ready, what?'

'Aye, sar. But a vampire to boot. Aldrich said you was fearless.'

Ah, Aldrich Kent has spread the word.

'Look Richard, I hate to spoil the myth but...'

'Caspy, Caspy. How's the head, matey?' Fabian walked through the gate, looking bedraggled but alive. 'By Jove, that was a good night's work, eh? And I hear yer took on our villain single-handed.'

I looked into Fabian's eyes; were they really that red?

'You're a dark horse, Caspy, a dark horse indeed.'

'And where did you hear of last night's... this morning's business?' I asked.

'Me fly driver told me,' he said, of the light horse and trap transport. 'All 'Obart Town talkin' about it.'

I looked at Richard Clincher, who was almost teary with pride, nodding his approval. Then back to Fabian. 'We need to talk.'

Fabian. 'I need coffee.'

They must have heard us walking up the stairs, for Jasper, Billings, Holly and Lantern Jaw Lincoln all applauded as we entered. My face reddened.

'Caspy the vampire killer!' Fabian slapped me on the back.

If you don't back off, I thought, *I'll kill you first.* If anything, I was dying of embarrassment.

'Let's get something straight,' I said, patting the empty space before me in a motion to silence my admirers. 'I did not kill anyone.'

'No, but yer nearly did.'

'Yer tackled 'im to the ground, we 'eard.'

'But he kneed yer in the tally wag,' Holly pulled a face as if she could feel the pain I experienced. I often I wondered if she did not sport a tally wag, herself.

I raised my voice. 'Listen to me. Listen. There is no vampire running amok in the streets of Hobart Town. I was attacked by Zachary Wolf, an ex-prisoner from Port Arthur, who is supposed to be dead and buried at the Sea o' Graves. Fabian and I have even seen his grave.'

'Zachary, you say,' Fabian asked.

'Yes. He is alive and well. And for some reason he wants me dead.' I turned to Fabian. 'And you too, more than likely. My guess is that Samuel Groundwater, who we chased last night to the rivulet, somehow warned Zachary, who we know is an acquaintance of his.'

'Now what?'

'I need coffee.' Fabian appeared to be wilting. 'An' Jasper, go see if Sergeant Clincher has any Weaver's Fluid Magnesia in the gatehouse.'

'Aye, sar.' Jasper left. Lincoln filled enamel mugs from the stewing coffee pot.

'Firstly we pay a visit to Lynch Savage at the Sea o' Graves,' I said. 'And see who *is* buried there.'

Fabian. 'Here, here.'

'Holly and Lincoln.'

'Caspian, Sar.'

'We need to get a lead on this Samuel Groundwater. We need to arrest the man for the murder of Molly O'Neil.'

'You think it *was* him?'

'Absolutely. He will also lead us to Wolf, of that I am certain.' I looked at Lincoln. 'Lincoln, the morning we found Mrs O'Neil dead in the alleyway, you said you thought the backyard had been disturbed.'

'Aye, it looked like something had been dragged over the garden and grass.'

'Then when you have the chance, you and Holly search that yard. Search it well; look for any evidence of a struggle, any unusual thing.'

'Good thinkin,' Caspy,' Fabian had finished one mug of coffee and poured a second. *How does he drink it so hot?*

'While you are at number 47,' I continued, 'trouble the landlord for a key, and search the O'Neil bedsitter. Look for evidence that the woman conducted abortions.'

I sent Jasper ahead to Waterman's Dock to warn Ben Swain, our police sloop skipper, that we were on our way to the Sea o' Graves. Fabian stepped into the middle of Campbell Street, waving down a buggy parked outside the Good Woman Inn, some way further up the street, when a fly carriage hurtled around the corner from Brisbane Street.

'Caspian!' My name was called as the fly galloped towards us. 'Caspian! A word if you please.'

It was Warren Boyles, *The Hobart Town Gazette* editor. And he was displeased. The fly slowed and the editor sprang from the passenger seat onto the long step and jumped to the road before the vehicle stopped. He immediately tripped, making a half dozen short skips to stop himself from falling face first into the gravel. I reached out and took him by the crook of his arm before he did himself an injury.

'Easy, Mr Boyles,' I said, supporting him. 'You forget your years, old friend.'

The man was not in a charitable mood. 'Forget my years. I could give you a run for your money, young man.'

'Sorry, I did not mean to offend...'

'Why have you not been to see me? I thought we had an agreement.'

'I... I...'

'Now I hear you personally had an experience with this... this vampire.'

This annoyed me. 'Firstly, sir, it is not a vampire...'

'I know that. But the rest of the colony doesn't.' And he poked me in the belly with a rolled-up newspaper and grunted.

'What's this?' I groaned.

'Read it.'

I unrolled the paper. '*Courier*. Great.' I read the headline for a one-page supplement. '*Vampire attacks lawman on Kelly's Steps.*'

'That was a bit quick. How on earth?'

'They have spies, Caspian. Spies! I need to see you in my office more often.'

'I've been so busy, Warren.'

'Oh! And I haven't. You've even been to Adelaide recently. What's that all about?'

'How did you know?'

'I have spies too, lad.' Our carriage pulled alongside. 'Where are you going?'

This query raised eyebrows.

'Look, Warren, I...' I turned my back on Fabian and Billings climbing aboard the buggy, and lowered my voice. 'There is much afoot this day. I will come and see you soon, I promise.'

'See you do. Caspian,' he harrumphed, as I too, boarded our transport. 'See you do.'

Sea o' Graves Inn, Browns River

'Really Caspian,' Lynch Savage called to me, as his esteemed yet grossly overweight self was carried towards us in his sedan chair. The four bearers lowered Lynch in his chair, anchoring him on four carefully placed kegs on the riverbank, where the Sea o' Graves maintained a small cemetery. Here, Lynch watched in protest. 'This is too much.'

'I am sorry, Lynch, but we know the man you knew as Zachary Wolf is not buried in this grave,' I said. 'I personally saw him in Hobart Town.'

'Impossible!' Savage's multiple chins wobbled, seemingly amplifying his words. 'I was witness to 'is internment; sat right here where I am now, as 'e were lowered into the ground to a verse or two from the good book.'

'Zachary Wolf lost an ear, I believe,' I said, 'when he was resident at Port Arthur.'

'Aye.'

'And the man who attacked me last night in Hobart Town also had one ear.'

'Attacked you?'

'Yes.' I went on to explain my experience, describing Wolf in detail.

'A few coves 'round 'ere have lost an ear, or an eye,' Savage said. 'But I must concede 'e were partial to capes, were our Zachary.'

Lynch bunched his lips briefly, in contemplation. I had always been on good terms with Lynch Savage and did not wish to ruffle his feathers. However, the law was the law, and although the larger-than-life innkeeper respected that, he did manage to run his business on a fine line between black and white.

'Dig if you must,' Savage surrendered with a flick of the back of his hand. 'But are you prepared for the consequences, should you be mistaken?'

'Consequences?'

'Aye. If you are wrong, you shall join me in my cabin for a roast emu that Jean has been slow roasting all day. It's a decent size bird and a rare treat these days, as I do believe they are almost extinct.'

'Sounds wonderful,' Fabian cheered, slapping his hands together and rubbing them vigorously. Savage was never keen on Fabian and this showed. But he had grown to accept Fabian as my *baggage*, should he wish to enjoy my company.

'And if I am right?'

'You'll join me anyway,' Lynch fished a gold pocket watch from his shroud-sized waistcoat and flipped the lid. 'It's after five already. Best yer be getting on with it.'

Billings and Jasper looked to Fabian and me for orders. I nodded. Jasper was reluctant, looking at me defiantly.

'What is the problem, Jasper?' I asked.

'Are you certain you want to be doin' this, Caspian sar?'

'Yer not still afraid o' vampires, are yer lad?' Fabian jeered.

'Well, sar, what about them killin's, they ain't been explained.'

'Vampires!' Lynch laughed. 'I've been hearin' stories, comin' down the river. People gettin' their throats sucked.' Jasper shivered at Lynch's words. 'You'll be believin' in werewolves next.'

Jasper's eyes bulged. I do believe he believes in werewolves, as well.

'Come now, Jasper,' I said. 'I thought we agreed there's no such thing as vampires.'

'Stop bein' a milksop,' Fabian barked. 'An' get in there, boy.'

They started digging. On a positive note, the digging was easy, the earth soft and damp, as it was a recent burial.

The sun disappears behind Bonnet Hill early in mid-winter. Now we were in gloom. Lynch called for refreshments and lanterns on poles and lanyards.

While Fabian entertained himself chatting to Fannie Peach, one of his favourite filles de joie at the inn, I stood alongside Lynch.

'I have a lot of faith in you, Caspian,' Savage muttered over a quart of his own porter. 'So I trust you are right this day.'

So did I. If, by chance, I had made a mistake I stood the chance of losing a friend, as well as a mentor. We all stared in silence as Billings and Jasper took turns digging. We had entered the gloaming, that silent, still moment of semi-darkness before moon-rise. The river was chilly, still, and a thick mist was gathering, creeping slowly towards us on its way out at sea, like the spectre of whomever we exhumed was paying a visit from purgatory to keep an eye on proceedings. With the mist in the lantern light the atmosphere was ominous. I tucked my jacket tight about me, buttoning the collar and lifting it high. Fabian had an arm about Fanny, keeping the wench warm, god bless him. Lynch watched on with interest, a possum skin rug draped about his huge body.

'Got something!' Jasper called out nervously from where only his head appeared above the hole. To make his point clear, he tapped his shovel to a hollow sound. He reached up for Billings to give him a hoist to the surface.

'You may as well finish it, now you are down there,' Billings said matter-of-factly.

'But it's your turn, Billings.'

'You're down there now Jasper,' Billings insisted. 'Lift the lid.'

Jasper was clearly having reservations about disturbing the dead. 'But it's...'

'Jasper lad.' Fabian tore himself away from Fanny Peach a moment. 'Just open the bloody thing.'

Jasper's bottom lip dropped. He looked to me for support, but I looked away, feigning a conversation with Lynch, while Billings leant in, passing Jasper a crowbar. Finally Jasper disappeared below the lip of the grave and we heard the squealing of rusting nails and the splintering of timber boards.

'Jaysuz!' Jasper's head appeared once more, gasping for fresh air.

'Well then?' I asked.

Jasper was gagging from the stench. 'Dunno, sar, you'll have to come see for yerself.' I approached with trepidation, a handkerchief before my nose, and looked into the dark hole where Jasper's lantern flame crackled and flickered from the unexpected gases, casting just enough light onto the corpse's head. Lynch ordered two of his bearers to join me.

'Jasper,' I said staring at a mummy-like body wrapped in a shroud.

'Sar?"

'Here.' I passed Jasper a small pocketknife. 'Cut the shroud from his face.'

Jasper looked at me as if I had asked him to climb into the coffin with the putrid corpse. 'Well come on then,' I waved the blade in his face impatiently.

He grudgingly took the knife and a deep breath, crossed himself and went about his macabre chore. He pulled the wrapping free to expose the face, complete with thread through the nose where a sail needle had passed – a seafarer's custom to ensure the person is truly dead. We studied the rotting corpse.

'There is a large birthmark on his neck,' I said aloud. 'This is not Zachary Wolf.'

'A birthmark?' Lynch queried. His bearers agreed. 'Like spilt wine down his neck?'

'Yes. Do you know who it could be?'

'Well it could only be Sir Eugene Oldham.' Lynch was as shocked as I.

'Sir Eugene Oldham?'

Fabian, Billings and the other bearers joined me, peering into the pit of death. By all appearances, the interred had the physical measurements of Wolf and was of a similar age, but there was no denying the birthmark.

'Who was Sir Eugene Oldham?' Fabian said.

'Oh,' Lynch grinned. ''e weren't a real *Sir*. 'e be the stable hand who mucked out the horse shite and tended to me pigs. Eugene, yer see, was an ex-lag from Saltwater River coalmines and then Port Arthur. 'e were transported for forging cheques in Sheffield. Apparently 'e was a well-ter-do what went broke. So when 'e came to work for me he acted all high an' mighty, even though 'e were shovellin' shit. So we gave him a sobriquet, *Sir* Eugene Oldham.'

'So was Oldham his real name?'

'Aye. He was a happy enough cove. Looked after the animals and I looked after him. But he died over two months since and... well bugger me!' Lynch had a revelation. 'It were Zachary

Wolf what insisted on taking Eugene's body to be buried at St David's Cemetery in the town. Said 'e made a promise to Eugene before 'e fell off the perch. Now I see what's happened. 'e's faked his own death.'

'Who? Zachary? Fabian said.

'Your quick off the mark today lad, ain't yer?' Savage couldn't resist the jibe at Fabian.

It all made sense. So, had this Zachary Wolf relapsed into a taste for human blood? 'My God!' I gasped involuntarily.

'What, lad?'

'Was Wolf after my blood on Kelly's Steps last night?'

'So how did Zachary falsify his death?' Fabian asked, looking to Fanny Peach as if he was the greatest sleuth on earth.

Beware, the rooster is preparing himself.

'He were found dead in his lodgings,' Lynch said. 'One o' the girls found him.'

'Which one?' I asked.

'Luella Mellow.'

'Can someone fetch her? Is she at the Graves this day?'

Lynch sighed heavily and his shoulders slouched in defeat with another revelation.

'She hasn't been seen since Zachary was buried,' he said in a hushed voice.

'Oh, how convenient.'

Savage felt totally deceived. It made sense now that she was in cahoots with Wolf.

'So who tended the body?' Fabian asked. 'Who boxed 'im up and buried 'im in the ground?'

Fabian booted a small mound of dirt back into the hole, forcing Jasper to duck.

'Jean,' Lynch sighed.

'Jean Parton,' I said surprised. 'Your cook?'

'Aye. But 'e weren't in on this caper, no sar.'

It was clear that Lynch would do anything to defend his cook. This French magician of the kitchen was irreplaceable to Savage.

I felt Lynch's urgency. 'So, Jean prepared the body for burial?'

'Aye.'

'It is possible, of course, that Zachary fooled the cook,' I said.

'Of course, Caspian,' Lynch's eyes brightened. 'That's exactly what happened. Zachary has played dead.'

'But someone else must have been party to this deceit,' I said. 'At some stage, Zachary has slipped away and Sir Eugene Oldham's body has been nailed into the coffin. Then, I assume you all paid your respects when he was buried and the deception was complete.'

'I had no idea.' Lynch was incredulous. 'The sly old fox.'

'Wolf, more like it,' Fabian laughed. 'Well, it's bloody cold out here. May I suggest we partake o' that emu you was talkin' about earlier?' he directed at the innkeeper.

'Out of respect, you better change that headstone also,' I thought I should mention.

Lynch Savage nodded in defeat and we retired, leaving Billings and Jasper to rebury Sir Eugene Oldham, while we followed Lynch and his struggling bearers as they bore the obese innkeeper across the gangplank and into the warm embrace of the Sea O'Graves.

Once we were seated at Lynch's stern cabin table, I decided to discreetly interview the cook. I excused myself on the pretext of visiting the inn garderobe, and took the risk of entering Jean Parton's galley instead. Jean Parton was Lynch's long time cook, whom he had rescued from a French expeditionary vessel visiting Hobart Town some years passed. I say, *'I took the risk of entering Jean's galley,'* as the Frenchman and I had a falling out some time ago, after I questioned the sanitary condition of a duck dish he had prepared. The ducks in question lived in the river waters surrounding the Sea o' Graves, and in particular, the waters beneath the lavatories. I shall leave the rest to you, dear reader; suffice to say, Jean's attitude towards me at the time bordered on aggression.

Stupid Frog!

Little had changed. Jean looked at me with undisguised contempt. In all fairness it was the frog's domain. *Sa cuisine.*

'Bonsoir, Monsieur Parton,' I said in greeting.

Grunt.

'If you do not mind, Chef Parton, I am here on official business and need to ask you a few questions.'

'Can you not see I am bizz-ee?' he said, and commenced banging pots and pans and making a general racket, pretending he was *bizz-ee.*

But this action was only to divert my attention from what really occupied the great *chef du galley.* I had walked into the galley as he inspected the evening meal's meat, scraping flyblows and cutting decaying parts from various joints; dressing the worst managed parts with vinegar, unless they were too far gone. Spices and fire would disguise the rest.

'I need to ask you about Zachary Wolf, the butcher.'

'He ees dead, non? You know thees thing.'

'Ah, but you are wrong. He lives.'

'Non, non. He ees bur-eed near the reever.'

'No, Jean. We just dug him up and it weren't him.'

'You what?'

'We exhumed the grave site of Zachary Wolf, in the name of Queen Victoria, I might add, and discovered the body of Sir Eugene Oldham, instead.'

'Thees ees bull-sheet.'

'No. It's fact.' I must say here that Jean Parton looked genuinely surprised. 'Have you any idea,' I continued, 'how the body of the said stable hand ended up in the butcher's coffin.'

'Sacre bleu! 'ow should I know thees things?'

'Mr Savage tells me you prepared his body for burial.' I looked to the joint of tainted meat. 'What are you, a cook, doing preparing the deceased for burial?'

'This ees always my... my... how you say, duty, 'ere at the Graves.'

'And you saw Zachary Wolf dead?'

'Oui. 'e were wrapped in 'is shroud and I passed the needle and thread through his nose to be cer-tain 'e were dead.'

'Wait a minute! You said he was already in the shroud when you prepared him?'

'Oui. Luella Mellow, she wrap 'im 'erself.'

'This Luella Mellow, she found Zachary dead in his cabin, did she not?'

'Oui. They were lovers, I am thinking.'

'Oh!' The plot thickens as they say.

'But you passed a needle through the nose?'

'Oui. Luella, she leave nose unwrapped.'

'Have you any idea where I might find this Luella Mellow?'

'Non.' Jean thought a moment. I had the impression he really wanted to help. 'But... ah... she did tell me some-theen once.'

'Oh?'

'er mother... she ees in Cascades.'

'You mean the women's factory?'

'Oui. She ees in pris-on for stealing reams of cotton from 'er *employeuse*. An' Luella, she tell me she visit 'er sometimes.'

'Do you know her name by chance?'

'Ivy, I am thinking. Oui, Ivy Mellow.'

'Thank you Jean, you have been a great help.'

Jean wiped his hands on a cloth hooked through his apron. 'Ah Casp-ian... ah, we have past differences, but I am thinking you ees a good man. Monsieur Sav-arge, 'e speak 'ighly of you.'

'Thank you, Jean. Lynch speaks highly of you, too.'

Jean beamed a huge smile and grinned modestly, almost blushing at the compliment. We shook hands. 'Tell me, Jean,' I asked.

'Oui.'

'Where is this emu Lynch was so excited about?' I could certainly smell something delicious.

Jean opened the oven door and vanished briefly into a steaming cloud of deliciousness before, with some difficulty, he managed to extract the roasted carcass of a very large bird sizzling in a deep tray, with lard and crunchy potatoes cooked in their jackets. The skin on the bird was golden and crisp, and a bread and walnut filling escaped from under the rib cage like stuffing exuding from a damaged mattress.

'Viola! Now you must seet at the table, eet ees ready to eat.'

'It smells divine. And I must say it looks awfully like a large turkey.'

'Ha!' Jean laughed. 'It ees turkey.'

'Oh?'

'Emu, she extinct in Van Diemen's Land now. I theenk Monsieur Sav-arge, he eat last emu last year.'

'But he thinks he is getting emu.'

'Ees good. I tell him emu. 'e believe me. Truth ees, Monsieur Sav-arge, he eat any-theen, any time an' always 'e enjoy eet.'

'And that joint over there?' I waved a finger at the joint of meat scraped of flyblows and other distasteful anomalies. 'Who's that for?'

'I cook that for downstairs,' he said of the drunkards in the taproom.

I returned to the table, but Jasper and Billings had still not returned. Confused, I stepped over to the stern windows and could just make out the small graveyard off to the right by the river, faintly lit with one lantern. Billings, I could see clearly, and as I focussed, I finally made out Jasper standing with the shovel over his head in one hand and in the other hand what appeared to be a...

'Jesus no!' I said loudly without thinking.

The chatter at the table stopped.

'What is it, lad?' Fabian asked.

'Nothing,' I said unconvincingly.

Fabian hurried to join me. 'Christ! Is he doin' what I think he's doin'?'

Fabian did not have to wait long for an answer. Jasper brought the spade down on a long stake he held in his left hand, driving it through the *vampire's* heart. A geyser of putrid decomposition squirted high from the grave and Billings dived aside.

'Now,' Fabian grinned. 'Thart's somethin' yer don't see every day, Caspy.'

When the two finally re-interred the unfortunate occupant and joined us for dinner, I asked, 'Was that really necessary, Jasper?'

'What's that, Caspian sar?'

'You know very well of what I speak.'

Billings looked sheepish.

'Well I weren't takin' no risks, sar.' And as if it made all the difference, Jasper added, ''e *were* already dead.'

The *emu* was the best I had ever eaten, accompanied with relishes and mustards all prepared by Jean. The potatoes had crusty skins, seasoned well with salt, while inside they were fluffy and buttery. The wines were from the red grape of Burgundy and the young ladies of the inn from dubious backgrounds. I tried hard to maintain sobriety, but after the adventures of last night I thought we could let our hair down for once. Besides, Fabian and I were topping up from the green fairy the night before, and even Jasper, with his wife and bairn at home, let his guard down. Oh well, I thought, we'll have him home by midnight, as long as the tides and winds are in our favour. And then I remembered Ben Swain our skipper, waiting on the beach. I sent word, only to learn that Ben, the righteous skipper who never missed his scriptures on Sunday, had actually come in out of the cold and was in the taproom downstairs, nursing a large brandy.

God bless his woollen socks.

Wonderful, I thought. All is good with the world. I excused myself from the dark-skinned doxy sitting on my knee, a Bermudian who called herself Chastity – I guess, with the real name of Hattie Crapper, why wouldn't you change your name – and made my way down to the taproom to find Ben and invite him to join us, when I heard a familiar tune in the packed inn...

What will we do with the drunken sailor?
What do we do with a drunken sailor?
What do we do with a drunken sailor?
Early in the morning.

The tune was familiar. All too familiar. I hurried down the last few treads, glancing through a cloud of blue smoke and a fug of spilt grog and debauchery. I peered over a hundred bobbing heads, and there she was, playing that fiddle like there was no tomorrow. She stood on a stool in the centre of a sea of aroused rum-spilling drunkards. The alluring minx had the taproom around her little finger. I was absolutely smitten. Was this fate? To meet this siren of the inns again. So soon. At inns so far apart. She teased that bow across the strings and into the verse...

Hey ho and up she rises,
Hey ho and up she rises,
Hey ho and up she rises, early in the morning.

By the next chorus I had shoved my way to the front row. Absorbed in her music, I watched that bow dance. I studied that driving elbow. Her tapping foot. Her intense concentration. Her devotion to the art. She had let her amber hair down, and silky in the lamp light, it whirled to the music...

Then she turned and saw me.

Oh Christ she saw me!

Our eyes locked.

She grew even more animated. The crowd went crazy, but I held her gaze and she bowed her head ever so slightly, looking directly up at me with her large cow eyes like she was peering over a pince nez. It was almost subservient...

No. No. No!

She teased me. Lured me in, like a big fish. A coquette plucking at my very heart strings. I felt my breathing grow heavy. My heart skipped a beat and I feared she would miss a beat also. Third verse down, she launched into the last chorus. I was fascinated. Together we climaxed. Me, mesmerised and clapping my hands like a giddy schoolboy, while she threw herself into a musical lather.

Well that is how I perceived the situation, anyhow.

With her set complete, she jumped from the stool with the agility of a gazelle and walked directly to me.

'You stalking me or what?' she said, her face as serious as a gaoler's bribe.

'I... I, ah...' I was lost for words. I felt myself flush. Damn!

I am such an idiot.

I must have looked ashen.

'I'm pullin' yer leg,' she said, bursting into laughter. 'Yer gonna buy a girl a drink or what?'

Jesus Christ!

'You had me there,' I snorted. I actually snorted. *Get it together lad.* 'A drink? Absolutely. And what would this girl like to drink?'

'Whiskey.'

'Whiskey. Of course. What else would beautiful Irish woman drink?'

'Careful who yer call beautiful, soldier. A girl might get the wrong idea.'

Jesus! Was this really happening?

To put this in perspective, she had a strong Irish accent, and her voice was husky. I shot her a scandalous smile. At least I think it was scandalous. 'I'm Capsicum... Caspian.' Christ I was nervous.

'Kathy.'

I offered Kathy the crook of my arm and she accepted it with good humour, and I escorted her to the bar.

'I heard you caused quite a kerfuffle at The Cutlass and Keg last night,' Kathy said, before gulping her whiskey in one mouthful. *I should have purchased a bottle.*

'Who told you that?'

'A little birdie.'

'A little birdie, huh.' I gulped my whiskey and with my confidence restored, I said, 'I'll be right back.'

At the bar, I looked around for Kathy's male companion, the one collecting their busker money, when I caught him across the taproom pressing drunkards for a donation. I returned with a bottle of whiskey.

'Thirsty, huh?' she said.

'Does it show?'

'Let's drink it elsewhere?'

Jesus. Now this was too much.

'Ah, what about your... ah...'

'My brother?'

'Brother!' I said aloud in a pathetic falsetto. 'Your companion, he's your brother?'

'Yes. Do you have a problem with that?'

'Problem? Huh! No, of course not. Brother, eh?'

'Why? Did you think he was my husband?'

'No... I... I just wondered.'

'Come. Let's find somewhere quiet to drink that. Inns make me ill.'

'Somewhere else?' I tried not to act like the giddy schoolboy, but the fact was, I had never been with a woman so forward, except the ones that took my silver. *Somewhere else?* I looked back to where I had seen our skipper, Ben Swain. He was content, people-watching, and sipping his brandy. He was preoccupied.

'Follow me,' I said, and we braved the chill, hurrying across the beach to the police sloop, *Fabian*. Tripping over our anchor rope in the sand, I hefted my fiddler onto the bow of the vessel, wading knee deep as the tide was changing. Below deck, I struck a tinderbox and lit a candle, pleased that the tiny cabin had retained reasonable warmth, for outside was at freezing point. I filled two glasses and had a mind to say *up yours* but said, 'Salute.'

Kathy tossed her drink back in one mouthful. I did likewise.

'So where do you come from?' I started.

Kathy did not answer. She leant forward pressing a finger to my lips. Then, as if burning coals had been thrown over her, she ripped off her woollen-netted shawl, tore off her blouse and exposed naked breasts hard and firm as baby pumpkins. Those cow eyes widened. Her hair teased forward, half covering her face and she pushed me back on Ben's bunk, unbuttoned my britches and lifted my shirt over my head. Suddenly I was blinded. With my attire over my face, my chest exposed and my britches juggled to my ankles, I was putty in the fiddler's hands. Well more the rigger's fid than putty and I remember thinking; I didn't know you played the flute as well.

I forget how many times we made love. I remember we finished the bottle of whisky between bouts of passion, nay, lust. We lay in each other's arms for what seemed hours. We chatted incessantly. We seemed to have so much in common. And... exhausted, we fell asleep.

I woke first. It was light. I thought a dream had woken me. I felt the sloop lift on a wave. I heard shouting. Voices approached, at speed.

Jesus!

I rushed the companionway and threw open the hatch...

Jesus Christ! We were at sea!

The shouting was advancing directly behind me. Almost on top of me. The sloop rose sharply on a steep wave. I spun about.

This was no dream, but a nightmare.

The whale was the size of a house. It rushed broadside with the sloop, only inches to spare. The vessel listed forty or more degrees. I was drenched in seawater as I saw the harpoon buried in the monster's back. The rope trailed away to a whaleboat manned by eight men filled with bravado and fear in equal measure. They were being towed.

'Hold to, lads,' the helmsman screamed. 'Hold too!'

I had a vision of colliding at sea. The whalers passed at arm's length, at speed. It was the famous Nantucket sleigh ride, as being towed by the harpooned whale was called. And I was inches from the action. They passed as fast as they approached. Within a moment, they were hundreds of yards away and I watched, still in shock, as the brutal hunt continued. Immediately the sloop settled onto an otherwise calm sea and Kathy's head appeared above the hatchway.

'Wh... what just happened? Where are we? Oh – my – god! We're floating.'

Floating?

'We've drifted out with the tide,' I said, looking about. Now I realised we were out on Storm Bay. About a mile distant, I saw the Yankee whaler had stopped, using sea anchors in the deep water, and black smoke billowed from the tri-pot fires, as the whale blubber was rendered to extract the oil. All around the bay we now noticed the whales, some panicked, thrashing their great tails, diving, splashing. Mothers protecting their calves, gigantic males trying to protect the mothers. All in all, it was a sickening sight.

Hastily, we dressed. On deck I tried to put on a brave face, but truth be known, I was battling to avoid panicking.

'Do you know how to sail?' Kathy asked.

'Ah, no. Do you?'

'How hard could it be?'

On several occasions I had watched our skipper set sail and knew enough to raise the mainsail. Kathy took the helm as a gentle breeze filled the sail.

'Uh-huh!' I said with some satisfaction. 'How hard could it be, indeed?'

But we were still heading south and out to sea.

'Ah, Kathy,' I called out, my eye on the whaling activities. 'Hobart Town is that way.' I pointed over her head north.

'It won't steer.' And to prove a point Kathy tugged on the tiller in both directions but the northerly breeze was pushing us further towards the great Tasman Sea,

Bugger!

My attempts at the helm were met with the same problem. 'The rudder's stuck, or broken.' I felt anxiety cloud my thoughts. *Get it together, Caspian,* I reprimanded myself. I struck the mainsail and the canvas collapsed untidily to the deck. We now drifted. With no other option I started waving to the whale ship. Kathy looked less than amused. I felt my manhood challenged.

Christ, I'm a lawman, a sleuth, and a bloody good one, I assured myself. 'Sorry, I am not much of a seaman, I'm afraid.'

Kathy said nothing, stood at the stern and, gripping the backstay with one hand, she waved for help with the other.

We were soon boarded by two crewmen from a returning whaleboat, who passed us a line and towed us back to their ship.

The 371-ton *Merlin,* a converted fifteen-year-old merchantman, I was informed, was a godsend; for I had not a clue how I would have saved us from drifting out onto the open ocean. Her name, *Merlin,* rang bells, but for the life of me, I couldn't make the connection. Apparently, word of my lack of seamanship had shot about the deck, much to my chagrin, I was the centre of undisguised sniggers.

'Welcome aboard, Cap'n,' some jester greeted.

I tried to keep face in front of Kathy, with whom I knew I was foolishly besotted, but now doubted *her* commitment. The ship was a beehive of activity, and with five of the six whaleboats still out chasing, and two whales already secured to the portside ready for flensing, the captain was busy. I cast an eye towards the bridge, hoping to attract the captain's attention.

'Where's the old man?' I asked in a confident voice, using seafarers' jargon for *captain*.

'Right behind yer,' the jester said.

I turned to face a Maori: six-foot-six, face tattoos, long, soot black hair tied in a chignon, arms like hams, stretched into a navy tunic with three quarter calico britches, bare feet and wearing a chimney stack top hat.

'Cap'n Pania, at yer service.'

'You're a woman, sir!' *Oh – my – god* did I open my mouth to change feet? I was totally dumb-struck. 'Pardon me, sir, madam... ah captain... I... ah... I am so grateful for your assistance.'

If there had been a crack in the deck wide enough, I would have crawled into it.

'Yes. I am woman.' Pania's voice was a deep baritone and matter-of-fact. 'At least, I was woman last time I looked, eh?'

And the crew, now gathered about, roared with laughter, again at my expense. Clearly, I had not offended the captain; she and the entire crew were used to this occurrence.

Captain Pania looked at Kathy and the geometric patterns tattooed on her entire face shifted into what I assumed was a smile.

'What are you two doing out here, anyways?'

I explained how I was showing Miss Alderson below deck on the *Fabian* when the tide went out and we were not aware until it was too late. That was close to the truth, I thought. But I don't think the captain believed any of it.

'Hmm. Someone cut your anchor rope.'

'I don't know what happened,' I started.

'No! I tell you. Someone cut your anchor rope. My crew tell me rope is cut.'

Oh, a statement, not a question.

'Come,' Pania put an arm about Kathy's shivering shoulders. 'We drink welcoming drink in my cabin.'

'Oh, I ah...'

'Your sloop, she safe. Crew will secure her off the stern. We go to Hobart Town when we finish here.'

Captain Pania poured muscatels from a cut-glass decanter and told us how Pania was a beautiful sea-maiden in Maori mythology. She told us they were one year out of the New Zealand port of Munganna and were sailing into Hobart Town for supplies when they unexpectedly came upon the pod of whales in Storm Bay.

'It is a rare thing to find whales so close in, these times,' she said. 'The Van Diemen whalers fish 'em out years ago, I'm told.'

Yes, I knew that to be true. Thirty years earlier whales were captured within sight of Hobart Town. I told Pania how we had been accidentally cast away on the outgoing tide from Browns River and mentioned the Sea o' Graves Inn. But she knew of Lynch Savage and the wreck of the *Sea Wolfe,* which had been stove in by a rogue whale some years ago, right here in this bay.

It was now late morning and I daren't think of what Fabian, Ben Swain and the others were thinking. Had I gone mad and sailed away, deserting them? Surely they would be sending out a search party, if they had returned to Hobart Town by some other means and realised I was not in town. Had Kathy's brother sounded an alarm about his missing sister?

'Is there not some way we can return to port sooner than later?' I asked Pania.

She laughed and filled my glass. 'We will surpass one thousand barrels of oil after today's catch. I have saved your sloop and your skin. You cannot expect me to stop now.'

I explained I was a lawman and on police business.

'Cannot your carpenter repair the rudder and maybe you spare one sailor to see us back to Hobart Town?'

'Are you blind as well as deaf, eh?' The tattooed face rearranged into a grimace. 'Can't yer see how busy this ship is? No, Hunter! I cannot spare the carpenter, who is working with the cooper right now, putting more barrels together, and all sailors are on the chase.'

But there was more afoot than I had imagined. Was it my imagination, or was this behemoth Maori sea captain, albeit a female, sharing lascivious glances with my Kathy?

My Kathy?

Not anymore it seemed. I had lost credibility with my lack of seamanship. I looked morose. I did not mean to, but my bottom lip dropped. *Don't sulk, lad,* I heard myself think.

The crew worked hard, far into the night. The deck was awash with oil, blood and spillage. The incessant smoke permeated clothing, along with the stink of rendering blubber. After the cutting in and trying out, the oil was stowed in barrels in the hold. The stripped carcasses were now cleaned for the bones and the waste thrown to the sharks. The baleen from the mouth, used for items like corset stays, buggy whips and umbrella spokes, was scraped and cleaned.

The thousandth barrel was stoppered and, as was the tradition taught to the New Zealanders by the Americans, donuts were fried in the oil of the thousandth barrel. Exhausted but exuberant, the crew tapped a barrel of rum and the celebrations began.

All the while, I had been in the galley, sharing adventures, sharing woes and sharing the cooking brandy with King Pip, the ship's cook. King Pip was a half-caste Maori Irishman. A weird mix, to be sure. He told me how he ran away to sea when he was fourteen. That was back in '32.

Silent From The Shadows

As was the custom of the sea, any man with a missing limb, and unable to carry out normal seamen duties, was delegated to the galley. King Pip lost an arm during a whale chase, his limb having been caught in the harpoon rope attached to the whale. 'It were torn clear from me body. That were five year ago now, an' the lads reckon I still don't cook great.'

I was sitting on a bushel of barley with a rather large brandy in my hand, while next to me, a cauldron of Irish stew simmered, smelling quite tasty, in my opinion.

'Hey,' he wanted my undivided attention, prodding me with his one arm. 'I made the boys rissoles for their midday meal.'

'Oh yes.'

'I roll 'em in me armpit see, on account o' me missin' limb.'

I felt my stomach churn.

'An' one cove complained 'e found hairs in his rissole. So, I explained I've only one arm, so I 'ave to roll 'em in me armpit. That's disgustin' says he. Oh that's nuthin', says I, you should see 'ow I make them donuts.'

His laughter caused a coughing fit and I heard something snap loose in his chest before he gripped the wooden spoon and gave the pot a stir, while I racked my brain for excuses not to eat this night.

King Pip told me resupplying the ship was only one of the reasons the *Merlin* was calling at Hobart Town. Many of the crew were suffering *ladies-fever*, as he called syphilis, from sharing women at the Bay of Islands, also known as the whorehouse of the Pacific.

Speaking of women, I wondered what my fiddler was up to. One thought was troubling, but the other mischievous side of me was envious.

Midnight. The ship's crew was drunk. Those who weren't conscious were dead asleep. I was propped against the barley bushel, comatose on brandy, while King Pip, it seemed, had deserted me for his bunk, hours ago. I woke briefly by the galley fire. My brain was yet sober enough to feel the hangover approaching like an unwanted squall. I felt my body slide from the sack, where I curled on the deck, cosy before the hot coals. And slept.

Daybreak. I awoke, lying on the deck with men stepping about me, helping themselves to a salty gruel simmering on the stove to start their day. I was parched, aware that my mouth opened and shut like that of a fish landed on deck. Words eluded me while my head felt like it was being hammered into shape by a blacksmith.

'My head!' I groaned. I watched as bare feet and britches brushed by my face, and finally managed my second sentence. 'Where am I?'

'Up yer git.' A short, half-native half-Caucasian looking man offered me his one hand to pull me to my feet. 'Yer in the bloody way, that's where yer are, Caspian lad.'

'Caspian? You know me?'

'Firk. You was more stewed than I thought.'

'King Pip!'

'Aye. Ship's cook. Now on yer feet.'

I stood and the world spun before me. I held onto the cook.

'Water!' I rasped.

Gulping down a quart mug, I spilt half down my shirtfront, but the chill woke me. The day before flooded back. I could see that it was morning. No! I've spent another night away. I also felt we were under sail. 'Where are we?'

'Headed to Browns River.'

'Browns River?'

'Aye. Thart's wha' I said.'

'But we were supposed to be heading to Hobart Town.'

'Tomorra matey, Cap'n wants to visit the famous Sea o' Graves. She been itchin' to visit ever since she 'eard of the place, back in New Zealand.'

On deck the breeze was fresh, fresh enough to fill the mainsail and propel us to Browns River, yet not strong enough to clear the air of the strong smell of urine. As I watched on, several sailors were lifting their grease-sodden whaling clothes from barrels filled with urine, where they had soaked since the night before.

'That's the only way ter clean them slops,' one man informed me. 'All that whale oil and muck ... soak 'em in piss, eh.'

The dungarees are then tied to a line and dropped overboard to be towed behind the ship before finally boiling them in the tri-pots of saltwater and ley, a type of solvent, I am told. With so much rigging aboard ship there was never a shortage of clotheslines. Laundry was secured with whalebone pegs carved by the scrimshanders and I was informed it was not uncommon, in a stiffened breeze, to lose an item overboard, including the captain's bloomers.

I was fortunate that two sailors of sober habits were keen to visit Hobart Town, ahead of the *Merlin* and her unpredictable captain. They would sail the sloop for me. But to give credit where it is due, Captain Pania had had the carpenter fix the rudder and make *Fabian* shipshape for the sail back to Waterman's Dock. Pania waved goodbye to me from the bridge and I was about to thank her in person, when it was made clear I should climb over the stern and into *Fabian* before the captain changed her mind. There was no sign of my fiddler, leaving me somewhat heart-broken. Had my lack of seafaring skills annoyed her? Had I offended her in some other way? Or did she prefer the company of a female sea captain?

It was almost noon before we reached Waterman's Dock where a greeting party, including Fabian, and the skipper, awaited.

Well maybe not a greeting party. More a war party.

The harbour watch had sent word to the barracks that the missing sloop *Fabian* approached. Fabian stood with his hands on his hips.

'Caspy, Caspy, where have yer been lad? We thought you were done for.'

'I... ah... we...'

Skipper Ben Swain was not so forgiving. He snatched the rope from the sailors and, securing it to a bollard, he pushed past me without a word. He was not a happy man.

'So who are these coves?' Fabian nodded to the *Merlin's* sailors.

I quickly explained, finishing off with how I had fallen asleep, alone, on board the sloop while waiting for everyone to return when some clown had cut the anchor rope. Well at least that part was true.

'*Merlin* huh?' Fabian stepped away. 'An' yer stink like a whale ship, too. Well hurry lad, Governor Young wants to see us.'

'Now?'

'Aye. 'e were expectin' us at half eight.'

'Half eight!'

'Yesterday. I put him off a day. It's now midday. But you'll be glad to know I sent word to say you were on police business.'

'Police business my hat.' These profound words from the Ben Swain the skipper, who had seen his abused cabin below deck. He poked his head from the hatchway and threw the empty whiskey bottle into the water.

'Fabian, I need to wash and change my clothes.'

'Forget it, Caspy. You've messed the governor about too much already.'

'But...'

'We'll tell the gov'nor yer been out all night on a stakeout looking for this vampire.'

Fabian waved down a fly carriage and we climbed aboard. 'Ah, Caspy,' Fabian asked, as the carriage sped off along the docks and towards the Queen's Domain. 'I don't suppose you know anything about that fiddler playin' at the Graves the night we were there?'

'Ah... no.'

'You certain? It was the same tasty titbit what you was eyein' at the *Keg* the night before thart.'

'Oh her.' I feigned a devil-may-care attitude. 'It *was* her was it? I thought I recognised the music.'

'I bet you did.'

'Why do you ask, Fabian?'

'Well her husband was ropable.'

'Hu... husband?'

'Aye. Angry as a cut snake, they said. Apparently, she took off with some cove and a bottle o' whiskey.' And Fabian pushed his bottom lip out as he tapped his finger on the side of his nose.

CHAPTER TWELVE

Government House. Queen's Domain

The governor's butler, Rupert Claiborne, an understandably stuffy individual, showed us to Sir Henry Fox Young's study, where the great man greeted us in a formal manner, with his swallow tailcoat buttoned at the front. The governor was displeased.

'Mr Winter, Mr Hunter, take a seat if you will.'

If you will?

I sat stiffly, as if it were an honour. Fabian fell into his chair, leant back easily and crossed his legs. I feared he was about to pull the servant's bell for tea. Immediately the governor caught a whiff of my far-from-sanitary clothes.

'My God! What is that smell?'

'Caspian, governor,' Fabian dropped me right in it.

Thank you, traitor.

'Fabian is correct your Excellency. I have been working all night on a stakeout that required me to be amongst whaling folk and their wretched tri-pots.'

'Is this to do with vampires?'

'Yes, Sir Henry.'

'Hmm,' the governor stood and walked to the window, which rolled up easily on its recently oiled sash. *Whale oil, I may add.* A cold breeze filled the jib like a curtain, but the chill, it appeared, was more acceptable than my aroma.

'Vampires, gentlemen?'

The governor sat once more, launching directly into business. He pinned *The Courier* to his desk with stiffened, arched fingers and spun the rag to face us, so we would not have to read the headlines upside down. 'What is this humbug? Are we to fear werewolves and screaming banshees in the streets of Hobart Town next?'

'It's the townsfolk, sir,' Fabian started. 'They are generally an ignorant superstitious lot...'

'Maybe so, but we will have anarchy next, if you do not solve this crime, if indeed it is a crime. I heard one report that the victim died of heart failure and those little black devils got to him.'

'We are looking into it, sir,' I said and went on to explain our suspicions of the ex-convict Zachary Wolf and his shenanigans of falsifying his own death and the fact that I suspected him of propagating the vampire myth amongst the ignorant of Hobart Town. 'And also, Your Excellency, I believe he planned an assault on me, at my own cottage only nights ago and I was again attacked on Kelly's Steps.'

'What?' The governor was ropable.

'Both times, I was fortunate enough to defend myself. He wore a long black cape and I strongly suspect, Your Excellency, that it was Zachary Wolf.'

'Then that is a crime on its own, and falsifying one's own death. The man must be brought to justice.'

'Yes, sir.'

'And see that these...' he pointed at the newspaper, 'these stupid rumours are quelled swiftly, nipped in the bud so to speak. Vampires, indeed.' Governor Young seemed to have a vague moment, staring at *The Courier*, which I had restored to its original position. 'While on the subject of vampires and monsters, we have another problem in the river.'

'What's that Your Excellency?' Fabian asked.

'Well with all the whaling activity, understandably, came the sharks. The river was infested with ravenous monsters of the deep. Nowadays we don't see so many, however, recently the harbour master requested that I insist a warning be issued, for bathers in the River Derwent to beware.'

'Oh?'

'Well the half-devoured body of a coolie was found, washed up on the beach at Clarence Plains across the estuary...'

'Thart's the first I heard of it, Governor,' Fabian said, rather defensively.

'Well, it was not suspicious, you must understand. On investigation, it was discovered that the body had been committed to the deep in the River Derwent, within sight of Hobart Town.'

'You mean a burial at sea, sir,' I said.

'Yes. Only 'at sea' was but a mile or so down river. Thrown overboard from the merchant ship *Lady Montagu*. It appears this coolie was the ship's cook, who had died of heart failure on the approach to journey's end, and instead of delivering him to the authorities here, they tossed him over the side.'

'And 'e's been nibbled by sharks, yer say?'

'Mauled, more like it. I deemed the act extremely reprehensible. The ship's master has been reprimanded.'

'I'm pleased to hear that.'

'It did, however, affect the sale of fish caught in the river for a few days.'

'I suppose it would,' I said, feeling slightly ill, as I had enjoyed a plate of baby salmon recently.

For the first time, the governor seemed to notice my unruly dress. 'Been up all night Caspian? You look dreadful.'

'I've been working on a case all night sir. A lead, to do with this damned vampire business, took us to the Sea o' Graves down river, where I was set adrift at sea and only managed to make it back to Hobart Town at noon.'

The governor eyed me cautiously and grunted something obscure. He straightened his back – and his dignity. 'On a positive note, I have read the coroner's report on the body of Albert Hartley you exhumed from the well in Evansdale. I commend you for that, Caspian. Well done.'

'Thank you, Your Excellency.'

'Now, what are your thoughts on the omnibus?'

'Omnibus, sir?' Fabian sat upright, keen not to be left out of the conversation.

'Yes. You know what an omnibus is I hope?'

'Aye, o' course. Double storey passenger transport. I know they are used in London and Paris.'

'Yes... and?'

'Well I think they are practical, Sir Henry,' I said.

'And would you like to see them on the streets of Hobart Town?'

'Aye,' Fabian said. 'Why not?'

'There are some aldermen pushing for the vehicles to be employed here, but I have reservations.'

'Reservations?'

'Yes. I had a cousin crippled for life after an accident involving one.'

'Oh?'

'He was on the open top deck and fell.'

'That's no good,' Fabian said in a devil-may-care tone.

'No, it is not, Mr Winter. There was no warning sign. You see, when mounting an omnibus one should do so cautiously, carefully, one step at a time. Then once on top, hold the rail tightly, for if the horses start suddenly, or jerk over a rut, one is liable to be pitched off the top and onto the road.'

Fabian. 'Like yer cousin.'

Sir Henry's next appointment was making himself known in the waiting room. It was time to leave. 'Nipped in the bud, gentlemen,' the governor reiterated. 'Nipped in the bud. I'll expect a full report within days. Good day to you both.'

Stuffy Claiborne was summoned and we were shown the door. 'And Caspian,' the governor said as we were leaving.

'Sir.'

'Tidy yourself up, man. You are representing Her Majesty Queen Victoria are you not?'

'Yes, sir.'

'Now what?' Fabian jammed his hands into his britches pockets for warmth and walked stooped, as if to avoid the chilly breeze in off the harbour.

'I didn't have a chance to tell you before,' I said. 'But we need to visit the female factory at the Cascades and talk to Ivy Mellow.'

'Oh?'

I went on to explain what I had learnt from Jean Parton, Savage's cook. Instead of telling me how brilliantly I had done, Fabian said, 'Women's prison, huh?' I imagined him smirking with a lascivious dribble. 'I'll come with yer.'

Cascades Female Factory

A smaller version of Port Arthur penal settlement, but for women, that would be the best way to describe the female factory. Situated at the foot of Mount Wellington, a few miles west of Sullivans Cove, and a little too close to DeGraves Brewery, I always thought.

Built on twenty acres of land originally reserved by Governor Sorell for a failed distillery over thirty years earlier, the property was refurbished into a walled prison complex for women repeat offenders. Women prisoners who, for one reason or another, could not settle into a term of servitude in the home of a free settler, as was often the case.

Warder Patrick O'Donohoe showed us through the gatehouse, out into the courtyard, pointing to half a dozen women standing about an upturned pork barrel outside the cookhouse, used for a worktable. They were skinning rabbits for the pot – not the prisoner pot either, but for the officers and warders.

'Ivy Mellow,' I called out on the approach. The gaggle stopped and all looked upon us, some flirtatiously.

'Who wants to know?' one older woman said, peeling the skin from a rabbit with skill.

'We're from the police department, Barrack Street,' Fabian answered, flashing his brass badge, hidden under his lapel.

'What do yer want wiv Ivy?' another asked, but Ivy stepped forward defiantly, wiping gore from her hands onto her apron.

'I'm Ivy.' The woman had an oval face with a low forehead, long nose, large mouth, round chin and a mole on the left side of her neck.

'I'm Mr Winter and this 'ere's Mr 'unter,' Fabian said. 'A word, if'n yer please.'

Ivy looked to the other women, who would have preferred to have seen some kind of resistance from her, but.... 'We can talk over 'ere.' Ivy led us a short distance within the prison courtyard.

'Your daughter, Luella Mellow,' I started.

'What she gone done now?'

I explained that we would not arrest her daughter, should she lead us to the whereabouts of Zachary Wolf.

'Who?'

'Zachary Wolf.' Fabian explained the situation and the ongoing rumours about a vampire on the loose in Hobart Town.

'Vampires! Aye!' Ivy crossed herself and said a quick Hail Mary. 'I've 'eard the stories.' She looked over her shoulder towards the other crones before squinting up at the mountain dominating the vista from the prison yard. 'Aye, we've all 'eard the stories. Eight been sucked to death in them 'ills,' Ivy shivered. 'Eight, we 'eard.'

'Only three madam,' I said.

'So it be true then, eh?'

'Well... no. There have been three deaths, not eight. And there are no such things as vampires.'

'Ooh!' Ivy looked at me as if I had just said there was no god. 'Yer either a brave man or a fool, Mr 'unter. A brave man indeed. Or I'm thinkin' yer just a fool. Were yer mother a dullard, son?'

Fabian burst into laughter.

'Mrs Mellow,' I raised my voice unintentionally. 'Do you know where we can find your daughter? Yes or no?'

She scrutinised us a moment. 'What's it worth then?'

'Worth?'

'Aye. 'ow much for information.'

'Christ!' Fabian said. 'You'd sell out yer own daughter.'

'Bah! She'd do the same to me. There's no love lost there.' She put her hand out rubbing forefinger against thumb. ''ow much?'

'I will see your daughter is not arrested,' I said. 'How's that?'

'I can get an ounce o' baccy for sixpence,' she hinted.

I weighed up the issue and deduced that sixpence would save a lot of trouble. I fished the coin from my purse. 'Here.'

Ivy snatched the coin. 'The Crown 'otel!'

'On Battery Hill?'

'Aye.'

I knew the Crown Hotel well. It was close to my Blue Whale Cottage on the corner of Hampden Road and Arthur's Circus. The two storey Hotel was popular with whalers, and in particular the whaling captains and their mates. As far as I knew, it was not a general haunt for ladies of the night. I must have looked doubtful.

'She be a wench in the taproom, Mr 'unter, not some whore like what yer was thinkin'.'

The Crown Hotel, Battery Hill

Innkeeper Freda Charles ran a clean house, and she was proud of it. We introduced ourselves.

'Luella Mellow, she's not in today,' Freda said. 'But she's back tomorrow at noon.' Freda looked at Fabian and me closely. 'Luella's not had a run in with the law has she?'

'No,' I said. 'We are from the Prisoner Barracks and are keen to ask her some questions about a man we are searching for.'

'Hm, because I will not engage troublemakers.' Freda turned to a young bar wench washing pewter tableware in a bucket. She was a horsey lass, and by the way Freda shot me a disapproving look for staring, I guessed she was the daughter.

I imagined this heavy hand was one of the reasons the bar was near empty. I looked around the taproom. One wily old seadog sat next to the window, staring into his tankard of frothing ale with a tumbler of rum to accompany his memory. He looked eighty if he was a day, and I imagined him with a wooden leg, stepping from the pages of Herman Melville's popular novel, *Moby Dick*; a new novel selling like fresh pork pies around America and the colonies, I am told. He was too preoccupied with visualising a Nantucket sleigh ride travelling through his ale foam to notice me.

Sitting close to the generous fire, an old lady, a street vendor, sipped at what looked like a sherry. She sat with her uncovered basket of assorted breads and cheese on the floor next to her, a little too close to the spittoon, I thought.

Three men made small talk amongst themselves at the bar while two others sat by the window, drinking from tall pewter tankards. One of these men, I noticed, was disfigured with a damaged upper lip. Maybe it was a cleft palate. The other man listened with intent to his mate, from time to time embarking on an involuntary facial spasm.

I turned at the sound of a florin spinning on the bar top. 'Two porters, good lady,' Fabian ordered from the innkeeper. I looked at my watch. *Two porters, why not?* The purchase put a half smile on Freda's face. She poured; we drank heartily and discussed our plans. Ten minutes passed and I presented my florin for refills. 'Back in a minute,' I said, and I left for the privy, a long drop within a shelter looking more like a soldier's sentry box than a lavatory. Minutes later, I walked back into the taproom when the man at the window turned to face me and I recognised our wanted felon.

"Samuel Groundwater!' I shouted.

Fabian stood poised at the counter, tankard in hand. His mouth dropped open. 'Caspy!'

Samuel Groundwater, whom I had met at the slaughter yard and whom I was now certain had murdered Mrs O'Neil, the abortionist, bolted.

Now I knew he was guilty. I shot after him. Fabian followed. Samuel Groundwater may be built like a brick shithouse, as Fabian put it, but by Jove he was fast on his feet. He tipped over a table near the door. I tripped, falling out onto the street. I was lucky I didn't break my neck. By the time I was around the corner, he was crossing Arthur's Circus, heading for the cove.

'Damn, that man is fast.' This was the third time he had eluded me.

'Was that 'im?' Fabian asked. 'Samuel Groundwater?'

'Yes. And I think he just admitted his guilt. Didn't you see him enter the inn?'

'Well... no.'

'The bar wench, huh? You were preoccupied.'

'Now now, Caspy.'

Immediately remembering the accomplices, I rushed back into the taproom. The two had gone.

Of course.

'Those two men by the fire,' I asked Freda. 'Are they regulars?'

'No. I've never seen them before.'

'And Miss Mellow will be here at noon tomorrow?'

'Yes.'

'I don't suppose you know where she resides?'

'No, Mr Hunter. And as I said, I will not abide trouble.'

Billings found me in the officers' mess catching hasty nourishment. He looked pale, white as a ghost, some would say.

'Billings. You all right?'

'It's my brother, Caspian. He's been arrested.'

'Arrested?'

'Yes. My younger brother, Nathaniel. He be a cabinetmaker with Button and Company in Melville Street.'

Whilst I knew Nathaniel Billings to be a sober, twenty-seven-year-old Hobartian with a clean record, I had never met the man. 'Yes Billings, you have spoken of him before. Why, pray tell, was he arrested?'

'He has been arrested for a crime of which he is innocent.'

'Oh?' I nodded to a bench seat opposite. 'You had better start at the beginning.'

Billings sat and I poured him a tankard of small ale from my stoneware jug. 'Like I said, he's a cabinetmaker. Two nights previous, he and his two co-workers finished late; they are building a display cabinet for Mr Rudall, the importer, and, as they often do on Saturdays, they imbibed a refreshment or two at the Jolly Hatter, also in Melville Street.'

I was only too familiar with the Jolly Hatter, named after a hat factory that was on the same site back in the '20s. There was a brewery next door that made the finest of ale and porter.

'But last night they imbibed longer than usual,' Billings continued. 'Talking shop mostly as they do, and the time slipped by.'

I knew the feeling only too well.

'It was late when they finally retired from the inn.'

'How late?'

'After midnight, Nathaniel was certain.'

Yes. I knew exactly.

'So they were making their way to Argyle Street where the other two have lodgings at the top of the hill, and Nathaniel lives with his wife in a cottage in Newdegate, north of Hobart Town....'

'Any children?'

'Pardon?'

'You said Nathaniel lives in a cottage with his wife. Do they have children?'

'One girl, four-year-old Scarlett.'

'Please go on.'

'Well Nathaniel said that, although they were singing and being rather boisterous, they were not aggressive, when Nathaniel stepped into a side lane to relieve himself. The other two had walked on some fifty yards by the time he stepped back onto Melville Street. Nathaniel ran to catch up but collided with another man, apparently as equally drunk as my brother. He asked the other man if he was all right, but he answered in a foreign language, which Nathaniel could not understand. The other man was short, expensively dressed with brown skin and oily hair, Nathaniel said. Unable to understand him, Nathaniel offered his hand in greeting, but the man gripped it firmly, and throwing his arm around his shoulder he held him firmly.'

'Who held who?'

'The stranger held Nathaniel. This was in a friendly manner, I might add. At first Nathaniel thought lightly of the matter and, as he could not understand him, he made to pull away, but the foreigner would not let him go.'

'And Nathaniel's friends?'

'They were up the street calling out for him to join them.'

'So then, what?'

'Well, this is where the problem started. Nathaniel was getting impatient and annoyed. The drunken stranger had him in a firm grip and as he struggled, other men walking by stopped to watch, thinking this was the makings of a fight.'

'Typical.'

'The harder Nathaniel struggled, the more tightly this man held onto him. Now, I must tell you here, Caspian, that my brother has not an aggressive bone in his body. But angry and struggling to free himself, he punched the man. This is most uncharacteristic of him. The man fell and hit his head on the ground the very moment a passing watchman passed by, attracted to the commotion. He called out from across the road for Nathaniel to stand to, but Nathaniel ran.'

'He took flight.'

'Yes.'

'Now I can see where this is headed.'

'His friends ran off home while my brother escaped through back alleys onto Elizabeth Street with the watchman on his tail. His plan being to lose the watchman before making his way up Harrington Street and across to Newdegate Street and home.'

'Something tells me he did not make it.'

'Oh he made it home all right, but please... let me explain.'

'Be my guest.'

'At Elizabeth Street, he turned right into Collins Street, where he was certain he had lost this pursuer. He took cover a moment in another narrow alleyway running alongside the Bank of Van Diemen's Land, when he saw a suspicious character lingering behind the bank, a man in a cape.'

'A cape!'

'Yes.'

Could this be the figure perpetuating the vampire myth? 'Did he get a look at the face of this man?'

'No. It was dark and the figure was well cloaked.'

This fact alone had me thinking. 'But what has this to do with your brother?'

'Nathaniel, unaware of the stories and rumours of vampires, yet fearing for his own safety that he had maybe interrupted a burglary, quickly made his way home.'

'Successfully?'

'Yes. But the watchman, a particularly dedicated lawman supposedly, returned to the scene of the crime, where he found the drunken foreigner still sprawled in the alleyway semi-conscious.'

'Please do not inform me that the man was deceased.'

'No. Thank the good lord. But he had been robbed. Apart from a swelling on his forehead and swelling around the mouth, the man was unhurt. The watchman, whom I now know is Constable Mortimer, wrote in his report that the man's breath was strong of liquor. While he was on the ground, he had been taken advantage of and was robbed.'

'So who was this foreigner? Do we know?'

'Yes. He was a looking glass merchant from Venice.'

'Italy?'

'Yes. He has been residing in Launceston the past two months, where he had opened a business in Charles Street, a quite successful business too, by all accounts. And he was in Hobart Town on business.'

'So why does he not speak the Queen's English?'

'Apparently, he has not as yet been able to grasp our language, and normally travels with an interpreter.'

I took out my little black book and started pencilling in notes. 'Name?'

'Marco Stefano. I heard he is a jovial man who enjoys the inns a little too much.'

'Was he robbed of much?'

'Seven pounds in Bank of England notes, fifteen sovereigns, a gold pocket watch and gold chain, a gold seal, two gold rings, a silk handkerchief and a purse of spending change amounting to eleven shillings.'

I whistled. 'That is a lot to be carrying.'

'Well some of it were recent sales.' Billings looked at me a moment, lost in thought, more so of concern for his brother, I imagined.

'But your brother escaped apprehension, did he not?'

'Yes and no. One of the passers-by who witnessed the altercation recognised Todd Brighton, the older apprentice cabinetmaker with Nathaniel. When interviewed by constables the next day, he gave them my brother's name and address. Nathaniel was arrested yesterday and is now locked in the watch house.'

'Oh.'

Billings' face was twisted with stress. 'Assault and robbery will fetch him fourteen years hard labour, much of it in irons.'

'But he did not rob this... this Stefano fellow, did he?'

'No, Caspian. Of course not. But there is mischief afoot. That is why I come before you; I need your help, desperately.'

Yes indeed, I thought, the man does need my help. Why, less than twenty years ago, this crime would be a hanging offence.

'I have made some enquiries already,' Billings said. 'One witness, who saw the kerfuffle and moved on that night for personal safety reasons, came to see me when he found out that Nathaniel had been charged. He said that two other men lingering in the shadows were known pickpockets and small time criminals. One, he knew by name, James Dick, but refused to go further, and said he would not be a witness in court. I have spoken to the innkeeper of the Nag's Head on the corner of Melville and Harrington Streets.'

'Nag's Head.' I had fond memories of that inn. 'Why Nag's Head?'

'That is where Stefano was last seen drinking.'

'My, you have been productive... and?'

'I learnt that Stefano had been in the taproom there often of late. It seems he was particularly fond of Agnes Brine, a resident prostitute, who has lodgings behind the inn.'

Agnes... Agnes... I think I remember her.

'Well, I learnt she is good friends of James Dick, isn't she?'

'Small town, I must concede.'

'It appears this Constable Mortimer has some grudge against my brother. When the two other cabinetmakers came forward as witnesses to the fact they were with Nathaniel drinking that night and he was innocent of the robbery, Mortimer convinced the arresting clerk that their testimony was biased and unreliable because they were drunk.'

'Come, let us first pay a visit to this prostitute, Agnes Brine.' I slipped my fob from my waistcoat pocket and flipped the lid. 'Twelve minutes past noon. I trust she should be up and about by now.'

The Nag's Head had opened nineteen years ago – in 1839, Billings informed me. The unexpectedly handsome two-storey building had three rooms on the first floor over the ground floor taproom. A dormer window in the centre serviced an attic room beneath a shingled roof with three chimneys. Built of red brick, it boasted a stucco veneer. The front door was topped with an arched lead-glass window allowing light into the entrance hall. Although, with the winter's day gloom, the light on entering took some time to adjust to. The first thing to hit me was the smell off manure. I looked back at Billings, who looked down at my boots. I had stepped in horse shite out on the street and had not noticed.

'Thank god for boot scrapers I say,' I said, attempting to find humour in the situation as I used the boot scraper outside the door. Billings was already at the bar.

'Agnes?' the innkeeper repeated the name. The innkeeper was a hard-faced woman in her forties with a sour expression and knuckles that warned me she could fight with the best of them . She looked us up and down with unbridled suspicion. 'Agnes? What yer be askin' 'bout 'er for? Yer don't look like punters.'

'Punters?'

''er usual cup o' tea if'n yer knows wha' I mean.'

'If it is customers you speak of,' I said, 'well no, madam, you would be correct in that assumption.'

'You sure squire, *you* look familiar,' the innkeeper directed at me, her eyes narrowing a moment as she searched the confines of her memory. 'Aye,' you been with Agnes before, ain't yer lad?'

'Look, is Agnes here or not?'

'Not,' she spat back. 'She be asleep, I'm thinkin'. But if'n yer desperate, an' I gotta say yer look it, go knock on her door, two cabins up 'arrington Street.' And as an afterthought she added, 'She's got a horseshoe on the door.'

Agnes's cottage was a one-bedroom affair, a wattle and daub construction hardly big enough within to swing a cat. It had an earth floor. I can only surmise that she conducted her business in a room above the inn. A scrawny, half-starved cat rubbed against my leg, miaowing, but suddenly moved away. It must have been the horse shite. The door was opened on the second knock and I was pleasantly surprised. Agnes Brine was of mature age but a most toothsome figure. Her soot black hair was down over her shoulders and covering one eye in a most seductive manner.

'Ag...' I cleared my throat. 'Excuse me. Agnes Brine?'

'Aye.' She immediately launched into a jolly and friendly smile. 'I know you, don't I?'

'I should not imagine, madam.'

'Mademoiselle, please,' she almost purred.

Billings stood aside. My guess was that he thought this interaction best left to me. 'Ah... Marco Stefano. You know him, I believe?'

'The mad Dago! Wha' of 'im?'

'I do believe he was a... shall I say, a patron, of yours.'

'Aye. And a drunken one at thart.'

'Did you see him the night before last?'

Agnes thought a moment. 'Nar, don't think so.'

'Well yes or no?'

'No then.'

'I believe you are an acquaintance of James Dick?'

'Little Dick! Aye. What's 'e done now?'

'Little Dick? Am I to believe the man is short?'

'Oh, average height really. But the man was born well endowed, so 'is mates, in all their wisdom, call 'im Little Dick.'

I smiled. Billings did not. 'Any other attributes? I asked. 'Well, 'e can be bad tempered, especially if'n anyone makes fun o' his facial twitch.'

'I'll try to remember,' I said.

'Why yer askin', any'ow?'

'We have reason to believe he and an accomplice were party to robbing Marco Stefano the other night, a crime for which the wrong man has been charged, which is, I might add, a very serious offence.'

Suddenly the mood swung. 'Don't know wha' yer talkin' about.' She swung the door closed, but I managed to shove a shite-reeking boot in the gap.

'This is a serious allegation,' I said. 'Can you at least tell me where I can find James Dick?'

'Hangin' inside 'is britches, like any other cove's,' she snapped, kicking my foot out of the way and slamming the door in my face.

'I must admit that was a good answer,' I grinned, remembering I should not appear so cheerful to Billings.

Billings ignored my comment. 'She knows more.'

'Aye, thart she does,' a voice said ever so softly, from the doorway of the next cabin.

'Pardon?'

A woman, whom I immediately thought could step into the limelight, treading the boards of a theatre, and play the role of the witch in a Hansel and Gretel play without requiring makeup, beckoned to us from her doorway.

'You have something to say, madam?' I said.

The old woman made certain Agnes was out of earshot before tipping her head for us to follow her inside.

'She knows plenty more, sirs,' the witch said.

'Oh?'

'Aye, thart friendly Dick o' whom she spoke is a right bastard. An' his accomplice o' whom you spoke would be William Norman, a mean bugger an' all. It's them two what's been gettin' Agnes there to spend a lot o' time with that Dago what yer mentioned. 'e's got plenty money, has 'e not?'

'Apparently.'

'Aye. Well Agnes 'as been groomin' the fella, so as they can rob 'im in his lodgings.'

'Well,' I said. 'They did that last night, but in the street.'

'I'm thinkin' that was a mistake. I'm thinkin' that them two was opportunists, just out an' about like they often are, robbin' drunks. But they've never met the Dago so they didn't realise they robbed the fella what Agnes was groomin', for bigger rewards.'

'Why are you telling us this?' Billings asked.

'Let's just say, me and Agnes have a difference of interests.'

'And do you know where we can find these men?'

'I think I've heard talk that Norman lives in Wapping, along the rivulet.

'We need to catch these men and convince them to testify as witnesses,' Billings said, stepping from the witch's cottage and into a patch of welcome sunlight.

'So, we will pay a visit to Wapping and see if we cannot root out this William Norman,' I insisted. As if I did not have enough work on my hands. But Billings was a friend as well as a colleague, and I only hoped that his brother Nathaniel *was* innocent, and we could prove it.

If ever poverty represented itself in Van Diemen's Land, it was at Wapping. Although the *Cessation of Transportation Act* had been passed five years ago, the convict stigma still haunted the poor; most were unable to drag themselves out from their pit of despair. Wapping nests in low-lying, flood-prone marshland where the Hobart Town Rivulet divides this community. The crystal-clear water from Mount Wellington supplies dozens of enterprises from breweries to tanneries. These businesses, in turn, discard their effluent along with human waste, which drains through the township, through the slums of Wapping, where it spills into the River Derwent as a nauseating discharge. Wapping's population, I am told, is around one thousand and is not a place to let one's guard down.

Any acquaintance of William Norman did not have to think too hard when asked if he knew the whereabouts of William Norman.

'What's the time, gov?' the acquaintance asked me when I enquired.

I looked at my fob. 'Twenty minutes past the hour of one.'

'Then William Norman, what you seek and fer whatever reason I don't give a shite, will be drinkin' in the Shades. 'e be a creature o' habit, that one.'

'And you are well acquainted?' I asked, thinking it suspicious that this man was so forthcoming with Norman's whereabouts to two lawmen.

'Aye, acquaintances only. 'e be no friend o' mine.'

'And tell me, kind sir, could you describe the gentleman to me, so I should know whom to approach.'

'Aye. He be an ugly bastard, forty-five or thereabouts, with long black hair and a cleft palate.'

Billings. 'Cleft palate?'

'Aye. It's a...'

'I know what it is,' Billings was uncharacteristically abrupt. 'I was just verifying the fact.'

The Shades is a small taproom beneath the Theatre Royal on Campbell Street, which borders Wapping. The carved stone building was completed just over twenty years ago in '37, designed by Peter DeGraves, the founder of the Cascade Brewery, and financed by a consortium of businesspeople. The music hall is very popular, offering all types of entertainment, even cockfights, I am told. Although the Shades has its own entrance in Sackville Street, patrons can also enter the theatre through a stair door in the theatre pit, which causes a dilemma occasionally, with noisy drunkards creating their own entertainment; much to the displeasure of upmarket patrons in the wing boxes.

We stepped down the steep treads and into the gloom and taproom fug of the day drinkers.

'What will it be?' I asked Billings, hefting my purse free, with a jingle of coin that turned heads of those attuned to the clinking of silver.

'Nothing.' Billings said, his acute eyes had acclimatised smartly to the darkness. He scoured the bar, like a hawk searching for a mouse. Two well-dressed men – albeit Billings and I – one holding a kangaroo leather scrotum purse full of coin, were attracting unwanted attention in the busy bar.

'Billings.' I elbowed the man. 'What would you like to drink?' I hissed in his ear, 'We must look inconspicuous.'

'Ah... a ginger beer then... thank you.'

We leant on the bar, Billings with his ginger beer and me with a quart of porter, and I could not help but feel like I was one of a two-prawn centrepiece on a platter of mussels. 'Well?' I said out the corner of my mouth.

'Well what?'

'Well, can you see William Norman?'

'Not readily, no. There are two booths back yonder with coves in them, but it's too dark to tell.'

Immediately, a young woman over-painted with makeup – and dressed in the attire of a woman one would not wish to take home to meet mother – stood to allow her male companion slide from the booth seat. He headed for the bar... and he had a cleft palate.

Billings saw him too. He straightened. 'Steady captain,' I pinched Billings's arm to be certain he understood. As the witch had warned us, Norman was a big bastard. He pushed up to the counter with four empty pewter tankards.

I leant in and whispered to Billings, 'Pay the man no attention. Wait until he returns to his companions and then we'll strike.'

Billings was stewing, but these words seemed to placate him. We waited. Norman returned to his seat, armed with drinks.

'Now,' I said. This was perfect. He was sitting in a booth, there was no escape.

'William Norman?' I said, sitting heavily on the seat next to the female companion, forcing William to shove across, closer to the wall. Billings, sitting opposite me, did exactly the same, also pinning the other couple against the stone wall of the taproom.

Norman stiffened. 'What the firk?'

'It is William Norman?' I reiterated, sitting my tankard on the tabletop like I was in for a friendly chat. 'Is it not?' Pause. 'Well?'

'You know it is,' Norman scowled back.

'Excuse us, ladies,' I said to the sporting girls. 'My friend and I won't take up too much of your time.'

Billings, at last, was beginning to enjoy himself. The other male's hands disappeared under the table, so Billings pulled his cosh from his jacket and pounded it on the bench. 'Hands where we can see them.'

'You from the barracks?' Norman finally asked.

'Clever lad,' I said. 'but not clever enough to rob an Italian merchant in the street and get away with it.'

'Now look 'ere....' Norman tried to stand but it was an impossible move with a rack of barrels stored over the booth. He cracked his head and cursed.

'Sit down, Norman.' I had taken my Yale double-barrel pocket pistol from my jacket and kept it in my left hand, resting it discreetly on the table, and pointed at the man. 'Keep your britches on. We just want to ask a few questions.'

I was about to ask who Norman's accomplice was when the man's face suffered a short bout of spasms. *The facial twitch!*

'Small Dick!' I exclaimed loudly. His whore burst into a cackle.

'Little Dick,' Billings corrected me, mouth curling into a smile.

'Small. Little? All the same to me. Empty your pockets!'

'What?'

I leant in towards the two men, each with his woman betwixt us.

'I'll not repeat myself again,' I said slowly, gritting my teeth. 'I am in no mood for shenanigans and lies. *Empty – your – pockets.*'

'Who do yer think you are?' Norman spat back defiantly.

I was so decisive I even surprised myself. I pounced; reaching in front of the whore, I jammed the Yale into Norman's cheek so hard I thought I heard a tooth chip. His cleft scar widened, reddened and winked back at me. Norman's bravado instantly dissolved. He glared back like a fox in the hunter's sights. I cocked the hammer. Now he looked terrified.

'Take care, sir,' he said in a stammer, beads of sweat appearing on his forehead. 'I'll do as yer ask.'

'Slowly,' I ordered, as Norman's hand disappeared from sight. Moments later he pulled a pouch of tobacco free and two clay pipes, one with a broken stem, some loose coins, copper and silver, a pewter crucifix and a brass key. He laid the items on the tabletop and looked at me hopefully. I pushed past the woman and tapped his pocket with my spare hand. His pockets were not yet empty.

'Keep going,' I said.

Grudgingly, a gold watch chain and a gold seal appeared, along with several pound notes tied in a tight roll. Billings picked up the seal, read the stamp and presented it to me.

'Well, well. M.S. Would that be for Marco Stefano, the Italian man robbed in Melville Street last night?'

'I bought that fair and square,' Norman cried innocently.

'Where?'

'Off a man at an inn, last night.'

'Oh how convenient. Which inn? What man?'

'I... I... ah... *we* went to so many.'

'We?' I looked at Little Dick who was trying to distance himself from his friend. 'Would that be you, Small Dick?'

'My name's James. James Dick,' he answered defiantly.

'Oh yes. That's right,' I said. 'Put your hands on the table where I can see them.' He complied reluctantly. I leant close to Billings's ear. 'Irons,' I said in a cautious voice. Billings understood immediately. He slipped wrist irons from his belt and cuffed James Dick's right hand, screwing the cuff closed with the screw key. I stood.

'Out,' I demanded.

'You said you just wanted to ask a few questions,' Norman started.

'I lied.'

'Bastard.'

'Bastard, I am not. I know who my father is. A cad I maybe. Sometimes. But at least I am not a common thief.' I told the two women to make themselves scarce and Billings hand-cuffed Dick to Norman's right wrist. 'Let's go for a walk.'

Chapter Thirteen

Prisoner Barracks, Campbell Street

At home that night at Blue Whale Cottage, something hounded me. I was certain I had seen the two men before – recently, very recently – but I could not for the life of me work out where. Then I realised that they were the two men whom Samuel Groundwater turned up to meet at the Crown Hotel on Battery Hill. At the time, I had not taken much notice of them and they had changed clothes, or at least their jackets. Now it hit home. I warned Billings as we met at the prison gate.

'So,' Billings said, also refreshed from a night's sleep and confident he could save his brother. 'There is more to these two villains than meets the eye.'

'Yes Billings. Birds of a feather and all that, eh. Let's interrogate them, see what mischief they have really been up to.'

'You 'ave company,' said Sergeant Richard Clincher, Keeper of the Gate, eager to alert us as we entered the prison.

'Who?'

'Some ambitious constable, Mortimer, a night watchman by all accounts.' And Clincher huffed at the inferior rank. 'And an officer from the watch 'ouse, Lithgow, I think 'is name be.'

I had heard of an Officer Lithgow from the watch house and knew him to be a right turkey. 'What are they doing here?'

'Come to demand your prisoners Small Dick an' Norman be released.'

'Over my dead body.'

Constable Mortimer had heard of our unusual and unexpected arrest at the Shades and had turned up at the prison at eight o'clock in the morning with his superior for support. I suspected immediately that something was amiss, for the constable was *so* bent on protecting Norman and Dick and so determined that Nathaniel Billings was guilty as charged.

William Norman and James Dick were sitting together in the interview room, looking very smug. I was furious. I had had them locked up in separate cells for the night so as not to let them concoct some story together. Now here they were together, chatting away merrily as if they were planning a holiday.

'What is the meaning of this?' I demanded.

'You have no right to arrest these men,' Officer Lithgow started.

'Who are you?' I spat, although I already knew.

'Officer Lithgow from the watch house and this is...'

'Constable Mortimer,' I cut in. 'I know, the man who arrested Nathaniel Billings on false charges.'

'Excuse me,' Mortimer bristled. 'There are witnesses to testify that Nathaniel Billings struck and robbed the victim, and...'

I held my finger up in an angry gesture. *Shut it!*

'I arrested these men for being in possession of one gold chain and one gold seal belonging to the victim.'

'I bought them off a cove in the street,' Norman swore.

'You told me you bought them off a man in an inn.'

Norman reddened. 'No, I couldn't remember, I had been drinkin'.'

'How convenient,' Billings said.

'Regardless,' I said. 'You are in the possession of stolen property, namely from a robbery.'

'Senor Marco Stefano has made a statement, saying he recalls Nathaniel's hand in his pocket before the assault,' Mortimer said.

Billings. 'Nonsense.'

'The victim was very drunk,' I said.

'He swears in his statement that he was as sober as the day he was born.'

'Really,' I laughed. I had read the statement and the fact that he was drunk was never challenged. The night before, Billings and I had also shown our two prisoners to Nathaniel in his solitary cell and they both swore they had never seen him before. I told Lithgow and Mortimer this. They shrugged.

'And don't forget,' Billings told the room, 'Nathaniel has an alibi. The two colleagues he had been drinking with all evening. They were together the entire time, up to the altercation, when my brother hit Stefano in self-defence.'

'Horse shit!' Officer Lithgow roared. 'He struck the man and robbed him.'

'How could he rob him if he fled the scene immediately?'

Constable Mortimer was having none of it. As far as he was concerned, Nathaniel Billings was as guilty as hell. 'I put it to you Mr Hunter, that Nathaniel Billings's role in this dastardly crime was to start an altercation with the victim and then do a runner if the law came along, which they did, so as to fetch the said law away from the crime scene, while his accomplices did the robbery.'

'Accomplices? You speak of Norman and Dick?'

'No, I do not! I speak of Nathaniel Billings's accomplices, who are yet to be arrested.'

Billings weighed in. 'But these men are Nathaniel's alibis, you pillock.'

Pillock! I liked that Billings, and it's so out of character.

'Nonsense.'

'I beg your pardon? Nonsense!'

'Yes, Mortimer. I've never heard such poppycock. Nathaniel Billings just happened to be in the wrong place at the wrong time.'

'I put it to you that he fled the scene, doubled back and robbed him.'

'You can put it wherever you like, Mortimer!' I yelled.

Billings. 'And where were you, *Constable*?'

'Chasing the villain.'

'But when you lost him, you returned to the scene and Stefano was on the ground, dead drunk.'

'Unconscious from hitting his head, when he fell to the ground from the punch.'

'And these two?' I stabbed a finger at Norman and Dick. 'Were they there? No. They fled after they robbed Stefano.'

Billings. 'Witnesses saw these two rifle the unconscious victim's pockets.'

'What witnesses?'

Now *this* was a problem. It appeared someone had got to the witnesses and they were now off the record. There was the briefest of silence as Clincher joined us, struggling with a large kettle, steaming off the fire and the pleasant aroma of Indian tea brewing.

'How do you know Samuel Groundwater?' I asked the two detainees, out of nowhere.

James Dick answered, 'Who?'

'Samuel Groundwater. He is engaged as a slaughter man at the Hobart Town slaughterhouse.'

'Never 'eard of 'im.'

'He met you at the Crown yesterday and bolted when he saw the law. Strange set of affairs, that one. Now, why would he bolt, and moments later you two bolted as well.'

'Don't know wha' yer talkin' about?'

'I was witness to your suspicious behaviour also,' Billings said.

'Look,' Officer Lithgow said. 'If you aren't going to arrest these men on any solid charge, you have no choice but to release them.'

''e's got a point there,' Richard Clincher the gatekeeper put in his two bob's worth. He sat the fresh brew on the table. I shot Clincher a filthy look and he realised his mistake. 'I'll go and fetch the mugs,' he said. 'Shall I?'

Moments later the old gatekeeper returned, clanging enamel mugs and carrying a crock of brown sugar. On his heels was another police messenger from the watch house. Clincher came directly to me and said quietly in my ear, 'Look wha' the cat dragged in.'

The messenger ignored Billings and myself and passed a sealed letter to Lithgow, who cracked the wax seal, read the contents and nodded victoriously. He showed Mortimer who smiled like a winner.

'You, gatekeeper,' Lithgow ordered Clincher. 'Unlock those irons. William Norman and James Dick are to be released.'

Lithgow thrust the letter towards me with outstretched arm. I read the contents. There it was, an immediate release of the prisoners and signed by Magistrate Orpheus Fry; a known black-hearted devil, if I ever knew one.

'How much did this cost you?' I said angrily. 'A crate of burgundy?'

'I beg your pardon!' Officer Lithgow was ropable. At least he *acted* suitably angry. But it was true. I held his stare. 'You would do well to hold your tongue, Mr Hunter.'

I answered by stuffing the crumbled communication into his tunic breast pocket.

'Mortimer... Mortimer...' Billings mulled the name over in his head. 'Now I remember. Years ago. I arrested a Mortimer for assault. It was quite a vicious attack, if I remember correctly.'

'Who? The constable, man of the watch Mortimer?'

'No, Caspian. It was his brother, Marcus, I think his name was. Yes, Marcus Mortimer. And he was gaoled for two years, if my memory serves me correct.'

'You arrested the watchman's brother?' I said incredulous.

'Yes. It was his younger brother. It was a real kerfuffle in court with his mother screaming and his father threatened me when the verdict and its punishment were given.'

'Well then, there lies our answer. This Mortimer has a grudge against you, and this is his chance for retribution... *your* brother, behind bars.'

Billings was exasperated. 'They have released the men who should be facing imprisonment and imprisoned the man who should be free,' he said when we were alone. 'It's a damned disgrace.'

'Something else bothers me,' I said.

'What's that Caspian?'

'Samuel Groundwater, William Norman and James Dick; they are up to no good. And we know Groundwater is in cahoots with Zachary Wolf, who I suspect is perpetuating the vampire myth around the colony, or in the south at least.'

'And that bar wench Luella Mellow is in this up to her pretty neck also.'

'Absolutely.' I had another thought. 'When your brother was being pursued by Mortimer, he said he saw a man hanging about in the township wearing a cape and black hat did he not?'

'Yes.'

'It was at the Bank of Van Diemen's Land?'

'That's correct.'

'Then I would like to talk to him.'

Nathaniel had suffered solitary for days now and I really felt for him. He was younger than Billings, three or four years maybe, and shorter. But he was solid of character, from a good family and looking like he would not hurt a fly. I saw him as a victim of circumstance and believed everything he told us was the truth. And punching Marco Stefano to free himself from the drunkard's grip seemed logical to me. I would have done the same. Billings entered his cell before me and his brother ran to his arms. 'Can't you get me out of here?'

'Sorry Nat,' Billings said. 'You know the magistrate has signed a warrant for you to remain incarcerated until your trial.'

I knew this to be the same magistrate, Orpheus Fry.

'Nathanial,' I said.' The night you were chased by Constable Mortimer you passed the Bank of Van Diemen's Land on the corner of Collins and Elizabeth Streets, is that correct?'

'Yes, sir.'

'Tell me what you saw. Tell me exactly what you told your brother.'

'I saw a dark figure, tall, slim, well built, he was lurking in the alley next to the bank. He appeared to be taking measurements.'

'Measurements?'

'The distance between the rear windows, or at least the furthest windows from the street.'

'So this was around two o'clock in the morning?'

'Yes, sir.'

'Were there any other witnesses?'

'No. I was alone. I thought, I am in enough trouble, I just wanted to get home.'

It was midday by the time I had a chance to inspect the bank, taking note of the furthest windows down the alley and their proximity to anything of importance within. The sturdy stone building would not be an easy nut to crack. The windows were also a good ten feet from the ground and I could not for the life of me see why anyone would tackle such a fortress. Inside, I was told in no uncertain manner, how secure the vaults were. They were underground, behind bars, and the gold was well secured in the most modern of vaults. It seemed ludicrous anyone would even attempt such a robbery.

Whoever he was, I felt his intention was to maintain the vampire on the loose myth for his own nefarious ambitions, maybe a bank robbery. But I also felt it personally. What was he doing in the backyard of my Blue Whale Cottage?

My other priority this day was to investigate this magistrate, Orpheus Fry, who was so intent on charging Nathaniel with assault and robbery and keeping Nathaniel in prison when there was so much evidence in his favour. I had never met him, but I knew of the man and did not like what I had heard. He was corrupt and I was determined to find a chink in his armour.

Using all the resources I had at hand, from Bonnie Nettle at the Sailor's Rest to Baldwin Cheek in the Court of Requests, a clerk who owed me favours, I was able to find that chink in Orpheus Fry's armour. That chink being a Chinese lover, and a young one at that. On further investigation, I discovered the lover was seventeen years old. That was hardly illegal, though Orpheus was in his sixties. But on further questioning amongst the Chinese community of Hobart Town, I discovered the lover's name. He Chong. He Chong was a *lad*. The magistrate was a Molly.

'Appropriate,' I told Billings my findings.

'What?' Billings looked confused. 'Appropriate that he's a Molly?'

'No Billings. Appropriate He Chong is a he.' Billings wasn't as amused as was I, by the phonetics. '*He* means *lotus flower*, I am told.'

'With all due respect, Caspian, what are we going to do about it?'

'Use it to our advantage, Billings.'

So it was that night, that Nathaniel Billings walked free of his cell, with all charges dropped. But it was not easy. I knew we would need witnesses. Reputable witnesses. Conveniently for us, Magistrate Fry was a creature of habit. He enjoyed dining on Mondays and Fridays in the saloon parlour at Harvest Home Hotel on the main Road to New Town. It was a relatively quiet inn with a lady landlord, Mrs Edith Tarbell, unperturbed by the magistrate's choice of companion. Besides, they were good customers, coming regularly to the Harvest Home Hotel for several weeks now. After dinner they retired to lodgings upstairs. Room five. Always room five. On further inquiry, I learnt Orpheus Fry had gone to great lengths to conceal this secret and, for the icing on the cake, his brother was a senior member of the Christian clergy. Namely the Bishop at St John's Anglican Church in Launceston. The perfect scandal for blackmail. I had the reputations of two big fish to fry. *Sorry dear reader. I could not resist the second phonetic humour.*

I called the operation a sting. For that's what it was. And none of us had any issues about blackmailing a magistrate who twisted the law to suit himself. It was a team effort. Fabian, Holly and Jasper kept the innkeeper busy in the taproom downstairs, Jasper, being the youngest and smallest, squeezed into a large double wardrobe in room five while the magistrate and He dined.

Oh! I hear you ask. But how did Jasper enter the locked guest room?

I should mention here that some months ago, I had had a set of skeleton keys crafted for me by a locksmith, Fletcher Coote, who owed me a favour. Twirls, the prison lags called them. Completely illegal of course, but by golly, I am a lawman, not an outlaw. Fletcher explained how locks are warded by a set of obstructions to prevent the lock opening unless a key, with notches to match the wards, is inserted. A skeleton key is a key with all the centre filed away allowing it to pass by all the wards without interference, hence opening the lock.

'So why is it named the skeleton key?' I asked the locksmith, and he explained it is because the key has been reduced to its essential parts.

So, with Jasper safely hidden in the wardrobe, the plan was – when he was certain the two were up to mischief – he was to pounce from the wardrobe like a Jack in the Box, blow a whistle for effect and unlock the bedroom door. This was our cue to enter as witnesses to the act, the act of sodomy, and an illegal act to boot.

But it did not go exactly like clockwork.

Jasper heard the men enter, held the wardrobe door closed with a cord he had affixed earlier and prayed neither required the use of the clothes cupboard. He heard the cork pop from a bottle. He heard amicable chatter, albeit murmured words through the wardrobe door. Talking ceased. He heard giggles. He was certain he heard groans but still he waited. He waited and waited and waited. It was now very quiet and he feared they were onto him and that any minute the doors to the cupboard would fly open and he would have to face an angry magistrate.

Nothing.

Silence.

After what seemed an awkward ten or so minutes, Jasper allowed the door to open slightly. He heard the subtlest creak of an unoiled hinge. Froze. Waited. Nothing. He managed to position himself to steal a peek. He could see the magistrate's feet; shoes off, socks on. Jasper allowed the door to open further. He saw hairy old man legs, white and knobbly...

Argh!

Jasper saw the man naked. It was not a pleasant sight.

Where the bloody hell's He Chong? Jasper hissed silently. He opened the door wider, another inch. Yes, the magistrate was totally undressed. Anxiously Jasper opened the door even further ...

Christ, no!

Jasper saw a pillow bathed in blood. He involuntarily gasped.

Jasper's focus sharpened. Where was He Chong? He leapt from the wardrobe hollering like a madman, bouncing across the room spinning in mid-air. He pulled his pistol free, cocking the hammer ...

Out in the hallway I waited his signal. We heard a kerfuffle. 'Jasper?'

Jasper pirouetted about the room, pistol drawn, expecting to be attacked any second.

Suddenly we heard an explosion. Jasper's gun discharged. In all the excitement he fired at a shadow shattering the plaster ceiling rose into crumbs.

We didn't wait. We shouldered the door open. While Billings searched for He Chong Holly danced into the room, a pistol in each hand. Lantern Jaw Lincoln joined Billings in the search for the killer. But Chong was long gone, the open window and the chill in the room testament to his departure minutes earlier.

Over at the bedside I looked at Orpheus Fry, the blackguard. Naked as the day he entered this world, socks not included. But it was his method of death that fascinated me. He had puncture marks in his left carotid artery. Two neat holes made by a Chinese eating stick, or chopstick as they are called. One stick, two holes well placed. The bloodied stick lay on the bed. Fry had bled out in minutes. His face was the colour of chalk. Jasper would tell me later he remembered the magistrate sucking short gasps the moment he jumped from the wardrobe. However, there was naught he could do.

Now the magistrate was before his maker, standing before the great judge himself. I watched as the last of his blood oozed onto the feather pillow and promptly heard Holly vomit out the open window. It was then that I had the weirdest fantasy of He Chong, should he be hiding down below, in the trajectory of Holly's last supper.

The landlady stormed into the room. 'What's going on? Oh my God! Police!' Mrs Edith Tarbell was clearly a stranger to death, especially someone murdered with a chopstick, and in her own hotel. 'Police!' she screeched. 'Someone get the police.'

'We are the police, madam,' I said. But the woman threw her hand to her forehead and spiralled into unconsciousness. Lincoln, god bless the man, leapt to her cause and caught her before she hit the floor.

'I hate to tell yer this, Caspian sar,' Lincoln said as he dragged her over onto the bed, resting her next to her lodger. 'But she's fainted.'

'Now what?' Fabian said, pressing tobacco into his clay pipe before lighting it in the open fire grate.

I knew what Fabian was thinking. We *were* to extract a retraction from the magistrate allowing Nathaniel Billings be released from prosecution.

'I can't think,' I said. 'It's too cold. Holly,' I said, as she continued retching out the window. 'Holly. Have you quite finished?'

'Oh gawd,' Holly blubbered, but pulled her body back in the window before closing it. 'Thank you, Holly. Bit nippy.'

'Aye.'

'Jasper... Billings.'

'Aye, sar.'

'Go to the watch house and report this murder and give them a description of He Chong. He is a seventeen-year-old Chinaman and there are not too many of them in Hobart Town. In fact, they are as rare as hen's teeth.'

'Aye.'

'And Jasper,' I suddenly noticed his hair, white as snow. 'What is that in your hair?' But I realised the moment I asked, when the last piece of plaster fell, clipping Jasper's ear.

'Oh! I see... ah... Lincoln, go to the hospital and organise a cart and orderlies to remove this body.'

'Should I fetch Mrs Rowley from the photographic studio, sar?' Jasper asked, brushing his hair best he could. 'To make a photographic image for the courts... like yer always ask me, sar.'

What a pleasant thought. And the room's warming up nicely. I looked at my watch – twenty minutes after nine in the evening – and looked to the landlady who was stirring. 'Ah, it won't be necessary, Jasper, thank you.'

'Are you quite certain, Caspian sar?'

Cheeky sod.

'Yes, Jasper. Now go.'

I was about to have Lincoln carry innkeeper Mrs Edith Tarbell to another guest room when she regained consciousness. Her eyes opened and she twisted her head - face to face - with the corpse. There was no scream this time. The woman simply collapsed back into her world of darkness and nightmares.

'Quickly,' Fabian finished his pipe, tapping the spent tobacco on the grate. 'Get 'er feet,' he ordered Lincoln. 'We'll get 'er to another room an' she'll think she dreamt it all.'

'See if she has a maid or someone downstairs,' I suggested. 'We haven't time to deal with this.'

With the aid of a sister who lived at the hotel, we were able to continue with our urgent police business and I knew our priority number one would be tricky.

'Holly.'

'Caspian, sar.'

'You come with Fabian and me.'

'What's the plan Caspy?' Fabian asked. Now that's what I liked about the man. He was in charge of our moderate crime investigation office, but he rarely had a brilliant idea. Well, not as brilliant as mine. 'Caspy?'

'The plan. Yes... hmm... the plan. Well, all the records are at the Court House. We, that is myself, Holly and your good self, Fabian, need to pay a visit to the records library and retrieve all warrants and orders signed by yours truly, the magistrate, there.' I pointed to Orpheus Fry who now appeared completely drained.

'Ah Caspy, the Courts are closed, matey. It's half the hour past nine.'

'I know.'

'So there won't be anyone there to aid us.'

'I know.'

'I see. I think I understand. You want us to break into the law courts.'

'Exactly.'

'Clever.'

I always struggled to understand if the man was serious, attempting sarcasm or satire... or, dare I suggest, stupid.

'Had you gentlemen forgotten the courthouse is still under construction?' Holly offered casually.

'Oh, you're right, Hol'.'

'O' course I'm right.'

I too had forgotten. The old courthouse built back in '24, on the corner of Macquarie and Murray Streets, had been demolished and the new building was under construction. It was still months away from opening its doors.'

'Bugger! Now what?'

'Well, where are the records kept in the meantime?'

'It'd make sense to me,' Holly piped up, 'that in the meantime, the old bugger had kept 'is warrants and other records in 'is own office.'

Fabian and I looked at each other, as if we had just experienced an epiphany. And maybe we had. 'By golly, Holly. I think you are right,' I said.

Fabian said, 'Makes sense.'

We left before the landlady recovered. The barmaid had been mostly understanding. This was serious police business; it was just the manner in which we conducted ourselves that bothered her.

Fabian groaned as we curled up collars, buttoned up jackets and pulled hats low from the chilly winter mist, roaming the streets like the unsettled crew off a wrecked ship looking for trouble.

'As if we 'aven't enough on our plates,' Fabian muttered. 'We have another bloody killin' to solve.'

'Worry not, good sir,' I said full of cheer. 'But I am confident I can solve tonight's unfortunate turn of events without too much effort.'

'Oh, and how's that, Caspy?'

This time I sensed a hint of sarcasm.

'I will keep you informed,' I said. 'Tomorrow, after I have sent a telegraphic message to Launceston.'

We were fortunate to manage to find a hansom cab returning from delivering a drunken sea captain from Sullivans Cove to his home at Runnymede at the base of the Domain Hill. Although the short trip was painfully slow due to the icy conditions, we three were comfortable behind wood, leather and glass.

We alighted at the Sailor's Delight Tavern on the corner of Despard Street and Murray Street, near Waterman's Dock, where a welcoming lantern over the front door invited us in for warmth and sustenance. We had not eaten since noon and were famished. Besides, it was too early for our nefarious plan and a little Dutch courage would not go astray. Magistrate Orpheus Fry's office was back towards the township two streets, on the corner of Murray and Macquarie Streets, third building in, diagonally over the crossroads from the new courthouse being erected. Unfortunately, a guard sentry box was situated on that very corner for a night watchman. However, we had no choice but to strike this night, as once the word was out that the magistrate was dead, his staff would be sorting through the records immediately.

With the kitchen closing, we were grateful for a platter of cold mutton – in fairness, it was still warm – with boiled potatoes, heavy rye bread and a lump of Gouda cheese scented with caraway seeds, purchased by the innkeeper from a visiting Dutchie. We were ravenous and relished the food.

'What's the plan then, Caspy?' Fabian searched for answers over the creamy froth spilling from his quart of porter. He smacked his lips noisily. I was familiar with Fry's office, having been in there six months earlier on other business.

'Fry's office is the main room, first on the left on entering the building. There is a small reception area, then the office. I would wager a bet that the files would be stored in his own office, especially files that are falsified, like we know Nathaniel Billings's are.'

Holly joined us with three whiskey chasers. ''ere we go, Fabian sar, Caspian sar, this'll warm yer cockles.' She sat heavily and tossed the whiskey back with a sudden jerk of the head, sighed deeply and sucked the head off her porter. 'What's my post then?' Holly asked.

'We have a nightwatchman in a sentry box diagonally across the street, outside the courthouse,' I answered, drawing an imaginary crossroads in spilt swill on the table and jabbing a finger to one corner. 'Your responsibility will be to entertain that watchman while Fabian and I find the file.'

'Break and enter yer mean?' Fabian redefined.

'Under the circumstances I would rather call it a retrieval mission,' I said quietly.

Holly shuffled anxiously, the way she always did when she was, well... anxious. 'Caspian, sar.'

'Holly.'

'How do you suggest I... ah... entertain this 'ere watchman. I 'ope yer aren't suggestin' anything... well... ah, dishonourable to my reputation.'

'No Holly, absolutely not, unless you call getting the watchman the worse for drink, dishonourable.'

Holly grinned. 'My kinda post, sar,' and she tapped the side of her nose with a cheeky finger.

'Now, here is a half guinea, Holly,' I said, pushing a well-worn gold coin stamped with George IV's head, through a puddle of ale. 'That will purchase you a square rigger,' I said, of the tall AVH Geneva Gin with its maritime sobriquet. 'I suggest you get a head start on that watchman. Keep an eye out for Fabian and me and detain the guard. Be certain he has his back turned against us.'

'How will I know it's you, sar?'

'Jaysuz, Hol',' Fabian said. 'It's brass monkeys out there. There's no other bastards mad enough to be wanderin' about in this weather.'

'Got yer. I'll be off then.'

'Good luck.'

The sentry box was placed well back from the edge of the road, next to a tall picket fence that totally surrounded the new courthouse-building site, to keep out riffraff. As Holly approached, the guard was nowhere to be seen and the interior of the sentry box dark as porter. With the gin nestled securely under her arm, hands buried deep in her coat pockets, collar up, hat low, head down, Holly crossed the icy street toward the guard and began to sing a shanty. Whether it was the fact she was a little nervous, encumbered by extra winter clothing, affected by two quarts of porter and four whiskeys, or her hobnail boots were no match against black ice – halfway through the shanty *Haul Away Joe,* Holly's feet flew out from beneath her and she landed heavily on her backside. 'Firk!'

The bear in its cave stirred. 'Yer right there, matey?' the sentry appeared from the blackness within and came to Holly's aid. He was Holly's age and a large man in all respects. Holly's first thought was, *Christ how did he fit in that sentry box?*

'Aye,' Holly looked up at the advancing *bear*. 'Jus' slipped on the firkin' ice, thart be all.'

Immediately, enough of Holly was exposed in the lamplight to identify her as a member of the fairer sex. 'Ah! Yer a woman.'

'Well I were the last time I looked.' Suddenly Holly felt she would not have to act the drunk, for she now felt the effects of her rushed repast. ''elp me up, fer Christ sake.' Holly proffered her hand. The nightwatchman chuckled, clamping Holly's hand in his, and tugged. Holly lifted two inches and fell back pulling the hapless guard on top of her, where he landed like a lump of lard and started laughing, close enough for Holly to whiff onions and rum on his breath.

So that's what he was doin' in the sentry box, tryin' to keep warm with a rum.

'Phew,' he cackled. 'My apologies, love. The road ain't half slippery eh?'

'Yeh, well it threw me on *my* arse.' Holly passed the man the Geneva. ''ere, 'ang onto this.'

Remembering her grandmother's advice, should she ever be stuck in a bathtub, Holly rolled over onto her hands and knees and finally stood, legs spread for balance, like some novice ice skater. 'Now give us your hand and don't drop the bottle.'

How Holly managed to assist the fifteen-stone watchman back onto his feet was a miracle; however moments later, the two were back at the sentry box.

'Holly Smith,' Holly introduced herself, lying about her surname.

'Jack Drummond.' Jack had a pleasant jolly and round face without beard or moustache but several days' growth of bristle. Although a man of large proportions, he had the height to balance his figure; *bit like Goliath*, Holly fancied.

'What yer doin' out on a night like tonight any'ow?' Jack asked.

'Got in late from D'Entrecasteaux. Sawyer's camp cook, see. We got becalmed down river an' never thought we'd make it in until this southerly picked up.'

Holly alluded to the cutting breeze edging over the dip in Murray Street, fresh off the harbour, stalking the night like some amphibious sea serpent.

Jack looked somewhat vague. 'Ah... yeh. All right then, 'ere's yer gin.' He made to pass the Geneva to Holly when she suggested, 'Fancy a wee nip before I head on?'

'Aye... yeh... why not,' Jack backed into his sentry box like a hermit crab might return home to its shell. 'Shove in a bit pet, get outa the cold. It ain't much but yer outa the wind.'

Holly shoved in beside the man and there could not possibly be a tighter fit. At least, Holly thought to herself, it was too bloody cold and too bloody cramped for the man to harbour any ideas of hanky-panky. Besides, as it was, they would have to lift the gin bottle out through the door opening so as to bend an elbow to bring the gin to their lips.

Holly took first swig, wiping her mouth on her sleeve and shuffling the bottle for Jack to take hold.

'So how long have yer been doing this... this nightwatchman lark?' Holly asked, watching Jack's arm stretched out into the night before arcing into position to level the bottle to his lips. He took a generous swallow, sighed appreciatively and stared at the buildings across the street like a watchdog in a kennel.

'How long have I been doin' this lark? Near on a year now.'

'Got yer pardon?'

'Aye. Got done fer burglary in Kent. That be back in '46. Done a stint in Port Arthur for stealing grog on me first ticket. Been a good lad since, an' here I am. It's all beer and skittles in 'ere, love.'

Jack's second imbibe was a hefty guzzle.

Jesus, Holly thought, *the man wants a shoulder to cry on and to get maudlin drunk.*

'Where is she?' Fabian hissed in the dark. I couldn't see anything either, for the sentry box's opening was facing away from the nearest street lamp. This was frustrating our plan, plan A. And we certainly did not have the luxury of plan B.

'She's there somewhere,' I whispered, feeling extremely vulnerable, standing on the doorstep to the Magistrate's office fumbling through my pockets with frozen fingers, searching for my set of skeleton keys. 'Holly would never let us down.'

'Aye,' Fabian was less confident. 'But she does have a bottle o' Geneva with her, an' yer know how much she loves that Dutchie drink.'

This, I had to concede. The lass *was* fond of a tipple.

Back at the sentry box, Holly had had a twenty-minute head start on us, and the Geneva, straight from the bottle, was taking effect rapidly. Large-portioned Jack, the nightwatchman, was also making the most of the situation; bottle of gin, female company and snug sentry box; what was there not to love about tonight's post. Unfortunately for Holly, Jack being a large man, meant that he could handle neat spirits better than she.

'Yer say yer a cook,' he asked Holly, handing her back the gin. Holly's eyes crossed over locating the bottle in the murky shadows. She raised two hands awkwardly before her, elbows pressed into her stomach, so as to grip the bottle and not drop it.

'Aye, an' a bloody gooden' too,' Holly boasted as she belched, feeling a rumbling as something shifted in her belly. *The cold mutton, maybe.*

'What's that?'

'Me guts.'

'No, I thought I seen somethin' loiterin' in the shadows.' Jack nodded across the street to the adjacent corner.

It took Holly a moment to realise Jack could have seen Fabian and myself.

'I thought I seen somethin' over there.' Jack shuffled but Holly had him well and truly wedged in.

'Got a pipe, Jack?' Holly interrupted the man, who couldn't even manoeuvre his arm behind himself to grab his Brown Bess musket, let alone exit to investigate.

'Got a wha'?'

'A pipe. Do yer not smoke, Jack?'

'Oh, aye.'

I found the keys and, feeling about in the darkness, I managed to slip it into the keyhole.

'Ah, there they are!' Fabian drew my attention to the sentry box that suddenly blossomed with the flame light of a match. 'Holly's in the box with the night watchman.' As we daren't move a muscle we watched on, the two faces profiled, one unmistakably Holly's. 'They look a mite cosy, eh?'

'I have to agree.'

The match burnt itself out, but a glow of kindling pipe tobacco framed their faces fire-red for a moment, as the night about the sentry box was stippled with sparks.

Click!

'We are in,' I sighed with relief. We stepped inside the office reception, closing the door behind us, and not too soon either. Holly told us later she was watching us out of the corner of her eye the instant we entered, and the watchman looked back towards us.

Being familiar with the layout, I felt my way in the dark; helpfully, some vague lamplight filtered into the magistrate's office on the Macquarie Street side. We found the filing cabinet, locked. A second, cabinet-style skeleton key soon had it open.

'Adams... Ahearn... Andrews,' I whispered aloud, sorting through the alphabet, holding each file on an angle to the faint light. It was a good thing I had excellent eyesight. 'Christopher...' I had jumped into the 'C's. 'I've gone too far... Chong. Chong! He has a file on Chong here.'

Fabian kept an eye out the window. 'Interestin'. Now can I ask yer to make haste, Caspy.'

I studied He Chong's file, but besides the name in bold writing at the top of the file, the document was difficult to study at this minute. I folded and pocketed it.

'Barley... Billings... Ha! Excellent. I've found it.'

'Brilliant. Now hurry lad. Let's get the hell out of here.'

I inspected the file. It was the warrant against Nathaniel Billings, all right. 'Yet to be lodged officially,' I whispered. 'What were they waiting for?'

'Who cares? Let's go.'

Across the street in the sentry box, Holly felt boiled potatoes and fatty mutton change partners for the final dance with macerated Gouda and mulishly bread, to the lively tune of excessive stomach rumbles. Jack passed Holly the gin and she managed to tip a measure down her throat, all the while attempting a semi-focussed eye out for activity over yonder. This was all very well, but Jack was a seasoned drinker and for him, the fun was just beginning. Holly felt the sentry box spinning. It was fortunate she was wedged in, otherwise she felt she would crash to the roadside.

Fabian and I covered our tracks, stepped out onto the front steps and back into the cold dark night. With my back to the street, I carefully relocked the front door, when I heard a yell.

'Who goes there?' It was Jack, the watchman. I turned in time to see him struggling to free himself from his tight tryst. 'Who goes there I say?'

Holly also struggled to keep the man where he was until she could plan her own escape. Jack managed one leg out of the box and into the night. He twisted about, wriggling, and reached for his musket. Holly threw her arms about the man.

'Give us a kiss,' she slurred, puckering her lips over theatrically.

'A wha'?' Jack reeled backwards, horrified.

'I said give us a kiss you big brute...'

Holly retched.

Jack's body popped from the sentry box like a champagne cork. Immediately, his feet went from under him on the ice. At first it was as though he was working the tread wheel at Port Arthur. There was no traction. Holly made an attempt to vacate her stomach in a ladylike manner, but Holly was no lady. Jack succumbed to gravity, crashing heavily to the roadside. Holly herself slipped, arms flailing for balance while releasing the remnants of dinner and drinks in a wide arc, screaming *Ralph*.

By the time Jack gathered himself together, Fabian and I were long gone. We positioned ourselves to keep a sharp eye on Holly, whom we watched stagger back down Murray Street, before intercepting her and ushering her to my cottage on Battery Hill. Holly had lost her usual joviality. She was white as the approaching mist from up river. Her eyes were red and she shook uncontrollably. We tucked her into my bed and placed my piss pot where she could hopefully see it, should she be ill.

Back in the kitchen, Fabian shook his head. 'Geneva, huh! Have trouble with the stuff meself.'

My watch read ten minutes past eleven.

'We've done well today,' I said. 'And Billings will be thrilled.'

'Whatya got to drink?' Fabian asked, looking about the kitchen.

Haven't you had enough, I wanted to say, but said, 'Green Fairy!'

'Christ, no!'

Of course, I did not have any absinthe and doubted I would ever drink the beverage again myself, after the Keg an' Cutlass kerfuffle. Fabian looked in the cupboard.

'No porter... ah ha... what's this?' he freed up a stone bottle.

'Brandy.' I threw my jacket over the back of my chair, retrieving the files from my pocket. Fabian poured two brandies and took a draught of his. 'Jaysuz, Caspy, my grandmother wouldn't use this shite in 'er Christmas pudding.'

'Yes I agree; it is a little... ah...'

'Cheap!'

'Well it was being sold at a reduced price.'

'Well, there yer go, lad. I bid yer good night. See yer on the morrow.'

I bid Fabian farewell at the door. 'And I advise you to walk by the battery and not down the Kelly's Steps, where I was accosted the other night.'

After Fabian left me in peace, I made certain all doors and windows were locked and prepared myself a bed on the flagstones in front of the smouldering coals of the fuel oven, where I studied He Chong's file. Another Chinese name was mentioned – Klaw Hong – and I wondered what else this magistrate had known. I made a mental note to use the overland telegraph wire communication to contact the Launceston police office on the morrow...

And crashed into a heavy slumber.

Chapter Fourteen

I walked through St David's Cemetery opposite St Mary's Hospital in Macquarie Street. It was that short period between afternoon and dusk. Twilight, one might say. I was alone, alone with my thoughts, my mind struggling to shift all the pieces into position. Someone, I convinced myself, was behind this vampire game of death.

'Good day to yer, squire.'

'Hell's Blood!' I gasped, stopping abruptly beside a family vault. I had not seen the young tyke perched on top of the stone vault. He was about ten years old, scruffy, yet dressed reasonably and wearing boots and a straw boater. 'You scared the devil out of me, lad.'

'That probably be a good thing squire.'

I looked about. We were alone. The cemetery was swiftly losing the last vestige of twilight and we seemed awash with a surreal redness, as if a distant bushfire masked the horizon west.

'What are you doing here?' I asked.

'Watching you, Caspian Hunter.'

'C-Caspian! You know my name?'

'Course. Everyone knows you in Hobart Town.'

I was flattered, yet I hoped this was not true, after all, I needed some anonymity in my business.

'Where are your parents?' I looked about, but we were definitely alone.

'Passed, squire.'

'Oh, I am sorry to hear that.'

'That's all right. Me mum, Bernice, and me dad, Henry Cage. They've been dead some years now.'

'Oh.' I was lost for words.

'Drowned at sea, squire.'

I was beginning to feel uneasy. Did the lad want money? 'What is your name?'

'Timmy.'

'Well Timmy, who looks after you?'

'I do. I live around here.' I fished my purse free. 'Oh I don't want your money, Caspian. Thank you. It's nice to just talk to you. I see you here a lot.'

'Oh, I've never seen you before.'

'Yeh... well. I keep to me self mostly.'

'You should present yourself at Ragged School in Wapping,' I suggested. 'Get an education. They will clothe and feed you, as well.' Although the lad looked well fed and clothed.

'Thank you. I might just do that.' Timmy looked seriously interested.

'All right then Timmy. I must be on my way.'

'Be seeing you then.' I made to walk on. 'Oh Caspian, don't mind if I call you Caspian, do you?'

'Not at all.'

'I just wanted to ask ... well, would you stop by and say hello more often, when you're walking through like.'

'Yes of course, if you are here.'

'Thank you. I'd like that.'

I walked on, feeling quite disturbed. A lad that young all alone, and in the cemetery. Surely, he could find a more pleasant place to sleep. *Timmy*, I mulled over and over. *Timmy* who? I didn't ask. I twisted about. 'Timmy who? What's your family name?'

Timmy stared back vaguely. He seemed to stare through me. His face turned the colour of the vault. His eyes rolled back exposing white orbs. His mouth opened wide with blood red lips and I saw sharp canine teeth. They dripped blood. I heard a guttural growl and Timmy leapt from the vault, flying towards me...

I screamed like a banshee.

'Jaysus! Caspian, sar!'

I woke to see Holly standing over me, nudging me awake with her boot.

'H-Holly! What...?' then I remembered. She had slept in my bed and I was on the flagstones before the stove. I had kicked my blankets free and sweated profusely in only my undergarments.

'You was havin' a bad one, then.'

'Bad one?'

'Dream, nightmare, whatever yer wanna call it.' She smacked parched lips. 'Where's the water pitcher, then?'

Hobart Town's telegraph communication was connected to Launceston and opened one year earlier in Morrison Street on the waterfront. What a wondrous time we live in, I thought, as we returned on foot towards the prisoner barracks.

'Hopefully, I will have an answer to my enquiry in two or three hours,' I told Holly. Feeling pleased with myself, I suggested we celebrate by partaking of a hearty breakfast at Mrs Adkins Tea Rooms in Collins Street before taking up our posts. Holly, who had managed a wash in my basin, had improved her humours somewhat. She pulled her purse from her pocket but it did not exactly jingle with coin.

'My treat, Holly.'

Holly stood gaping in the window at the pies, pastries and sweet treats and was hardly subtle. She moved her weight from foot to foot, salivating, and I am certain I heard her stomach groan. 'By golly, Caspian sar,' she said, her eyes downgraded from red to a pink. 'I'll take yer up on that offer, by Christ I will. I'm so hungry I could eat the...'

'Yes Holly,' I interrupted as two society ladies swept by me and in through the door I had propped opened for Holly. 'After you.'

I managed a Cornish pasty and a bacon pastry while Holly devoured three of the Cornish miner's tiddy oggies, as they called them. We shared a large pot of Darjeeling tea, from Northern India, Mrs Adkins informed me, drunk with creamy milk and spoonfuls of sugar. 'And fresh out of the oven, Chelsea buns,' Mrs Adkins insisted we have one of the cinnamon, lemon rind and mixed spice buns each, with her compliments.

Holly and I were intercepted by Jasper on our trek uphill towards the prisoner barracks. 'Doctor Crawley wants you at the morgue, Caspian sar.' He was breathing heavily after his search to find us.

'Oh really?'

'Aye. 'e be pokin' and proddin' the dead magistrate and he has a theory, nay... not a theory. 'e reckons 'e *knows*... yes, knows the vampire killer.'

The Morgue, St Mary's Hospital

Formaldehyde, congealed blood, rotting flesh and other seepages from human corpses are not the type of after dinner 'cigar and brandy' one wants to inhale after a delicious repast. The cellar morgue was as gloomy as usual – dank, damp and particularly cold this day. Probably a good thing, as the cold weather discouraged the fat flies full of their eggs that were such a feature here in the colonies. Orpheus Fry lay on the stone mortician's slab, looking paler than when I last saw him, even with the warm light from the oil-fuelled lanterns in their wall sconces that made the place look more like a medieval dungeon. His face was waxy white and his body had been sponged with spirits. There were no signs of blood, which accentuated the two, neat, deep, purple puncture marks in his neck. I noted two other dead Hobartians awaiting the mortician's attention, both on stretchers on the floor. But there was no sign of the eccentric, elderly Doctor Crawley.

I stepped over to the corpse, all the better to study the fatal chopstick stab wounds. It had taken a minute or two, but I became used to the foul odours. As my eyes adjusted to the poor light, I leant over the dead magistrate and the pale, grey face of the young boy Timmy, in my nightmare, came back to me.

'What was your game then, what were you up to?' I whispered into the cadaverous ear. 'I'll find the truth,' I muttered, carefully inspecting the neck. 'I'll figure it...'

'Boo!'

I must have jumped two feet. 'Jesus Christ! Doctor Crawley you...'

'You should have seen your face, Mr Hunter,' Crawley threw his head back in uncontrolled laughter. 'You nearly had an accident in your britches.'

The morgue always bothered me and now this. But the doctor thought it was a great joke. I nearly said, *at seventy-one don't you think that was somewhat immature?*

'You frightened me, sir,' I said in an attempt to save face.

He turned an ear in my direction. 'What was that?'

'You frightened me, sir.'

'Excellent. You've crept up on me often enough.'

Truth was, I never *crept* up on the man; it was only because he suffered an acute hearing loss that I managed to surprise him. Doctor Crawley dropped a cheesecloth with something greasy poking from it onto the slab next to the magistrate. He wiped grease from around his mouth and swabbed his hands with a mortician's rag.

'So why were you having a wee tête à tête with the magistrate here?' he pointed to Fry.

'What... oh... a tête à tête. Was I?'

'If you weren't talking to the dead, then I don't know what you were up to.'

A sudden flare of flame in the lanterns startled me as methane from the corpses rose up the stairwell. This bothered me. I do not know why, I was used to this morgue and its eccentric tenanted doctor, but today seemed different.

'Can we get on with it, Doctor Crawley?'

'On with what?'

'You asked me here, sir,' I said impatiently.

'I asked you here?' He screwed up his face, bunching his lips a moment. 'I asked you... oh yes.' Instantly, he remembered and his face lit up like someone had given him a bottle of Napoleon's personal cellar cognac for his birthday. 'Vampires!' he said aloud, and stood his six-foot-two scrawny body erect, with hands out like claws to make his point. 'Vampires, Mr Hunter. I know who or what your vampire is.'

Not expecting a sensible answer, I said. 'Excellent,'

'What was that?'

'I said, excellent.' I waited. 'And?'

Doctor Crawley took in a deep breath, pushed out his chest and hooked his thumbs through his braces. 'Your vampire, sir, is no less than the Tasmanian hyena!'

'The striped tiger!'

'What?'

'The striped tiger, Tasmanian Hyena.'

'That's what I said. Call it what you want, striped wolf, dog-faced dasyurus, zebra wolf... why, I've even heard it called the dog-headed possum.'

'Well,' I puffed out my cheeks. 'I knew it was not a vampire.'

'I should hope so.'

'And do we have proof?'

'What?'

'Proof... doctor?'

'Well I took it upon myself to have a chinwag with that hunter fellow that found the first victim, what's his name... ah...'

'The victim?'

'No... the hunter.'

'Oh, Hester James.'

'Hester James! That's him. Nice fellow. I purchased that duck from him.' And Crawley poked a finger at the greasy parcel he had brought with him. 'Delicious,' Crawley was vague in the land of gourmands temporarily. 'Matron cooked it the way the frogs do it, confit she called it. Cooked the bird in its own fat. Sounds awful I know, but I've got to tell you, Mr Hunter, it is superb.' He picked up a leg and chomped down on the meat like he'd missed dinner and breakfast.

'Doctor Crawley...'

'Here, try some,' he said through greasy lips, shoving the oily limb towards me.

'Ah,' I stepped back. 'No, thank you. Hester James, doctor.'

'Ah yes, where was I? Hester, whom you informed me, sells his wares on the corner of Liverpool and Murray, and that is where I found him... I must thank you by the way...'

'Uh-hum.'

'Yes, quite. Hester was convinced the killer was some deranged person who drank human blood. Like a vampire, but not supernatural mind, an insane soul who is blood and bone like you and I, who should be locked up.'

'Yes. He told me that, too.'

'What?'

'Go on, sir,' I persisted.

'Well I would have none of it. I had my own suspicions, suspicions I tried to tell you some time ago, I might add.'

'The Tasmanian hyena.'

'Yes. You see, I measured the canine teeth indentations, and they are exactly the same distance apart on all victims. Three inches to be exact. There are also incisor marks, but these are far less obvious, and these are the same also.'

'So what has this to do with Hester James?'

'Well Hester gave me the name of a colleague, Horace Kelly.'

'The trapper who lost his wife.'

'That's him. Lives way up behind the mountain.'

I knew exactly where he meant. 'Collins Cap,' I said.

'Collin who?'

'Collins Cap doctor.'

'Yes. Well I managed to send him a message to contact me next time he was in town.' Crawley sucked the final morsel of meat from the bone and it came free with a slurp. He threw the bone into the amputation basket beneath the slab and gazed back into the cheesecloth. 'All gone,' he muttered with a crestfallen frown.

I was forced to give the man another reminder. 'Horace Kelly.'

'Ah yes, Horace Kelly. Well, I spoke to him this morning and he told me of a rogue tiger out there.'

'Rogue?' I repeated the word as if it were *vampire*. 'Are they not all rogues, doctor? Surely this dangerous beast is simply doing what Mother Nature intended.'

'What, kill people?'

'That is not what I meant, but...'

'No Mr Hunter. This animal is unique. A rogue in the sense that it is huge and a fearsome creature to behold, and the trapper, Horace Kelly, is convinced it has a taste for human blood. It must be silenced.'

'You mean destroyed?'

'Say what?'

'It must be killed.'

'Dead. Yes.'

'Horace Kelly, Doctor Crawley, did he happen to tell you if he was returning to the hills immediately? I need to speak to him, and sooner than later.'

'Yes, you do that.' Crawley lifted the greasy cheesecloth to be certain it was empty.

'Doctor Crawley,' I raised my voice.

'What?'

'Did Horace Kelly happen to mention if he was returning to the hills immediately, after you spoke with him?'

'Well, he told me he had to visit Mary Kelly's sister. Mary's his dead wife.'

'Yes.'

'He had some business with her. Said more than likely, he would stay the night with her and her husband and then head back to the hills.'

'Did he by chance say where his wife's sister lived?'

'Well, yes, her husband is Captain Rogers in charge of the semaphore on Mount Nelson.' Crawley's face mellowed as if he had had a fond memory. 'Horace had two black swans in a sack that he was taking to her as a gift. Never tasted swan, have you?'

Later that day

It made sense, a wild tiger being the culprit, and I was determined to prove the trapper right. But why did I not simply have a bounty put on the animal's head instead of going after the damned thing myself, I hear you ask? Maybe it was the sense of adventure or some fool's errand to see this creature in the flesh, so to speak. Either way, I was on a mission. After a lengthy discussion, Fabian did not argue with my decision to accompany the trapper, Horace Kelly, and find this vampire tiger, as my colleagues started calling the animal. Besides, we were desperate to arrest Zachary Wolf and his cohorts before they committed whatever crime they were planning. Also, Samuel Groundwater was wanted for murdering Mrs O'Neil, and He Chong, the magistrate's killer, was still on the loose, although I had my own suspicions about him.

'Fill yer boots, lad, and good luck to yer.' Fabian gave me a slap on the back, fell into his chair and hoisted his boots onto his desk.

'Now,' I said. 'All I have to do is make contact with this Horace Kelly before he retires back to the bushlands.'

'Easy,' Fabian said out of the corner of his mouth as he focussed on lighting his pipe.

'Easy?'

'Aye. 'e be at Mount Nelson signal station is 'e not?'

'Yes.'

'Well, Caspy. You live on Battery Hill, go ask them soldiers there to flag the mount for yer. Message. *Is-Horace-Kelly-on-site?* Somethin' like that.'

'Brilliant. Why did I not think of that?'

'Do yer really wanna know?'

I ignored the comment and took to the stairs three at a time.

The men at the battery semaphore were most obliging and I indeed, had a return message instantly. *Yes. Horace Kelly was in situ and would await my arrival.* All I had to do was make the trip to the top of Mount Nelson, a southern foothill of the great Mount Wellington. I managed a buggy to the bottom of the mount, where I joined a supply cart taking provisions to the signal station.

Jeremiah Marlock, the cart driver, was only too glad of the company. 'Keep a sharp eye, Mr 'unter. There's villains about 'ere what would 'elp themselves to these 'ere vittles and other vitals what we're takin' to the semaphore.'

'Oh.' I looked about. There were a few people watching our progress but I sensed nothing untoward.

'Aye. When they abandoned Norfolk,' he said, speaking of the penal colony on Norfolk Island in the middle of the Pacific Ocean, 'most o' the buggers were sent 'ere to live, in an' around Sandy Bay and its environs. Villains and scoundrels, matey. So keep a sharp eye.'

On the climb we passed chain gangs working to build a quality road up and over Mount Nelson. 'It's goin' to continue on to Browns River, sar, this 'ere road. Be nice when it's finished, all smooth like and covered with gravel.'

I knew Mount Nelson joined Bonnet Hill, which lead down to the foreshore at Browns River. 'Browns River, eh?'

'Aye.'

I wondered whether Lynch Savage of the Sea o' Graves approved. I knew he enjoyed his isolation the way it was now. With thick bushland making an overland approach very difficult, it was really only approachable by water. Then again, it would increase his business ten-fold. I made a mental note to discuss it with Lynch on my next visit to his inn.

The ride was slow, passing by the road gangs, and I could not help it feel sorry for these devils. Being second offenders, they were chained together in groups of up to thirty men; all in leg irons and connected together by chains. Some recognised me as a lawman and their hatred was palpable.

'Stop yer gawkin',' the overseer, carrying a whip on the end of a pole, yelled at the men. As we passed by, twenty or so men hoisted a huge trimmed log onto their shoulders. The weight would have been tremendous and I noted the taller men took most of the load.

'Human centipedes, they's called,' Jeremiah told me. 'Dawn till dusk, poor bastards.'

I had to agree.

On the final approach to the signal station, up a gentle incline for the last mile, Jeremiah told me how there had been a semaphore here, in one state or another, since 1811. 'If'n a prisoner absconds from Port Arthur, they can flag a message to 'Obart Town within half the hour.'

'Really. Fascinating.' I wondered if this would be replaced by the modern telegraph line any time soon.

'The original three-arm semaphore was restrictive, sar, an' back in '38 they modified it to a six-arm system with a code book of three thousand signals and 999,999 possible settings. That's nearly a million, sar. A bloody million!'

He was totally awestruck but I had used the more modern communication of the telegraph and could only surmise that the telegraph was the future. I thought I would tell him so, when a man dressed in kangaroo skins with a large fur hat that resembled a skinned possum, wearing sheepskin moccasins and carrying a musket, appeared from behind a huge eucalyptus tree. Two great hunting dogs pulled at their leads.

'Whooa!' the driver pulled the cart to a halt as his horse whinnied and pawed the dirt. It was no wonder the horse was spooked; I could smell the man from where I was. Or was it the dogs?

'An' who might you be, sar?' Jeremiah questioned brusquely. 'Davey bloody Crockett?'

Damn, I thought, is this driver biting off more than he can chew? Immediately Jeremiah cackled a laugh, coughed and spat.

'Marlock, yer mangy prick,' came the answer. I felt my breast pocket to be certain my Yale double-barrel was on my person, but should have known better. My driver jumped from his seat and the two men exchanged a cheerful greeting. I relaxed. Finally the stranger looked up at me. 'You be Mr 'unter?'

'Aye... I mean yes... are you...'

'Horace Kelly, aye.'

We continued at walking pace. Jeremiah and the trapper caught up on old news. I remained vigilant. Two hundred yards further on, we pulled alongside the signal station, where a red coat soldier wearing a shako and with a bayonet fixed onto the muzzle of his Brown Bess brought us to a menacing halt. His captain, with his shirt-tail hanging loose from an overhanging gut, was directly behind the soldier.

'It's all right Maurice, 'tis friends not foe,' the captain said, full of cheer.

Maurice eyed me with suspicion, albeit briefly. He saluted his superior and disappeared back to his guardhouse.

'Jeremiah,' the captain greeted my driver. 'I trust you had no problems from those islanders back down the hill? Bloody thieving sods, what.'

'Nay, Walter. I had the fearsome Mr 'unter 'ere to ride shotgun, so ter speak.'

'Aha.' The captain studied me as I alighted. 'You're the man from the prisoner barracks, the man here to meet with Horace and help him avenge his wife's death. Caspian Hunter, if my memory serves me correctly.'

Help Horace avenge his wife's death? What mischief is this?

'Ah... well, yes and no... Captain.' I shook the captain's hand.

'Nice to make your acquaintance lad, my title is Captain Rogers, but call me Walter.'

'Thank you... Walter.'

'Novel use of our semaphore system, Caspian,' Walter said of my earlier communication from Battery Hill. 'And one way to hold this reprobate, my brother-in-law, Horace.' Walter slapped Horace on the back. 'Whom I see you've already met.'

The single storey brick and timber signal station with its shingled roof, I thought, looked a pleasantly comfortable lifestyle for those lucky enough to man its semaphore; away from all the hustle and bustle of the busy port of Sullivan's Cove. The harbour stood out prominently, off to the north. The view was exceptional; I felt that if I had a spyglass strong enough, I would be able to see all the way to Port Dalrymple, on the north coast of Van Diemen's Land. A sheltered porch, facing north, was shaded with a large awning. I counted five chimneys, extended taller than usual to allow the smoke escape freely.

'It blows like a bastard up here some days,' Walter assured me.

Positioned to make the most of the sun, an extensive vegetable garden was laid out to the east, surrounding the semaphore pylon. Several native trees, I noticed, also remained around the property.

'Wind breaks,' Walter informed me, noting my interest in the trees. 'Need the bloody things up here. Speaking of which, sea breeze's picking up. It'll be bloody freezing here in a minute.' Walter slapped his hands together and rubbed them vigorously.

'Come, let's go inside. It must be time for high tea,' he chuckled and his belly wobbled. 'Eh Horace? High tea, what?' And Walter thumped his brother-in-law on the back once more. I followed last, and became aware we had female company.

A short woman, whom I at first thought a child, crossed the garden towards the house carrying a basket of what looked like a cabbage, beetroots, potatoes and turnips.

We settled into the large dining room, set up like a mess, really. One long table, a dozen dining chairs and a fireplace loaded with burning logs. I was impressed. Life looked grand for these lucky folk. They even had their own cook, an ex-convict called Jonathon Tamworth. We sat at one end of the table and Jonathon brought in a tray of decanters, including a freshly opened bottle of Madeira wine and half a dozen cut glass wine glasses. 'Ah,' Walter smacked his lips in theatrical anticipation. 'High tea!'

Now I knew why the others were so keen on high tea. Jonathon – who, I realised, fitted in quite well with this lot, with his shaggy full beard, untrimmed moustache and ringletted head of unkempt hair – filled all the glasses to the brim and promptly sat to join us.

Ah, what a happy family they were.

Outside, the soldiers quickly unloaded the cart and the lady with the basket joined us. 'Abby, Abby darling,' Walter said of his wife, 'You've come to join us and meet our guest, lovely.' Abby was five foot and a quarter of an inch tall, I was told, without shoes. She had a dark complexion; dark eyes with black hair and was boisterous like her husband, with a reedy nervous laugh. Whether natural or not, a white-grey slash of hair swept through her black mane, reminding me of an illustration in a book I had seen, of a New England skunk.

'Abby Rogers,' Walter said loudly as if she stood in the next room. 'Meet Caspian Hunter, sleuth extraordinaire, so I am told.'

'Oh, did my reputation precede me?' I wanted to know.

'Sort of.' Walter had a sparkle in his eye. 'Jeremiah here gave me the heads up a moment ago.'

I wasn't aware I had told the driver that much about myself. While Abby placed the vegetables around the coals for baking, the Madeira flowed. The sun was now below the yardarm. Suddenly, I was aware of two things. Well, three things, actually. It was late, I wasn't certain how I was to return to the township and I was enjoying myself too much. What lovely folk, I thought.

Jonathon finally left us to check on the roasting black swans brought to the party by Horace the trapper and I had a moment at last to speak with Horace, who insisted we remain in the dining room, although I offered to talk with him in private.

'I wish to offer you my condolences, Horace, for the loss of your wife – from my colleagues also.'

'Aye, I thankee for it. 'Twas an awful death.' It certainly was; I had seen her body, but did not convey that information. Horace finished his Madeira and looked vaguely at the bottle a moment before reaching for the whiskey decanter. He filled his glass. 'She could be a whining old cow,' he started, 'but I miss her so.' Horace was a large, strong man who lived a rough and basic life, but now I saw vulnerability.

'Yes,' I said. 'It must be a lonely life out there.'

He said nothing, gave his two dogs lounging before the fire a good head scratch each, downed his whiskey and poured another, finally turning back to me. His face hardened.

'So tell me, Mr 'unter. Why exactly are yer here?'

I explained we had a criminal on the loose, who was perpetuating the vampire myth amongst the more ignorant and gullible of the township. He laughed, but not in humour, more in ridicule at how easily deceived were the unlettered.

'A vampire there is not, Mr 'unter. We both know thart. What we're dealin' with is far more scary.'

'Yes, well I have reason to believe it is a Tasmanian hyena.'

'Aye. There be no doubting thart. But it's a big bastard.'

Outside had grown dark and a sudden squall rushed up the mountain from off the estuary, rattling the window sashes. At the same moment heavy rain pummelled the roof and a clump of soot loosened, falling down the chimney and into the fire. Walter stabbed at the mess with the fire poker and the flames rekindled, casting an eerie glow across the room.

'I seen it twice, this 'ere striped hyena, an' it's a big bastard. A male. Normally, these animals kill for a meal, eat their fill and leave the remains for the black devils to finish off. They ain't known to return to a carcass. But I seen this bastard hangin' about, after he killed my Mary.'

It was a sobering thought. Like a murderer may return to the scene of the crime. 'Are you confident you can kill this animal, Horace.'

'Aye. I been lookin' for him ever since, and I'm certain I now know where 'is lair be, a few miles north-west o' me hut on Collin's Cap.'

'Then I would like to join you on the hunt,' I said.

Horace looked at me like I would be an encumbrance. 'I dunno 'bout thart.'

'I assure you, Horace, I am in better shape than I may appear.'

'I ain't accustomed to company, Mr 'unter, only me and Black Billy.' He read my mind. 'Black Billy be a half-caste, an aborigine and me father's accident.'

'He's Horace's half-brother,' Walter revealed.

'I would still like to join you. What do you say?'

'You take Mr Hunter with you Horace,' Abby Rogers said. 'You need all the help you can get. I want my sister avenged. Kill that damned beast and nail its hide to yer hut. It'll keep other hyenas away.'

Horace drained his glass and sucked in his lips. He turned back to the fire and spoke into the flames. 'Can yer use a gun?'

'Ah... well... well certainly. I am a lawman.'

'Aye. But can yer use a musket and shoot true.'

'Of course.' I swallowed.

'Cos your life might depend on it, Mr Lawman.'

'Then I *can* accompany you?'

'Aye. We leave at dawn.'

'D-dawn?'

'Do yer have a problem with thart? Will yer be wantin' a little sleep in?'

Quiet chuckles surrounded me.

'No. No, not at all. I was expecting to return to Town and prepare myself, meet you the following day maybe, up at your hut.'

I dare not tell the man I would like to enjoy a bath and dress suitably. Now I fancied I would be away for days and smell like the trapper himself.

'I have oil skins yer can borrow, I have a spare musket, powder and shot an' you'll be eatin' bush tucker like the rest us, savvy.'

'Savvy... I mean... fine.'

'Speaking of tucker,' Walter came alive. 'Jonathon,' he hollered down the passageway. 'How are those bloody swans?'

The swans looked amazing, pan roasted with onions, and the fresh vegetables fired on the coals were the perfect accompaniment. I was thinking it was a lot of food for six people, when Maurice and another guard, their wives, a gardener and a scullery maid joined the table.

'One big happy family,' I said, moving my chair along to make room.

'Oh, I'm glad you approve, sar,' Abby Rogers said. 'Cos Maurice there is me boy. Well, he's not a boy no more, he's all growed up.'

'He certainly is.' And I noted his wife was with bairn.

'I had an older son and all,' Abby continued, 'but he were killed five year ago.'

'Oh. Sorry to hear that.'

'He were a botanist, David, and he fell into a pit trap in which a bull had previously fell into. He was gored and horribly crushed.'

'Oh! I am so, so sorry madam.'

'Abby,' the woman corrected.

'Abby. That is awful.'

Walter heard this conversation and leant across whispering in my ear. 'Take no heed Caspian, my wife is delusional; David died of a snake bite.'

I had enjoyed myself immensely and the reason why I was even here had been sidestepped for joviality and camaraderie. We finished the meal with an egg and currant pudding. Jonathon had done himself proud. Sated, stifling yawns, the party ended as smartly as it had started. The clock chimed nine o'clock.

'Well, that's goodnight from me,' Walter stood and stretched. 'Come Abby, time for nigh-nighs. Jeremiah, you know where your usual bunk is, and Caspian...'

'Captain.'

'You can sleep on the chaise-longue by the fire. June will find you a spare blanket.' June being the scullery maid, smiled cheekily, looking up at me through large green eyes from a down-turned head. Cheeky minx, I think she fancied me. Or was that the wine playing tricks again? I too, stood and stretched, and swayed to starboard. I must have had more to drink than I thought.

Horace, I feared, had turned a little morose from the whiskey. I turned my back briefly to see if June was still about, and when I turned back, Horace and his dogs had vanished. 'No goodnight to you then?' I muttered to myself and was considering one more nightcap when June appeared with a blanket. 'Here you are, Mr 'unter. This'll keep yer nice an' cosy.'

'Thank you, June.' I was having lascivious thoughts and sought to make conversation. 'So tell me,' I said. 'Where's that Horace sleeping? Out in the yard curled up with his dogs, stinky and pong?' I snorted a laugh.

'No Hunter.'

I spun about. 'Ah!' Horace was directly behind me.

'Me an' me *boys* sleep in the guard's quarters. if'n yer must know.'

'Good night Mr 'unter,' June said, pink-faced, embarrassed on my behalf. And she left the room with Horace and his *boys* in tow.

Chapter Fifteen

I woke to the sound of a rooster directly outside the window. I was parched, desperate for water, and my bladder was in serious need of attention. I could smell bacon and heard cutlery scraping a plate. Horace was sitting at the far end of the table, eating alone. He heard me stir.

'Up yer get, 'unter. We've got a long trek ahead of us.'

I muttered a morning's greeting and found the kitchen unattended, where I drank greedily from a pitcher of water before making my way to the privy. I rattled the door handle. Locked.

'Be a minute or two yet.' I recognised Jeremiah's voice. *Bugger.* I was in dire need. I hurried behind the outhouse and unbuttoned my britches. My relief was enormous. I closed my eyes, tipped my head back and allowed the morning sun to wash across my face. My relief seemed inexhaustible. I groaned with pleasure. Suddenly, I heard a giggle. My eyes flew open. 'June!' She stood holding a bucket, while I stood aiming directly at her.

'Sorry Mr 'unter, I was just fetchin' water from the well and...'

I fumbled clumsily to secure my private parts, leaving nothing to the scullery maid's imagination, and promptly wet the front of my britches. She hurried inside. It appeared all I could ever manage with this young lass was to embarrass her.

Inside, I stood before the fire, hoping to dry myself with haste.

'Piss yerself, 'unter?' Horace observed, ever the astute trapper.

Walter entered the dining room full of cheer. 'Ah, Caspian. A good morning to you. Did you sleep well?'

'That I did, thank you.'

Abby followed and Walter gave his wife a slap on the bottom. 'So did we, eh pet.' The following chuckle was an unnecessary boast.

'Did them cats disturb you?' Abby asked me.

'Cats?'

'Aye. Native cats climb under the floorboards at night for shelter and scratch about. Sometimes they fight.'

'Yes. Noisy bastards,' Walter agreed.

'Then no, I heard nothing. Slept like a babe, thank you.'

So, it was with fond memories of the good captain and his eccentric *family* that I sat on the rear tray of Jeremiah's cart, my feet dangling just off the road, and watched the signal station shrink into the distance. Horace sat up front next to Jeremiah while I shared second class with the dogs. We were blessed with fine weather, albeit chilly at this altitude. Jeremiah left us a few miles further on, to descend back to civilisation – where he promised to notify Fabian at the barracks of my intentions – while Horace and I walked to his hut. A day's walk. Indeed, it was a good thing we had risen early and now, I fully realised, my life was truly in this wild trapper's hands.

Silent From The Shadows

Foothills behind Mount Wellington. The trapper's hut

The trapper's hut was more than I expected. Horace told me it was originally a one-room cabin of horizontal and vertical hand-hewn timber boards. My guess is, as his family grew, an annexed wing was attached to one end with an apex roof with gabled front. The roof was lined with sheets of bark. At the opposite end to the wing was a chimney that appeared one quarter the size of the dwelling. There was no glass in the windows; simple hinged shutters were installed to keep the warmth inside and allow in the light during the day. Two abandoned hogsheads, their lids removed and positioned one each end of the building, caught rainwater from off the roof. The chimney had a stone base and the smoke was led skywards through a chimney of timber, tapering towards its top. Frankly, the place looked a firetrap.

Uncleared tufts of mountain grass grew all about the dwelling, including a lavatory pit, housed in a smaller version of the homestead. It was leaning on such an angle, I feared it would topple any minute.

As I stood by, I watched one of Tasmania's large tarantula-looking spiders crawl under an eave and I dreaded what other indigenous creatures shared their abode.

The half-caste, Black Billy, who I believe had more of his mother in him than Horace's father, greeted us. Horace had been less than talkative the entire hike, but Billy was amicable enough, and now I started to realise Horace just wanted this sorry saga over with. Loose tongues in Hobart Town had pointed the finger at Horace as being responsible for his wife's death; which was a ridiculous notion. But the capture of this brute would clear any such suspicions.

We spent a sober yet restful night at the hut and kitted up early, before daybreak. Billy prepared a breakfast of damper, plum jam and black sweet tea. I was given spare oilskins, a musket that looked like it was used at Waterloo, powder and shot and limited supplies in a satchel – damper, cured meat and a tinderbox for making a fire. Billy packed other provisions for an overnight stay. Although the sun was rising lazily to the east, black clouds gathered and the horizon was a palette of pink. What did my mother always say, *pink sky at night, shepherds delight, pink sky in the morning, shepherd's warning*. With rains threatening, the black cockatoos came calling loudly down the gully.

'Noisy bastards,' Billy muttered.

'Are we sleeping out in this?' I asked Horace who was taking pleasure in my discomfort.

'Where we are headed there be caves, we'll shelter in one o' them.'

Fine.

The hunt was on.

I was beginning to wonder what on earth I was doing here. The landscape was desolate. A land as bleak, as miserable and as wild as one could imagine. I had heard stories of the highlands in Scotland in winter, but standing here with a blizzard approaching, I could only imagine that this was far more intimidating.

I was in the vicinity of Collins Cap northwest of Mount Wellington's pinnacle and a few hours hiking and climbing from the trapper's hut. Winter had well and truly arrived in the colony and nowhere was it felt more than up here, thousands of feet above sea level. I wore furs and oilskins with knee-high wool-lined boots and thick woollen gloves, yet still, I felt the cold. It sliced through me like a cheese knife. My thoughts went to Sir John Franklin, missing in the Arctic, missing now for eleven years – since 1847.

Until now, both men were comfortable in this environment. We had ventured several miles from the trapper's hut, where Horace told me he eked a living, hunting wallaby, kangaroo and the egg laying mammal, the platypus. Horace had eventually warmed to me enough to tell me of his horrific discovery, the morning he returned from the hunt, to find his Mary mauled. He knew immediately it was the work of the rogue tiger.

'I first seen the mongrel last summer. 'round 'ere it were.' He waved a hand across a barren landscape that could be on the moon for all I knew, and spoke quietly, his eyes alert.

'Biggest bastard I had ever seen, and these hyenas ain't exactly known for their size.'

We sat on boulders a moment to rest, and shared water from a leather bottle.

'So how will we catch our beast?' I asked. 'Hunt and shoot like you do the kangaroo?'

'No 'unter, it ain't thart simple.' Kelly clucked his tongue, as was his habit, and thought best how he could explain to me, a townsman, not accustomed to life in the bush. 'Yer can't poison 'em neither,' he said. 'You gotta snare 'em in traps.'

'I see. What about baiting with poison?'

'Nay. They is cunnin' bastards, cunnin' as can be. They knows when the meat is poisoned.'

'Not even if you poisoned a carcass already killed by other tigers?'

'Nay. They is wasteful bastards, too. They always kill in the same way.'

'Oh?'

'Aye. They near tear out the jugular vein, suck out the blood, and sometimes eat part of the shoulder. The rest they leave to the black devils, the scroungers.'

'They never come back to same kill,' Black Billy added. 'Wasteful buggers, them tigers.'

Kelly nodded. 'I'll tell yer a story what'll make yer hair stand on end.'

'Oh,' I took a strip of kangaroo jerky offered me by Billy. 'Please go on,' I said.

'I were in the old stringy bark forest some miles west o' here... about three year ago now. An' I was returning from a good day's 'untin', it was late afternoon, when I had this feeling I was being watched.'

'Watched?'

'Aye, stalked like. You must remember, I had a large bundle o' skins I were carryin' also. The smell o' death was all around me, not to forget I was sweatin' like a cart 'orse and the bugger would 'ave my scent as well. Anyways, I was still miles from me cabin and the sun was on the horizon and I thought, Jesus, I better move or I'll be stuck 'ere all night. Finally I heard somethin' in the bushes real close. I dropped me furs and spun about to face the biggest tiger I had ever seen. He just stood there, three paces away, staring me out with his yellow eyes, without a fear in the world. In fact it let out a guttural growl, threatenin' me, when *it* should be afraid.'

'It was definitely a tiger,' I said. 'Not a wild dog.'

Kelly sighed, irked at my doubt. 'Its huge yellow body was marked with a dozen or more stripes.'

I nodded knowingly, feeling a little foolish in the company of experts.

'Now, I've seen a few in me life, but this bastard was mean, real mean. He had a huge jaw salivating with fangs at the front, them same fangs what the folk in 'Obart Town thought were vampire teeth marks.'

'Are you suggesting this is the same animal that has taken three lives, of late?'

'Aye.'

'Clearly you did not kill the animal; what happened?'

'We stood lookin' at each other for what seemed ages. It was a standoff. Could you imagine that? The bloody thing wasn't a bit afraid. I feared that if I made a sudden move, it would attack. Clearly it were 'ungry. Eventually I thought, Jesus, yer can't stand 'ere all night. I loosened me twelve bore from off me shoulder but remembered it wasn't loaded. I thought, I'll hit the bastard with it, club it like. I took me eyes off the bugger for a second and when I looked back, it had gone. Vanished as quick an' as silent as it appeared. I hurried to where it stood but it had taken off. There was just this awful stink where it'd been.'

'What sort of smell?'

'A pungent, rotten carcass smell. They all stink like that. I've smelt it before.'

'You got home safely, then?'

'That I did, 'unter. Soon after, I reached the edge of the forest and hiked across the plain, just as darkness approached.'

Black Billy looked to the sky and then to Horace. 'We better get a move on; that's a blizzard headed our way.'

So how did I manage to find myself lost, you ask?

I really don't know how exactly. It all happened so quickly. So unexpectedly. I desperately needed to answer the call of nature and told my guides.

'Make haste, 'unter,' this storm ain't waitin' for no man. We need shelter.'

Fine.

Once I regained order, I ventured to the clearing where I had left my companions. At least it was where I *thought* I had left my companions. They were nowhere to be seen.

The blizzard thickened. I cried out for help. There was no answer. It was then I realised I was lost. I blundered on, thinking I had picked up their trail. I had not. I climbed on, aware that I was somewhere near the tiers we had discussed the night before. Now, a fog as dark as night descended and I could not see more than two paces before me. For the first time since I was shipwrecked on Tasman Island, I felt anxiety creep across me. I had heard of people, unprepared for such excursions, dying out here.

And I was unprepared.

Fighting panic, I looked for shelter as a freezing wind cut to the bone. It was some time before I found a tall narrow crevice between two cabin-sized boulders at the base of a cliff. It was tight, but I managed to squeeze into the space and was relieved to see it opened up into a small cave. By now, the snow was settling and I realised I would have to spend the night in the cave. I pushed in a safe distance and made myself as comfortable as possible, sitting with my back to the wall and hugging my knees. All I could do was sit the night out and pray that in the morning the sky would be clear.

Slowly circulation returned to my frozen hands and I remembered a tinderbox and a folded copy of last month's *Colonial Courier* in my inside coat pocket. Groping about in total darkness, I gathered kindling. Finally I managed a small flame when... I caught movement at the rear of the cave.

I froze.

A pair of eyes stared back at me. I daren't move. The fire and kindling took hold and the cave filled with light...

And there, staring me out, was my first sighting of a Tasmanian tiger. As large as it was, I had a sense it was a female. Now for the first time, with the blizzard raging outside,

I became aware of the putrid smell. The cave floor was littered with the bones of her prey. The animal stood glaring at me, panting, viscous saliva drooling from her fangs. Now I saw her cubs, two young tigers off to her side. Instantly, the trapper's advice came flooding back... *Never come between a tiger and her young.*

The word terrified is but a shadow of how I really felt. I was afraid to move. And if I were to leave, I would perish in the blizzard; there was no doubt in my mind about that. I lowered my eyes and looked away, staring into the flames hoping my actions did not appear threatening. Carefully, ever so subtly, I fed more bracken onto the fire, my reasoning being that the tiger, hopefully, was afraid of fire, and prepared myself for a long and unpleasant night.

It would be a fair assumption to say I did not sleep. Sometime, early in the morning I guessed, the storm had eased away and the snowflakes finally fell steadily. Outside was total silence. By first light, the snow had settled a foot high at the entrance. I was cramped, freezing and every bone ached. The tiger and her young had not moved either. Keeping my eye on her, I backed out through the narrow slit of an entrance that had protected me from the elements. The tiger watched me distrustfully. She took steps towards me, baring her teeth, snarling. Sensing my fear, she herself must have felt the victor of our most unusual encounter.

Outside, the wilderness was a picture of beauty. The sun was a rich golden orb on the horizon. My apprehension, my anxiety of being lost was replaced with gratitude. Gratitude for the fact that I lived to tell this most bizarre tale. Elated, I trudged east towards the sun, for I reasoned Hobart Town was in that direction. I recognised the base of cliffs, tiers I had passed the afternoon before. Within the hour, I saw smoke in the distance and marched towards it into a forest.

But as the forest came alive, I had this unnerving sense I was being followed. *Surely not*. Then I remembered stories Horace had told me about tigers stalking their prey. Was I prey all of a sudden? I sped up towards the smoke. Soon I was back amongst large boulders covered with lichen, which I recognised as the pinnacle of Mount Wellington. As I entered another clearing, I heard twigs snap underfoot; something approached. It grew closer and closer.

Then I saw it.

The huge tiger had circled to cut me off. It stood its ground between myself and the only possible way I could see to escape. It was not afraid; on the contrary, it seemed to be enjoying itself. We faced off for what seemed minutes. I lifted the musket to my shoulder and slowly, ever so slowly, backtracked. Instantly it let out a guttural growl and started towards me.

I aimed and fired.

The old Bess bucked, pounding the butt into my arm. The shot flattened against a rock. I had missed.

Preparing to club the attacking animal I lifted the musket over my head. The tiger closed in, jaws wide, teeth salivating. I made to swing my club. It leapt. I heard a deafening boom by my ear. I dived aside the moment the beast's head exploded. Landing heavily, the Tasmanian tiger was dead before it hit the dirt.

I lay where I fell, on my back, my pride more wounded than the bruises I could feel developing.

'Where the hell have you been?' Horace asked. Billy joined him and together they rolled the tiger over.

I looked at Horace Kelly the trapper for what seemed ages. I was speechless. 'Well?' he persisted.

And all I could say was, 'Thank you.'

Black Billy and Horace gutted and skinned the tiger there and then. I watched on, glad to be alive – and glad it was not me being flayed.

'Eh, boss,' Billy called to Horace after he inspected the contents of the animal's stomach. Horace looked on and nodded silently.

'What is it?' I asked.

Billy showed me what appeared to be an undigested human ear. I was encouraged to inspect it closer.

'Is that what I think it is?'

Billy splashed water on the chewed bloody gristle and sure enough, a gold earring appeared, pierced through the lobe.

'That's Mary's,' Billy said. 'Boss give them earrings to Mary, years ago.'

I looked over to Horace who had accepted his wife's fate. I watched as he busied himself cleaning the skin for transport. One had to admire these tough men of the bushlands for their resilience. Horace found what he was looking for, made minimal fuss, and turned the venture into an economic gain. He sensed I was watching him.

'So, Mr 'unter,' he said over his shoulder. 'Here it is at last. Here's your vampire.'

Prisoner Barracks, early afternoon

Anyone would have thought I had returned a war hero from Crimea.

'Come 'ere an' give ol' Richard a hug, sar.' Sergeant Richard Clincher waddled towards me at the prison entrance with a wide gait reminding me of a huge goose in a red uniform. 'Bless your woollen socks, Caspian 'unter. Me an' the lads are so proud o' yer.' He threw his arms about me. 'Warm me cockles yer did, caught the bloomin' vampire and come 'ome safe 'n sound.'

I was about to tell Clincher what really happened when I heard cheering and clapping emanating from the guardhouse. I looked through the window into the guard's mess to see half a dozen guards lined up near the fire.

'Arh, yes, the lads want to congratulate yer too, sar.'

They might want to wish me well, but they weren't too keen on leaving the warmth of the fire. I waved. They clapped harder. 'Come on in, sar, the lads want to…'

'Sorry Richard, but I'm needed urgently up in the office.'

'Urgent. Yes, sir.' He released me. 'We'll see you a little later no doubt.'

'That you will.'

'What was that all about Caspy?' Fabian wanted to know, as I entered the office. 'I heard cheering and carrying on. It wasn't for you, was it now?'

'No,' I lied. 'Not at all.'

'Mr Boyles at the *Gazette* wants to see you urgently,' Holly said, barging into the office behind me.

'Oh.'

'Aye. Urgent. An' 'e's not at all that happy.'

Lincoln was on Holly's ankles. 'Hate to tell yer this Caspian, but them lads downstairs are mighty disappointed yer didn't stop to take a bow, sar.'

Fabian. 'Bow?'

'Aye, Caspian 'ere is a hero, they're saying.'

'Christ!' I angered. 'Does no one say morning's greetings anymore?'

'Morning Caspian,' in unison.

Jasper and Billings filed in. 'Did we miss something?'

'No!' I shouted.'

'Bit touchy this mornin' ain't yer, Caspy?' Fabian said.

Jasper passed me a letter. 'This come for yer this mornin', Caspian sar, with the Royal Mail on this mornin's coach.'

'Oh.' I snatched the correspondence.

'From our northern brethren,' I said, pleased that they had finally answered my enquiry, albeit days late. 'I was expecting a telegram.'

'What is it, lad?' I held up a finger for silence while I read its contents. 'Well?'

'Yes!' I pumped the air.

'What is it?'

'He Chong, remember him?'

'The magistrate's Molly.'

'Yes. Well, as I suspected, he was the same Chinaman who stabbed another Coolie to death in Launceston some weeks past, when I was up there on the *man in the well* case.'

'Oh.'

'It seems our Magistrate, Orpheus Fry, had a fetish for young Chinese boys.'

'We gathered that.'

'You mean there was more than one?'

'At least one other; a rival by all appearances.' I went on to explain how I had been witness to a murder in Launceston, on the riverside, where a Chinese lad, same age as He Chong, was murdered with a chopstick. 'You see, it was too much of a coincidence. I mean, really, dead Chinaman, chopstick, it had to be the same killer, right? The lad's name was Klaw Hong and he, too, had succumbed to the sodomising Orpheus Fry on his visits to Launceston, when he travelled north as the visiting magistrate.'

'Are you saying they were all Mollys? The Chinese lads, too?'

'Not exactly. The young men were paid for these discreet dalliances. They were, for use of a better word, whores. Klaw was He's rival. The two apparently had made quite the name for themselves in the goldfields in Victoria, and a small fortune. But these young men also succumbed to the Chinaman's curse of gambling. It appears that when the magistrate heard of Klaw's murder, he threatened to blackmail He into a future of unwanted attention, under the threat of the hangman's rope.'

'Blackmail eh? How low's that?'

'Yes, indeed.'

'So where is He Chong now?'

I waved the letter. 'Fear not, he's behind bars in Launceston.'

'Well, I never.'

'Brilliant.'

'That's another crime we've solved,' Fabian grinned.

We? I shrugged inwardly.

Chapter Sixteen

Hobart Town Gazette Office. Elizabeth Street

'So, the wild bushman returns.' Editor Warren Boyles opened his office door and worked his fingers before my face like a talking hand puppet, in a mime of vocal newspaper headlines. 'Caspian Hunter, the vampire slayer of Hobart Town,' he grinned.

'Please spare me, sir,' I said, in mock annoyance and pushed by him to stand by a hot potbelly stove.

'Why the long face?' he asked.

'I thought you were vexed with me?' I answered, throwing my wet weather coat over a chair to dry.

'I was. You were supposed to have been here days ago. I have a commitment here, you know. Schedules to keep. My compositor has come down hard with the cold sickness and is confined to his bed, and I have one day remaining to distribute this week's *Gazette*. But, I am a forgiving old sod.'

'My apologies Mr Boyles... Warren.'

'Well, you're here now Caspian and I hear you caught, and killed, the said vampire, albeit, a Tasmanian hyena...'

'I didn't kill the damned thing.'

'What are they like up close? These hyenas?'

'I said, I did not kill it.'

'Oh? But it is dead is it not?'

'Yes. The damned thing nearly killed *me*.'

'That's not what the townsfolk are saying.'

'Well, they are wrong.'

Warren recognised my dejected demeanour. He bunched his lips in that intellectual decision-making grimace of his, and fixed me a stare over his pince-nez.

'All right. The kettles boiled, let's make tea and you can tell me all about it.'

With the *vampire* saga behind us, I launched into other business afoot. I explained how Zachary Wolf fitted into the picture and how he and his cohorts were still at large and a police priority. I told Warren how my suspicions were that Wolf and his gang were planning to rob the Bank of Van Diemen's Land, a brazen and ambitious endeavour indeed. But their plans were thwarted, in my opinion, when Samuel Groundwater's young lover, Lizzie, died from a backyard abortion, and Samuel murdered the abortionist, Mrs O'Neil, in retribution, only to bring the wrath of the law down on his head, whilst attracting attention to the gang.

The loose end that rattled me had been Samuel Groundwater's relationship with the two low-life's, James Dick and William Norton, who were out and about, the night the black caped stranger, who I was certain was Zachary Wolf, was seen acting suspiciously at the Van Diemen's Land Bank.

'You see, if it had not been for Billing's brother Nathaniel requiring my help, we would not have discovered those two scoundrels.'

Warren was all ears. 'Marvellous.'

'It also eventuated,' I continued, 'that the Italian victim in all this kerfuffle, Marco Stefano, was an acquaintance of

Constable Mortimer the night watchman, having drunk with him in the past, and was considered generous towards the policeman. – Stefano, the ever-popular drunken businessman with coin in his pocket, kept the likes of a night watchman, Constable Mortimer, on a remuneration of a few shillings per day.'

'A bribe?'

'Yes. Why wouldn't the constable take advantage?'

Warren's quill and inkpot were being overworked. He was now a happy editor with plenty of material and I had no doubt he would embellish the facts somewhat.

'And this Groundwater fellow, you have evidence that will stand up in court?'

'Oh yes.' I explained how we found evidence of the address being used for feticide in way of surgical instruments at 47 Sackville Street. 'Also we discovered a brass button embossed with a deer's head in the yard behind the property. This button had been torn from the jacket cuff Samuel Groundwater was wearing when I interviewed him at the slaughter yards where he worked. From what we could ascertain, Groundwater waited for Mrs O'Neil when she used the privy at nighttime, possibly late, before she retired for the night. He had attacked her and dragged her body out into the laneway at a later hour.'

'Oh.'

'At least that is my theory. I will confirm it when we catch the devil.'

Warren poked a small log into the stove and studied his notes. He was clearly pleased. Warren had already read my report on the Hartley affair, the man lost down the well. 'That page is complete. What else do you have for me?'

'Ever heard of a magistrate, Orpheus Fry?'

'Orpheus Fry... Orpheus Fry...' Warren scratched the side of his head. 'Can't say I have. But enlighten me.'

'Well, you will love this.'

'Good.' Warren's eyes stared into mine in anticipation, only taking them off me briefly to pick up his teacup. It was empty.

'Hold that thought,' he said suddenly and slid off his drafting stool, dropping to the floor. He fetched a decanter of whiskey and pulled the curtain across in front of the street window.

'Yardarm was passed hours ago,' he said with a cheeky chuckle, taking two tumblers from a cupboard. 'Whiskey?'

'Please.'

'Now.' He perched himself back on his stool. 'I hope this is scandalous, because god only knows I need some scandal if I want to keep up sales. I've had to print some drab stuff lately. Did I tell you about the sea leopard that was captured at Kangaroo Bluff?'

'Ah, no.'

'This fisherman caught a giant sea leopard, some twelve feet long, and weighing several hundred pounds. Then Bill Wood, a well-known vendor of cabbages and cauliflowers, purchased the huge beast from the fisherman. Roping it to a cart, he moistened it with seawater and fed it fish occasionally as he exhibited it about the town, charging one halfpenny or any other small coin. He even took it to Government House, where the governor and his wife were most impressed.'

'Fascinating,' I lied.

'Sorry, I digress.'

I continued. The story of the magistrate stabbed with a chopstick was too much for the editor. He laughed. Yes, he actually laughed. 'Why, even Charles Dickens couldn't write better fiction. A chopstick!'

He drank the remains of his whiskey and the stopper was removed from the decanter in one practised motion. He filled our glasses and checked his notes. 'You have been busy.'

'There is more.'

'I know there is, lad.' He shot me a mischievous wink.

'Oh,' I feigned surprise.

'Yes, Caspian Hunter. Who is this fiddler called Kathy?'

Ah Kathy, my beautiful seductress and Irish fiddler Kathy. I had not heard that name mentioned for some days now.

'Well then?' Warren insisted.

'How did you hear about... oh never mind. Hobart Town – small place, right?'

'You got that bit right.'

'I never did get her full name.'

'Where is she now, lad?'

'I honestly don't know. With her husband I assume.'

'H-husband... no?'

'That's another story.'

Attentively, Warren Boyles listened to my 'lost at sea' and 'rescue by the New Zealand whaler' stories. 'You never let the grass grow under your feet, do you, Caspian?

'I guess not.'

By the time I had brought Warren up to date it was early evening – the township quiet, the streets empty. Just the muffled sounds of laughter and joviality emanating from the nearby inns.

I stood, arching my back in a stretch. The night in the cave caused me aches and pains that would not have bothered me a few years back. Warren held my heavy wet weather coat high for me to slip my arms into its sleeves, when a soft voice called out from the compositor's room in the basement.

I said, 'Did I hear a voice?'

'Ah... oh... maybe.'

'Maybe?'

'Warren,' the voice grew closer. Suddenly the door to the cellar opened and a dark-haired woman, some years Warren's junior, slim and half a Wellington boot taller, poked her pretty face around the doorframe.

'Oh, pardon me. I thought your company had left,' she said, rather startled.

'Oh.' Warren pretended to be indifferent. 'Mr Hunter, this is Miss Wilson.'

Mr Hunter! Being a little formal, aren't we?

'Fanny.' The woman corrected, looking a little bug-eyed from hours spent compositing the *Gazette* in the light of a lantern. 'Call me Fanny; everyone does.'

'Caspian,' I said, voiding the editor's formality, and looked Warren in the eye. He blushed.

What? Warren, you old dog you.

He read my mind also, and grinned sheepishly.

'Please excuse me, Caspian, a moment,' Fanny said. 'But Warren, do you still want me to fit this advertisement on the back page, the one from the diocese?'

'Yes, please.' Warren had a thought. 'Show Caspian – he might get a smile out of it after the week he's had.' Fanny passed me the handwritten note.

WANTED; A Church of England Clergyman – for the township of Sorell, to bury the dead, as the present incumbent has been missing about a fortnight. Two bodies are now waiting burial.

Chapter Seventeen

Four days later. Late afternoon

No news was good news, or was it? Not a word of the whereabouts of the would-be bank robbers was forthcoming. Clearly, they had been spooked. But in the end, it was one the oldest of motives that brought the pathetic quartet undone. Revenge. Revenge is sweet. You see, Luella Mellow was infatuated with Zachary Wolf; she idolised the man. For one thing, she risked her own freedom by helping Zachary Wolf stage his own death at the Sea o' Graves. She was devoted to him. She was also a most attractive single woman with her own means, so why Zachary Wolf proposed marriage to Luella and then bedded Susan Charity, an ironmonger's daughter from Granton, is beyond me.

Evil drink, most likely.

Evil drink or not, the words upon a letter addressed to me at the barracks were music to my ears. This forewarning of his whereabouts waited for me at the gatehouse when I arrived back at the prisoner barracks late one afternoon. Sergeant Richard Clincher was in poor spirits this day, with his gout arresting his good humour.

'You've correspondence inside, sar,' Clincher said, closing the iron prison gate behind us, keen to warm his aching bones back before the guardhouse fire. He passed me the folded letter, sealed with a blob of obscure red wax. There was no identification within the seal.

'Delivered by some scruffy, confident little tyke what called 'imself Mr Swift.'

'Little tyke?' I said. 'Mr Swift?'

'Aye. Cheeky sod an' all. 'bout ten years old. Stood right there where you're standin', and asked fer sixpence fer deliverin' the note an' all. I told 'im ter sod off.'

Dear Mr Hunter,

The man you seek, Zachary Wolf, resides, for now at 49 Molle Street, lodging in an attic room. Beware. He is a dangerous man.
Your most humble servant,
Signed,
One who knows

I sent Billings to notify Fabian, who I knew had retired early to the Good Woman Inn, while Jasper fetched Holly and Lincoln from the guard's mess.

'Tonight's the night,' I said. I could almost taste victory. Already the shrinking sun threatened us with darkness. It would be a moonless night with thick winter cloud gathering over the mountain. 'We will strike within the hour.'

We shared a last round of hot coffee and checked our weapons, while Fabian enquired at the officers' mess, where he spoke to Captain Taylor who was on duty.

'There are four guards what can be spared,' he informed us. 'That makes our party ten. We don't want to be undermanned on this one Caspy, eh?'

I nodded. *Sometimes I felt Fabian thought it was he who ran this show.*

Jasper, I discovered, was still struggling with the discovery that the Tasmanian hyena was the sole *vampire*. He still held the notion that an undead fiend was stalking out there in the night. Jasper and I have been colleagues near on three years now and I have grown fond of the lad. I am accustomed to the nuances of his gullibility. Ever since the first *attack* victim was found in the Mount Wellington foothills, Jasper has been cogitating over vampires and their blood-sucking ways.

'Vampires can't have their photographic portraits made, can they Caspian, sar?'

'No, I believe I have read that somewhere too, Jasper. But Jasper, there is no such thing as...'

'And babies born with teeth at Christmas time, they turn into vampires too, don't they?'

'Oh, I had not heard that one before,' I answered, tongue in cheek to humour the lad.

'And my dear old gran use to say if'n a cat jumps over a corpse, it too becomes a vampire.'

'Hmm, your dear old gran was a true believer, then?'

'Aye. She told me, *Jasper... Jasper*, she'd say, *Vampires can't abide sunlight.* It weakens them, yer see. Thart's why they sleep during the day and she also said the only way to kill a vampire is with a stake through the heart.'

I wanted to ask Jasper, *what kind of steak — beef or lamb*, but he was deadly serious and would read the attempt at humour as mockery. For this reason, I was compelled to send him along with Lantern Jaw Lincoln and the four soldiers to reconnoitre the address.

'Make certain no one leaves. If they do, follow them discreetly from a distance. Got that?'

'Aye, sar.'

'I will join you as soon as Fabian arrives.'
'Aye.'

By all accounts, 49 Molle Street was a run-down residence built for an army captain, Captain Gregory, who had arrived with Lieutenant Bowen and helped settle Hobart Town back in '04. The captain had retired from the army in 1817 and moved from the barracks, less than a mile south, to enjoy the winter of his life in this humble dwelling. Now, forty years on, the residence showed all the miserable signs of neglect, wrapped in a green shawl of ivy. It was the ivy, by all accounts, holding the crumbling bricks in position.

Yet, there was no attic in which our outlaws could hide.

Trying to be inconspicuous, which is difficult for four large men wearing red uniforms, the accompanying soldiers spread out and searched the property. The address was unoccupied and in a more dilapidated circumstance even than it outwardly appeared. The next-door property, separated by a spiked iron fence, was similarly unloved, although Billings later reported noticing a lone figure through a drawing room window. Once it was established that no one resided at 49 Molle Street, Lantern Jaw Lincoln took it upon himself to remove planks nailed across a side window and climbed over the sill through cobwebs and into darkness. The soldiers followed.

Jasper, however, ventured to a dilapidated barn at the rear of the property, certain, he told us later, that he had seen one of the redcoats enter before him. With the thought that he was not alone, Jasper cocked the hammer on his loaded service pistol and ascended to the attic room above the barn; illuminating his passage with a small oil lantern. The floorboards creaked with every tread and this alone would have heralded his approach.

Zachary Wolf was a cornered rat. There is no doubt he would have seen the redcoats when he looked from the single window into the yard below, and could only assume that

Jasper, ascending less than silently, was escorted by soldiers. In that brief moment, as he entered, Jasper recalled the attic room to be filled with decrepit old furniture. More a storeroom; although a table, two chairs and sundry items of home comfort were set up in the middle of the room, as if squatters were living there. To one side, a ladder led to a hatch in the roof. A candle stub, recently extinguished, smoked from its candleholder on the table. Behind the table, Jasper noted a partition wall to one side, hung with several paintings; landscapes, family portraits and gilt framed mirrors. They appeared to have been taken out of storage and hung in a neat row, almost like someone wished to feel at home.

Realising that he was, indeed, alone, Jasper became more alert. Night had arrived and the attic was dark, except for his meagre lantern casting spectral shadows with his every step. Jasper could feel his heart pounding. *What the hell am I doing here?* he thought. He stepped to one side, pushing his back to the wall.

Flight or fight… fight or flight…

His heart quickened.

'Z-Zachary Wolf,' he called out. 'Show y-yourself.'

Nothing. Not a sound.

'Zachary Wolf, we are here in the name of the Queen.'

Another shadow shifted. Jasper raised the lantern above his head only to shift more sinister shapes.

Jesus!

'Zachary Wolf…'

Wolf stepped from behind the partition.

'You are under arrest, sir,' Jasper announced, less than confidently.

Now Jasper saw his foe. His lantern barely outlining the black shape of a large man dressed all in black. Black cape. Black boater. Black britches and jacket. Wolf unsheathed a cutlass, and with arm outstretched, he waved its murderous point in Jasper's direction.

'Arrest me... huh... you an' who's navy?'

Jasper levelled his pistol at Wolf's chest from where he stood, less than three strides away. Immediately, Jasper was aware he had the shakes. His loaded Tower pistol felt made of lead.

His voice waivered, 'D-drop the sword and step out where I can see you.'

'Send a boy to do a man's work, eh?' Wolf grew in confidence. 'How old are you son, twelve?'

'S-stand to, I say!'

'Well, what is it to be, boy? Step out or stand to. Stand to or step out?'

Now he was making a mockery of Jasper's indecision. Wolf stepped to where Jasper could see his gnarly face. This man was twice his age, twice his strength and had nothing to lose. *He had been an inmate at the notorious Saltwater River coal mines. He had escaped at Port Arthur. He had eaten human flesh, for Christ's sake.* Jasper thought of his wife and bairn. He felt his bowels rumble. Wolf dared shift a half step closer, right boot before the left.

'B-back... back I say.'

'B-back... back I say,' Wolf mimicked in a girlie voice.

Jasper heard a voice in his head... *shoot the bastard; shoot him before he cuts yer throat, lad.*

Wolf's left foot slipped silently forward. Jasper felt beads of sweat trickle down his forehead. The salt stung his eyes. His pistol trembled. Wolf shifted slightly sideways. He passed before a mirror and... *no reflection!*

Jasper gasped and let out an involuntary cry, '*Vampire!*'

Wolf spun about, alert that he was to be attacked from behind. But no! They were alone. Thinking Jasper had called his bluff, Wolf pounced.

Vampire!

The word echoed in Jasper's head.

Vampire!

Wolf lunged with the blade. Jasper pulled the trigger. The attic reverberated with the exploding musket. The ball skipped across Wolf's shoulder splintering bone. Wolf screamed in pain, dropping the cutlass. Alerted by the gunshot, Lincoln and the soldiers mounted the stairs three at a time, shouting and crying out to Jasper.

Now panicked, Wolf mounted the ladder to the barn roof. With one powerful arm, he pulled himself up. Emboldened by the shouts of his approaching colleagues, Jasper spurred on bravely. He leapt after his assailant; following that flailing cape through the open hatch onto the steep barn roof and...

out into the blackness of night.

Jasper froze.

Heights were not his forte. The roof dropped away steeply and the ground below was hard. Lying flat on the roof, Jasper watched Wolf skipping confidentially along the ridge. Ahead was a tall, mature walnut tree with the full moon creeping out behind dark clouds to aid his escape.

Escape! The vampire was escaping!

This is when Fabian and I pulled up at the gate in a buggy. Billings and Holly rushed to join us.

'Look!' Holly stabbed a finger to the barn roofline. 'It's Zachary Wolf.'

Jasper rose to the challenge. He had an audience and help was climbing that ladder behind him.

'Halt!' Jasper cried out in a manly baritone. 'Halt or I'll shoot.'

But his pistol was spent. Lincoln poked his head through the hatch.

"ere yer go Jasper,' Lincoln passed Jasper his pistol.

Wolf didn't look back. With arms outstretched to the sides, he negotiated the roof ridge like a tightrope walker. He made it to the gable. The walnut tree was almost the height of the roof, and it was only a short jump to its upper branches.

Escape was possible.

Fabian, Billings, Holly and myself rushed to intercept his descent. But the walnut tree was on the next property and a tall, spiked iron fence separated the estates. Jasper stood, balancing awkwardly onto the roof.

'Halt, I say!' he cocked the hammer and took aim. Wolf turned briefly to stare Jasper in the eye. The moon lit his face and Jasper saw the devil. He saw death itself. Wolf's eyes were blood red and Jasper will swear later that he saw the canine teeth of a monster. Suddenly Jasper's nerve vacated him. He was intimidated. But lest he lose face, he called out once more, 'H-halt, or I *will* shoot.'

Zachary Wolf's mouth opened and he hissed like an angry tomcat... and leapt for the tree.

Jasper pulled the trigger. The ball whistled off towards Hobart Town.

From where we stood, we saw Zachary Wolf crash through the upper boughs. He missed his hold and dropped heavily, like the large man he was. Clawing at branches as he fell, Wolf landed face down on the spiked iron fence.

There was no scream. No groan of pain. Death was instant.

The *vampire* died with an iron stake through his black heart.

Two minutes later...

We all stood about, under the lantern light of the soldiers, who now joined us. All mouths were open. We were all incredulous. My first thought was how, or who, was going to prise our prize from his impalement?

Jasper was the first to speak. Nay, he gloated. 'I did it!' he crowed. 'I killed a vampire!'

'You what?'

'I killed a vampire. I killed a vampire....'

I fancied Jasper was about to break into a dance. Holly joined in the mood.

'Jasper, the vampire slayer!' she cried out, holding Jasper's arm up like a pugilist referee.

'I hate to tell yer this,' Lincoln interrupted, 'but 'e were nothin' but a common criminal.'

'No! No!' Jasper was deadly serious. 'I saw it for meself.'

'Saw what?' Holly was wide-eyed.

'He walked in front of a mirror, upstairs in the attic, and there was no reflection.'

Fabian was having none of it and said so. 'Horse shit.'

'I don't mean to argue with yer, Fabian sar, but that...' Jasper poked a finger at Wolf's body, now being inspected by the soldiers, who were working out how to remove him from the iron fence.

'That there Zachary Wolf walked in front of a mirror and, as god be me witness, there was no reflection.'

'What mirror?'

'I'll show you.'

Two minutes later, we stood before the mirror in question. Holly held the only lantern, her eyes darting about in a guarded manner.

'Here.' Jasper pointed at the mirror. Lincoln had noticed the mirror himself, earlier.

'Oh, this mirror?' Lincoln said, and he passed in front of it.

There was no reflection!

Jasper jumped backwards. 'What the bloody hell?'

Holly let out a nervous gasp, instantly holding the lantern up to Lincoln's grinning face. 'L-Lincoln,' she said, with a quiver in her voice. Surely she didn't suspect her friend to be a vampire.

I too could see the humour.

'I hate to tell yer this, Jasper,' Lincoln chuckled, 'but there ain't no mirror in the frame.'

An hour later

We all agreed a celebration was in order. With Zachary Wolf bundled into a sail cloth, heaved onto a cart and taken to the morgue, we decided a few rounds at the Sailor's Rest our best option, and on the police department's purse. Why not give our good friend Bonnie Nettle the money?

As the Rest is only a little over a mile away from the crime scene – as the crow flies – and the moon was bathing Hobart Town, on a crisp, yet still, winter's night, we walked. We walked to the Molle and Collins Street corner, where we wet our whistles at the Boar's Head. Sated, temporarily, we sauntered down to Harrington Street to Davey Street, where we partook of refreshments at the Freemason's Hotel. From here it was a quick stroll to New Wharf via Salamanca Place through St David's Cemetery.

Ah! Full moon. Cemetery.

But as we travelled in a cheerful group, slightly fortified on our indulgences, we feared not. That is, until I remembered my dream of ten-year-old Timmy sitting on the family vault.

'Where are your parents?'
'Passed, squire.'

'Oh I am sorry to hear that.'
'That's all right. They've been dead some years now.'
'What is your name?'
'Timmy.'
'Well, Timmy, who looks after you?'
'I do. I live around here.'

I was aware we were passing by the area in my dream. Under the branching umbrella from a mature oak tree, I noted several family vaults. I stepped closer to read their inscriptions, but it was too dark. 'Holly.'

'Caspian, sar?'

'Light that lantern, if you please.'

The others looked on impatiently. I don't know whether it was my imagination or not, but the chill had intensified. Holly fiddled with the tinderbox while I gave the others a brief rundown on my dream.

'Yeh, right,' Fabian's standard answer when he did not believe something.

'What was his name?' Billings said.

'Timmy.'

'Timmy Alexander Cage?' Lincoln called out from the next vault, as Holly's lantern cast more shadows than light.

'What?' I said.

'Timothy Alexander Cage,' Lincoln read aloud. *'Here lies Henry Sattler Cage, 47 Bernice Vera Cage 41 and Timothy Alexander Cage aged 10. Taken from this world by a cruel sea, having drowned. July 12th 1856. May they rest in peace.*

I studied the vault. It was the very same.

We left in a sober group after that, as Timmy's last words haunted me.

'Will yer come and visit me?'

The next day proved successful, three-fold. Lynch Savage at the Sea o' Graves was keen to make amends with the law, after the kerfuffle of the false burial, and on his property. So, when James Dick with his facial twitch and his mate, William Norman with his cleft palate turned up at his inn – hiding from the law – he made a citizen's arrest and threw them in the brig buried beneath the taproom. They had taken flight after Wolf was killed. We were indebted to him. These two villains, joined at the hip as Fabian described them, were quick to reveal Samuel Groundwater's hideout. Apparently, he had heard everything from a priest's hole he had fashioned in the deserted house in Molle Street, only to relocate when we vacated the property.

On our instruction, soldiers were dispatched to Austin's Ferry, where they captured Samuel Groundwater attempting to board the ferry, to traverse the River Derwent and escape north.

Epilogue

I had missed my trysts with the most inviting and irresistible Mrs Royle Rowley, the photographic studio owner in Liverpool Street. The woman charmed me like a queen cobra, if there ever was such a creature. And after her indiscretion with Cyril Hoffbrand – well I considered it an indiscretion, even if Royle did not – I had sulked somewhat. But *absence makes the heart grow fonder,* as my dear old mum would say, and we managed the most unexpected and unusual rendezvous.

George Williams had nothing to live for. Sadly, his wife Jane had left him for Huon Yews, the head clerk at Shaddocks and Company, where George was gainfully employed as a quill scratcher and stores man. God only knows why Jane fell for

Huon Yews in the first place. Yews was a man of frugal habits, nay, worse, he was mean as hell. *Tight as a fish's arse,* I heard sailors mutter. But love knows no boundaries – yes, my dear mother would say that, too. George had been at Shaddocks since he was indentured when he was fifteen. Now, on his forty-eighth birthday, he was released from duty. No doubt Huon Yews had influence in the matter; take the man's wife and then dismiss him. But for George, the prospect of starting life all over again was simply too much, so he blew his brains out. Literally. It took two shots. The first bullet ripped through his jaw, leaving him mortally wounded, but not where he wanted to be. Dead.

He barely managed a second bullet, which, fortunately, went through the top of his mouth into the brain. Now, here we were, Royle Rowley, my photographer companion and myself, sitting on either side of George in his Kangaroo Bluff cottage, drinking to our good health, but not George's. Royle and I shared a bottle of George's Geneva, flavoured with juniper berries and fresh lemons off George's own tree. With the cottage no longer a crime scene, my colleagues had departed, but not before Jasper fetched Royle with her photographic imagery equipment. That was an hour earlier.

I alluded to a stone crock of flour sitting on the table.

'It appears he contemplated cooking damper for his evening meal,' I said, feeling quite inebriated, after more than a few nips of the water of life.

'Maybe the monotony of his diet added to his depression,' Royle giggled, equally befuddled. How carefree we were. But lovers are, are they not?

I had had a most difficult time of late, without respite. I had been to Adelaide and back. I had dealt with 'vampires' and participated in a psychic phenomenon, solving the mystery of the man in the well. I had spent the night in a cave with a wild tiger, for Christ's sake. I knew of an abortion that had gone terribly wrong and arrested a husband for murdering his wife and dumping her in an alleyway, even though he was innocent. Yes, it had been a tumultuous few weeks.

Now I sat here with dear old George Williams, sitting in his kitchen chair with his cranium missing and his brains adhering to the ceiling and wall. His head was tossed back and his lower jaw dropped almost to his chest, like he, too, saw the funny side of our mischief.

Our mischief?

Maybe I should explain. You see, Royle and I were by now quite drunk. We had both endured difficult times of late and our relationship, for what it was, had been tested, what with me catching Royle in the company of that dandy, Cyril Hoffbrand. How could she! But then, I have not exactly been an angel myself.

We were alone at last.

I stoked the fire, closed the shutters and locked the door before filling our glasses from the black glass bottle of AVH gin, and toasted once again.

'To ush,' I grinned, showing off my pearly white teeth.

Royle reached in front of messy George Williams to clink glasses with me.

'To us,' she saluted, her voice husky from behind enticing, devil red lips.

Her beauty lured me in like a sturgeon baited by a fresh clam. Her eyes, green as starboard lights on a ship, danced over my body. Royle slipped the pin from her chignon and her silky red hair poured over her shoulders, cascading over one eye. She unbuttoned her bodice, exposing her white firm breasts. Nipples firm as thimbles pointed unashamedly in my direction... beckoning.

'R... Royle... I...'

'Hush, silly boy,' she purred. We stood, embracing each other – behind George's back. The macabre, I had noticed, remodelled this woman into a seductress. With the kitchen fire throwing out all the light we needed, our lips met, tongues explored. Hands fondled and groped. Soft whimpers became heavy panting. Finally, deprived of clothing, Royle lay face down on the table with arms outstretched and her boots planted firmly apart on the floor. I waited no longer, and with the past weeks forgotten, I shuffled forward with my britches at my ankles, taking Royle with the energy of Hercules. Royle balled her fists. She squeezed them tight and let out a chorus of most satisfying groans.

'Tally-ho!' I cried out. 'Giddy-up there.' I had visions of the Launceston bank manager on his desk practising his polo moves. 'More wrist Toby, more wrist!' I shouted in drunken cheer.

'M-m-more w-wrist... Toby?' Royle was as bemused as she was thrust forward.But there was no time to explain. I thrust my hand into the flour crock and dusted the wench's back like I was some debauched baker. 'Tally-ho! Giddy-up there.' We rode hard, going nowhere, but arrived the same time. Sated, breathless, lathered with sweat, we collapsed back into our chairs. I poured drinks. 'To us,' I said again.

Royle held her tumbler high. 'To us,' she repeated staring down the lens of the camera still secured on its tripod at the far end of the table. Royle giggled. 'Let's make an image of us,' she grinned, her words slurring from the gin.

I should have said, 'That's probably not a good idea.' But instead I said, 'How?'

'Elementary, beautiful boy.'

I watched Royle set up a fresh photographic plate. She prepared a dish of calcium carbonate with an oxygen flame until she had the required limelight. The kitchen was immediately basked in a bright light.

'We have two minutes,' Royle was giggling like a schoolgirl.

She fastened a ribbon to the lens cap before jumping on my knee, both naked as the day we were born. Except Royle still wore her boots – little minx. I took George Williams's right arm and placed it on her shoulder.

'Can't leave George out,' I laughed. Royle laughed and George laughed. Well at least it appeared so, as his dislocated jaw sat on his chest.

'Ready?' She said.

'Ready.'

Royle pulled the ribbon. The spring-loaded lens popped open. We sat still, stifling our giggles. Finally Royle released the ribbon. The lens closed, and we celebrated at our ingenuity with laughs and gin. 'I have always wanted to do that,' she said. 'I don't think anyone has ever done that before.'

'What? Make a self-portrait?'

'Yes.'

'What will we call it?'

'Oh!' I said. 'I have an idea...'

THE END

Van Diemen's Land.

A Short History.

Until the dawn of the nineteenth century, the island of Tasmania, then known to the European world as Van Diemen' s Land, was a forgotten land, a land roamed by tribes of aborigines living in harmony with nature. It was estimated somewhere between 3,000 to 15,000 Palawa natives called the island home at the time of European settlement in 1803. Appallingly, that was about to change.

These people had crossed into Tasmania some 40,000 years ago. Archaeological evidence excavated in the South-West's Warren Cave in 1990 has been dated to 34,000 years, making Tasmanian Aborigines the world's southern-most population during the Pleistocene epoch.

Tasmania was connected to the mainland by a land bridge during the last glacial period, but sea level rise following the last ice age, some 8000 years ago, separated these aborigines from their mainland counterparts.

The first recorded European visitor was Abel Janzsoon Tasman, a Dutch seafarer and merchant in the service of the Dutch East India Company, who is credited as the first known explorer to reach the southern islands, including New Zealand, in two separate voyages, 1642 and 1644. Tasman named the island Van Diemen's Land after the governor of the Dutch East

Indies. Interestingly, the expedition did not encounter any aborigines when they landed.

However a French exploratory expedition, under Marion Dufresne, did encounter the aborigines the day he rowed ashore in 1772. At first they were friendly. It was only when a second longboat was dispatched to join him on the beach that the natives grew anxious and responded by throwing stones and spears. Musket shots were fired and regrettably, one native was killed and several wounded. It would be twenty years before another European ship explored the region.

The French returned almost a generation later, and animosities were either forgotten or forgiven. Bruni d'Entrecasteaux's visit in 1792-3 and Nicolas Baudin in 1802 both enjoyed friendly encounters.

Meanwhile, from the 1790s the northernmost tribes on Van Diemen's Land encountered the sealers, a violent and determined group of (<u>desperate</u>) piratical characters, making a living by trading in sealskins captured from the Bass Strait Islands. Many of these men were escaped convicts from Port Jackson or whalers who had abandoned ship for a castaway lifestyle. Their treatment of aboriginal women was abhorrent: kidnapping them for their sealing skills and forcing them to gratify their 'companionship' urges. Many were kept tied up and treated like dogs. Many of the Aboriginal men were murdered by sealers.

British settlement and domination was not far off.

In December 1798, ten years after the first fleet arrived to settle New South Wales, Mathew Flinders and George Bass sailed to Van Diemen's Land's Frederick Henry Bay in their little colonial sloop *Norfolk*. They circumnavigated the southern lands, proving it was an island by exploring the strait between the mainland and Tasmania, which now bears the name, Bass Strait. In the southern estuary, now known as the River Derwent, they sailed parallel to the coast, along the seven-mile beach coastline, believing the bay to be the one Abel Tasman chartered as Frederick Henry Bay, 156 years earlier in 1642. They did not, however, come ashore.

Four years later, the wily French were prowling about the Pacific once more, spying on the British colony on behalf of Napoleon. The expedition of the French explorer, forty-eight-year-old Captain Nicolas Baudin, sailed into New South Wales's Port Jackson on board *Geographe* and *Naturaliste* in the summer of 1802. Like true gentlemen officers, the British entertained their enemy in Sydney Cove. Many of Baudin's crew suffered scurvy and were permitted recuperation time in the NSW sun, whilst the officers were entertained at government house. But over roast wallaby, Madeira wine and rum, the French bragged about erecting the tricolour on Van Diemen's Land shores, while recently there. (It is rumoured that they imbibed too much of their host's hospitality) This is supposition. They may well have had ideas of claiming territory for French settlement, kept their plans secret, and only at the end of their sojourn at Port Jackson did Baudin inform a relieved King that their expedition was purely scientific.

They told of discovering Pittwater with its good anchorage, rich black soil, tall timbers, white freestone for building material and an endless source of fresh water. Why, even Napoleon was keen to have a settlement here, they declared. After dinner that night, the French officers showed off charts of Van Diemen's Land with areas coloured in gold and red denoting the proposed French settlements.

Among Baudin's crew, a young Louis Freycinet and Francois Peron had gone ashore in what is now known as Freycinet Peninsula, ostensibly to collect flowers and insect specimens. This is confusing Baudin's expedition with D'Entrecasteaux, at Recherche Bay. The expedition's gardener was amongst the casualties earlier in the journey and the voyage from VDL to Sydney in Jun with a crew already sick and dying from scurvy was extremely wild and horrifying. Going ashore on Freycinet Peninsula to plant a garden would have been <u>the</u> last thing on their minds.

When the gout-pained NSW governor, Philip Gidley King, heard of this French boast, he was furious and his response was immediate. The southern island had to be colonised and staked British for George III before the French did likewise, for their rogue emperor, Napoleon. Before the French even sailed out of Port Jackson, King sent a young lieutenant, Charles Robbins, in the small schooner *Cumberland* to seize King Island for King George III, under the French noses. To make a statement, Robbins claimed Port Philip next.

I don't think Tasmanians today realise just how close we were to being a French colony. We might all be speaking the French language and eating our daily baguettes. The local snails would probably taste all right too, if we gave them a chance. Baudin's officers also sang the praises of the north coast of Van Diemen's Land, claiming the rich bounty of what would be Port Dalrymple, George Town and Launceston.

But with France's economy struggling through what would come to be known as the Napoleonic Wars, the French sailed for Europe, and eventually Colonel Paterson was dispatched south, where he settled this northern coast.

Tasmania could also very well have been Dutch, for that matter. Abel Tasman anchored *Heemskerk* and *Zeehaen* offshore, near Hobart, on 1 December 1642. But the surf was up at Seven Mile Beach and the Dutch could not land, causing Tasman to send a strong swimmer ashore, Master Carpenter Pieter Jacobsz, to plant the flag of the Prince Frederik Hendrik, as a token gesture of Dutch possession. Endearingly, today Tasmania bears the man's name. The Dutch East India Company was only interested in maritime trade for profit and could find no people or product in VDL or New Zealand that they could sell profitably in Europe. As there was no need to find a remote place to exile its convicted citizens, as had England, it had no use for settling there.

Hobart Town finally settled.

To spite the French further, Governor King sent a young, albeit foolish, Lieutenant John Bowen to the Derwent Estuary to claim southern Van Diemen's Land for King George III, arriving on board *Lady Nelson* and the whaler *Albion*, on 12 September 1803. He unwisely chose to settle on a marshy landing on the river's eastern shore.

Months later, on 11 February 1804 Lieutenant Colonel David Collins was sent by King to join Bowen and establish a permanent settlement. He sailed aboard the grossly overcrowded 481-ton convict transport *Ocean*, captained by Captain John Mertho. Accompanying him was his chaplain, the Reverend Robert Knopwood, and Lieutenant Edward Lord, with 25 Royal Marines and 178 prisoners from Port Phillip.

Previously, Collins had abandoned Port Phillip in Victoria declaring the settlement as an unsuitable, sandy waterless wasteland. It's now called Melbourne.

On arrival in the estuary, Collins was impressed with Pipeclay Lagoon and Pittwater on the eastern shore of the wide River Derwent. But this is well south of Bowen's chosen site, which Collins had yet to inspect.

Knopwood was also impressed, writing glowing reports in his diary, where he noted the reedy shores abounded in the game precious to him as a sportsman and a lover of good living:

We see a great number of wild fowl and one emu. Quails, bronze-wing pigeons and parrots. At 4 we returned to the party we left and got a great quantity of oysters. It appeared to me that the natives were much better supplied with fresh fish and birds than those at Port Phillip. Near the first lagoon which was large, more than 12 or 14 miles round, was a quantity of flax and very fine, ducks and teal, and I think woodcock was flushed.'

That was written the morning after they landed at Bowen Bay. The next day they encountered their first natives. A party of 17 appeared.

Knopwood wrote:

> *They were well made, entirely naked; some of them had war weapons; they had a small boy with them about seven years old, and did not appear to flee from them.*

But innocence was lost that day. Tragedy awaited these tall brown hunters with their ochre matted hair, carrying long thin spears, accompanied by their women, wearing gleaming necklaces of shell and carrying woven baskets and stone hand axes. The sight of the tribe passing by on their way to find fresh hunting grounds panicked an ignorant Lieutenant Moore and his charge of uneducated marines. They fired a carronade loaded with canister shot into the tribe. It is not recorded exactly in the history books, but there would have been many aborigines wounded, if not fatalities.

Collins was rowed ashore at ten o'clock on the morning of 16 February and inspected Bowen's new settlement, basically a few tents. He was not happy. What he saw was a desolate repeat of Port Phillip Bay, from where he had just sailed; a land of marsh and brackish water; a miserable trickle only, could be gathered as soakage, through the sands and into their sunken water barrels. Although it was obviously a poor choice. When Bowen's party made camp there in September 1803 it was spring. It was sheltered from the southerly weather; the surrounding country would have been green and the creek would have been flowing.

Come summer when Collins saw it, it would have been dry and the stream a trickle.

The next morning Collins, Reverend Knopwood, Collins's kinsman William Collins, two marine guards and a rowing crew, journeyed down river in search of a better location to start a settlement. En route, several points and landmarks were charted and named, with Collins naming Sullivans Cove himself, after the Permanent Under Secretary to the Colonies, John Sullivan.

The natural and deep harbour was surrounded by tall timber, growing back into the rolling foothills of a mountain they referred to as Table Mountain, due to its resemblance to the mountain at Cape Town. From Hobart, it appears to be anything but like a table top, but from Adventure Bay, where the first sea explorers saw it, it appeared flat. And this is how it got its name. This would be renamed Mount Wellington, in honour of the famous Duke of Wellington, some years after he defeated Napoleon at Waterloo in 1815. Now, in the 21st century Mount Wellington shares its name with the aboriginal name, Kunanyi.

The area appeared unsettled by the indigenous people. There were streams running east through the mountain forests of eucalyptus and the tea-tree forests closer to the shore. Here, the water filtered through reeds where bird life was prolific. The location for a settlement was idyllic.

Idyllic for the moment. It would not be too long before these fresh water rivulets ran with cholera and other pestilences of 'civilisation'.

The main stream poured into the harbour on either side of a rocky outcrop, a sparsely timbered islet, which, at low tide, was linked to the shore by an isthmus, or a bar of sand.

Collins made a short walk that day, into the woods with Knopwood, and immediately recognised the area as suitable for the new settlement. The water ran deep and swift through the forest and was clear, cool and sweet in the height of summer. Timber and stone, lime and clay were all there in abundance. The soil was black and rich and ideal for corn, which Collins preferred to grow. The islet, he named Hunter Island, would prove ideal for unloading stores and also protecting their precious supplies.

(Captain John Hunter was Second Captain of the First Fleet and governor of New South Wales from 1795 until 1800.)

Reverent Knopwood wrote in his diary:

The Lieut.-Governor, Collins and myself went to examine a plain on the S.W. side of the river, the plain extensive and continual run of water which is excellent, it comes from a lofty mountain, most resembling the Table Mountain at the Cape of Good Hope, the land is good, and the trees very excellent, the plain is well calculated in every degree for settlement.

Bowen must have felt supremely inadequate. He had arrived on the 12th of September. What on earth had he been doing for five months, swatting mosquitoes in the swamplands of a land now called Bowen's Park?

Within weeks, a village of wattle and daub dwellings had sprung up at Sullivans Cove, and a government 'house' was erected, mostly of canvas at this early stage, on the site now known as Franklin Square.

In 1807, the population swelled somewhat as the penal colony of Norfolk Island was abandoned and its residents sent to Hobart Town, as the new settlement was now referred to. Unfortunately, soon they all faced famine. Some corn and small gardens grew to supplement the meagre and rotting rations sent from Sydney Cove, like two-year-old salted pork and beef. Rice brought from India, however, was a staple.

Hunting parties were sent into the bush, with fowling piece, powder and shot, making kangaroo reasonably plentiful in the diet. Even convicts were sent, armed, into the bushland to hunt. As the native grazing animals had natural predators, except the Aborigine with spears and occasionally a thylacine, they were unusually tame and easy to kill compared with the mainland animals, which had to contend with the dingo. Many absconded, befriending aborigines where possible. But the reckless shooting of natives at Risdon must have made the natives wary.

Collins settled the Norfolk Islanders a few miles north of Hobart Town, at a place they called New Town. Here the soil was fertile and the more industrious made a go of it.

Eventually, as the decade progressed, younger convicts were sent to replace the 'old men' Collins had brought with him in 1804. However, these younger men, while stronger and fitter, were a dangerous breed, to be watched at all times. Cheap rum from India did not help stabilise the colony.

In those early years, government house grew to a three-room residence. Its walls were one brick thick; the roof was leaky, but it was not draughty in calm weather or damp on rainless days. Reverend Knopwood, chaplain to the young settlement, was better housed on Cottage Green, Battery Point, where he had a pleasant garden of fruits and potted herbs. Collins and Knopwood remained close friends and dined together regularly, often entertaining the masters of visiting ships.

Except for the fact that the population was outnumbered by convicted felons – many of them marauding bushrangers – resentful natives and general corruption amongst the constabulary, Hobart Town was shaping nicely...

Until the infamous Rum Rebellion of New South Wales.

Sydney Cove was becoming a maverick settlement. Disorder was the order of the day and the straw that broke the camel's back was the installation of Captain Bligh as governor, to replace Philip Gidley King. Yes. The Captain Bligh of the *Mutiny on the Bounty* fame. The British Government appointed Bligh on the strength of his reputation for being a tough leader. Unfortunately, his strict demeanour only replicated the situation on *Bounty,* and the rebellion – known as the Rum Rebellion – became the only successful armed takeover of any government in Australian history. The New South Wales Corps, under leadership of Major George Johnson and John Macarthur, deposed the Governor of New South Wales, William Bligh. The military ruled the colony until the arrival from Britain of Major-General Lachlan Macquarie as the new governor in 1810.

The reason I mention this is that the Rum Rebellion had a ripple effect, down in Hobart Town.

Bligh, you must understand, was put aboard *Porpoise*, to be sent back to England. But breaking his word as a gentleman, he ordered his ship sail to Hobart Town, much to the embarrassment of David Collins. Collins humoured Bligh with the intention of placing him under arrest and returning him to Sydney Cove. However, the wily fifty-six-year-old sea captain, once master of the *Bounty,* saw through Collins's ruse and once again escaped on *Porpoise* before Collins could arrest him, but not before threatening to blow Hobart Town into the Derwent. Had the great mariner, who had once served under the famed Captain Cook, lost his marbles?

Bligh waited out his time, anchored in Norfolk Bay on Tasman's Peninsula, continuing to be a thorn in Collins's side. Collins, by decree of proclamation, made it an illegal offence to aid or supply Bligh. All the same, Bligh waited out the year before returning to Sydney Cove, arriving January 1810. Before the new governor Lachlan Macquarie, Bligh demanded Collins be court-martialled. Unfortunately David Collins, Hobart Town's founder, collapsed and died suddenly, on 24 March 1810.

Shamefully, to this day, David Collins's body lies in an unmarked plot somewhere beneath St David's Park. Does it? I have read that his lead-lined coffin was exhumed in the 1920s, when the burial ground was being converted into a park, and reburied where the monument is today. This needs verification.

The settlement's first warehouses were built in the early 1820s on Hunter Island. The narrow isthmus offered security from theft by the aborigines and convicts.

A decade later, another group of warehouses was constructed on the opposite side of Sullivans Cove. Collins named Sullivans Cove after John Sullivan, the Under Secretary at the Colonial Office. These later warehouses now make up Salamanca Place, which was originally called New Wharf; probably named by the same creatively minded committee, which named the old wharf on Hunter Island, Old Wharf. I personally prefer the name Old Wharf; it has more charm, I feel, than Hunter Street. Salamanca Place was named after a town in Spain, which was captured by the famed Duke of Wellington, during the Peninsula Wars of 1812. The Old Wharf /Hunter Island area was too shallow for vessels to have linear quayage. So, after vast reclamation works by convicts on the western side were completed in the early 1830s, ships for the first time could tie up against a long new wharf instead of being serviced by lighters.

The indigenous Mouheneener people of the land had little choice but to move on, and the aboriginal name for the area has been lost to history.

Now Hobart is a thriving capital city and, in recent years, has become a tourist Mecca.

Books by the Same Author

Series:
Five Pipes
Twenty-One Steps Down
Fool's Hoard
Poveglia Island

Series:
Shadow Hunter
Hunter Hunted
Chasing Shadows
Darker Shadows
In the Gallows' Shadow
Taken to the Grave
Silent from the shadows

Escape the Hangman

Dark Valley

A Bitch Called Tracy
Where There's Smoke

1814

On the Devil's Knee

The Ghosts of the Drunken Admiral

Island of Secrets:
Volumes One & Two

All influenced by Tasmania's incredible history

www.craiggodfrey.info

Any similarities or names of existing people are a coincidence.
© Copyright Craig Godfrey
11 Alexander St
Sandy Bay
TAS 7005
Tel 0409 806 766

CRAIG GODFREY

Craig Godfrey was born in Hobart in 1952 and traveled extensively, which has given him many of the experiences and escapades he so enjoys putting into print. These include working in the early 70s as a chef for a restaurant owned by figures from Sydney's criminal underbelly, and cooking in Darwin when cyclone Tracy destroyed the city.

After decades in the hospitality industry—and nearly forty years after opening the Drunken Admiral Seafood Restaurant—Craig decided to hang up his apron and leave family at the helm in order to indulge in his other passion: writing fiction. And with Tasmania's fascinating past he has plenty to write about.

Craig loves nothing more than to weave adventure, mystery and mayhem together, incorporating colourful characters from all walks of life. He has published eighteen previous titles, and is currently writing the seventh book in a series called *Shadow Hunter*, in which Caspian Hunter travels to Van Diemen's Land from Birmingham in 1855 to take a position as second in charge of Hobart Town's fledgling police department. His adventures around the waterfront inns are boundless.

The chef of a Hobart waterfront restaurant called the Hook, Line and Sinker is the protagonist of a series set in modern times. He and his partner, the assistant curator of the Tasmanian Museum, continuously find themselves in trouble, whether it be solving the disappearance of rare art works on Tasmania's west coast, caught in hang-glider dog fights over the Caribbean Sea, finding their way out of the myriad of tunnels under the battlefields of Flanders, or being imprisoned by antiquity thieves in Venice. Number five in the series has recently been completed. Other action-adventure novels are set in 1830s Van Diemen's Land, the Tasmanian wilderness of the 1940s, and during a murder investigation in Sydney and Darwin in 1974.

In the 1990s Craig independently shot two feature films: a murder mystery set in Southern Tasmania, which aired on television, and a splatter comedy still available online. He wrote, produced and directed both.

Craig's life has been busy and interesting, to say the least.

1814

BY

CRAIG GODFREY

1814 is a tale of two hemispheres and a man and a woman who initially shared little but the English language. Of a man of peace – a doctor – ensnared in the violence of the American revolution, forced to flee the former American colonies of King George III. Of a very young woman fighting for survival amid the injustice, poverty and corruption of early nineteenth Century Britain. A woman who is unjustly sentenced to transportation to Van Diemen's Land. British 'justice' was harsh beyond belief at this time and at its worst in its treatment of female convicts.

At this point in history Britain and particularly the Royal Navy were all powerful and the American doctor sought anonymity under a new identity. He 'signed on' with a group of sealers who had their own notorious empire in the remote islands of Bass Strait. These sealers, to this day, are recognized as the most evil of men.

It is in this lawless world that two good people meet. This is a world the writer/ historian and master story teller Craig Godfrey understands very well. Though fictional his characters fiercely illuminate the times, the remoteness and the people that populate these colonies.

PENMORE PRESS
www.penmorepress.com

Taken to The Grave
BY
Craig Godfrey

This adventure continues....

Nineteenth Century Van Demonian sleuth, Caspian Hunter, is a colonial lawman deeply immersed in the life and crimes of Hobart Town, where convicts transported from Mother England form a majority of the population. Caspian and his decidedly unconventional associates are sworn to uphold the law where lawlessness is almost a way of life.

The fledgling colony includes newly pardoned convicts – 'ticket of leave men' – on a sort of parole. Misfits and unsavoury characters come this remote outpost of the British Empire to get as far away as possible from whatever lives they seek to leave behind.

But by the middle of the century, free settlers are arriving in ever greater numbers from Britain. Hobart Town is blessed with one of the world's most beautiful deep-water harbours, so it also attracts sailors and whalers. And it is rapidly becoming prosperous. There are inns aplenty, and a growing number of enterprising ladies are skilled in the arts of making sailors, whalers, gentlemen and even lawmen briefly happier and certainly poorer. This is Caspian's town.

A murder most foul committed with the most blunt of instruments, a hot flat iron, leads Caspian to the prison hell of Port Arthur, traveling on a railway man-powered by convict slaves, and an illicit liaison with a British Army officer's wife. The motive for murder: a diamond worth a king's ransom, hidden in a most incongruous place.

PENMORE PRESS
www.penmorepress.com

BELLERAPHON'S CHAMPION

BY

JOHN DANIELSKI

Deep within each man, lies the secret knowledge of whether he is a stalwart or a coward. Three years an un-blooded Royal Marine, 1st Lieutenant Thomas Pennywhistle will finally "meet the lion," protecting HMS Bellerophon at the Battle of Trafalgar.

Not only will Pennywhistle be responsible for the lives of 72 marines aboard Bellerophon but their direction will fall entirely on his shoulders since his fellow Marine officers consist of a boy, a card shark, and a dying consumptive. If he has what it takes to command, it will take everything he's got.

In the course of battle, he will encounter marvels and terrors; from valiant foes to women performing miracles, from the skill of acrobats to the luck of the ship's cat, from a dead man still full of fight to a coward who has none. He and his marines will meet enemy élan will with trained volleys and disciplined bayonets. Most of all, he will meet himself; discovering just how dark his true nature really is.

Europe will be changed forever by Trafalgar, and so will Pennywhistle.

PENMORE PRESS
www.penmorepress.com

The Captain's Nephew

by

Philip K.Allan

After a century of war, revolutions, and Imperial conquests, 1790s Europe is still embroiled in a battle for control of the sea and colonies. Tall ships navigate familiar and foreign waters, and ambitious young men without rank or status seek their futures in Naval commands. First Lieutenant Alexander Clay of HMS Agrius is self-made, clever, and ready for the new age. But the old world, dominated by patronage, retains a tight hold on advancement. Though Clay has proven himself many times over, Captain Percy Follett is determined to promote his own nephew.

Before Clay finds a way to receive due credit for his exploits, he'll first need to survive them. Ill-conceived expeditions ashore, hunts for privateers in treacherous fog, and a desperate chase across the Atlantic are only some of the challenges he faces. He must endeavor to bring his ship and crew through a series of adventures stretching from the bleak coast of Flanders to the warm waters of the Caribbean. Only then might high society recognize his achievements —and allow him to ask for the hand of Lydia Browning, the woman who loves him regardless of his station.

PENMORE PRESS
www.penmorepress.com

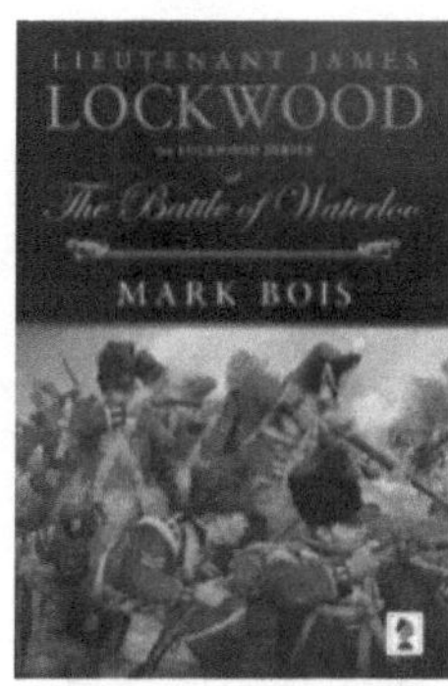

Lieutenant James Lockwood

By

Mark Bois

"Captain Barr desperately wanted to kill Lieutenant Lockwood. He thought constantly of doing so, though he had long since given up any consideration of a formal duel. Lockwood, after all, was a good shot and a fine swordsman; a knife in the back would do. And then Barr dreamt of going back to Ireland, and of taking Brigid Lockwood for his own."

So begins the story of Lieutenant James Lockwood, his wife Brigid, and his deadly rivalry – professional and romantic – with Charles Barr. Lockwood and Barr hold each other's honor hostage, at a time when a man's honor meant more than his life. But can a man as treacherous as Charles Barr be trusted to keep secret the disgrace that could irrevocably ruin Lockwood and his family?

Against a backdrop of famine and uprising in Ireland, and the war between Napoleon and Wellington, showing the famous Inniskilling Regiment in historically accurate detail, here is a romance for the ages, and for all time.

"... Bois' meticulous research and command of historical detail makes this novel a must read. He sets the standard for research and understanding... and the audience will demand more novels from this new author. Historical fiction welcomes Mark Bois with open arms." – Lt. Col. Brad Luebbert, US Army

PENMORE PRESS
www.penmorepress.com